PUBS, PULPITS & PRAIRIE FIRES

ELROY DEIMERT

Halifax '09
E Deimert

ROSEWAY PUBLISHING
AN IMPRINT OF FERNWOOD PUBLISHING
HALIFAX & WINNIPEG

Editing: Christy Ann Conlin and Eileen Young
Cover images: (front) Unemployed transient, Great Depression; Frank, Alberta, 1930, Glenbow
Museum Archives, Calgary, NC-54-3604; (back) Trekkers on the On-to-Ottawa
CPR train, Provincial Archives of Alberta, A5145.
Cover design: John van der Woude
Printed and bound in Canada by Hignell Book Printing
Printed on FSC Certified paper.

Published in Canada by Roseway Publishing,
an imprint of Fernwood Publishing
32 Oceanvista Lane
Black Point, Nova Scotia, B0J 1B0
and #8 - 222 Osborne Street, Winnipeg, Manitoba, R3L 1Z3
www.fernwoodpublishing.ca/roseway

Fernwood Publishing Company Limited gratefully acknowledges the financial support
of the Government of Canada through the Book Publishing Industry Development
Program (BPIDP), the Canada Council for the Arts and the Nova Scotia
Department of Tourism and Culture for our publishing program.

Library and Archives Canada Cataloguing in Publication

Deimert, Elroy, 1953-
Pubs, pulpits and prairie fires / Elroy Deimert.

ISBN 978-1-55266-320-2

1. Riots--Saskatchewan--Regina. 2. Depressions--1929--Canada.
3. Unemployed--Canada--History. 4. Canada--Economic conditions--1918-1945.
5. Regina (Sask.)--History. 6. Canada--History--1918-1939. 7. Co-operative
Commonwealth Federation--History. 8. Social Credit Party of Canada--History.
I. Title.

FC577 D45 2009   331.13'797109043   C2009-904174-X

CONTENTS

LATE-NIGHT RAMBLES

DR. PAUL WESSNER INTRODUCES HIMSELF AND HIS JOURNAL

ONCE THERE WAS AN EXTRAORDINARY group of friends who walked right into history over a few beer at BJ's Bar and Cue Club. I call them the Tuesday Club, and, if truth be told, it was not the beer that conjured that exit to history. There was a doorway, however, stage-right of the bar, which normally led to some pool, pinball, and extra tables. That, at least, was the case on regular days, but some Tuesday nights, for a few precious years in the late 90s, it was like Railway Platform 9¾; this doorway was an unlikely portal, not to Hogwarts, but definitely to the Great Depression, circa 1935, with some intriguing connections along the way. Through that doorway, the Tuesday Club had their own private corner of BJ's that no one else used during the slow times, like Tuesday nights.

I am a veteran history professor at the local college here in Grande Prairie, Alberta, but I may not be the typical BJ's patron if one judges by appearance or age or speech idiom; as Cam, an astute friend, once said, "BJ's is not a pub; it's a bar," in the middle of Northern Alberta's oil-patch. My reasons for choosing this bar over a pub like the Crown and Anchor are a bit complicated, but, if I'm a misfit at BJ's, there are other misfits there, like my good friend Charles Quamina, age seventy-eight, Trinadad-born ex-gospel preacher and ex-alcoholic who likes the atmosphere — maybe the fumes. Then there's Daniella, an ordained United Church minister. On Tuesday nights when things are a bit quieter, the three of us have an occasional round at BJ's. As well, rounding out the Tuesday Club with more than the occasional round, are Tom and Cam, two of the local heroes in the music scene who don't seems to think Charles, Daniella and I are out of place at BJ's; that is, because they are unusually intelligent and cultured "for way the hell'n gone," as they say, and past forty themselves.

Then there's Sammy, an adopted club member, sometimes called a rig pig by the less tolerant among us, but, hey, that's why he's at BJ's rather than the Crown and Anchor. He is a recovered crack abuser, rehabilitated (so to speak) by the oil company's program and their ultimatums. Unfortunately, he's a little more regular at the bar than the other regulars like Tom and Cam. After all, Sammy and the oil company (and any student of the local geography) all understand that alcohol abuse is apparently not classified as a drug problem north of latitude 55. So Sammy was the wildcard sixth, sort of like the turn in Texas Hold 'em when the stakes rise and the odds simplify. Don't ask me what that means, not yet anyway.

You see, a few years ago I started telling Charles and Daniella, and sometimes Cam and Tom, about these veterans of the 1935 On-to-Ottawa Trek that I had been interviewing. I live and breathe that kind of research. Sixty years earlier these men were the young single unemployed victims of the economic crash that changed the world. Thousands of them were herded into work camps — slave camps, where they organized, walked out on strike in B.C., and protested for two months in Vancouver, before riding the rails in mass to take their grievances to Ottawa.

When I share their stories with Daniella and Charles, it often leads to some heavy economic and social philosophy, which occasionally prompts a debate on our Canadian duty to positive social engagement, as opposed to the American right to the pursuit of happiness. This, in turn, often inspires some serious soul-searching for the three of us, depending on how many beer we've had. However, Charles and I are notorious for stretching one or two beer into a marathon philosophic discourse, while Daniella sometimes drinks lemonade. Sammy gets a kick out of this, so he often listens in, when he has worn out his welcome at other tables. Well, Charles and I can wax a bit rhetorical at times, and Sammy is often there to shoot down the flights of rhetoric in a bid to keep truth simple. Of course, "keeping *truth* simple" is the sad story of this province's politics for the last seventy odd years.

I remember my first real conversation along the bar with Sammy before there even was a Tuesday Club. One night Charles and I were mixing our personal history with Great Depression history, waxing more eloquent with the second beer, when I self-consciously started misquoting my namesake, an ex-acquaintance of ours, the Apostle Paul.

"When I was a child, I spoke as a child, I saw as a child, I reasoned as a child." I was speaking slowly, in confessional mode. "When I became a man, I *thought* I had put away the things of the child. Now... I see through a glass darkly... but then...?"

"Alright already! Is this poetry we're hearing or is this the goddamn Bible? I heard this somewhere before, and if it's the goddamn Bible like I suspect it is, you can't expect us to sit here listening to your bloody scripture reading for the rest of the night." That was Sammy, a high-school drop-out who at thirty-five years of age was earning more than I was as a tenured professor, but every now and then he could surprise you with his breadth of reading.

"Hey, could we get some more beer down here? Or are we cut off or something just 'cause some poet, smoking funny tobacca, quotes the god-damn Bible."

"Keep your voice down, Sammy, will you. Besides, I wasn't talking to you."

"So, you weren't talking to me. So who exactly you talking to in this bar, and who don't qualify? Maybe we should get that straight before the sermon, if that's coming next."

"Okay Sammy. Maybe… maybe I was talking to everyone, or anyone who happens to be listening. I thought I was talking to Charles here, but since we're all at the same bar, I suppose I'm talking to anyone who doesn't get bent out of shape just because they're subjected to a bit of poetry accidentally in the course of discourse."

"Course a discourse! Jesus H. Christ! He sounds like a bloody professor. Or preacher, ain't quite decided which is worse."

Sammy chug-a-lugged his beer, while we all laughed because everyone knew that he had nailed my identity faster than my psychologist. Well what could we do? We started telling him about the Ottawa Trek and the Regina Riot and my research. After that, he would often follow us to our private corner in the room off the bar or sit nearby if we didn't invite him to the table right away. Of late though, we finally credit Sammy for recognizing a world beyond the Patch and his beer, so he too, I admit, was a part of the birth of the Tuesday Club.

Anyway, when I fail to adequately communicate to my friends at BJ's the relevance of oral history from these veterans of the Great Depression, I come home to write down the stories, along with my tangential rambles. It is usually late at night, like tonight, when I furtively meet with you, my imaginary readers of this journal. And what can I say? Of course, I hope that someday the readers are not just imaginary.

Then again, why should anyone want to read someone else's journal entries? Fragmented sentences, fragmented stories. I suspect that a typical journal is often a sort of secret offer to posterity of some precious bit of history, precious to the writer, but not necessarily to anyone else. After all, the journal keeper is just one thin voice, such a small part of the really interesting story — that larger symphony. What attempt at writing history has ever managed to deliver the entire tragicomic symphony? The readers of history rarely get to experience how those singular voices can come together, sometimes in harmony, more often in a kind of counterpoint.

I think the lone journal writers, the amateurish raconteurs, these volunteer keepers of the lore, have often been privileged to hear a few of those voices come together. They've heard fragments of the greater score. They've become thirsty for the entire orchestral libation, not just to drink, but also to pour, to contribute to the symphony.

So although the great stories of our culture surround us in abundance, most people, like Sammy, for instance, have little tolerance for some pilgrim's late-night rambles, especially if the pilgrim speaks as if he were uttering undiscovered truth, as opposed to just a good story.

But that's the difference between Saint Paul and me. His truth was about that certain future, that certain resurrection, of which he was so confident. My truth at the moment has more to do with the resurrection of one small corner of Canada's past, a past that changes the more I listen to it, and that changes me too, I think. Saint Paul's truth included all of his people converting their truths to his truth, to think as he did. "One God, one faith, one baptism," one voice. I mean how many voices does one need if there is only one truth or one story line? So Saint Paul's story has become part of the dominant narrative of our culture, so much so that it seems to affect every story that I dig up here on the Canadian prairies, including this one. At least Saint Paul once admitted to merely seeing "through a glass darkly," but compare that modest admission to the certainties of "Bible Bill" Aberhart or Ernest Manning, two of Alberta's many colourful and dogmatic premiers.

I teach history for a living, but in my spare time, I've been digging up written and spoken relics from the Great Depression in western Canada, discovering the occasional phantom hero, though we all know heroes have been banned in serious history, and in serious literature. But there they are, shadowy wraiths from beyond the grave, resurrected from obscure pages in the Saskatchewan Archives or some such place. Sometimes the ghosts blend their voices with the quivering narrative of some still-living veteran, some skeletal ancient mariner, who holds me with his glittering eyes to tell his story one more time.

My fascination with these particular narratives developed accidentally, rather than through any well-planned research. I mean, it did not start as an academic plan. It was more of a series of eyes, ears, nose and throat experiences: voices from aging bodies, mingled with smells and tastes of human fear, the tactile sensations on my left palm of a mangled 38-calibre bullet dug out of a Regina citizen's shoulder blade late at night, on the night of the Regina Riot, 1935.

The voices? My wife's grandmother's was one of the first. She was about eighty-five years old in the mid 1990s. Her voice triggered my own trek. She and my wife and I were having our regular Sunday lunch in the same old café, the Trumpeter Hotel coffee shop, downtown Grande Prairie, when I mentioned something I read about the Regina Riot. That's what her generation called the infamous police action against the citizens of Regina, and against the "On-to-Ottawa" Trekkers in the middle of the Great Depression. In her laconic prairie voice she began to speak of "that evening," at first without a hint that her knowledge of it was of a different order than my knowledge, gleaned from cursory historical references. The night she spoke of was July 1, 1935, Market Square, Regina, Saskatchewan, Capital of the Canadian Dust Bowl.

Doreen Rust (my wife still called her Nanny) sipped her tea and began this story.

"I remember that evening, you know. We were at a movie theatre downtown 11th Avenue. I don't recall which theatre. There were several in that area. We were just going to leave after the movie finished. I don't recall what was playing, but I had Joyce with me. Your mother was only about five, I think. We were just getting out of the movie and getting ready to walk home. Anyway, this young man came bursting through the doors from the street and sort of huddled in a corner near us. He was kind of agitated you know and his nervous eyes caught me staring at him, and I just froze there. He looked at me and then at Joyce and back at me and said, 'Don't go out there, lady. They're shooting at people; they're trying to kill us.'"

"You were there? You were downtown Regina, the night of the riot?" I was amazed.

"Yes," she drew out the word. "And Joyce was there. At that age she loved those westerns. But there's this young man shaking in the corner, talking of real guns and real bullets. Then we noticed people staring out the windows of the theatre doors, pointing. But the young man's voice alone was enough to convince me. 'Well, if someone's shooting, let's call the police,' I said to him. I'm sure I sounded a bit doubtful. He shook his head, kind of annoyed maybe, but patient, you know, and he says, 'Ma'am! It's the *police* doing the shooting! First, they fired warning shots over the heads of the crowd, ma'am. Now they're firing right at us. Some of them that's hit went down in the middle of the street. Can't even get to them. The bloody cops arrested a couple of guys going out to help them.'

"I remember his off-colour language with Joyce there, not that I blamed him, but I'm sure my face reflected my shock, so he continued more forcefully, you know.

"'Aiming right at us now!' he said. 'There's a bloody war out there, lady — you and the girl wouldn't be safe. There's bullets bouncing off the bricks all over the street. They don't seem to give a damn who gets hit, ma'am. They're trying to kill us.'

"I was getting the message. I mean who do you call when you need protection from the police? By then some people who had left the theatre had come back inside. They didn't say anything, but I could see the confusion on their faces too. I told Joyce to stay beside me and I used the pay phone to call my husband. He borrowed a bread delivery wagon from his friend and drove the thing right up to the doorstep there on 11th Avenue. I can't imagine which direction he came from, because I remember looking back and seeing some sort of barricade of cars and men blocking the avenue behind us. It was dusk, but not completely dark yet, you know, that time of year, just about 11 p.m., I think, and still quite warm out."

She sipped her cold tea.

"It's so hard to imagine that you were actually there. You witnessed it."

"Yes," (that slow drawl again), "but I'll never forget that young man's face. We all knew about the Trekkers. Strikers, we called them. But that is the first one I remember meeting close up. I imagine he might be alive somewhere yet. He was younger than I was, I think."

Doreen has passed on now, but her voice is fresh in my mind. Mid-nineties, sixty years after the event, yet her voice still excites a sense of place. When Wallace Stegner writes of a sense of place that marks western Canadian writing, I think of the voices of fiction and poetry, sensual with landscape, but a history book rarely does the trick for me. However, the oral stories, the voices of the Great Depression veterans, the Trekkers, the unemployed, with their anger, their memory of empowerment, the healing that comes from the speaking, especially when someone is listening... now that is something different. And that is a history not yet chronicled. Together those multiple voices create something authentic — closer to Tom Thompson's sense of place, or Emily Carr showering light on a landscape in some inspired way that would never let you see that actual scene, those tangible trees, in the same old way again.

That is the way I see Market Square now, in Regina behind the old Fire Hall. Today, a modest parking lot shares the Square with the Regina City Police Building, a ponderous edifice with an embarrassingly small monument at the entrance that offers a few cryptic lines about this being the site of that July First evening. A riot is mentioned, but only the police death emphasized, and no real explanation of how it could happen. Yet when I walk through those parking lots, behind the old Fire Hall that witnessed it all, the people today look at me as if I'm lost, as I stare right through the asphalt at some ghostly cinder-covered Market Square beneath. I'm seeing it in grainy black and white like the old newspaper photos. I'm smelling the tear gas rising all over the north end. I'm seeing the clubs, and billies, and black-jacks, and riding crops doing their dance. And leather jackboots — the sound of nearly one-thousand jackboots. And shod horses trotting. The cavalry of the Royal Canadian Mounties in one of their darkest actions.

After that Sunday lunch with Doreen, I began listening... and taping those other voices — the voices of surviving Trekkers still living across western Canada: Regina, Saskatoon, Rocky Mountain House, Vancouver, Powell River, Quesnel. Finding them was my profession; it is the kind of research I'm trained to do, and I love it as much as teaching. Their voices recall the barricades, the Mounties, the ricocheting bullets whining overhead. And many recall the square-jawed face, the walk, and the words of a man they remember as Arthur, or Art, or just Slim.

Arthur (Slim) Evans, leader of the On-to-Ottawa Trek, was a carpenter, coal miner, and a union organizer for the One Big Union. But to Prime Minister R.B. Bennett and company — just a "communist agitator." Evans

Arthur Evans, 1911, organizing in the northern states with an IWW union card, learning his activism from the Wobblies. Glenbow Museum Archives, Calgary. NA-3634-1

was a Canadian Robin Hood, or perhaps Canada's own anti-Arthurian hero, suckled on the creed of the legendary turn-of-the-century Wobblies like Joe Hill and Big Bill Hayward and union activists like Ginger Goodwin. He joined their fight against the bare-knuckled exploitation that ruled the western lumber camps and mining towns. This was long before Alberta big oil supposedly liberated us all from the need for unions.

I first heard of Slim Evans in Drumheller, Alberta, in 1975. A First Nations counsellor named Wilf Cunningham in the Drumheller Federal Penitentiary told me of this union organizer in the mining heydays of Drumheller in the 1920s and '30s, when dinosaur bones were still being raided regularly from mines and coulees along the Red Deer River, and where Mary Roper's brothel was a major institution of worship on Saturday nights. Slim Evans led a couple of the legendary strikes in the Drumheller Valley that made the Safeway strike or the Brooks meat-packers' strike look like Sunday-school picnic scuffles.

I never knew at the time that the story of Slim Evans was larger than just a character of local miners' lore. I would never have thought it possible that a child of the Sixties Revolution, like me, could ride the rails of that Thirties Revolution, the On-to-Ottawa Trek with Arthur Evans. Still, I have made that box-car pilgrimage, not exactly riding the rods, but through the voices — some alive, some dead — voices of Doc Savage, Matt Shaw, Steve Brodie, Ronnie Liversedge, Red Walsh and scores of others of the 2500 young unemployed Trekkers. They were all refugees from the military-run relief camps where the Tory powerbrokers tried to hide our national shame of unemployment in the middle of the Great Depression — 2500 young men, and swelling at every railway stop, all bound to visit the Honourable Prime Minister Bennett in Ottawa to ask for "work and wages" instead of "bullshit speeches."

I don't mean to make it sound like some adventure story. Riding the rods is not romantic. Many of the young single men of the thirties rode the rails now and then to look for work, or to get away from the Depression of their particular small-town world. But the regular users, the uninvited guests of the mighty CPR and CNR, were desperate men. Lost men. Only men. Almost never women. So when a youth hopped a freight for his first time, the initial feeling was fear — fear that the harness bulls (the privately hired railroad police) would catch them. Or worse for some, that someone who knew their family would see them.

But the fear came in many exotic flavours: fear that your grip on the rusty iron ladder might not hold when the CPR security bull suddenly appeared above you with a club meant for your fingers; fear that you'd be dragged under the wheels; fear of guillotined limbs; or if you were lucky, fear of a quick but messy death for which your relatives should not expect an inquest.

And then there was the fear that your grip on the dream of a cash-paying job would fail somewhere — that the train wouldn't slow down for some particular jerkwater stop near a community rumoured to have farmers hiring or construction looming. Fear that your food would run out and you'd have to steal to eat, or that the freight car door wouldn't roll open enough to let you inside during the dust storm, or the thunder storm. Fear that it *would* open, only to let you into the den of a wine-sodden gang of tramps that had boarded from some hobo jungle up the line, closer to the core of hell — the hell of men who needed your pennies worse than you did. Or maybe these men had other more sinister needs concerning your body, from which your pennies could not buy exemption.

Then there was the fear that if you slept through one of the stops, some CPR hand would lock the freight car door, disdaining to check inside, preventing your chance to make an escape. Then under the summer prairie sun, the 95 degrees Fahrenheit heat outside would trap the prisoners inside the car in a suffocating gas chamber at 130 degrees and rising, on a siding out of the earshot of men, and out of the sight of God; a god who left the railroad freight of the Great Depression to Lucifer's fallen, to the domain of the unredeemable.

Only in gilded retrospect, after a few beers with the boys at the Legion could nostalgia gloss over the fears and realities of riding the rods. So it is difficult to imagine convincing 2500 young men — and hundreds and thousands more, eager to join all along the line to the east — to hop a freight with an army of unemployed, with the unlikely mission of visiting the Prime Minister in Ottawa to discuss work and wages, unemployment, and the western winters of our discontent.

And just like that, alone in my den, making speeches to my journal, I almost think that I can smell his beer breath as Sammy bushwhacks me.

"Western winters of our discontent? Lucifer's fallen? Jesus H. Christ, you gonna wreck a good story with those fucking literary allusions. Worse than the Bible verses! I mean, *Pulp Fiction* survived the Bible verses… but this ain't *Pulp Fiction*, you know what I'm saying?"

It is a bit infuriating — that voice, like some self-appointed sentimentality sensor from my subconscious. I just want to fire back: "Thank you, Sammy. I'll take that as a compliment. But kindly back off now, if you please. I wasn't talking to you." And then I continue talking to myself, more determined than ever to keep my ear to the narrative voices rising from those decades past.

Of course Slim Evans didn't exactly have to talk these men into riding the rails to Ottawa. Their frustration with the two-month strike in Vancouver and their increasing sense of solidarity was all it took to turn a brash challenge, from his confident voice in a general meeting of the relief-camp strikers, into a project that couldn't be brushed aside. But if anyone could organize such a Trek, keep it together and focused, forge it into a movement that could harness the dialectics of history, that person was Slim Evans.

"'Harness the dialectics of history'? Jesus Murphy man, you sound like a Marxist-Leninist professor from the sixties at that hippy-faggot Simon Fraser University. Nobody's going listen to that crap in the twenty-first century. You want us to listen? Then stick to the story line and forget the Fidel Castro bullshit."

See what I mean? That voice of Sammy will sandbag me just when I'm rolling, he and his bloody bigoted tongue. What the hell does he know about narrative voice? He should have no say here when I'm alone at home with the journal. Actually he's often a good deal more polite in person than when his apparition accosts me from my subterranean levels.

So I catch myself talking out loud to a bloody phantom? I tell him that I'm not talking to him. But… then who the hell *am* I talking to? There were many guys like Sammy that climbed on top of those CPR freight cars in June of 1935 in Vancouver, B.C., all bound to visit "Iron Heels" Bennett in Ottawa, to tell him what they thought of his fiction so far.

Okay, Sammy, wherever you are tonight. Maybe I *am* talking to you, but you've got to know that one has got to tell his story with his own voice, his own way, so cut me some slack here. I can't give you the legendary voice of Slim Evans. He died on the mean streets of Vancouver before I was born. I can only deliver on the voices of his compatriots: Robert "Doc" Savage, Matt Shaw, Andy Miller, Rudy Fedorowich. Guys who poured out their stories for me like a long-sealed bottle of aged whiskey, sixty some years after they put their youthful bodies and souls on the line against fascism, right there in the province of my birth and nurture. Okay, so you don't like my rhetorical flourishes, Sammy. But hell, I'm in this story too, whether we like it or not, because, for better or worse, I'm the one recording their voices, drinking their coffee and beer.

Some of them I met only once. Most have died since we talked. Some talked with an idiom more colourful than Sammy's. The profanity of the thirties was a bit different from ours. Some talked with a composed dignity, as if history professors and textbooks might be recording them. The few still living do not have a whole lot of years left to tell their story, and there isn't a long line-up of people now begging to hear them.

So now it is me, Sammy. Me, trying to put this all together, trying to resurrect the ghost voices of hundreds of Trekkers, many of whom wrapped up their Ottawa Trek only to start a new quixotic trek to Spain a few months later to join the Mac Paps. The Mackenzie-Papineau Division, Canadian youth fighting for the Spanish people and their elected government, fighting Franco and his mercenaries in the Spanish Civil War. Spain was the first breaker in that riptide of fascism. Imagine hundreds of young Canadian ragtag veterans of the Ottawa Trek, clutching outdated rifles, "the *Internationale* wrapped around their shoulders," as Al Purdy once wrote. Even so, half of them found that lofty mantle no protection against Franco's Stutka bombers, borrowed from Hitler, and mortar and machine guns contributed by Mussolini, as the Mac Paps simply became part of the warm-up, merely target practice for the machinery of the greater wars, for the greater good, of the greater reichs that were to follow, just a few months later.

So, this is about more than the Ottawa Trek. It is about those voices that hold the clues to what happened to this country, to my neighbours, in the seventy or so years since Regina's Market Square. I wonder how these twin virgin provinces of Saskatchewan and Alberta conceived and nurtured, in their identical twin wombs, such divergent world views, nurturing both Bible Bill Aberhart and Tommy Douglas, like Cain and Abel, from the same parched prairie.

Think of Tommy Douglas! Recently voted "Most Famous Canadian," the first CCF premier in Canada, who initiated, incubated, and mid-wived medicare in North America, thirty years before President Clinton impotently aborted his promise of public health care in the U.S. — aborted for fear of the same powerful interest groups that Premier Douglas chose to ignore.

And what about Bible Bill Aberhart? He, on the other hand, was the first Social Credit premier in Canada, father of funny money, and *Back-to-the-Bible Hour*, surrogate father of Ernest and Preston Manning, of Ralph Klein, and of the photogenic, meteoric Stockwell Day, one time western Pretender to the Canadian throne, not to mention their latest heir, Stephen Harper.

Late some nights, when only my journal and my quirky speculations entertain me, I wonder whether Tommy Douglas and Bible Bill both read the same newspapers the day following the Regina Riot? Did they both vote against Prime Minister R.B. Bennett three months later? Did Cain and Abel both participate in that moment of collective common sense when Canadians booted out a wealth-blinded demagogue who was plunging us further into the Great Depression, like Archie Bunker's favourite president, Herbie Hoover? Or would a Calgary Aberhart right-wing nut secretly vote for a Calgary Bennett right-wing nut, when push came to shove?

"From religion, to poetry, to politics! You gonna piss off every reader in the entire country before you even get this bloody story in gear, before you finally decide to pop the fucking clutch and let her roll."

Sammy again. Just when I thought I might include his voice in this story, he pipes up again like an ignorant rounder with a month's pay and one night to spend it.

"What did I say, man? There you go insulting the salt-of-the-earth working man again, Paul. Not one of whom will listen to your screwed-up story, if you mention another fucking politician. Like we should care about how the dickheads voted, you know what I'm saying?"

Sorry, folks. But I do hear what he is saying. I also know that he is occasionally good at smelling dead end tangents, so I owe him sometimes. I just wish he would shut up while I try to explain why I can't just "pop the clutch" on the story of Arthur (Slim) Evans without including people like Sammy and people like me from the dawn of the twenty-first century. Not to mention some from the last five decades of the twentieth century. It's like Ondaatje said, sometimes you have to meander to find the best route to town.

"All right, Numb Nuts, but I'm telling you straight. No one wants to hear your dick-head explanations. Who the hell's Ondaatje anyway?"

Forgive me for allowing this guerrilla voice to ambush me in the middle of my writing. It only happens late at night when I've had one too many beer. But you see, before I was a history professor, I worked in a federal penitentiary in Drumheller. That is the town where Slim Evans first walks into Canadian history and into my story too. I first heard his story in the slammer. Slim spent time in the slammer. And the slammer provides a whole other layer of literary consciousness and language, which surfaces late at night when I begin to doubt the orthodoxy of our realist tradition in literature. A kind of Garcia Marquez rye whisky seeps into my blood, and W.O. Mitchell's Saint Sammy loosens my tongue. Never mind. You'll like Sammy better when you meet him in person. I used to think he was just another red-neck Albertan in the audience, too ignorant to recognize his own best interest, too much in the moment to even guess that he and I might be a part of this history.

For now I see through a glass darkly that Sammy and I, for better or for worse, are in this story together.

2

SEEDS OF THE TREK IN MOUSELAND

PAUL HEARS T.C. DOUGLAS SPEAK OF HISTORY

W AY BACK IN THE MID-NINETIES when I began talking to Daniella and Charles about these veterans of the Trek and the riot, Daniella started talking about recording these stories on tape. I said that only the eyewitnesses deserved to be taped. A dangerous woman, that Daniella. She promptly pointed out that a number of the stories I told about growing up in Tommy Douglas's Saskatchewan were in fact eyewitness accounts and that she rests her case. So eventually we did record some of the stories that she and Charles insisted I read to our Tuesday Night History Club at BJ's. The now-notorious club was conceived, by the way, out of that first innocent intercourse about recording eyewitnesses.

I first met Daniella through Charles, a former friend of my father's, way back in the sixties in Saskatchewan. Sometime in 1996 Charles had met this new associate minister of the United Church at an Alcoholics Anonymous conference, where she was delivering a paper on youth alcohol abuse, while he was part of a panel about revision of the AA philosophy. She was intrigued with his clerical background, his life journey, and his unique philosophies. They started visiting regularly and Charles invited her to BJ's to meet an old friend of his (yours truly), over our semi-regular Tuesday-evening beer. I had just signed the divorce papers with my wife; I suppose Charles felt that I could use the consolation of any intelligent and mature company.

Daniella was a single mom who had been forced to put off her university and career plans until her daughter was older. Saint Paul's United was her first major assignment in youth and social outreach ministries. On our very first meeting I was shocked and delighted to find out that Daniella's grand-father happened to be the late Robert "Doc" Savage, the youngest of four division leaders on the On-to-Ottawa Trek. Since I had interviewed Doc in Quesnel, B.C., I started speculating about the chances of him visiting Daniella in Grande Prairie and telling his own story to us all. On our fourth or fifth Tuesday together I explained my idea of several casual lectures by Doc to our group; immediately Charles, along with Tom and Cam, our musician friends, all signed on to the project, some of them probably thinking it was merely pub-time fancy.

However, Daniella narrowed her eyes and stared at me, her lips doing this strange, tense dance that I had seen before. Ultimately, she made it happen, and before we knew it BJ's Tuesday Night History Club was alive and kicking in the womb. Cam was the sound man for the house band and for most of the live acts that played the BJ's stage on weekends. He was a huge man with a giant presence at BJ's; his pull with the management would be to our advantage. Tom, a slight wiry bass player with big hair and a mountain-man beard, performed with the house band. Roots, blues, rock and even bluegrass pulsed through his arteries as naturally as red corpuscles. Both of these men had professional wives whose income allowed for the luxury of middle-aged husbands addicted to music. Tom and Cam were into professionally recording Doc's lecture by putting it through the sound board or some damn thing. Finally months later we had a commitment from Doc and we enthusiastically planned a dress rehearsal, so to speak. So a couple of weeks before Doc came, Daniella insisted that I read a certain story, which she had discovered in an older version of my journals, to our embryonic Tuesday Club. You see, she and I had begun trading books as well as our own research and publications, and now she was making me go public with some unpublished autobiographical creative writing. Cam and Tom could try out the recording equipment before the real thing with Doc, she suggested.

So there we were in the south-west corner of BJ's Bar & Cue Club, between the pool tables and the stage, an area not normally used, except when the place fills up for the live music on Friday and Saturday nights. The main bar and sports lounge, with televisions tuned to hockey, are in the next room, although there is no actual door anymore, just a doorway between the two rooms. The place is old. From the outside it looks like maybe a couple of buildings were pulled together over a makeshift foundation. Inside, the walls, the exposed beams, the floor and the furniture are all an ageless wood, more or less preserved with a secret concoction of varnish and beer. If nails were ever used, no one can find a trace of them now, probably driven in, filled, and varnished over. A Mike Holmes sleuth could probably tell that long ago, probably when they joined the two buildings, an adjoining wall to the stage and dance-floor room had been partially cut away for a view of the action. Our corner acts as the last-choice overflow for those who don't care about sound quality, or for latecomers on the crowded weekends.

The owner has set up this separate room so that he can allow minors in to play the pool tables and two or three video games until 9 p.m., without technically violating the *Liquor Control Act*. Or maybe the normally strict laws on miners get grandfathered for places like this. That is why we start after 9 p.m. with our Tuesday Club meetings now. Monday and Tuesday are the only nights when there is neither live music nor karaoke. So there we were — Daniella, Charles and I with a beer each, and Tom and Cam with a pitcher of draft between them. Cam had let the management know about our semi-private party. Everyone was a bit more talkative, as if we really were throwing a party instead of pursuing our regular Tuesday dialogue. When Cam finally flipped a switch, I introduced the entertainment for the evening, standing at a little lectern that Daniella had brought for me, probably from Saint Paul's United.

T.C. (Tommy) Douglas, leader of the CCF/NDP. Glenbow Museum Archives, Calgary. NA-2864-997.

"The story is set in 1961," I began, "at a Masonic Lodge in Leader, Saskatchewan, near where the South Saskatchewan River and the Red Deer River meet as they force their right-wing Alberta currents into a decidedly left-wing Saskatchewan. At the age of eight, I've just sneaked in to the back row in a community hall a couple of blocks from home, to have a peak at the Premier of Saskatchewan, who is already speaking to the locals about his new plans for health-care. Political meetings didn't attract many children my age, but my teacher's daily current events session had piqued my interest in Premier Tommy Douglas.

"Question from the brother with the John Deere cap," said the Premier.

"I ain't so sure about the brother part, but I am sure about one thing — that politicians don't seem to make time for the man-on-the-street, less he's reduced to marching in the goddamn street. Normally politicians don't show their faces here unless they're about to lose the next election."

Scattered nervous laughter greeted the heckling, and at eight years old, I was torn between laughter and embarrassment, fearing that perhaps the farmers of Leader, Saskatchewan, did not know how to act properly in the presence of the Premier. The slight-of-stature Premier with the high-pitched voice did not look like the forbidding image I had conjured up from the teacher's words about "the Premier of Saskatchewan, Tommy Douglas." This was the same Douglas my father condemned through clenched teeth and with furrowed brow. My father was an evangelical preacher. At the moment though, I naively thought this short skinny Premier could use someone to defend his dignity before this uncouth stubble-jumper, but I was wrong.

"In my experience, you're absolutely right about the politicians," Tommy Douglas dead-panned, as if the Premier of Saskatchewan could never be included in that hated species called "politician."

"In the Dirty Thirties, wasn't till our boys in the relief camps took to marching in the street and riding the rails towards Ottawa that the Tories down east and the Liberals at the Regina Legislature finally started talking to them about work and wages and their right to dignity. The boys had to march in the streets, get their heads bashed in, and some of them took a few bullets in their bodies, before the politicians took their eyes off Wall Street and Toronto's Bay Street long enough to pay attention to Main Street."

Another man in sooty coveralls in the back row, a couple of chairs down from me suddenly went from sullen relaxation to rigid attention during the Premier's last two sentences. He had to be a railroad section-hand, and I cringed when he rose from his seat to wave a weapon-like finger, his voice drawing the attention of the entire audience to us in the back row.

"He's right about that, by God. I was there that night on Market Square."

I slumped lower in my chair beside him, trying in vain to disappear. With all these old folks there, I was afraid that someone would recognize me and remark on it to my parents, who expected me to stray no further than the alley behind the house and our half of the block. But now, suddenly, half the town seemed focused on this guy and me, the kid in the back row beside this angry man in the coveralls.

"Police charged the crowd yelling like banshees, swinging their clubs like we were wild dogs when all we were doing was standing peacefully listening to the speakers up there on the platform."

"You were there that night! You were on the Ottawa Trek?" The Premier looked like he appreciated the support.

"Hell, no. I wasn't a striker. I was just a section-hand on the CPR, just got off a late day shift, went over to hear the speakers. Most of the crowd weren't strikers that night, regular Regina folk mostly. The buggers charged the Square on a perfectly peaceful crowd, clubbed at us, knocked over a baby carriage not ten yards from me. The mother was screaming 'cause she'd been pushed by the crowd fleeing the cops, and couldn't get to the baby on the ground there." The anger on his face and in his huge frame rose till I thought I could feel his heat.

Premier Douglas cut in, "Some of you are too young to remember what happened that night in Regina. You need to listen to this man. He can tell you what it's like to live under governments that would rather blame the people than help them. Go on — tell them what happened that night, and why it happened, if you want."

The man's energy faltered then. I suppose he finally realized that the Premier of the province, already legendary for his oratory, had just turned the stage over to him, an uneducated CPR section-hand still in his coveralls from a late day shift, just like he was some twenty-seven years before.

"Well, I wanna tell you, them Mounties rode us down like they were on a bleeding fox hunt that evening; even when we tried to get out of their way or find an alley to hide in, they come after us. Some of them relief camp strikers finally got tired of running and stood up to them. Used a bus and some parked cars to barricade the street there on 11th Avenue, 'cause them Mounties and city cops kept coming at 'em, driving 'em. I mean here we were, already five or six blocks from Market Square, and they won't even let some thirty, forty of those boys walk in orderly file back to the stadium where they're camping, without blocking their path, riding down on 'em, beating on 'em, cracking skulls, firing over our heads. Then finally those city cops fired right into the crowd there on 11th Avenue, near the Post Office. Shot down damn near a dozen of them right before my eyes. Ambulances, local cars trying to take 'em out to emergency. It's a miracle more didn't die.

"They say none of them that was shot got killed, but I tell you, some of them boys that was cut down that night, those bodies disappeared from the face of the known earth. Family out on the Island never saw their son again, but lots of living folks saw him downtown Regina that night for the last time. And he wasn't the only one."

He had his fire back now.

Tommy Douglas jumped in as he paused. "So tell these younger folk here why a Tory Prime Minister would sic the Mounties on a peaceful Saskatchewan crowd in Market Square, Regina."

"Well, sir, I don't wanna take up the stage here. People come to hear you, not me. But you know, it weren't so different then, than now. They were telling everyone the boys were commies or led by commies anyway. Bunch a young unemployed kids get organized and stand up for themselves, ask the government for decent wages, 'stead of twenty cents a day. So right away they're all devil-led Bolsheviks trying to overthrow the government. Like you here, trying something new with this medicare so the average Joe can afford a doctor for the wife or kids, an' right away they raise the red bogey, commnist plot for sure, you know. What can you say? Maybe they gotta suffer more before they get the message."

Now that short, skinny little man in the suit, who had ruled the province for seventeen years, rose up to his full five feet five inches in the tense silence, and, like a bantam-weight boxer magically transforming into a heavy-weight, he took over the ring, growing in stature as his voice rode the emotion of the moment, like Billy Graham warming up for an altar call.

"Now you younger folk could pay some heed to these folk who have seen the thirties and the darker face of what my Liberal friends like to call 'free' enterprise. Free for whom, I'd like to know. 'Every man for himself!' said the Elephant as he danced among the chickens!" The crowd's laughter suggested they were settling in for the entertainment they'd been expecting. The man my teacher sometimes called Tommy was way past warm-up now; this was no shadowboxing.

"I'm all for healthy competition, as long as we don't force children, or the poor, to compete with Rocky Rockefeller in the same boxing ring. In that kind of perverted freedom your odds of survival are about equal in the Amazon jungles or concrete jungles of Harlem or in the Bank Manager's offices of the Saskatchewan wheat belt, for that matter. But we in Saskatchewan believe there is room here in this Canada of ours for compassion, and the same dignity for all of us. What our brother in the back row said about the red scare tactics reminds me of a story some of you may have heard me tell before.

"There was a kingdom that I'm sure you're all familiar with, called Mouseland. That's right, Mouseland. And the good mice folk of that land were preyed upon mercilessly by the cats that ruled that kingdom. Black Cats they were, and fat cats, but they got elected every four years as if it were their divine right to rule the mice. Finally the oppression and the misery became so unbearable the mice got together and voted for the opposition, the White Cats. Well, turns out the White Cats didn't seem to have the best interests of the mice at heart either and the predatory practices and misery for mice continued. So come another four years they voted out the fat White Cats and voted back the Black Cats who were a bit leaner but all the more anxious it seems, despite their promises, to prey on the mice.

"Finally, at a meeting like this, one of the young mice stood up in the back and says, 'Ehhh... excuse me folks, I... I'm kinda new to this politics, but... but it occurs to me that maybe we should stop electing cats there, and, uh, vote in some of our mouse folk!'

"Well! You should have heard the commotion. 'Socialist!' they called him. Some suspected he was a Bolshevik in league with a foreign government. Most everyone agreed that such sentiments were most un-mouse-like."

The crowd was smiling and chuckling now. Tommy was rolling, and even Liberals wouldn't be caught rooting for the fat cats at the moment. And there in the back was a young mouse, feeling some new exciting kinship with this applauding CPR section-hand two chairs down, with this brave new leader of Mouseland, visiting our lowly town. This was an important adult-thing going on here and I was a part of it. Somehow I knew that this new feeling was something not to be shared with my father if I wished to keep it intact. But the Premier wasn't finished.

"But, you see folks, when someone has the courage of conviction to speak up for truth, it's like the Sower broadcasting his seed. Much of it falls on soil so eroded or beaten down that the message can't take root, but some of it falls on fallow ground, you see. Are you with me now? Certainly the Bay Street brokers and bankers that bankroll the Tory and Liberal parties alike can't begin to understand the microscopic miracles we call germination, not to mention the devastations of drought, erosion, rust, and hoppers. Hence the truth of that venerable proverb: Liberal, Tory, same old story! But the mouse-like folks of this province have long since got the message about the fat cats, and haven't been so mouse-like or timid for some time now.

"I remember in that provincial election in '44, one crusty old codger piped up with the challenge, 'Young man, why should we move from a proven party like the Liberals or Conservatives to vote for this new racket called CCF?' I said, 'Sir, I think I can give you the reason if you can answer the question I have for you. Why would you vote for the same party your banker votes for?' There was a silence in that hall, till the farmers were sure no bank manager was present, and then one or two started clapping. And then more. And you know what? Folks in Saskatchewan haven't been voting the same as Bay Street bankers from that day till now.

"We've since moved from under a crushing debt left to us by our Liberal predecessors, from a time when we were the poorest, most indebted province in the whole dominion. During these seventeen years we've not only paid off the debt, got the bankers off our backs; we've also proceeded with rural electrification, telephone lines, sewer and running water to every corner of the province. We've moved from the dark ages into the twentieth century. You folks did that. But how did you folks accomplish those miracles? Through profiteering multinational corporations? Or through community cooperation! Through the generosity of the big banks? Or through the rural electrification co-ops! The grain marketing pools! Through common-sense community initiatives for the public good, for even the weakest in our society! Saskatchewan folk can be proud of the example they've set for all of North America.

"And now in that same tradition of community cooperation and compassion we are in a position to fulfil the promise of full, publicly funded medicare to all citizens of the province, from the unborn baby nurtured in the mother's womb to the eldest grandparents that might need a little extra attention and care in their twilight years after bearing the brunt of the hungry thirties. Not to mention the brunt of the callous ideologies of the Liberals and Tories. These parties have been talking about implementing publicly funded healthcare since the National Liberal Convention in 1919, doing half measures, reaching towards it and drawing back. Well... now we're just going to *do it*, folks. It's the democratic thing; it's the *right* thing! Most countries of Northern Europe, including England, and now the new state of Israel, have all done it.

"Here in Saskatchewan it is merely courageous mice looking after the rights of mice rather than the interests of fat-cat health-insurance companies, many of which take the profits from their gouging premiums south of the border, out of circulation here in Saskatchewan where they might do our economy some good. Why not keep our money here where it can create jobs for our children, rather than give it to whoever is using it down in New York or Chicago?'

People were clapping vigorously whenever the Premier made a point, and I was into it, too. Responding to this fire-brand preacher was easier than an "Amen!" or "Praise the Lord" at a Pentecostal revival meeting, of which I'd had some experience. However, I had noticed my former teacher from grade two, Mrs. Samuelson, in the second row, and I was nervous that she might recognize me and mention my presence to my father, thinking that was something he'd be happy to hear. I wasn't sure how late it was getting and whether or not the folks would be looking for me, so I slipped out the back while Premier Douglas was still in full stride, my mind full of these new adult issues. Like fat cats preying on mice. Like this medicare thing. And most of all this story of police beating and shooting citizens in Regina.

"I ran most of the two blocks back to the alley behind our house, thinking that my father was a teenager during the thirties. He had lots of stories about the dirty thirties, but he'd never mentioned police shooting folks in Regina. I imagined the Mounties on horseback chasing me down the alley. Then I stopped to catch my breath and walked over to peek through the cracks in the fence to see if Mom or Dad were in the yard looking for me.

"I began to recall with dread the time I joined a bunch of the guys wandering down past the tracks to play cowboys and Indians among the bales in the feed-lot. We had all lost track of time in the fantasy world of smoking guns and killer heroes, until the fear of God struck me full force with the low setting sun in my gunslinger eyes. The wrath of my father would be smouldering red and large across my horizon if it was as late as I thought it might be. Running toward home, I was out of breath and furtive then, just like this time, when I reached this same alley. I had missed supper that time, but I got away with a week's grounding rather than the usual leather-razor-strap licking. How to explain my absence this time? Mouseland seemed as much a fantasy world as the gunslinger's... beyond explanation or defence, at least before the Lord's prosecuting attorney, my own father.

"I don't really remember now if they did indeed notice my absence. I suppose I would remember if I got a licking, or the embarrassment of trying to explain the inexplicable: sneaking down to the Masonic Lodge into an adult meeting that wasn't even a church meeting. How would a kid explain a kid's curiosity about the CCF bumper sticker on Mrs. Samuelson's car, the only sticker of its kind in town, to my knowledge, and a premier called Tommy — a kid's name, almost."

3

WHERE THE TREK BEGINS

DOC SAVAGE ON THE RELIEF CAMP WORKERS UNION

IT IS MAY 1997, AND DANIELLA and I have brought Robert "Doc" Savage down to BJ's tonight. He lives in Quesnel, but he is staying in Grande Prairie a few days visiting Daniella, his granddaughter. Doc Savage has agreed to try a little talk, or reminiscence, for our Tuesday Club, because somehow this dedicated core of regulars have taken a genuine interest in this On-to-Ottawa Trek that I've been jawing about off and on for the past year. There are only five of us as audience to begin with: Charles and I, Tom and Cam, and Daniella, nursing our drinks at a couple of small round tables drawn together. We've been semi-regulars for almost a year now at these tables, but this night is the first time we have had a real eyewitness of the Ottawa Trek to tell us his story. Cam has got permission from the night-shift manager again to use the quiet part of the bar for this event; I'm sure he is secretly glad that we hang out in this deserted corner, and that we only do so on Tuesdays so as not to give his bar a grey-hair reputation with the younger crowd.

See, I was forty-four when this occurred, with a bit of grey, and Charles was seventy-eight with a lot of grey highlighting his angular Afro-Canadian visage. Almost nine months ago when Daniella started having the occasional drink with Charles and me, the manager asked me quietly who the new cougar was. Daniella was about thirty-seven then, but I thought the term was an insult for someone as young-looking as her. He looked quite sceptical when I introduced her as Reverend Daniella Arthur, United Church clergy. The manager, familiar with our habits now, realizes that there is no big money to be made from our tables, but knows we're no trouble either.

This night he has dubiously allowed us a corner for our own makeshift history lecture. So although we've been the Tuesday Club informally for almost a year; this is the night that most of us feel was the official birth of BJ's Tuesday Night History Club. We use the name ironically of course. But Doc has come prepared with an array of notes, newspaper clippings, and some photos; he obviously takes the club very seriously. Daniella does the introductions from her "portable pulpit" as she calls it. She explains what our little session is all about before Cam punches "record" on the tape recorder. She proudly tells us a bit about her grandfather who, at twenty-three years of age, was appointed by Arthur (Slim) Evans as the youngest leader of a division — Division Three of the Relief Camp Workers Union.

Then, for the sake of the recording, she says, "Gentlemen, I give you Robert 'Doc' Savage." Her grandfather rises rather spryly for an eighty-five-year-old as we applaud. He heads quickly to the pulpit but is intercepted by a hug from Daniella that he is quite unprepared for. When he recovers his composure from that he straightens his notes and begins.

"Hi folks. No, hell it's not 'Doc.' It's been years since anyone called me that. Just Bob. Some of the boys like Matt Shaw were calling me Doc for the papers again for the Trek's fiftieth anniversary that the Saskatchewan Federation of Labour had there in Regina. Sent us out on the rails to see Brian Mulroney, if you please, as if that somehow could complete the Trek of '35. The press want glamour stories, you see, and 'Doc Savage' sounds more glamorous than 'Robert.' Hell, 'Matt Shaw' wasn't even Matt's real name you know. Surdia was his family's name, but many of those that were blackballed took other names, you know. Especially the Ukrainians and Germans. Bennett was blaming everything on the 'foreign-born' and the Eastern European immigrants, you see, as if the true Canadians were all of good British stock, right?

"Oh yeah. That anti-immigrant bullshit had as much popular appeal in the general public in those days as it does in red-neck Reform country today. 'Foreign-born' the papers would say. They didn't beat around the bushes about it though in those days… like Preston up there in front of all of Canada. Did ya see'm there in the election debates? 'Now Reform is *pro*-immigration,' he sings like a bloody Baptist hymn. Alexa McDonough and Jean Chrétien are so baffled by that, they don't even think to ask him how cutting 300,000 immigrants per year to 150,000 immigrants (those with the right sort of cheque books and correct passports) — how slashing immigration in half could possibly be considered pro-immigration.

"Anyway I didn't have to change my name, back then, since I was born in Lancashire. My father and mother died in an influenza epidemic during the Great War, and the orphanage in Liverpool that took us kids used to pay their staff by selling the kids to farmers or families in Canada and Australia that needed free labour. So I was sent to Canada at twelve years old, a virtual slave to the Peterborough farmer who paid for me. It was bloody hell, folks, believe me. I think I was thirteen when I left him for good reason without saying good-bye. So I never had a chance to get an education or a trade. I just learned to survive with labouring jobs.

"Strictly working-class, my old man. That's why the orphanage could get away with that shit. Weren't any doctors in our family. 'Doc' was just a handle they hung on me after the Trek started, when one of the immigrant boys, who didn't understand our instructions well enough, cut up his elbow and hands when he jumped off a boxcar before the train had slowed enough.

He stumbled and hit the shale and cinders hard. I was the captain of Division Three, and felt responsible, so I removed the shale from the cuts, cleaned him up a bit, wrapped his arm and his hands, rigged a kind of a sling so he wouldn't be tempted to use the elbow, and the boys started calling me 'Doc' as a joke, you see. I've heard racier stories of where the nickname came from, but that's the way I remember it. Then Arthur Evans started calling me Doc and it kind of stuck. But it was only the boys on the Trek that ever called me that."

"Where did you first meet Arthur Evans?" I ask, as he pauses.

"Well, I'm getting to that. It all started in the relief camps. Evans was organizing the relief camp workers, and we first…"

"What the hell's a relief camp?" a voice from behind me interrupts.

"Sammy, if you wouldn't come in halfway through a story…"

"Can't help it. Just got off work."

"If you'd paid attention through high school you might've heard about relief camps in social studies," says Cam, the sound man.

"I made it through high school, most of it. Don't remember nothing about relief camps, mind you," Sammy replies. The waiter takes this opportunity to quietly drop off more peanuts, merely gesturing wordlessly to check for more orders.

"Sammy, this is Doc — Robert, I mean. And Doc, Sammy. Let him talk, will you Sammy? We got the tape rolling and I promised these guys I'd bring Doc down here and let them hear his story first hand." Actually we were all secretly delighted that Sammy made it because we thought he'd desert our area as soon as this club got too formal.

Typical unemployed men's relief camp in the B.C. interior, 1930s.
Glenbow Museum Archives, Calgary. NA-2279-1.

"Pleased to meet you, Sam," Doc says. "And you're right about those schools. High schools today are a dead loss for teaching your basic history or economics or politics. They don't teach about relief camps in any high school I know of. Couple history texts might refer in passing to the 'Regina Riot,' as they called it. Some don't even mention it. The thing about the relief camps, well, you see, there just weren't any jobs by '33, less you had a sure trade or a Longshoreman's Union ticket. And hell, they were laying off men on the docks, and on the CPR, the CNR — everywhere. Only union men with seniority had any sort of job security, and the young single guys, general labourers couldn't get work for love nor money. The most recently hired all got pink slips by the summer of '32. Bloody hell, over half the single guys seventeen and over were unemployed. You either joined the bums riding the rods, hoping for a temporary farm job, or you made your way to a relief camp. No single man seventeen or older qualified for relief, you see, and, hell, their families couldn't feed them. We still had some pride, you know, and the government promised us road work and at least some chicken-shit wages if we moved to these relief camps.

"Now let me tell you, these camps weren't the glorious democratic communities Steinbeck praises in *The Grapes of Wrath*, by God."

"Hey, we had that sucker in high school. Fuckin' turtle crossing the road, right?"

"Sammy, it's Doc's turn now," Daniella suggests gently. As a United Church minister she was in charge of youth programs, peace and justice programs, all the interesting stuff. When she speaks Sammy listens.

"Sorry, Daniella. Excuse the language. Forgot you were here for minute. Just trying to prove to Cam I wasn't totally comatose through high school. Alright, sorry Doc, I'm listening."

"Well these relief camps weren't FDR's Okie havens, that's for damn sure. The bloody Department of National Defence took them over and dropped the wages to twenty cents a day. No one in their right mind could call them wages. Forced labour, slavery, call it what you will. The thing is Bennett got elected boasting that he'd fire the Canadian economy right onto the international stage, so, you see, he couldn't have a ragtag army of unemployed kids hanging around to remind voters that his cowboy version of economics was pushing most of the Canadian economy further into the crapper. So he tries to herd all us single unemployed boys into these work camps away from the public eye. Bennett tried to suggest that all transient workers were bums and derelicts. 'This government is not going to be a wet nurse to every derelict in the country!' he said, sort of like Ralph Klein when he was mayor of Calgary.

"Trouble is that in the fall of 1929 road work was paying fifty cents an hour, but when they set up these relief camps in B.C. (fall of '31, I think), they cut the wages to two dollars a day with an immediate eighty-five cent reduction for board and room. A year later in the fall of '32 the feds and province joined forces in running these camps with wages dropping to seven-fifty a month as the relief camps started filling up. When Prime Minister Bennett turned these camps over to the Department of National Defence, in July of '33, he reduced the so-called wages to twenty cents a day. We were being humiliated as unpaid labour. Slave labour, basically, because there was no alternative besides theft or the life of a hobo. Like I said, relief was not available if you were seventeen or older and physically able. Some provinces cut them off at sixteen, I heard.

"The men in some of the camps were forced to do military drills and basically lick the boots of some camp foremen who thought they were big shots. When we met with Prime Minister Bennett later during the Trek, Evans had to stick the evidence for this right in front of his face, before Bennett would admit that it might be going on. Hell, if we wanted to march and drill, we could have joined the army and got paid for it.

"The camps were pretty crude, but the worst of it was they robbed you of any hope. There was no proper recreation; the food was bland and basic. We heard all kinds of stories of government supplies being ripped off by the local camp bosses and contractors. The boots were these ugly black army-issue things that had been sitting around for fifteen years since the end of the Great War. The stitching was rotten and they tended to fall apart on you when you put the boots to the shovel in a serious way. The dorms were crowded and smelled like hell. Wet socks drying over the stove, some of the boys not having a clue how to take care of their laundry.

Relief camp workers were paid 20 cents a day to pull tree stumps.
Glenbow Museum Archives, Calgary. NA-2279-4.

31

"I remember Camp 333 — Beaver Ranch they called it — near Merritt. Primitive shacks. Forty-five-gallon-drum wood stoves. Had to have a regular wood gang to keep enough firewood stacked up in the winter. No electricity in the bunks, just these coal oil lamps, so it was too dark to read when the sun went down. There was nothing to do, and monotonous evenings and bad food were the routine. There was no first-aid there of any kind beyond a supply of aspirins and laxatives that you could borrow from the cook.

"The conditions were depressing, but worse than the physical conditions was the isolation. Nothing to do. Nothing to read. No women, of course. Some of you maybe know what that's like in a barracks or in the slammer. And there was no hope, you see. A man can survive if there's a bit of hope. But every new fish that came into camp had no encouraging news from the outside. 'Cause he wouldn't have been there if he hadn't given up on finding a regular job that could give him some dignity. One of the boys made a sign for the entrance to one of these camps that read 'Abandon hope, all ye that enter here!' I think that's from a novel by Kafka or one of them existentialists, or maybe Dante, but damned if I can remember which one. Where's that from, Paul?"

"You're right with Dante. Dante's *Inferno*."

"Thank you. That man is a walking library, case you haven't discovered. Anyway, the sign had a dark sense of humour and profound truth at the same time.

"So in June of '33 this guy comes into camp, only works there for a few days before they run him out, 'cause he's passing out copies of the *Relief Camp Worker*, this underground paper, and explaining that we should send delegates to this conference in Kamloops in July where all the relief camp workers in B.C. were gonna decide whether to organize into one big union — amalgamate any unions that existed in the camps, with the eventual goal of a national relief camp union. Well I can't remember none of my camp going, but sure enough we hear that they voted to form a national relief camp workers union. Some of the guys had a good laugh at that, but they weren't laughing long, 'cause, sure as hell, if they don't send out an organizer from Kamloops to sign us up.

"Now we'd all heard rumours of relief camp unions, and the names of Smoky Cumber and Malcolm MacLeod were floating around, but it was that summer that we all signed up, right across B.C. apparently, can't speak for the rest of the country. Bloody hell, we had nothing to lose. They say MacLeod was the first secretary of the union, but Matt Shaw seemed to have taken over as secretary by the time we all got together in Vancouver, after the bosses locked us out of camp for refusing to work. Smoky Cumber was still president and Ronnie Liversedge — he wrote a book on the Trek, you know — Ronnie was on the executive and in charge of the presses. The

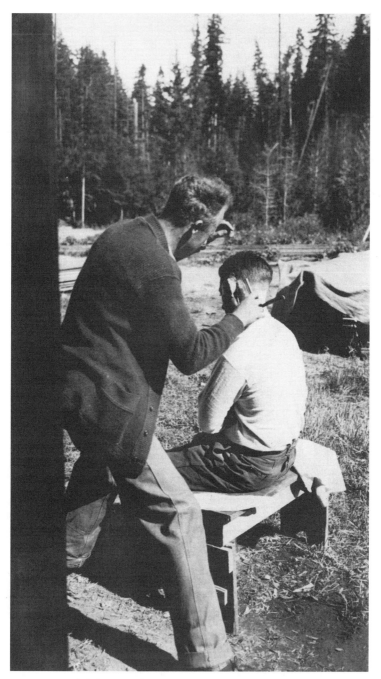

Relief camp workers cut each other's hair to avoid head lice.
Glenbow Museum Archives, Calgary. NA-2279-8.

Relief camp worker washing his clothes.
Glenbow Museum Archives, Calgary. NA-2279-7.

irony is that most of these guys were blackballed from the camps and so they became the activists in Vancouver.

"A guy needs to understand the summer and fall of '33 if you're gonna understand the Trek of '35. There were more guys blackballed that summer of '33 than ever. I mean they were always shanghaiing someone in those camps. Speak too much at a supposedly secret meeting, or get caught passing out *Relief Camp Worker* papers and pretty soon you disappeared in the middle of the night. In B.C., blackballing was especially vicious and extremely organized. McCarthyism was tame compared to the 'dirty thirties.'"

"Sorry Doc. What's this blackballin'?" Sammy has waited for Doc's slight pause this time.

"Sam, working in the patch you probably know that from the push on up, they don't have any use for the unions. Normally the bosses are just ignorant about what they're all about, but sometimes the big shots are just greedy and think they might not get to retire to Phoenix soon enough if they give their workers decent benefits. So whenever they find a worker that's talking up the union or signing up their workers, they fire them and blackball them. These days they fax and email their names to everyone in the Chamber of Commerce or anyone in business in their network of contacts, warning them that this lad's a troublemaker. 'Commie agitators' is what they called us back then. Department of Defence had a list of them, which they shared with relief agents, camp foremen and anyone else who cared. Lot of us back then that were blackballed ended up working in union headquarters in Vancouver, because the government relief offices in Vancouver wouldn't allow us back in the camps."

"So they blackballed you, too?" Sammy asks. "What were *you* nailed for?"

"I spoke up at one of the meetings we had one evening. Said I didn't think we had anything to lose by hitting the bricks — walking out, that is. I took a few RCW Union cards to help sign up the guys that hadn't signed on. A day later at breakfast they read off four names to report to the boss. They drove us out to the middle of nowhere, near what's now the Coquahalla highway, and told us to get out and walk. We hiked sixteen miles to Merritt where we pooled our coins for a loaf of bread and sausage, hopped the freight in to Vancouver.

"So Vancouver is where their blackballing backfired, as I was saying. All of us on the lists weren't allowed to work so eventually they had to give some of us relief money to keep us from starving and dropping dead on Hastings Street. So of course we all kept busy helping the Relief Camp Workers Union any way we could — distributing the papers and bulletins for public meetings, which Ronnie and Matt put out.

"Now Slim Evans had quite the reputation there already as the man behind the scenes, especially when it come to the underground press and organizing meetings. He'd led a major Hunger March in Vancouver a year earlier, where 3000 unemployed marchers swelled to a 30,000-strong crowd to hear the speeches on the Cambie Street Park Grounds. But, by the time I got to Vancouver in '33, he wasn't in charge, due to his arrest and trial for organizing the miners in Princeton. He had been the Vancouver organizer for the National Unemployed Workers Association, till the Workers Unity League drafted him as their main B.C. organizer. Now the Workers Unity League was the union face of the Communist Party of Canada in those days. So it isn't any wonder they were hounding Slim. He managed to find some time in the midst of his legal battles and speaking itinerary to plan the conference that reorganized and revitalized the Relief Camp Workers Union in the summer of 1933, but he spent the next eighteen months in the slammer in Okalla while we were on the ground organizing all the camps.

"But I remember some of the boys saying what a pleasure it was to work with him 'cause he would tell all these stories about the Wobblies and the OBU. Big Bill Hayward, Joe Hill, Ginger Goodwin — he'd worked with them all. He'd hit the bricks with the best of them. Guess that was before he came up to organize the miners there in the Drumheller Valley. Anyway, when he told a story, it just kinda lifted a guy, hearing some off-the-cuff retort Joe Hill had fired back to some copper boss in Utah. The boys would work their butts off for Evans; if he asked one of us to go up country with a message or papers for one of the relief camp locals, by God, it felt like we were in the vanguard of the revolution."

"So Doc, are you telling me you boys were commies and proud of it, or did you even know they were behind this?" Sammy is leaning forward on the back of his backward chair, hanging on his every word by now.

"Sam, we'd all been told by the camp managers or heard the rumours, but you gotta understand what unemployment and a bloody relief camp can do to a young man's self image, and, to be fair to the Communist Party, they were the only ones offering to organize the unemployed and the un-skilled workers at the time. You folks in these parts have grown up all your lives hearing folks talk about the scary 'red bogeyman,' but if you were an unemployed lad in the Great Depression with the whole world telling you that you're worthless, and stepping on your balls, well all I can tell you is that signing an RCW Union card wasn't anything like an intellectual joining the Communist Party. And you gotta understand that working for Slim Evans and the Relief Camp Union was like being touched by the Good Samaritan, you see. No priest nor politicians were about to dirty their hands with the likes of us. So 'who then was neighbour,' by Christ, to the beat-up and bloodied unemployed stiff lying on the Jericho road? The Workers Unity League.

"And Slim Evans, you see, he was something else. 'Cause you sensed that

Slim was part of something bigger than the Relief Camp Workers Union. Something that was part of the working man's history on this whole damn continent, but something that was especially alive and strong in the lumber camps and mining camps of the American northwest and the Canadian west.

"That's where the good union jobs were — in those camps and on the docks with the Longshoremen. Many young relief camp kids dreamed of landing a job like that some day. So working for the Relief Camp Workers Union made us all a part of that greater movement, and, sure as hell, Slim Evans was part of all that. Carpenter, miner, union organizer.

"It was Slim Evans who managed to break the stranglehold the United Mine Workers of America had in the Alberta coal fields. He brought some of the Drumheller locals into the One Big Union, to start with. The OBU they called it, back about 1918. We were stronger, more together, just listening to him talk about the old days in the OBU and the Wobblies. Hell, we sometimes just itched for Slim to say the words, 'Down tools!' 'cause we'd a hit the bricks with our heads high, if he gave the word.

"So, you see, by November of 1934 we were ready for the whole B.C. Relief Camp Union to walk. December 4th we cleaned out damn near every camp south of the Caribou and we all hit the bricks together in Vancouver, by God, and with about 1500 of us marching, people had to pay attention. They couldn't ignore us then.

"And so they set up this huge common front, which we initiated. A coalition of unions, CCFers, some veterans groups, even some churches, and they chose a delegation to go see Premier Patullo over in Victoria. So our Matt Shaw, must have been all of twenty-five years old, Matt led this delegation of six across on the ferry to Victoria to get an audience with the Premier. And they did, by God. When thousands march in the streets of downtown Vancouver, the politicians make time for you then, you see."

Well, that wasn't all Doc Savage said that night but we forgot to turn the tape over for the last bit. I was impressed with the group; all of a sudden they knew they wanted more of this, and so did Sammy. Others in the main room of the bar started looking in on us and some came to sit at tables nearby for various lengths of time. Word was out that Tom and Cam, two characters known by virtually everyone who tilted beer in this town, had joined up with two old philosopher farts and a foxy looking cougar rumoured to be moonlighting as a United Church minister. And they were running some kind of Tuesday Night History Club at BJ's. I swear that business picked up on Tuesdays from the curious coming to peek through the doors to verify the rumours.

4

EVOLUTION, MCCARTHY
AND MEDICARE IN MOUSELAND

HISTORY TOUCHES PAUL

I THINK I MENTIONED THAT BY the time Doc spoke the first time in May
of '97, Daniella and I were already trading recommended books, and
somehow she had talked me into lending her my original journal a couple
of times. So Daniella the Dangerous started pestering me to show Charles
my autobiographical stories about the socialization of a preacher's kid. He
liked them so much that the two of them coaxed me to share several with
the club. These early Pauline epistles started the tradition of each of the club
members sharing their humorous and sordid childhood history stories when
we didn't have any official or semi-official guests to entertain us. Political,
social or historical interests were preferred, but anything with a decent narrative was fair game since none of the nation's archivists were beating down
our doors just yet. Then again some nights we just argued about history or
current political stories.

"May I remind you, Paul," said Daniella, who was capable of the occasional moral lecture, "that you were an eyewitness to street-level debate
about the one of the greatest social changes and one of the greatest traumas
in Canadian history."

"And a great example of early '60s socialization of youth, in fundamentalist families," added Charles the sociologist. How can you win against these
two? So I promised I'd deliver the story the following week.

So the next Tuesday Daniella introduced me as if I were a famous novelist
reading at Harbour Front in Toronto. All of the Tuesday Club were there
except for Sammy.

"Thanks, folks. This is another Leader, Saskatchewan, story, 1962,
starting at the kitchen table in the Evangelical Church manse, which was no
mansion, let me tell you. As usual, I was tired of responding to my mother's
eternal question about what I'd learned in school that day, so I told her the
truth for a change, so here goes."

"Russell said that all that stuff about God creating the world in six days was
bullshit," I said, keeping a wary eye on my mother's reaction. The muscles

38

in her arm relaxed from pushing a wet rag over the sink counter, but face muscles tensed as she turned to face me.

"Paul, if I hear you use that word ever again, you are going to get a lickin' that you won't soon forget. You understand me?" I just stared back at her, with all the defiance of an eight-year-old going on ten. My father wasn't home and she hadn't threatened to tell him yet.

"I'm going to speak to your father about you playing with Russell. That kind of language is not going be used in this house, or at school, or at all by you, young man. Understand?" My eyes dropped and I nodded.

"Did Mrs. Nikish allow him to use that kind of language in the classroom?"

"He didn't say that in the class. They're not allowed to swear in school."

"Well I should hope not."

"He showed us this book with chimps, and apes, and these shaggy-haired cave men at recess before he showed it to her. She let him show it to the class. But she didn't seem all that excited about it."

"Well, they shouldn't be allowing him to bring any picture books about apes and evolution into your classroom. I just hope Mrs. Nikish had the sense to tell him to take it home again. I'd like to know what that Mrs. Gill is thinking of, letting her son bring that kind of garbage to a public classroom. How do you think God feels when he hears you repeating something like that?"

Now, I knew when Mom brought up God's feelings that my relationship with her had deteriorated precariously. I could tell that her angry admonishment had not satisfied her at all, and that the subjects of Russell, apes and bullshit were far from closed, considering her husband, my father, was a strict evangelical clergyman.

The next day was Saturday, and I had to work with my father, handing him the hammer, the saw, the nails, while we constructed a playhouse from salvaged two-by-four studs and some cheap grade of plywood that Beaver Lumber was trying desperately to liquidate. Not that I knew the grade of the lumber then. It all looked like the stuff of romance to me: a future hideout for Robin Hood and his locally drafted merry men. And if my older sister refused to play Maid Marion like any altruistic Christian sister should, well the boys would deal with that as only devious school boys could.

The future romance, however, was jarring against the realism of a father who constantly berated his son for being a dreamer, or lazy, as in "You don't want to grow up to be a good-for-nothing ditch-digger."

"Sounds just like my old man," Tom said as he set up a beer for me beside the lectern.

"Thanks Tom," I paused for a swallow (it was even my label), and continued reading.

Such comments were due to my attention straying from the disciplined concentration my father knew was required to make a practical man out of a plodding day-dreamer of a boy. Why couldn't I figure out when he needed the hammer without his having to ask for it, he wanted to know? Why couldn't I concentrate on the task at hand?

Fortunately our neighbour, Doc Cousins, was having a local underemployed carpenter build a fence between our properties that same day, so every now and then Doc came out to ensure that his money was being properly spent. Normally, that wouldn't have entailed speaking to my father. In fact, Doc Cousins rarely spoke to anyone, though occasionally he could mumble a few words of cross-examination to a patient he was attending.

This day was different though. Who is to say whether initiating conversation was penance for building a fence without first talking to his neighbour about it (a high-privacy fence at that), or whether the issue of the conversation had become so urgent that his normal British aloofness and professional reticence had to be jettisoned temporarily for the sake of the common good. Well, 'common good' might not have been his chosen phrase, you see — the particular menace that loosed his tongue into the fray was those godless socialists in Regina.

"So what do you think about this T.C. Douglas and his medicare?' He spat out the final word like he had accidentally chewed up his cigar butt.

"Oh I know! Well, that seminary in Brandon where Douglas was educated is well-known for their commnist sympathies,' said the preacher. 'They've brainwashed many a young man, I've heard. Young fellows go in there with ideals and a calling, but maybe a lack of practical grounding in common sense, and they come out preaching this social gospel. Now, Doc, some of these guys are just too wet-behind-the-ears to know that "social gospel" is just a fancy name for socialism — preaching socialism instead of the Gospel they were called to."

"Huh. Not surprised," Doc wasn't used to such complex responses. "Well this CCF racket is going to run decent medicine into the ground in this province. Why, every self-respecting physician worth his salt will be pulling up stakes and moving south of the border."

Now the Doc knew about south of the border. Every year, come goose season, his wealthy doctor friends from American Medical Association conventions came north to the Canadian prairie flyways with their well-oiled 12-gauges, digging goose pits before the murky frosty dawn in order to shoot down the Greater Canada Greys. The Americans were the guests of their good friend Doc Cousin, and a mickey of medicinal fortification for the coffee thermos was as important as the 12-gauge. There's been precious little historical analysis of the role the goose pits played in forging Canadian-American alliances in the late fifties, against commnist infiltrations. For these doctors, it was not a question of silly swagger so much as pluck, and perhaps the hint of earthy metaphor, to suggest that slightly bigger calibre guns in slightly bigger goose pits and, who knows, maybe we could shoot down those incoming ballistic missiles the Ruskies were stockpiling. The American doctors were fans of the late Senator Joe McCarthy, whose House Committee on Un-American Activities was still powerful, with definite opinions and files on Douglas and medicare.

However, my father wasn't exactly the model Chamber of Commerce audience for the Doc's tirade against medicare and the CCF. That was the Co-operative Commonwealth Federation Party that had swept into power in Saskatchewan during the war, like some perverse prairie fire that refused to respect proper boundaries and influence. You see, the Doc lived between the parsonage and the church, a situation I'm sure he did not appreciate. This was not a proper respectable church like the United or Anglican varieties, or even the Catholic Church down the block. This was an upstart immigrant church, and no doubt Doc Cousins could hear them singing those German hymns right through the humble evangelical walls on Sunday mornings.

The church-owned manse on the other side of his property was a hovel cobbled together by the parish farmers who, according to local lore, pulled three granaries together over a hole in the ground. The hole was for the coal furnace, a potato bin, plank shelving for preserves and dark crawl spaces for children. They'd hammered the bins together, run the joists beneath for support, framed a couple of extra walls dividing the two outer granaries into two bedrooms on one side and a tiny living room and bedroom on the other, cutting the necessary doors and windows, stuccoing over the outside walls, and adjusting a few trusses and roof tiles to make it a house. Perhaps labour was cheaper than lumber at the time. The home came with a cistern under the crawl space, a pump on the kitchen sink, a coal stove and an outhouse — no permanent indoor bathroom, except for a ten-gallon pail under a sanded plywood seat downstairs in the hole in the ground upon which the shack squatted. That pail was reserved for forty-below winter weather and midnight emergencies. We had special concoctions of lye or lime for those slop pails to battle the stench. Fortunately, I only had to empty them once, to my recollection.

"Empty it where?" asked Daniella, slight awe in her voice.

"Outhouse. Two-holer. Larger of the holes. Carefully. Because if you messed up, you cleaned up." That drew my biggest laugh of the evening and it wasn't even in the script.

There was a garage of sorts, but this had no disguise like the house. It was still barn-red over shiplap siding, as much a barn as it had ever been, before its relocation. So Doc wasn't likely to ask what new hovel the good pastor was hammering together out of salvaged scraps, although I'm sure my father, Reverend Wessner, was careful to explain his children's need for an eight-by-eight-foot, walk-in playhouse with an unpainted plywood roof like a squatter's shack.

The Doc was used to ignoring many affronts to civilization all around him. Instead of a sombre, manicured graveyard in the church's double lot next to his, the congregation graciously allowed the pastor a huge potato garden, so that he could fill up the cold-storage bins in the manse's basement. Keeping the pastor's family fed through the winter was the bottom line for this practical congregation. Regular salary, for example, was understood to be a matter of the best of intentions, but largely dependent on the state of the books, the cash flow and the progress of the treasurer's farm work.

The Doc's new fence was probably the result of an ultimatum from his wife, whose pedigreed golden Labs got rather excited at the sight of our pet rabbits that my father occasionally let loose in the yard; he just couldn't bare continuous captivity or squalor, even for soulless animals, without a few moments of relief or hope. The rabbits lived in a chicken-wire hutch stretching all along the back fence, but my father had dug and laid a stovepipe tunnel under the sidewalk and into another hutch inside the garage.

There were liberal amounts of straw in both hutches, and especially in the stovepipe tunnel, where the rabbits responded to the pastor's warm thoughtfulness with appropriately prodigious fecundity — spring, summer, fall and winter. We could never give away or liberate the rabbits fast enough, and, although we managed to recycle the local grocery-store's waste vegetables and our own leftover porridge, not all our neighbours had the same unconditional love of God's smaller creatures that we children and our father had. I am not sure that the new by-law against captive rodents within the city limits was aimed particularly at us. Nor am I sure that the Doc or his wife had any lobbying role in it. I do suspect that her Labs ate better than the parson's progeny.

But now, despite the rapidly rising fence between the properties, the immediate goal of the Doc was clearly a holy (if temporary) alliance against that dual threat to both moral and fiscal order, Premier Tommy Douglas himself, and his public health-care initiative. The Doc's overtures were not aimed at anything so grand as the classic European alliance of the privileged class and the clergy, which struggled to uphold the interests of landowners against those insatiable European labourers. After all, this particular clergyman had a social etiquette and heritage closer to the "little Europes" of the immigrant communities, rather than to the Tory establishment. Nevertheless, as Doc explained, respected professionals in towns like ours had a duty to speak out for the good of the community, for small-town values.

To my knowledge he did not use the term *noblesse oblige*, and I'm not sure my father would have been familiar with it, but Doc understood it and lived the concept. The upshot of the conversation was that Doc wanted the Reverend Wessner to come with him to Regina for a "day-of-action" rally against the medicare legislation, led by the doctors, of course, and financed by the American Medical Association. In 1962, the CCF Government in Saskatchewan was seen, by many businessmen and some workers, as a toehold for socialism in the western hemisphere, even though Douglas had been in power for seventeen years and hadn't nationalized any banks or seized any assets yet. Sure, they had retired the seemingly unconquerable Liberal debt and brought electricity, running water, roads and telephones to a largely rural population. Nevertheless, a toehold for socialism, even as Cuba was the "foothold" for the Kremlin and its plans for "world domination" — these beliefs had taproots tougher than dandelions, despite the continuing American Munro Doctrine that had graciously "protected" Canada and Latin America from such apocalyptic soviet dangers.

"In this medicare fiasco, Douglas is finally showing the CCF's true colours," Doc said. "Nationalizing potash mines, destroying medicine. They're out to destroy free enterprise, plain and simple."

"Sounds like he and Ralph Klein would have seen eye-to-eye," Cam chuckled.

Well, Doc Cousins was a bit to the right of Ralph Klein, but he certainly would have appreciated Ralph's efforts to reverse public health progress. My father certainly agreed that the CCF were against free enterprise. In retrospect, however, I wonder if he might not have had some doubts about opposing publicly funded medicare. He had buried his first wife, my mother, during the polio epidemic seven years earlier, and the hospital costs had almost buried us all. A miscarriage and the birth of two babies to his second wife involved medical bills that dwarfed our monthly food budgets. They kept the family as a permanent charity case for the few farmers in the congregation who could spare a side of beef, or the weekly donations of gallon jars full of fresh Jersey milk.

In fact we were a charity case for Doc Cousin, too, who frequently tore up, or discounted our medical bills, or found sample drugs to replace expensive prescriptions. Ten percent discounts for "men of the cloth" were common in those days; however, the Doc had a standing discount of 50 percent for our family, probably the result of the uncomfortable affront to decency, at least to Doc's definition of decency, when a member of a supposedly white-collar profession like the clergy had to suffer poverty conditions imposed by the local rural depression and the 'cultural-backwater' values of some of Saskatchewan's 'immigrant communities.'

My father finally excused himself from the Doc's crusade to the Regina

Legislature by explaining that many of his parishioners expected his spiritual duties to preclude political partisanship. Now, if he'd been asked to join the 'back-to-the-Bible' Social Credit crusade, still running strong in the 'promised land' of Ernest Manning's Alberta, his answer might have been different. Nevertheless, I think my father was flattered to be asked to join a common front of white-collar decency against the socialists.

Ironically, the only times I remember hobnobbing in a truly white-collar home was when we would sheepishly invite ourselves next door to the Doc's for tea on the occasional Sunday night, in the name of neighbourliness, as an excuse to watch the end of the *Ed Sullivan Show* (television being a luxury beyond our means). That kind of spontaneous visit was more common in some circles then than it is now. But more important than Ed Sullivan was the show that followed it, *Bonanza,* starring Lorne Green in. Some of my father's most venerated sermon illustrations came from the pastoral settings of the Ponderosa, from the wholesome melodramas of Pa Cartwright and his strapping sons: Adam, Hoss and Little Joe. The living room TV lounge in Doc's house was idyllic, too, in comparison to his neighbours' quarters, but I can't say that I ever felt comfortable at the Doc's, as I did, later on, in that playhouse we were constructing that day of their almost holy alliance.

The medicare issue was timely for me that day, because I suspect that my repetition of Russell Gill's forbidden language and my reference to Russell Gill's books on evolution ('creeping first into the schools and then into our homes') was indeed a real threat to the family, one that my father would have confronted directly on another day. But that day God's champion against evolution was not quite as glamorous a role for my father as Doc's invitation to spiritual warfare against those closet communists in Regina.

By the end of the day, Robin Hood's hideout was constructed and Billy Gill, Tim Wilson and Kim Krump were enlisted into my Sherwood Forest warfare against the wayfaring gentry on the Nottingham road. The only issues that disrupted our modern version of that venerable romance was Billy Gill's refusal to play Little John as subordinate to Robin Hood, and my sister's insistence that her friends would use half the new playhouse for playing house with her baby dolls.

In that prairie hideout, in our child-world community, we were unaware of the real or the perceived perils of Darwinism, McCarthyism and social-ism. Rich and poor were just characters for romance and fantasy to us, not to mention for some of our parents, there in Leader, Saskatchewan, a couple blocks from Sinclair Ross's false-fronted stores on Main Street, surrounded by W.O. Mitchell's horizons of land and sky, three hours drive from Regina's Market Square.

Funny, but I was disappointed that Sammy wasn't there the night I read this story. When I wrote this chapter of the journal many months earlier I imagined his reaction to the ending.

"Jeazuss Murrrphy, man. Darwinism, W.O. Mitchell. Will you pop the clutch on this story, connect the pedal to the metal, 'cause I'm having trouble seeing Mitchell's horizons in downtown Regina, you know what I'm saying? Thirties, sixties, nineties, how many decades is this story gonna cover? You can't sneak your Regina Riot into this one!"

In fact Sammy is a good deal more polite in real life these days than when his guerrilla ghost ambushes me at home alone with my journal and my flights of rhetoric. As I've said before, his macabre voice has morphed into some sort of late-night sentimentality sensor. And thus I now have this compulsive need to have Sammy in the audience, and not just at BJ's. I used to think of him as part of that "great crowd of witnesses" from the Book of Hebrews. But also, I suspect, he's becoming part of the players on stage.

5

VANCOUVER, SPRING 1935

MATT SHAW ON THE RCW UNION'S
FIRST MILITANT ACTIONS

I INTERVIEWED MATT SHAW IN THE summer of 1995, just after the Saskatchewan Federation of Labour included him in their Sixtieth Anniversary Celebration of the On-to-Ottawa Trek. I was impressed at his continuing ability to entertain and enlighten his audiences on the issues of the "hungry thirties" and their relation to contemporary issues. Next to Doc Savage, Matt was my most productive source for material on the Trek. I have a close friend in Regina, where Matt lived, who comes to visit friends and relatives in Grande Prairie every summer for a week. So Daniella convinced me to approach him about bringing Matt Shaw along to do some guest appearances at our BJ's Tuesday Club.

The idea was that I would put him up at my place and that we would take up a collection to pay him to do a couple of slightly more formal sessions at BJ's, on the early days of the Trek. It turned out that Matt had a friend here in the Peace Country, and that he was delighted to come up to visit and to talk to us. He accepted the ride, but refused to be paid. When the BJ's Tuesday regulars heard this, Daniella, Charles, Cam and Tom started brainstorming as to where these sessions might lead.

"Listen Cam," Daniella said. "We need you to think about how all these sessions can be put together technically. See, we might be just the audience but I have a feeling we're participants in the history as well. Like Paul's stories. They fit in, don't they?"

"Probably," Cam said. "We could import the sessions to a CD with a bit of editing."

"Unedited, Cam!" said Daniella. "Paul's stories, Sammy's firecrackers, your jabs Cam, it's all good, as the kids say. Our own voices intersect the narrative, you know what I'm saying?"

It took some of them a while to get excited about her theories, but everyone was excited about the archives someday including our recordings of BJ's Tuesday Night History Club. Our archivists at the museum in Grande Prairie were definitely interested and I had a feeling that the provincial archives or the Glenbow Museum might also be interested.

We walked Matt Shaw through our BJ's portal on a Tuesday night in late June 1997, with early summer heat from outside still defying any air-conditioning BJ's might have had operating. With the odours of pretzels, peanuts, beer and sweat all around, I could just barely imagine a stage at Maple Leaf Gardens in Toronto where Matt Shaw had been the guest speaker sixty-two years earlier, addressing a crowd of thousands of leftists and sympathizers who had turned out to hear about the relief camps and the On-to-Ottawa Trek, which Prime Minister Bennett had stopped in Regina by royal decree. Art Evans had chosen Matt Shaw as the youthful voice and face to represent the story of the relief camp workers, to speak to the growing crowds of urban supporters in central Canada and to prepare the way for the anticipated showdown on Parliament Hill between Prime Minister Bennett and the unemployed youth of Canada.

Here he was before our humble assembly — a motley crew of six regulars from the History Club, a couple of our friends and a handful of the curious who had heard some strange rumours infiltrating the city from BJ's Bar and Cue Club, about Tuesday nights. You'd have to know BJ's to realize how cut-off our corner of the establishment could be from the main lounge on a Tuesday night. Yet everyone in the next room at the sports monitors, at the bar, at the booths and at the pool tables knew that something slightly strange was going on in the pool room left of the stage; but somehow they respected our space.

Mr. Shaw came fully and formally prepared, still like the inspiring orator he had been in 1934 and '35. Now in June of 1997 he was a lean, dignified, silver-grey-haired gentleman in his late eighties. He walked with an aluminium cane partially due to his extremely poor eyesight, but he had brought notes printed in large font, as well as books and clippings.

Danielle took him by the arm and guided him to our corner. "It is wonderful to have you with us, Mr. Shaw. My grandfather mentions your name whenever he talks about the Trek, so I kind of feel like I know you already."

"A grandchild of Doc Savage," Matt said. "Hard to believe. I met him again in Regina a couple of summers back."

"That was that sixtieth anniversary of the Trek, right?" she asked.

"Yes. You know, Doc was a looker when he was young. And I might be legally blind now, but I can still see that you've inherited some of his good looks."

"Finally we have a gentleman in this bar," Daniella said, smiling right at me.

"Here's your pulpit." Daniella took him to the lectern, which had apparently downsized its permanent residence from Saint Paul's United to BJ's Bar. "You can put your notes on that and we'll put these books and folders on the table here. I'll help you with whatever you need. Paul's going to introduce you, of course."

Doc Savage (left) and Matt Shaw (right), Regina, July 1, 1995,
On-to-Ottawa Trek Sixtieth Anniversary.
Saskatchewan Federation of Labour document.

So, with the tape rolling and my introductions complete, Matt took over
the pulpit amidst our applause.

"Very kind of you folks to ask me here, and I understand that my good
friend Doc Savage has told you about the relief camps — slave camps really — how we organized, walked out and descended on Vancouver in early
December of 1934. You've got to understand the larger dreams of these guys
at the core of the Relief Camp Workers Union if you want to understand
our little confrontation with Premier Patullo that December. When the
RCW Union was consolidated in '33 as a chartered affiliate of the Workers
Unity League, they voted themselves an ambitious and lofty constitution. It
committed us to organize all relief camp workers in Canada (starting with
B.C.) into a militant union to lead the struggle not just for real work and
wages, but for higher living standards for everyone. This constitution of
ours defined higher living standards as a hell of lot more than just decent
wages. It included a campaign for adequate old age pensions; imagine these

young guys concerned about old age security? It included a campaign for disability and sickness benefits, and social insurance in general. And what we called non-contributory unemployment insurance, a much brighter, more just unemployment insurance compared to the current UI fund that the Honourable Paul Martin raided regularly to pay down the deficits. Of course those deficits included the inflated salaries of fat senators and gold-plated pensions and pet projects for their partisan big business supporters, all lining up at the troughs.

"You know about that of course, don't you? The fact that they've been using your surplus unemployment insurance premiums for everything else under the sun rather than using it to support decent UI benefits? They continue to cut back UI benefits while the UI surplus grows and they skim funds to help balance the deficit on the backs of the unemployed and the poorest of the working stiffs. Please forgive my habit of digressing.

"Now this Relief Camp Workers Union constitution didn't even stop there. It included a section on international proletarian solidarity against fascist and imperialist wars, as part of a larger struggle for more worker control, worker input and worker-friendly governments right around the entire planet. How do you like them apples for a bunch of unemployed kids duly and democratically represented at some convention in Kamloops in July '33 or Salmon Arm in August of '34. Okay, I know those words like 'proletarian' and 'imperialism' and 'fascism' sound kind of academic and doctrinaire today, but back in the darkest part of the Great Depression, with the stories of Hitler's thugs, Franco's mercenaries, and Mussolini's brown-shirts beating and imprisoning the most progressive thinkers and activists of Europe, and machine-gunning Ethiopian tribesmen in the name of the greater glory of the empire, you've got to understand that imperialism and fascism were a street-level, everyday reality for our generation.

"And these guys we elected to represent us were the ones most aware of the connections between war and empire and the right-wing agendas in general, you see. Guys like Ronnie Liversedge, George Black and Jack Cosgrove had experienced the trenches of the Great War and how little value the competing empires placed upon the foot soldiers that supported their entirely fascist visions of glorious empires.

Now I can't say exactly how complete an understanding I had of all this then, and how much I've read into it since, but we younger guys were right in the middle of this awakening to a larger world out there, realizing that all these unemployed youth were created by certain economic philosophies and vested interests. Interests that were quite willing to sacrifice the many for the few in the time-honoured tradition of Western and Eastern empires (and business empires) throughout our recorded and unrecorded history from time immemorial. And by God, our little union's constitution reflected that knowledge, and I'm damned proud of that to this day.

"Thanks Daniella," Matt paused, acknowledging the glass of water that she had put beside the lectern on the table. He took a slow drink and glanced at his notes for the first time.

"So, you see, the big argument those first few days of the strike was whether our demands to Premier Patullo should be broad enough to reflect the greater needs of the unemployed and the working class in Canada and throughout the world, or should the demands be practical and specific to the relief camps. Well the case for the narrower agenda won out, much to the chagrin of myself and Liversedge and some of the newly elected executive. The boys wanted to keep us focused on achievable goals, so we went with the basics: number one, work with real wages, forty cents an hour, seven-hour days and a five-day week. Secondly, the camps wanted out from under the Department of National Defence. Thirdly, they wanted decent medical protection and compensation for injury or disability sustained on the job site. And fourth, the right to vote in provincial and federal elections. That's right. You didn't know that, eh? Disenfranchised because the camp didn't qualify legally as a domicile, or something like that.

"Hey, don't be fooled into thinking we've come such a long way. Blacks still have to fight to get registered before they can vote in Florida, Louisiana, Mississippi, and all across the south; one of these days, in a close election, it's going to cost the Democrats the White House, man. The homeless and transients in this country still don't get to vote.

"And I guess we had a fifth point about ending the blacklisting. Far as I could tell, blackballing was more systematic and more wicked in B.C. than anywhere else in Canada. Anyway, I was nominated to lead an elected delegation of six to Victoria to present our case to Premier Patullo. Since I was secretary of the Relief Camp Workers Union, they probably figured I'd be the one to keep a written record. Patullo had just won an election and the Liberal Party of Canada had high hopes for his leadership of a 'new deal' type of populism. So he of course told us how he personally supported our work and wages agenda, but that the province was broke from the previous regime and the recession. However, he promised to investigate the blacklisting, and to issue scrip and lodging for the boys in Vancouver. The larger issue of work and wages he claimed was more of a federal issue, and he promised to push Ottawa for an inquiry into camp conditions in B.C.

"Of course, old 'Iron Heels' Bennett wasn't going to cooperate with some bleeding heart, Johnny-come-lately Liberal. Later we found out that Bennett personally intervened to cancel our scrip after less than one full week. As far as he was concerned there would be no commission of inquiry since the camps were open to public and press at any time. How's that for imperial logic?

"Well, we marched a thousand strong in downtown Vancouver. We paraded through some of the bigger department stores. We made the press and the people of Vancouver take notice, till finally Patullo promised that, if the rest of the boys went back to the camps, the province would supply temporary relief again for those blacklisted members not allowed back into the camps. He promised to hold a provincial inquiry into blacklisting as well as camp conditions in general, and into any specific grievances along those lines that were brought to his attention. So, with no food or lodging forthcoming for most of the boys, and a hungry Christmas for many, the strikers finally voted to return to the camps under the conditions of Patullo's offer.

"Well, the Premier was a typical Liberal: fairly good at making the talk, but fairly tardy at walking the walk, as the kids say. January, February and halfway through March nothing was done. Rumour had it that the Premier was back to lobbying for a federal inquiry commission."

"Matt, what was the role of Arthur Evans in this strike?" I asked, a bit fearful that I would interrupt his rhythm.

"Well, you see, Slim was in the slammer for the first part of December. He had spent most of '34 not to mention the last part of '33 in Okalla on a notorious frame-up job, for organizing the coal miners in Princeton. They charged him under the infamous Section 98, "belonging to an organization or ideology that intended the overthrow of the government." The trial is somewhat of a legend already in leftist circles. Somehow it wound up in some kangaroo court in Vernon, Justice MacDonald presiding, and Slim conducted his own defence with the help of the Canadian Labour Defence League. Apparently Evans had more affidavits introduced than a Philadelphia lawyer, and was cautioned for turning his questions into speeches so many times that they burned out the caution light. You want to hear about all that, or am I way off topic here, Paul?"

"Heck no! I mean, no it's not off topic. So yes, go for it. That was part of that whole fight against Section 98, with Tim Buck and Tom McEwan and all in Kingston Pen at the time for being on the executive of the Canadian Communist Party, right?" What could I say? The crowd was hanging on his every word, as if we had an exam on it tomorrow. Even Sammy was leaning forward, peak of the baseball cap aimed straight at Matt's eyes.

"Okay. You got it, then. The defence in this trial was an important part of a broad movement across Canada at the time to have this law declared unconstitutional. Of course we didn't have any Charter of Rights and Freedoms back then, so it wasn't so easy. Under this law an activist didn't have to commit a crime in the usual sense of the word. They only had to prove that he held some ideology deemed to be a threat to the ruling elite, which included the local mining company. Even if you aided an activist in certain ways you were guilty. One of the paragraphs of Section 98 said something

Union members guard Arthur Evans' house against bank attempts to foreclose while he is in Okalla prison. Glenbow Museum Archives, Calgary. NA-3634-2.

like, 'Any owner, lessee, agent or superintendent of any building or place, who knowingly permits any such meeting shall be guilty of an offence under this section and shall be liable to not more than five years.' How about that!

"The irony is that even the Canadian Communist Party by this time had moved away from advocating direct violence or from publicly advocating revolutionary overthrow of the state. They wished to emphasize the popular front ideas, which mainly translated into union activism. On the other hand the governments of the day often encouraged the police to act as thugs against picket lines, if they couldn't stir up local vigilante red-necks to do the dirty work. In Princeton and throughout B.C. at the time, the police squads that volunteered for goon action against the unions were called Pooley's Hooligans, a reference to B.C.'s Attorney General, R.N. Pooley. He presided over a justice system that turned a blind eye not only to police hooligans, but to Ku Klux Klan activities also aimed at intimidating and punishing union activity. Slim told us that the KKK's fiery crosses dominated the skyline many a night on a certain hill above Princeton. They were a regular feature of the terrorist campaign against the strikers."

"Jesus!" Sammy swore softly, his beer all but forgotten.

"Mike McCaulay, who also did time as a result of activity at that strike, once told me that men who were seen on picket duty were beat up by the Klan. One lost his hearing. Homes were harassed constantly. Evans himself was kidnapped by armed men, carried seventy-five miles from town and put on a train to Vancouver. He got off and returned to Princeton, laid charges against the men that he recognized, including two police constables and the president of the local board of trade. These charges and all other charges against police hooligans and KKK goons were dismissed, but, after a famous week-long trial in September of 1933, they put Arthur Evans in Okalla for twelve months under Section 98, which ended up being eighteen months, if you count the time he served waiting for trial and the three months tacked on for who knows what.

"So here's a guy that gets put in the slammer for belonging to an organization wrongly accused of advocating violent revolution against democratic institutions. Yet the police and courts that put him inside resorted to violence all the time. They routinely employed illegal violence, intimidation and protection of criminals in their support of every tawdry local strike-breaking effort that came along, like the one in Princeton. These same courts and government officials helped the bank foreclose on Slim's house in Vancouver, once they had him securely in prison. His wife and kids were kicked out on the street and told to find rental accommodation. Some of the boys tried to picket the house to stop the foreclosure, but it didn't stop them. It was a standard story in the thirties, when it came to dealing with union organizers, and we're not so far from those days as you might think." Matt paused for a drink of water.

"So you see, Slim Evans wasn't involved in that first walkout in December of '34 till after we were well into it — about mid-December. When we agreed to go back to the camps around Christmas, Evans knew that we really hadn't won anything significant or concrete, so he began to lay the groundwork for the next walkout, once it was clear that they weren't keeping even the meagre promises that we'd achieved. Evans was the man who spearheaded the Kamloops conference of the RCW Union in early March of '35. He was the district organizer for the Workers Unity League. The League was responsible for the organization and support of both the National Unemployed Workers Association and the Relief Camp Workers Union. I was the Union secretary, but I wasn't able to be at that conference. I had a recurring respiratory problem that forced me to take a leave from those duties. But I recall seeing the minutes, hearing about the decisions, hearing some colourful stories about the debates.

"The delegates' decision to walk out had to be ratified by a majority of the members in the camps. Nothing was done without democratic votes and full membership input throughout the entire action, yet the press constantly intimated or speculated that the boys were the dupes of radical agitators and victims of communist enforcers and Soviet-style intimidation. Heck, most of our meetings were open to the press, and anyone present knew the truth: that we were a hell of a lot more democratic than any level of government in this nation, then or now.

53

"I remember Red Walsh telling the story of how he was chairing the meeting and trying to maintain a bit of Parliamentary order, with some of the young men shouting out their opinions or frustrations from the floor. One of the older delegates, a huge well-read gorilla called Charles Sands, was officially the sergeant-at-arms to tile the doors on important votes or to carry out the instructions of the chair if necessary. But Charles was a dedicated leftist, veteran of World War I and in the commnist resistance in Germany after the war — a member of the Spartacus Bund underground. It was only a few years since his immigration, but it was hard to keep him out of any debate. His fifty-two years of experience included more leftist readings and study than could be claimed by all of the rest of us young buggers put together. Charles had a slight speech impediment, but that couldn't stop him when he got wound up.

"Walsh was trying to make a point-of-order clear to one of the delegates and Charles interrupted him for the third or fourth time on the same issue, shouting, 'What about Lozofsky?'

"Apparently Lozofsky was a famous Marxist theorist, author of a treatise called *The World Economic Crisis*, which Charles was fond of quoting. By this time his intense voice had taken the floor, point-of-order notwithstanding, and he was bellowing.

"'K...k...Comrade Lozofsky says th...th...that when ap...p...peals to government ceases to b...b...be...'" but Chairman Walsh had had enough and whirled on him with a voice booming straight back from all five foot four of his fearless frame right into the face of the Goliath, Charles Sands.

"'Comrade Sands, if this Lozofsky fella knows so much, let him get the hell up and speak for himself.' Well, the boys just roared with laughter, even those that had never heard of Lozofsky."

Mr. Shaw paused for another drink and glanced at his notes while a waitress gingerly tried not to interrupt us as she set up more beer for Cam, Tom and Sammy, who tended to go through more of it than the rest of us.

"Anyway, my point is that nobody forced us into our decisions. We debated, voted, then took collective action. The reasons for the walkout were similar to all the other walkouts, but this time we felt particularly motivated, since the Premier had failed to fulfil any of the promises he made to my delegation in Victoria four months earlier. Hell, we were just a political football kicked about between three levels of government that all just wanted us to disappear. It wasn't till April 1, just days before our walkout, when the planned action was already public knowledge for days, that the federal government finally appointed the MacDonald Commission to look into relief camp problems. Even then their terms of reference, as I recall, did not allow them to address any of our major demands.

"The March Kamloops conference had cited seven demands, and

they didn't really change at all throughout our Vancouver action, nor on the Ottawa Trek to follow. First and foremost, the central demand was for fair work and fair wages, not twenty cents a day in slave-labour camps. We asked for a minimum of fifty cents an hour for unskilled workers and trade union wages for those with recognized labour skills. Five-day week, six-hour workday, not counting lunch and coffee-breaks, but we wanted a minimum of twenty days work per month. Hell, we wanted *work*, not just part-time token crap at their whim, when they thought they could use us. Secondly we wanted the relief camp workers under the *Compensation Act*, because we had guys injured seriously: one guy lost an eye; another guy got his back badly buggered; many were seriously disabled for various lengths of time; and not one of them ever got compensation. And part of this demand was that we have immediate access to first-aid supplies right on the job site.

"Next we wanted all relief camps out from under National Defence, and an end to the blacklisting, which we associated with their management. The fourth demand was related to this, in that we demanded recognition of our democratically elected camp committees, our basic union structure. Today that's covered in the Charter under freedom of association.

"The fifth was the call for non-contributory unemployment insurance, an old standard workers' issue in those days. It was a good idea and beats the hell out of what we got today. Sixth demand was for all workers to have the right to vote. Now isn't that radical! You see our union gave them democratic respect, but their country wouldn't even recognize their right to vote, much less listen to their opinion.

"Our final demand was to repeal Criminal Code Section 98, and the vagrancy laws, and sections 41 and 42 of the *Immigration Act*. These were the laws most often used against RCW Union members and the unemployed in general. The *Immigration Act* allowed them to deport any immigrant who was unemployed or active in unions or organizations of any kind. This was supported by the widespread bigotry against immigrants. A few months earlier, Prime Minister Bennett himself had boasted to a pro-deportation lobby from the Confederation of Catholic Workers that his government had deported, in the previous year, 7000 'Bolshevik sympathizers,' as they called them. Their lobby was to deport all communists and to ban the immigration of any German Jews. You see? Your Jim Keegstras and Zundels would have fit right in there back in the thirties. Wouldn't have stood out a bit."

Daniella stood up during his slight pause. "Mr. Shaw, we've got a chair for you, if you'd prefer…"

"No, but thanks for the thought. I don't get a chance like this much anymore so I'll hold on to the pulpit, if I need to, for a few more minutes here before we call it a night.

"Well, there we were. By the end of the first week in April we were between 1700 and 2000 strong on the streets of downtown Vancouver. That was the highest the RCW Union membership had been. Two months later in our strike, over 1600 union members were still with us and dedicated to winning our fight. Even though spring farm jobs were luring some, we still had over 1400 who chose to board the boxcars to take their demands to Ottawa. The membership grew to between 2400 and 2600 before they broke us up in Regina. But, during those two months in Vancouver, our impact was far beyond 2000 strong. Looking back, they remind me a bit of Gideon's Band: hard-nosed, disciplined, capable of generating a lot of noise and attention beyond their puny numbers. And I credit a lot of that to the organizational skills of Arthur Evans.

"There was an eighty-man Central Strike Committee elected, which met every morning, and Evans was on it but didn't chair it. The Central Committee's decisions all had to be endorsed by the entire membership in their four divisions. Each division had a captain, a secretary and a chairman. Doc Savage, there — you've all met him here — well, he probably told you already that he was captain of Division Three, probably the youngest to be designated captain, I would guess. He and Paddy McElligott, captain of Division Four, were largely responsible for the divisional organization into pods of twelve, each electing its own leader, sort of like the IRA model, of which Paddy was a former lieutenant. Red Walsh was captain of Division One; Perry Hilton was chair, I think. Jack Thomas led Division Two.

"Now each division had its committees, like Finance Committees, Card Committees, Food Committees, Soliciting Committees and Clean-Up, each functioning to ensure the survival and cohesion of such large groups. The Central Committee also had subcommittees like Finance, the Card Committee, Tag Day Committee and Publicity, which was led mostly by Ronnie Liversedge and myself. Ronnie wrote a book on the Trek, you know. Tells all about this stuff."

Matt searched for his copy of the book and held it up. "Hard to come by now, but you've got to find this book if you're really interested in the Trek. Don't think it will be easy to find anymore though. University libraries maybe. It wasn't exactly a bestseller. Been out of print for years.

"Anyway, just a few days into our action we decided that among the many other subcommittees of the Central Committee, we needed a small but special Strategy Committee made up of one leader from each division, usually the captain or chairman or secretary, plus Arthur Evans. Arthur has to be credited ultimately for the incredibly disciplined organization. I mean all those committees and democratically functioning institutions arose out of the chaos of 1800 hungry, homeless men. But Slim always knew that efficient militant action depended on confidential, realistic, and detailed strategy.

"So Arthur Evans always emerged as a leader whether he was buried deep in some subcommittee or merely the representative of the Workers Unity League on the Central Strike Committee. Everyone with any degree of objective perception soon realized that this was the best organizer this union, or any other union, was likely to see in action. He wasn't pushy, but people always asked him to speak. And when he spoke, his passion and inspiration was catchy. In spite of his passion for order and reason, one sensed that order and reason were not ends in themselves. Order for Slim was never a means toward comfortable routine so much as a means toward effective militant action. Militant yes, but it had to be united and effective action or he wasn't interested. Maybe he'd seen too many disappointments with the Wobblies and the OBU to risk a less disciplined approach. Everyone who'd been around him much, soon sensed that, and fed off that energy and focus.

"It was that energy that turned this compact Gideon's Band into a force that focused the common front that spring in Vancouver and scared the hell out of the Vancouver corporate elite, who pretty much had their own way with high unemployment, low wages and a sort of imperial disregard for the social problems and economic conditions in the middle the Depression."

"Excuse me, Mr. Shaw, for interrupting." This was Sammy taking an advantage of Matt's pause for water. "But what's this Gideon stuff? The way my old man told it, guys like you were Bible-banning godless commies. No offence. But you and the professor here seem to quote the goddamn Bible like Socred politicians. You're blurring my stereotypes here."

"Exactly Sammy," Daniella's low but firm voice intervened. "You just identified an Alberta stereotype. So then, you can't very well continue pretending to be a red-neck, can you."

But Sammy wasn't finished, "Apologies to the Reverend Arthur too. But red-neck? Hell. I thought it was a fair question. I thought them universities encouraged questions?" I could see a twinkle in his eyes under that ball cap. He loved attention from Daniella. I think female clergy who drank lemonade and the occasional beer at BJ's fascinated him.

"We love your questions Sammy. We just have difficulty explaining your behaviour to strangers from the civilized world." That was Tom, from Trout Creek, Ontario, originally, which didn't lay any special claims to civilization. Tom didn't look particularly civilized, but he was.

"Well, Sam, I don't know the university rules, but I say let the questions fly. As for the Bible, most of us 'commies,' as your father called us, learned to be a bit suspicious of hierarchical religion after seeing the church siding with old money against the unions time and time again. But then many of us were brought up on the Bible long before we heard anything about socialism, you know. Anyway, I didn't mean anything religious in calling them Gideon's Band. Just that they were small in number, but damned effective."

Well, that was the beginning of the end of the formal lecture and we more or less degenerated into a Q&A dialogue when Matt sat down and joined us for a beer. Cam eventually remembered to shut off the tape. Daniella hovered over Matt making sure he had his cane, his books and his files and notes where he could find them. I remembered that this man never did really need those notes, back when I interviewed him, either. He had honed his ability to speak to the issues of his day under the mentorship of Arthur (Slim) Evans, the most famous organizer and activist that Canada has ever known. By all accounts, he had learned those skills in the heat of combat, and now we had heard him in his waning years: tall, straight and ever so clear-sighted, way the hell 'n gone in BJ's Bar.

6

GIDEON'S BAND [OR] WHERE WERE YOU IN '62?

PAUL ON THE APOCALYPSE, CUBAN MISSILE CRISIS AND MRS. NIKISH

T HE FOLLOWING TUESDAY AT BJ'S we had a disappointing surprise
because Matt woke up sick and had lost his voice by the evening. We
talked him into staying around another full week so that Daniella and Matt's
friend could nurse him back to health. We didn't want him travelling home in
that condition. When I told Charles about it, he had this idea that the show
must go on since we now had this reputation in the community. He also had
decided on the performance and the performer. Me, again. It was my own
fault, too, because I talk too damned much about my personal journal entries
when I've had more than one beer. Charles, who has been a close friend ever
since he retired here in the early 1980s, has read all of my journal entries
that are set in Leader, Saskatchewan, because that is where he met my father.
He remembered one entry that mentioned Gideon's Band and he thought it
was a good segue from Matt Shaw's closing comments the previous Tuesday.

I couldn't see any real connection, but one has to understand Charles to
catch why it was important to him. We'd nicknamed Charles "the Rev" as
in The Reverend, because Charles was once a Pentecostal pastor. Ironically
we had never called Daniella, Reverend or Rev. It had something to do with
that salt-and-pepper grey dignity of Charles. My father and he were close
friends in the late fifties and early sixties, in Leader, Saskatchewan. Charles's
father was a black Trinidadian self-styled preacher who was a bit of a scary
authoritarian man, if I read Charles's comments correctly. He had come north
to Pine Creek, Alberta, just east of Athabasca, to start a "holiness movement"
in home churches of Afro-American farmers, in the community later known
as Amber Valley. That was in the early twenties, just after Charles was born.
I guess that he thought the local African Methodist Episcopal Church was
not lively or holy enough and that the Lord had called him to start a brand
new holiness prairie fire there. He sent his son south to Prairie Bible Institute
for high school at the relatively young age of sixteen, so Charles's fate was
sealed.

Charles served as a Pentecostal pastor in several churches before winding

59

up in Leader, Saskatchewan, at the Apostolic Church. After my family left that town, Charles's secret problems with alcohol grew in proportion to his doubts, and soon he left the ministry and eventually his father's faith behind. Ironically, years later in the early eighties, his personal trek intersected with mine in Grande Prairie. There he finally overcame his addiction, after a love-hate relationship with Alcoholics Anonymous and various other forms of addictions counselling. He never has more than a beer or two at BJ's, and that just once a week now. So naturally Charles was interested in any stories about the socialization process of young fundamentalists.

Charles introduced me by telling a bit of his own story and how he met my family in Leader. There was a gravelly warmth to Charles's voice, sort of like Satchmo introducing a song. The Tuesday Club and I were perfectly mellow by the time he turned the pulpit over to me with some polite applause.

I began to read the story.

They called us Gideon's Band because, in Leader, Saskatchewan, there were precious few kids (an elite group in my father's eyes) who could sit through daily vacation Bible school in the dog days of summer. Eventually, we would forget to worry about what our schoolmates would say if they found out we were stuck in a church basement at that time of year. Then we could occasionally even appreciate the odd morning lesson from the Old Testament; that is, if it was war-like enough, and if they included those pictures of the Midianites, more ferocious and evil than Viking raiders. Raven black hair and hooked Arab noses with leering countenances that had none of the redeeming character of the warrior sheik, played by Anthony Quinn in *Lawrence of Arabia*. Once you've seen those Sunday school paper caricatures, there is no mystery to the origins of the Reform Party policy on Israel, the PLO or the Palestinian Intifada.

We were a rare breed of child warriors trained in those church basements in the early sixties. We barely tolerated the half-hour of arts and crafts, but could occasionally be brought around to full participation by some lively action choruses. "We may never... *march* in the infantry [we marched], *ride* with the cavalry [we bounced], *shoot* the artillery [we clap-fired the big guns]; we may never... *fly* over Germany, but we're in the... *Lord's army.*' It was supposed to be 'fly o'er the enemy," but we were schooled in war games and knew good guys from bad guys.

The afternoon sessions were the real challenge. It was tough slogging for the brave young 'missionary' teachers — Protestant 'Jesuits' all of them — who signed away their summer breaks from Bible College, in pursuit of higher service for a meagre allowance, plus room-and-board, in some pastor's manse or elder's house. For one thing, after lunch they had to switch to the New Testament, with fewer battles, less bloody gore and less intrigue. The artists' renditions of Palm Sunday or the Damascus Road couldn't muster the chutzpah of such classic stories and paintings like those depicting Captain Jehu, the wild Chariot musher assassinating the King of Israel and the King of Judah, then ordering Jezebel to be thrown from the second-storey window to the street below where the dogs would eat her flesh — all in an afternoon's work.

Even tougher was teaching the last half of the New Testament, where watching paint dry on the arts and crafts could well have scored higher ratings with the kids than the finer points of the Pauline Epistles. Thus, the Apocalypse of Saint John, all the way from his exile on the Isle of Patmos, came to our rescue, and to the rescue of these dauntless boot-camp trainers of our Gideon's Band. They outdid themselves with artists' renditions of the new Jerusalem descending to earth like a vast Vulcan space station. Or the beast with seven heads, ten horns, the body of a leopard, the feet of a grizzly, the mouth of a lion, empowered by the dragon. And riding on the beast was the Great Whore, the Mother of Harlots in purple and scarlet, the golden bejewelled chalice of her fornication in her hand, toasting us and the world. We understood why Saint John beheld her with 'wonder and great admiration,' though I was as yet unschooled in the mythological significance of chalices at the time.

The paintings were not to be outdone by their banner-length flow charts detailing the epochs of history and the future with equal precision. These were formulated from the conceptual viewpoint of the Creator Himself who had divided mortal history into seven thousand years, and seven dispensations of His grace. We were completing the sixth millennium and dispensation, of course. Why some liberal scholars would later challenge Stockwell Day's six-thousand-year history of humankind, not to mention the planet itself, would not have been a mystery to these trainers of Gideon's Band. They knew that the Spirit of the Beast himself was at work to deceive folks about the signs of the times and about Truth itself.

I had not yet seen Bergman's classic movie, *The Seventh Seal*, since movies, along with dancing and cards were worldly, carnal, of-the-flesh, bound to lead the young into deception, in my father's tradition. But Bergman could not have imagined some of the delicious horrors we in Gideon's Band were treated to. The imagery was often a good deal more surreal than the twelfth century plagues and mass hysteria featured in Bergman's flick. The chess game with the grim reaper was a civilized affair compared to the Beast and his minions of triple-sixers in the Great Tribulation.

The Seven Seals, the Seven Trumpets and the Seven Vials of God's Wrath poured out on an unresponsive human population, positively riveted us, especially since our boot-camp officers came from such renowned institutions as Alberta Bible College, descended from the Calgary Prophetic Bible

Institute, founded and fostered by Aberhart and Manning. Some were from the very buckle of the Bible belt, the Prairie Bible Institute, in Three Hills. These teachers were reputed to be learning the secrets of the Revelation. It seemed just a matter of time before we, their students, could predict the rise and fall of present day powers and perhaps identify the Beast himself. After all, our teachers already knew that the ten horns of the Beast represented the ten nations of the European Common Market, who had been much too conciliatory with Kruschev and Communism of late. They had clearly fallen away from Reformation Christianity, like the Laodicean Church, and God was about to 'spew them out of His mouth' because they were 'lukewarm' backsliders (Revelations 3:16).

We were all convinced that the conspiracy to introduce the mark of the Beast would no doubt come from the great financial centres of Europe. It was clear from the last verse of Revelations 17 that the Great Whore, Mother of Harlots, represented Rome; therefore the Vatican must be in league with the Beast and the financial powers of Europe. Those 'tiny' leaps in logic must have teased my brain even then, because I questioned how the parents of my Catholic schoolmates could avoid the obvious implications of these verses. We were told that the Catholics were not allowed the English-language Bible, by which they meant the King James version — we were not told of the Duhai Reims translation, the early Catholic English translation. The Catholics, we were told, only heard the Bible on Sunday and only in Latin; incredibly the only Bible to which they had access was chained to their Church pulpit.

These contributions to multiculturalism and religious tolerance were supplemented, a few years later, when the adult Gideons passed out the little red Gideon New Testaments in grade five. Now, our town never had a Catholic school, and though some of the Catholic families in town bused their children to a school in Prelate, the next town down the line, many Catholics could not afford the busing and preferred the convenience of the neighbourhood school. One of my Catholic schoolmates behind me at the back of the row, leaned over to a Catholic girl and asked, 'What do *we* do with these?'

"Take them home and burn them. They're not our Bible," said the redhead. He nodded as if to say, "that's what I figured."

Years later I realized that the mutually "heretical" Bibles, that we in our two solitudes imagined to be so different, were just similar translations of the same Greek and Hebrew — equally vulnerable to "reader response" theory. Back then though, I just felt sorry for my Catholic schoolmates who were deprived of our fundamentalist world-illuminating interpretation of the Apocalypse.

I paused to accept a glass of draft from Tom. "Thank you."

"You're welcome," said Tom. "And on behalf of all us Dogans across this fair land, I thank you for your youthful sympathies. God knows we needed them."

"As did we Orangemen Prods," I replied with a chuckle and continued reading.

In retrospect, our summer catechizing in DVBS (Daily Vacation Bible School) was possibly not quite as colourful as that of the young IRA Provisionals or that of the youthful suicide bombers in Hamas. But I suspect a historical study of it would be illuminating to the far-right politics of Alberta. Then again, perhaps Armageddon was just so much closer then. My father knew the imminence of Armageddon, too. It was a special area of study for him. When attendance at Sunday evening services began to lag a bit, and tithe money was no longer meeting salary, let alone other church expenses, the young Reverend Wessner began his series on prophecy and the Apocalypse. As those four grim Horseman rode on inexorably Sunday after Sunday, as Armageddon loomed larger in the Four Riders' pathway, we managed to turn the corner on attendance and tithe. My father, I'm convinced was not into Revelation and prophecy for the enhancement of the members' tithing. He loved apocalyptic prophecy for its own sake and lived for it. And what the father loved, so loved the son. But who could not thrill to those warrior locusts swarming from out of the bottomless pit, like *horses prepared unto battle… breastplates of iron; and the sounds of their wings was as the sound of chariots of many horses running to battle. And they had tails like unto scorpions, and there were stings in their tails.* Who could doubt that the great seer of the Isle of Patmos was seeing modern-day attack helicopters, the Reverend suggested.

Apocalypse Now had not yet thundered across the silver screen, though those impressive 'warrior locusts' were already manufactured and just a few short years away from swarming over the Mekong Delta. *And the four angels were loosed, which were prepared for an hour, and a day, and a month, and a year, for to slay the third part of men. And the number of the army of horsemen were two hundred million… having breastplates of fire, and of jacinth, and brimstone. And the heads of the horses were as the heads of lions; and out of their mouths issued fire and smoke and brimstone. By these three was the third part of men killed, by the fire and smoke and brimstone.*

An army of such large number was no doubt referring to the Red Chinese army, he assured us, which was growing daily beyond their vaunted strength at the end of the Korean War.

What books of vision and imagery: Daniel, Revelations, Ezekiel, Zechariah! I still marvel at them, but not like then, when they spoke directly to the evening news, when Vietnam was flickering into flames from the ashes of France's would-be colonial empire, when every week a larger atom bomb was tested over Siberia or over some unlucky Pacific island not yet freed from their American liberators.

"Where were you in '62?" asked the ads for the award-winning movie *American Graffiti*. We were under our desks in nuclear attack drills. We were in a grade-three classroom that started each morning with the Lord's Prayer and "O Canada." Sometimes with "God Save the Queen" or "The Maple Leaf Forever," with its thistle, shamrock and English rose. Then came Current Events.

"Now, boys and girls, how many of you listened to the news this morning?" Eager hands went up all across the room. Mrs. Nikish was a progressive teacher for small-town Saskatchewan, especially for the dust-blown, drought-stricken, hopper-eaten, poverty-riddled, staunchly conservative, south-west fringes of Saskatchewan.

She was the only one in town to have a "bomb-shelter," as we called it — a fall-out shelter actually. We had been hearing about the effects of the fall-out radiation drifting over us from the new atomic bombs being tested in the atmosphere above Siberia, equivalent to fifty megatons of TNT, then one hundred megatons of TNT — thousands of times the power of the Hiroshima atom bomb, with Russia and America each cranking up the rhetoric and the stakes of the Cold War. Scientists recommended a well-stocked fall-out shelter, but only Frank Nikish, the local barber, had one in his basement, having bowed to the 'foolishness' and 'paranoia' of 'that woman'; so went the gossip on the street, and in our home. Imagine Frank having to field those subtle jests about fall-out shelters from his short-haired customers, surrounded by commentators-in-waiting.

In class, I always raised my hand to share some current events gleaned from the CBC Radio News, which my father and I monitored faithfully. In our family it was important to keep up with current events, since one needed to correlate them with the complex time lines of Revelations and Daniel, our coded blueprints for the end times. To be a good Bible scholar, and a good Christian, one needed to be found "watching" — anticipating the Second Coming. So at school, I reported excitedly the increasingly powerful H-bomb explosions. I drew a cartoon in art class of Uncle Sam shackled in his attempts to invade Cuba, yanked back from the Bay of Pigs and out of the action by a dim-witted U.S. Congress. After all, my family had cheered for Nixon to succeed that lovely Christian warrior, Dwight Eisenhower, and to uphold Republican militarism in the face of the godless communists, so the election of a Catholic Kennedy was another sign of the end times for us. Mrs. Nikish looked with growing horror at my cartoon drawing, probably realizing not only the unusually prodigious interest in political detail on the part of an eight-year-old, but also the horror of discovering a right-wing hawk and its brooding nest this far north of the forty-ninth parallel.

She could not be expected to understand that the rising tensions and the mushrooming hydrogen bombs meant that Armageddon was close at hand, and that meant the Rapture and the Second Coming. Why worry about fall-out shelters when the good Lord had this all under control, and had it all prophesied and revealed for those who studied the Great Code.

Yes, the Great Code in '62 was not the one Northrop Frye envisioned in his hallowed halls at the University of Toronto. It was those delicious and macabre passages of prophecy in Revelations, in the Gospels, in Daniel, Ezekiel, Micah and Zachariah that could be creatively interpreted to refer to the end times, the final apocalyptic years of planet earth. For evangelical Protestants, that was our Great Code. For the Catholics, Vatican II was nowhere yet to be spotted on the far-eastern horizon. Some United Church members, faced with a troubled planet, timidly embraced the social gospel that advocated social activism, but, for most of them, that was just the talk of idealists influenced by radicals from Winnipeg and points east of our horizons. As for the Pentecostals, Baptists and evangelicals of all stripes, the Great Code offered the hope that the Ruskies and their H-bombs might well force the good Lord's hand, so that the Second Coming would then render rust, hoppers, drought and two-dollar wheat all as a single moot point. It was like some of my Albertan friends who see a profit in global warming.

I stopped for a drink from a tepid beer.

"Another beer, Paul?" Sammy asked.

"I think I'm fine, Sammy. Thanks," I smiled at him, and glanced at Daniella, who winked just before I looked down to find my place on the page.

I remember that day when I gleefully reported on the recent American supremacy in the hydrogen bomb race. I believe it finally overwhelmed our grade three teacher's beautiful belief that an interest in current events might help us blossom into more responsible adults, who could save the world from senseless destruction. She launched into a heart-stopping explanation of the follies and horrors of confrontational Cold War politics. With the Cuban Missile Crisis just a few weeks away, she spoke not as a misunderstood Cassandra, but as a feminine Jeremiah warning her nation from her third-grade pulpit. In mid-passion she glanced at my face, a face still halfway to the Rapture, knowing Armageddon meant my salvation. Then she burst into tears, there at the head of the class. A young classmate of ours in the front desk began sobbing with her. Seeing this, our teacher rushed out of the classroom to regain her control in the nearest women's washroom, and to rally her spirit against the forces of darkness.

It took her a while; I thought to myself there and then that obviously our teacher did not share the "faith of our fathers." With our young classmate still sobbing in the front row, I went to get Mrs. Samuelson from the next classroom, explaining that our teacher and leader had deserted us, fleeing the front, in tears. Mrs. Samuelson met our crisis calmly, walking into our classroom, asking us to close our eyes and to put our heads down on our desks for a few minutes of silent rest — a lovely variant, I thought, on our compulsory nuclear-attack drills.

Mrs. Nikish recovered soon enough in the washroom, but the rumour went through town that the woman had had a nervous breakdown, and that she was not fit to be instructing the children. After all, children did not need classroom-induced nightmares, they reasoned, to add to the nightmares of their home lives. The consensus seemed to be that to weep in front of children not only showed weakness in the face of the enemy, but mental imbalance and incompetence. I believe the Home and School Association had its way, and she was eventually talked into taking some leave, for 'health' reasons.

In retrospect, remembering the behaviour of Kruschev and Kennedy, and of their military and civilian staffs a short time later, I have begun to suspect that Our Lady of the Weeping Jeremiah tradition was perhaps the sanest person in that town and that her reaction more appropriate than we could possibly know.

I closed the journal, smiled at the audience and nodded.

Charles led the applause heartily, getting up to thank "our guest reader." He said some very kind words to the effect that the history of childhood and the socialization of children had been profoundly ignored in our studies of rural Canadian history. I'm sure that it meant more to him, having known these characters and that town. I suspected the other four Tuesday Club members would rather have heard Matt Shaw, but we promised his return the following Tuesday. However, sitting down with the others, I soon was enjoying a beer on Sammy who joined in with Tom and Cam, sharing Catholic versus Protestant stories, confirmations, confessions — we were hilarious, and I regret that Cam had killed the tape.

Daniella fussed over me as if I were a celebrity novelist on an international tour, which flattered me and embarrassed me at the same time. Daniella the Dangerous and Charles the Rev — I was in love with them both.

7

VANCOUVER: BREAD AND ROSES

MATT SHAW ON THE
VANCOUVER PROTESTS, SPRING OF 1935

W E MANAGED TO KEEP MATT Shaw for another week in Grande Prairie. I phoned Mrs Shaw, back in Regina, saying that it wasn't his idea to stay longer, but that we didn't want him travelling when he was sick, and that we were going to spring for a plane ticket for his return in a week's time. I had had tea with Matt and her two years earlier. I assured her that we were checking in on him daily, at his elderly friend's place. Actually Daniella accompanied me each day, making chicken noodle soup for both Matt and his friend John, making sure Matt took some antibiotics that she had bullied out of some doctor at a walk-in clinic. She even insisted on taking the both of them for a daily walk around the reservoir to watch the young ducks and geese learn to fly. She seemed to understand the broader connotations of "ministry," so Matt was enjoying his extended holiday and he recovered quickly for someone his age.

On Tuesday night we were all in our places, including Matt's host John, sitting at the table with Charles, Daniella and me. Sammy was lurking at the bar in the next room hitting on the waitress, who looked like she could hardly wait for our session to start in order to be rid of him. I knew that he had made a point of being on time this time, so I sent Tom to collect him. They came back with two extra beer each, which meant that they were here for the long haul.

"Hey Sammy, good to see such a keener." Cam pulled out a chair for him. "Two Buds should hold you till recess, eh?"

"One was for you, Cam, but I guess I'll change my mind on that." Sammy replied.

"Cam, you lay off Sammy's case awhile so we can get started here," Daniella said just before addressing us all. "Everyone is so delighted that Mr. Shaw could stay with us for another week. His throat is better, he tells me, and we're looking forward to the rest of the story of that remarkable Vancouver Spring of 1935."

"Thank you, Reverend Arthur…" Matt Shaw was headed to the lectern, his cane moving ahead of him, Daniella taking his arm just in case.

"Your notes are on our portable pulpit there," Daniella said, "and the

67

books are on the table beside it. There's water and a mug of tea. Careful, it's hot."

As usual the pulpit stood near the two deserted pool tables, facing three tables of audience with their backs to the empty stage and dance floor in the next room.

"Evening folks," Matt began. "If my wife knew what great care I'm getting from a certain single United Church minister, she'd take the first flight to Grande Prairie out of jealousy. But seriously, I'm getting on in years, and my eyesight is all but gone. Legally blind now, so they let me carry this white cane, but I can still see good enough to check out the occasional date. No not that kind, Sam. The dates in my journal here. Brought it along in case my memory fails me. Or in case some young hockey player stumps me with a question or two."

He and Sammy grinned at each other, and Sammy adjusted his cap. "Back in '35, I jotted down notes about the Trek those first two months in Vancouver while I was held in prison after the police attacked the boys in Regina. I had a good month, mostly in Regina police cells before they sprung Evans and the rest of us on bail. One month to try to figure out dates and details. I had my trial coming up in December, not to mention the Riot Inquiry, which was interested in the origins of the Trek, too, so I wanted this stuff down on paper so those government lawyers couldn't undermine my credibility on the stand.

"Anyway, as I was telling you last day, within a week or so of our planned arrival date in Vancouver, we went from 1600 to nearly 1800 mouths to feed, and that was growing daily during April. We got some initial donations from various unions and citizens groups that carried us for several days, but we clearly had to feed ourselves from then on. We had created a coalition of delegates from labour, civic, ethnic and even religious groups. Plus the CCF. The CCF volunteered more help than we wanted from them at times, because some of our leaders thought they cared about their own electoral agenda more than our welfare; but they were there through thick and thin, and spoke up in the Legislature several times on our behalf. Spoke at all our public meetings."

"What the hell's the CCF, Matt?" Sammy was leaning forward, forearms on his knees.

"Jesus Murphy, Sammy! You really were sleeping in history class, weren't you?" This was Cam, of course. Since he was a big man he could get away with this. "They're the NDP now. CCF's what they called them back then. Only difference is I hear the CCF had more balls back then, than today's NDP. Right, Paul?"

Daniella gave Cam an annoyed look which we all caught and I deferred my supposed authority on the matter to Matt with a polite hand gesture toward the lectern. He didn't seem phased at all. For an orator of repute, he was remarkably unpretentious.

"Well, that's basically true," Matt weighed the question. "They weren't quite the same party as today's NDP. They were the Cooperative Commonwealth Federation, a political party that had been conceived as a political movement at a Calgary conference in '32 and became an official political party in Regina in '33 with their Regina Manifesto. It came out of Depression desperation I suppose. They were a coalition of prairie farmers, teachers, clergymen, some modest union representation from B.C. and a few intellectuals and writers from the east, mostly from Montreal, called the League for Social Reconstruction, or some damn thing. They formed a moderate social-democratic party, something like the British Labour or the German Social Democrats. But to listen to parts of their manifesto, boasting about ending capitalism, you might have actually thought they intended to be real socialists. They started to try their wings in elections about the same time we were organizing the Relief Camp Union.

"Well, they were a hell of a lot more effective than Liberals or Tories, and given little choice on the left sometimes, in later years, I've been known to mark the occasional ballot for them — more than occasional, truth be known, especially when Tommy Douglas was bringing them into government in Saskatchewan, end of World War II. They brought in the first public health care to Canada in Saskatchewan, just about the time Tommy Douglas was resigning as premier to take on the leadership of a new federal party called the NDP. The New Democrats are a coalition of the old CCF federal party and the Canadian Labour Congress and its union affiliates. So the NDP modelled themselves on the British Labour Party and left some of their more colourful grass-roots tradition behind them.

"Anyway, these CCFers in Vancouver were right in there with our Action Committee, along with the Communist Party, the Socialist Party, the longshoremen and of course the Mothers' Council, all lobbying for our right to hold public tag days for fundraising, always making sure we had a crowd at any of our rallies. They used to meet in the Lumberman's Hall on Hastings Street not far from our headquarters at 52½ Cordova. Over forty different organizations were involved — it's a credit to the Relief Camp Union executive and the Workers Unity League that they actually took workers' unity seriously enough to put aside ideological differences. Hasn't happened too often since.

"Well, the day after this Action Committee's first meeting, they sent a delegation back to Victoria — a more diverse delegation than the one I led in December. They came back with Patullo's answer that providing relief for the boys was not within the provincial jurisdiction, nor were any of our demands. Although they expressed some sympathy with our plea for work and wages, they ultimately washed their hands of it. Well, we had the fellows parade in the downtown street the next day to protest their yellow buck-passing. Heck, Patullo was more seriously engaged with my December delegation than with this one. Hearts had hardened now that the feds had struck the MacDonald Commission.

"Of course Slim Evans, Smoky Cumber and some of the boys addressed the commission as witnesses. Evans pointed out that one of the three commissioners was a ranking member of the Gault firm that held the contract to supply overalls and mackinaws to the B.C. relief camps — a bit of a conflict of interests. He didn't bother to point out that MacDonald, the Chair, was the retired judge that had sentenced Evans to serious time in Okalla under Section 98 for belonging to a 'revolutionary organization that plotted to overthrow the government' — this for helping to organize the Princeton miners' strike.

"The commission had already told the RCW Union that their demands did not fall under the scope of the commission. Their mandate was merely to 'investigate camp conditions,' not to change the structure or nature of the camps. How's that for a great example of a paper-shuffling commission to pacify voters with no intent to change the status quo? Hell, that might just define the real nature of a royal commission right there."

Matt took a breather finally, slowly sipping the tea. "Still warm after all this time. She's even got a choice of sugar or sweetener. Neutered sugar I call it. For all of us watching our figures." He stirred in the Splenda, took a more substantial swallow; Daniella beamed.

"So on April 12th we stepped up the pressure," Matt continued, "parading in our ranks of four with files a mile long, but this time we had a target. We had already held a couple of mass meetings in the evenings at the Cambie Street Grounds, and people were beginning to congregate whenever we assembled, so we had quite an audience when we paraded downtown and marched right into Spencer's Department Store, up and down the aisles, four abreast where we could manage it. Brought commerce to a screeching halt you can bet. The riot squads and police responded to their pleas naturally, but what can you do when the 'customers' just check out every aisle, then leave through another door, not harming nor touching a thing. Lots of organized marching customers, but no cash registers ringing. What were they supposed to charge us with? By the time they figured that one out, we were marching back to our respective division halls.

"In the meantime, Art Evans had organized a clockwork-efficient tag day for the next day. A tag day is just organized begging with tin cans on a grand scale, tagging everyone for a few bills and their loose change. Art never did obtain official permission, but he'd advertised, promoted and planned it down to the details. So we had crowds of people around the street-corner canvassers, and he sent his special envoys to canvass offices, union headquarters, boats, churches, beer-parlours, civic leaders — hell, the boys all had assigned targets. Collecting, counting, recording, with cans of loose change dumped on tables, they processed it more efficiently than the Royal Bank, running totals, with food always available to every canvasser, counter, recorder. The police in New Westminster started arresting everyone with a tin can in their hands, but Art had it worked out to replace two for every one that got arrested. When the Chief of Police figured out the strategy he just turned them all loose, not having the facilities or the budget to keep up with it. Vancouver city authorities backed away from any action against us, because the Vancouver people were impressed with the resourceful, determined effort to feed ourselves when everyone knew the authorities had denied us relief.

"Well, when the total went over $5,000, Arthur says, 'Boys, this kind of money needs protection. Somebody might rob us.' So he gets on the phone and gets the Vancouver Chief of Police on the line. We're holding our sides from laughter as he explains the serious predicament of potential crime with that amount of cash, and we couldn't believe him when he says, 'Boys, they're sending a couple of Vancouver's finest to protect the union's money. Now ain't that progress!'

"We couldn't believe his audacity, but sure enough, they show up officiously, and we are giggling in the background watching the paper work. And it didn't help our lack of control when, just as they're about to escort that 'dragon's horde,' as Slim called it, of loose silver and wrinkled bills, Evans addresses the cops, without cracking a smile, 'Now you've seen it for yourself, boys — Moscow gold. Moscow gold backing those bloody unions.' And off they marched to put it safely in the police station vaults till Monday, when we picked it up again to open an account."

He paused to drink most of his tea.

"Could I get you a beer, Matt?" Sammy looked pained to see him drinking tea.

"Thanks, Sam, but I'm going to stick with tea, if you wouldn't mind getting me another. No, that's fine, Daniella. Sammy offered." He motioned her to remain seated.

Sammy winced as he stood up, "Should be quite a scene, me ordering tea at the bar." The laughs and the comments made us feel like we had all been let out for recess.

Matt started lecturing again as if he were being paid by the minute. "That tag day, let me assure you, took some miracles of publicity and organization — miracles made out of tireless effort. I know, because I was in charge of the publicity committee and we had some printers in sympathy with us, so that every major action was well advertised by leaflets. We could distribute between ten and thirty thousand, sometimes more, before a major event.

We organized our first large mass meeting at the arena on… April 19th, my journal tells me. That building held more than ten thousand people and we made a damn good effort to fill it. Evans spoke. All the major union organizations from B.C. had their turn on the podium. People began to dream of a concerted action, perhaps a general strike on our behalf, but we didn't have the labour unity that Winnipeg had in 1919. Give us another year of organizing and we just might have.

"Then on the 23rd of April we moved to crank up the pressure, because, though all levels of government were involved with correspondence and discussion, nothing concrete was happening, and our boys did not have even their basic needs met. One of those needs was hope, and another was encouragement. Hell, Evans had even sent a cable to King George just before Prime Minister Bennett was to meet with him over Easter. So, April 23rd, we marched downtown. The police managed to talk Spencers and Woodwards into closing their doors, but Hudsons Bay decided to stay open, assuming we'd just march through peacefully and leave, as in past demonstrations. Well, we marched in and stayed put. Malcolm MacLeod, one of the union's long-time executives, got up on the shoulders of his comrades and told them to stay put until we got some answers to our central demands. He went over our seven demands to the public and staff in the store.

"The city police showed up and decided to clear the building — not one of their wiser decisions. Naturally, with the guys packed in like that, when they started to jostle the strikers, people had nowhere to move. Things on the counters started falling off as people were jostled. As glass broke on the floor, tempers flared and fists flew when the police tried to advance. About three other display cases toppled or broke in the melee. People's heads were getting smacked with billies, blackjacks and clubs, so men staggering away from that kind of terror weren't necessarily aware of the furniture. The leaders were finally able to ease the congestion by marching the strikers out one exit that wasn't blocked, into Seymour street, east to Dunsmuir and into Victory Square, where they rallied around the Cenotaph, with a huge crowd of Vancouver citizens who had joined the throng to see what was going to happen, now that the police and strikers had clashed seriously for the first time.

"Police were already starting to surround the Square — Mounties and city police mainly, coming from who knows where, in increasingly dangerous numbers. I jumped up onto the side of the Cenotaph along with Slim Evans. Joe Kelly was up there too, as well as Harold Winch, a CCF MLA. Amazingly, we all delivered the same message, quickly and pointedly. These guys are looking to crack heads; don't give them a pretext for action of any kind. We quickly chose an ad hoc delegation of twelve to head over to the Mayor's office to negotiate our way out of this peacefully. I was one of the twelve."

Sammy was already standing just inside the door, waiting for the waitress to tell him the tea was ready. He didn't want to miss anything.

"Mayor McGeer's office wasn't far down Hastings Street; we were escorted by a police officer upstairs to his office, and there he was on his throne. With sort of a grimace, he starts barking questions: 'Your name sir!' 'Place of residence!' Well, we all gave them our Vancouver addresses, but he had his mind made up not to talk to us and had the police usher us back downstairs where extra paddy wagons were awaiting us. I balked when they tried to herd me into the wagons with the rest of them. I asked if they were arresting us. Yes. On what charge? Vagrancy, no visible means of support. Well I showed him the cash in my wallet and my identification as an employed union executive member — this in front of several officers — so they all would have had to agree to lie if they took it from me. They hadn't rehearsed what to do in such a case, so they let me go, but booked the rest of the delegation.

"I was fuming. I jogged back to the Square, but slowed down when I saw it ringed completely by police. At one point the police were on the opposite side of the street, so the intersections were more or less clear to slip through their lines, though they seemed more worried about people getting out than in. I got back up to the Cenotaph and reported to the crowd what had happened. A couple more speakers addressed the crowd, and Evans decided we should send another delegation comprised of established long-time residents of Vancouver complete with identification. So Harold Winch, the CCF MLA, led this one, but apparently they ran into McGeer in the rotunda on his way out to Victory Square, so they dutifully followed him right up to the Cenotaph.

"There Gerry McGeer gets up on the elevated base of the Cenotaph and starts reading something in a conversational voice, and, though not very many of the crowd knew what he was saying, those of us close enough figured out that he was reading the *Riot Act*. We shook our heads incredulously. Here was a perfectly calm crowd listening to the speeches, and this clown has the nerve, with his blue-shirted security goons and an army of police on the perimeter, to insult the crowd by calling them rioters. Harold Winch got up when he was done — he bellowed out to the crowd that the Mayor had just read the *Riot Act*, and that we should all be careful not to do anything in haste that would justify such a distortion of truth. He then got down to negotiate with Foster, the Chief of Police — who was a damn sight easier to talk to than McGeer at the moment, asking for an orderly withdrawal so the men could march back to their division halls. When he got down Slim Evans took the stage and, with characteristic humour and colour, lightened the atmosphere a bit. The crowd had taken to booing the Mayor and the police, and Evans picked the appropriate tone.

"'So,' he says, 'His Worship Gerry McGeer has responded to the multitude's cry for help. We humbly petitioned him for bread to feed the hungry men, and Jeremiah Jesus McGeer offers them bullets. Blessed are the peacemakers.' He waved his hands in the direction of steel-helmeted RCMP patrols, mounted police and city forces all around us. Well, Slim entertained the crowd during these tense moments, when it could have gone either way, and diffused the potential for indignation boiling over into confrontation, while this Harold Winch just took charge of negotiations and made sure the police agreed to let the men march out of the Square in orderly fashion. He also made sure the Mayor made time to see a delegation of the men at City Hall, which McGeer agreed to, as he should have done in the first place without all the theatrics.

"So Cosgrove, our parade marshal got the word, and notified Doc Savage, and Red Walsh and the other division captains, and they give a whistle and pretty soon there we were marching in formation right out of the jaws of that planned police riot. No question about it; these boys had riot equipment, helmets, shields (some of them) and weapons enough to start another world war. But we marched out of there and a crowd of four or five thousand, according to the press, came with us, and more lined the streets. No riot. No disturbance. Maybe a bit of heckling of the police by citizens mainly. We were proud of the boys. They won the hearts of Vancouver that day even with the Mayor's office attempting to slant every news article on it."

Sammy tiptoed in and set his tea on the table near the pulpit.

"Thanks, Sam. Well, McGeer's duplicity wasn't over yet. Paddy McElligott told me about how he was one of the delegation to go with McGeer, and how Jack Taylor had the presence of mind to ask him for a guarantee this time that there wouldn't be any more harassment or intimidation. McGeer swore they were safe with him. Paddy says they got off the elevator on the second floor only to meet the police who hauled them off to more waiting paddy wagons. The man was a coward, not to mention a liar. He could only discuss something with you from a position of power.

"I think the man that summed up McGeer the best — other than Slim Evans, perhaps, with his caricature cartoons that we printed up and sold all over Vancouver, but that's another story — the man that described McGeer the clearest was Steve Brodie. He was chairman of Division Three, a good friend of Doc Savage. Steve had lots of experience with McGeer — I saved this interview of his." He held up this lined paper from the pages of his tattered files.

"Read this for the folks, would you, Paul? That script is way too fine for these eyes." He squinted at the text. I got up to help and he showed me a handwritten letter. "Does that say Steve Brodie on the top there? That's the one. From a written statement he made for Jean Evans Shiels, Slim's daughter, years later when she and Ben Swankey wrote this book on the Trek and her father's role in it. Best damn research done on the Trek in many ways. They interviewed more of the boys and used lots of stuff she'd managed to get Art to write down. Lots of articles from the union papers that covered stuff from our point of view, unlike the mainstream press. Hell, they had research from the archives, the hearings in Regina. You name it — they dug it up. I don't doubt Paul has a copy of this book, if you're interested. Don't know if he'd like to lend it out though. They're hard to come by. Where's my copy here? There it is. *Work and Wages*. That was sort of our main slogan for the strike and the Trek, you know.

"Here, I've got the article marked in the book here too... And it's probably more legible, Paul. Best damn thing on McGeer I know of, from a guy that knew him better than he ever wanted to." He handed it to me, pointing at the page, so I stood beside Matt and read from *Work and Wages*:

McGeer was a publicity hound. I studied that man very closely. In his own mind he was a real demi-god. He was a big blowhard. He never missed an opportunity to glorify himself.

He was an absolute physical coward. Everyone who knew McGeer knew the story of how he had a paranoid fear that there were international gangsters about to get him. This man thought he was a power in the world. He thought he had improved on Major Douglas' Social Credit theory, that he had a monetary system that would stun the world.

This man wasn't quite right in his head and he dreamed up a vision that international bankers of the world had a price on his head. No car was ever allowed two car lengths either in front or behind the Mayor's car. McGeer wouldn't leave his house unless he was chauffeured by city policemen. Nor would he leave City Hall unless he was chauffeured by a policeman. I don't think he went to the bathroom without making sure there was a policeman within reach.

He was completely paranoid and actually believed that he was the saviour of the city when he read the Riot Act to us. He knew no violence was intended by the unemployed so this was a publicity stunt.

But later that night McGeer demonstrated what he was like. He marched his policemen up and down until a crowd accumulated and then they attacked the crowd. I was trapped at the foot of a stairs in a little hotel at 52☐ Hastings. I couldn't get up the stairs because people were trying to get off the street. I was trapped and beaten unmercifully just because I happened to be there. (I had just come out of a show at the Beacon Theatre.)

He pretended to save the city from a riot when he read the Riot Act at the Cenotaph, but at night he arranged a riot with his police attack on a crowd on the street. It was a savage attack, deliberate and without provocation...

He always had the press to glorify his actions even if it involved lying to convince people that the unemployed were under communist control and riotous revolutionaries.

I closed the book and handed it back to him, and dismissed myself.

"That's it? Thanks Paul. Alright, there you go. That was Jeremiah Jesus

McGeer. The boys kept calling him that for the next month. They loved Slim's brazen humour. He used to call the Mounties "yellow-legged hummingbirds," especially if they showed up at meetings. But that wasn't the last time Steve Brodie would get beat up by McGeer's goons. Steve led a famous unemployed labourers' sit-down in the Vancouver Post Office in '38 that got busted up by riot police. Heads cracked, bones broken, but no charges laid. That's what his goons loved to do. Steve was beaten unmercifully till he lost consciousness that time. That was Bloody Sunday.

"But back to April of '35, the day after reading the *Riot Act*, McGeer negotiated with the union. Smoky Cumber, Evans, three CCF MLAs and General Ashton on behalf of the military, as well as a bunch of union officials from around Vancouver were all in the Mayor's meeting, but it was really McGeer and Evans who were drawing the battle lines. McGeer would always swear that he was much in favour of a work and wages program, but go on to blame the feds for not acting on it. He tried to strike a deal for us to return to the camps, if we were fed in the meantime and if he gave his personal guarantee to pursue a work-and-wages agenda with the Mayor's council and with Ottawa. He was always displaying the telegrams he'd sent off to Ottawa supposedly in sympathy with our cause. On the other hand, he'd tell the local press that we were dupes of the communists. He was a typical right-wing nut-case B.C. politician. Wacked out Social Credit type, carrying a Liberal Party membership, just like this Gordon Campbell character, now. Champion of the neo-right-wing charge to help B.C. surpass Klein and Harris in the race to the bottom.

"Anyway, Evans took his proposal to the Strike Committee, who pointed out to the divisional meetings that they'd been conned into returning in December without anything concrete in return, and look what happened. The general vote among the men was overwhelmingly against returning to camp.

"We had astonishing support from the majority of people in Vancouver at this time. We'd caused quite a stir. Front page news almost daily. The one citizens' organization that impressed me the most, I suppose, was the CCF Women's Group. The CCF as a whole was very active on this issue by the end of April, but that women's outfit, they went and organized a city-wide Mothers' Council representing a membership of thousands of progressive Vancouver women. Some of them might have been a bit old-fashioned in their liberation, but by God, they never waited for the CCF leadership to tell them what to do. They just took over. They threw a picnic for the boys in Stanley Park that none of us will ever forget. They invited the public to come as families to adopt one of 'our boys' for a few days, or at least for that day. The response was moving, as we all met at Lumberman's Arch in beautiful sunny weather — families had huge hampers of food, blankets for all. No speeches, just an MC with a loudspeaker who cheerfully made sure that each of us had a family and that each family had at least one boy. We ate, we laughed, we talked about our families, we left the tensions of the strike behind for one wonderful idyllic day. I know of a few of the boys that met their future wives that day, and quite a few carried on relationships with those families for many years to come."

The waitress had slipped in with another round for everyone and a pitcher of draft for Tom, Cam and Sammy.

"The women were also instrumental in planning this huge rally at the arena. The CCF initiated it but they were careful to try to make it a united front effort. Nevertheless, we had problems right away, when this darn Mothers' Council sends an envoy to Cosgrove, our marshall and parade leader, and requests that the Mothers' Council lead the mass parade to the arena. This parade happened to be the largest yet, with about ten thousand sympathizers from the CCF, the unions and general public following the boys in their disciplined ranks. The audacity, assurance and public nature of the request made it impossible to refuse. This rally turns out to have the biggest attendance of any political event in memory, some 16,000 in the arena and some in overflow. So some of the leaders of the Communist Party and, to a lesser extent, the Workers Unity League got a mite touchy when the CCF MLAs and Dr. Lyle Telford, the CCF leader at the time, got a lot more stage time than, say, Smoky Cumber and RCW Union speakers. I think I might have been the only RCW Union speaker that night, aside from a brief appearance by Ernie. To top it off, one of them darn CCF women organizers is quoted in the press as saying something like 'Enough of these commissions,

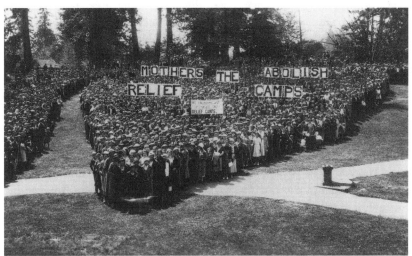

Picnic sponsored by Mothers to Abolish Relief Camps, Stanley Park, Vancouver, 1935. Glenbow Museum Archives, Calgary. NA-3634-10.

delegations, petitions. Now we'll take over.' Some read that to mean the CCF thought they could take over the strike after such a successful rally — after the Workers Unity League had done such a great job of forging a popular front for this event, and also for the May Day parade, which was just a few days away.

"So, later that night, some of the Communist Party members met, and several felt their stake in the strike, via the Workers Unity League connection, was being challenged and upstaged for CCF electoral expedience. Jack Taylor and another party functionary, whose name I can't recall, expressed anger at the CCF, but Evans stood up to them with an explosion of anger himself against the comrades.

"'Jesus, Jack!' he says, 'go get yourself a union organizing job. Get yer hands dirty for awhile again, an' rub shoulders with some workin' folks for a change. The rank and file loved what happened there tonight. Every one of their speakers condemned McGeer. Every one of 'em supported the strikers… supported our demands… pleaded for funds — and not for Telford or Woodsworth or CCF — funds for our boys, for food. We agreed that they participate — to cooperate. So when the women want to lead, what in the name of mothers would you like Cosgrove to do? Say "no we're not really a United Front with these folks at all?" Come on, Jack. Get real!' Evans says.

"Well, they argue a bit more. Taylor tries to give orders to one of the Evans supporters, but he tells Taylor to shove it. That was that! Evans had been elected leader of the strike back at the Kamloops conference that called the walkout, and Evans was still the leader that night of the rally, that's for damn sure. The boys knew damned well who had negotiated face to face with McGeer, who had made officials back down time after time and who it was that came up with ideas for their meal tickets. See, Evans was a Communist Party member, probably for a good ten years by then, but he was a small 'c' communist, if you get my drift. He wasn't an ideologue. He wasn't dogmatic about doctrine, theory, party, what have ya. He was interested in sound strategy more than correct theory. He had his eye set on the more tangible immediate ends, which was making a better life for the average working stiff, which in this case meant both the boys in the RCW Union and every other man, woman and child whose consciousness might have been raised by our actions.

"And for those of you who cringe at the word 'communist,' because you were brought up to fear the bogeyman, well, there you go. You get this mean little morsel of a fact that Slim was a commie stuck in your craw, but goddamn it, Slim was a human being *first*, before he was a communist. Are you with me here? He was a first-rate human being *first*, by God. He sure as hell wasn't any saint. But he walked the walk if anybody ever walked it."

Sammy looked down, adjusted his cap. I think he suspected that people were all thinking that Matt was indirectly addressing him.

"Anyway, the powers-that-be had their spies and their infiltrators, and they knew Evans was the man they had to hit, so they spread leaflets all over town, and to the strikers especially, copying our underground style of leaflet. It was an exposé on Arthur Evans, criminal, manipulator and communist agitator, out for his own interest and not for the interests of the unemployed. Well it bothered Evans, because he never really got a chance to answer the charges publicly, before the strikers had a vote of confidence on his leadership. But the boys weren't fools. They voted damn near unanimously to back his leadership of the strike.

"Well, this same alliance that planned the Stanley Park picnic put together a May Day parade just a few days later. There'd been lots of talk about a general strike, but I think the most we got was a token one-hour work stoppage, May 1st. I guess if the issue doesn't affect the worker's pocket-book directly it's hard to get him to down tools and hit the bricks. But the May Day parade was something else that year. Over 15,000 marched with us, crowds lining the streets all the way, and thousands more waited for us in Stanley Park to hear the speeches. We had pipe bands, drum and fife, banners galore for every group represented, and there were hundreds I guess. Our own banners stuck to two main themes: 'Abolish Slave Camps,' and 'Work and Wages.' Those were the battle cries of the strike and the Trek.

"Speeches on May Day could get awfully doctrinaire and full of jargon. Even I got bored with some of them, and I was scheduled to speak last so I had to listen to them all. Jack Taylor of the Communist Party started things out, but every major union and ethnic group had their turn. The Wobblies even had a speaker there, though most of us thought they'd been hunted to extinction years before."

"Excuse me, Matt," Sammy had his grin back. "Spare a moment for the red-necks again. What the hell's a Wobbly, in sixty seconds or less?"

"Yeah. Sure. You're not alone on this one, Sammy. They're not only almost extinct, but almost forgotten, too, in many circles. Wobblies were the IWW — Industrial Workers of the World. Bit of a legend, even back then, among union circles, not to mention with paranoid anti-unionists too. They were a militant industrial workers union that organized a lot of the lumber camps and mines in the north-west of America, and Canada too, I suppose, especially before World War I. They fought all the big fights back then. We take for granted the right to free speech and the right to organize, but their members fought in the streets against clubs, bullets, tear gas, KKK raids and vigilante terrorism that none of us can even imagine today. Their leaders were killed in the streets, and at night in their beds... some of them disappeared off the face of the earth like union leaders today in Indonesia and Columbia, or in Chile, under Pinochet."

"And you're telling me this stuff happened in Canada?" Sammy squinted, with a beer in hand.

"You bet your bottom dollar, in Canada. More often in the western and mid-western states, especially the north-west for the Wobblies, but in Canada, too. The mining companies hired a Pinkerton man, not an actual Pinkerton employee, but that's what we called them. 'Special constable' they called him; his job was to track down Ginger Goodwin near Cumberland on Vancouver Island, and he shot Goodwin in the back. Evans used to work with Ginger. 'Course that shooting was well-known, but many of these executions weren't even published in the papers. Everybody's heard of Joe Hill of course, shot inside the Utah Penitentiary. They even shot into Tim Buck's cell in Kingston as late as 1932, I think it was, but they missed him. Tried to make it look like an accident.

"You know, we learned a lot about the Wobblies from Slim, himself, 'cause he was a Wobbly before he came back to Canada. He had all kinds of stories about Joe Hill and Big Bill Hayward and them. You see, the Wobblies were committed to the workers like us with no particular trade or licensed craft credentials. They organized anyone that no other union wanted to bother with. The Wobblies believed that every worker, no matter what your trade or job, should go to bat for any other worker that was getting a shit-kicking from the bosses. Excuse my language there. Forgot about the tape for a minute there. The Wobblies used to say 'An injury to one is injury to all!' More than anything else, that's what today's society could learn from the Wobblies. They figured the more that walked out, the sooner the bosses had to bargain. And the sooner the bosses had to talk, the better it was for every worker on the planet. Hence their name — 'Industrial Workers of the World.' The OBU in Canada had the same ideas."

"Why they call 'em Wobblies?" Sammy asked.

"Everyone asks that, and nobody really knows. Apparently, Joe Hill used to say that when the IWW organized the Chinese immigrants in Seattle and Vancouver and in some of the mines, the Chinese workers couldn't pronounce WW and they would say "Wobbillie" instead of W. Nobody really knows. It's all part of their legend now, but lots of the old farts, like me, still think the Wobblies had the right idea. Evans learned his strategies and militancy and workers-first philosophy from the IWW, that's for sure.

"Anyway, the Wobblies were represented on stage along with every other left-wing outfit in the province and there were scores of them. By the time we got to the end, many had left or were leaving, but they estimated 35,000 people at its peak. When it was finally my turn to speak, I just got up and thanked folks for participating, and especially those that had downed their tools at work and walked out on our behalf, like the longshoremen. And I thanked all those that had contributed money. I said that there was a time for speeches and a time to finish with speeches. They all cheered one last time. Then everyone went home. I'd have loved to make a speech to 30,000 people but there's a time to shut up, too, I guess.

"I actually think the folks enjoyed our Relief Camp Union informal parades more than the May Day pomp. Somewhere about that same time, we started doing this snake-parade that we became famous for. This was another case of Slim Evans' strategy. Instead of marching straight down the street we'd zigzag from one sidewalk to the other, four abreast, blocking the street and giving great aerial shots for the press on top of buildings. More importantly, it made it damned difficult for the police to outflank the marchers, which was a favourite intimidation tactic. It'd give the crowds on the sidewalk a bit of entertainment; they'd hear some of our marching songs and get a longer look at us.

"Colonel Foster, the Chief of Police, usually tended to let the boys march. He learned early on that there was no violence or destruction intended by the strikers, even when we marched through the big department stores, so he usually resisted the hysterical right-wing wacko calls for martial law, especially leading up to our May Day parade. But that didn't stop him from telling the press that communist agitators were trying to lead the boys into trouble, all the while making sympathetic comments about the unemployed. In a report on the May Day parade, Colonel Foster sent a memo to the Mayor suggesting that the parade was rife with 'notorious criminals, foreigners of a low type, and communistic organizations intent upon destruction.'"

Matt Shaw paused for some more tea but promptly started again. "Probably our most satisfying and memorable protest during the Vancouver action was the time Division Three occupied the Museum. This was classic Slim Evans and the Strategy Committee. No one knew what was happening or which division was marching where, except the division captains. In our division meetings we'd been asked to trust the Strategy Committee to make the calls on where to march and what to target, so that no stool pigeon could pass the plans on to the police. In most divisions the vote to trust them was unanimous. So Walsh led Division One towards Spencers first, and a few minutes later Thomas took Division Two towards Woodwards, making it look like we were going to march through the department stores again, diverting the police forces in those directions. Division Four headed down to the Vancouver Ferries.

"Then the word came, and Division Three quick-marched straight for Main and Hastings, turning into the Public Library's main entrance, and up the stairs to the second floor, which housed the City Museum. So we pack close to 500-odd men upstairs within minutes and Doc appoints a crew of four to guard the rear exit, which was a single-person metal stairway, steep and narrow, a kind of indoor fire escape leading down to an obscure back exit to the Library. The main entrance and exit we sealed off with this sliding steel security grille dividing the main Museum from a lobby at the top of a narrow stairway, which descended to the Library vestibule. It was virtually unassailable from inside and tear gas would have caused untold damage to precious artefacts, exhibits, and paintings, with the men crowded in there and no place to escape.

"I know this sounds like an extreme measure, but our funds were too low to feed the men by the second week of May, since the feds had recommended that McGeer not supply relief. And no solutions were in sight through our regular negotiations. So the strategy committee was careful to choose a site where the elite of the city were not likely to allow violence or police action. It was extremely well planned.

"Immediately on entry, Doc had someone requesting the staff to leave, and someone securing the window ledges — they had this banner to unfurl for the outside of the building: 'RCW Union: When do we eat?' He had someone commandeering the phone to call Evans that the Museum had been secured, and Evans sent word to the other three division leaders to march to Victory Square for a rally in support of the occupation. Evans had a phone tree arranged so that we were phoning the press, the CCF, the unions, the citizens groups, and each contact was asked to phone their contact lists. So between Evans on the outside and our phone on the inside, we drummed up an instant afternoon rally based on the news of the union's occupation of the revered Museum.

"Before we secured the steel grille at the Museum entrance the curator came out to talk with Doc Savage. The curator was asked to leave immediately with the rest of the visitors and staff. He passionately tried to impress on us the value of the exhibits, many of them being irreplaceable, and Doc guaranteed him that nothing would be damaged as long as the police didn't attempt eviction by force or gas, in which case the safety of the treasures could obviously not be guaranteed. I'm sure the fellow immediately called some of the mucky-mucks on the Museum board before he notified the police, because one could see in his eyes that he anticipated a certain lack of cultural sensitivity in the police forces.

"Steve Brodie and Shaparla were running the Maintenance Committee which was supposed to feed the boys for as long as it took. They discovered a wicker basket and a couple hundred feet of cord coiled in a corner of the Museum. I'm sure it was planted there for them. They lowered the basket to the gathering crowd below from this substantial ledge just under the second floor window. Then from beneath his banner, Steve started his speech to the crowd about what was happening, how and why, and what they could do about it. Steve was higher than a kite out there. I don't think his speech ever really stopped for the entire eight hours that we occupied that place, except for working breaks, as he drew the basket up full of donated food for the boys, and took a bite himself to fortify his lungs and energy. He could have given endurance and elocution lessons to Fidel Castro himself that day."

Daniella and I glanced at each other, eyes locking with a grin — I'm sure she was thinking that Matt Shaw, at eighty-seven or so, was pulling a Fidel Castro himself. The man's kidneys were holding up better than ours.

"With the banner focusing the issue, and Steve gearing up the rhetoric, the word spread on the street that we'd taken the Museum and that we needed food and support. Well it was almost unbelievable. The bakeries, coffee shops and little delis along Hastings, and in a several-block radius, responded with a massive variety of food, pastries — all ferried up to Steve with this cord and basket. And coffee — I mean someone eventually sent up coffee in these huge stainless steel ten-gallon cream cans. Within the first half-hour, thousands of people gathered outside blocking the streets, and our other three divisions came marching from Victory Square, snake-parade style, to help our cause. Inside, almost none of the boys could see what was happening outside, but we could hear this incredible din out there. From the changed pitch of Brodie's voice we began to imagine the scene outside.

"And over all that we could hear the boys from the other divisions as they got closer, singing the union version of 'Hold the Fort,' accompanied by Comrade Marsh on his concertina — that's a sort of compact, poor-man's accordion. He'd always lead us in that song. In fact 'Hold the Fort' became the anthem of the Trek, you know, and, for Division Three, whenever we took up its refrain, we would think back to the first strains of that marching hymn wafting through our tension-packed crowd in that upstairs room, as-suring us that if the police attacked now, well... 'Ho, my comrades, see the signal... reinforcements now appearing,' our comrades were there below to help us."

Daniella and I glanced at each other again. His voice was getting stronger and his body more animated as he rode the emotion of the story. He looked right at Tom and Cam.

"Never heard 'Hold the Fort?' You'd probably have to be brought up Baptist, or Methodist. Or maybe Pentecostal, Salvation Army or some evangelical denomination like that, to know that hymn. We got it from the Wobblies probably. They'd modify the hymns to more appropriate union lyrics. Sang them on the picket lines and at the rallies. Music was important to the movement back then. Don't know what happened to it since. The NDP and the Canadian Labour Congress meetings now are about as musical as a sack of hammers. Anyway the actual church hymn starts out, 'Ho, my comrades, see the signal waving in the sky, reinforcements now appearing, victory is nigh.' Then the refrain, 'Hold the fort for I am coming, Jesus signals still...' and it's all downhill from there as you realize they're not talking about

RCWU march, singing their anthem, "Hold the Fort for We Are Coming, Union Men Be Strong."
Saskatchewan Archives Board, Regina. R-A21749-1.

real comrades — neither leftists, nor actual men in the trenches, nor even friends. It's basically about ignoring the condition of your neighbourhood and the world around you, with eyes away from the streets, and looking to the sky for the Second Coming to relieve all your problems, to remove you from your neighbours, whose problems you haven't bothered to understand. A variant on 'pie in the sky, when you die.' So naturally we rewrite the refrain a bit. 'Hold the fort for we are coming; union men be strong...'' etcetera. Anyway it lifted our spirits in there and we gave a cheer.

"Brodie, every now and then when he takes a breather from his speeches to the crowd, hands in some food an' tells the boys about how big this crowd is getting and the cars having to turn around at the next intersection, and some of us think he's exaggerating a bit, but clearly something big is happening out there. And below us we hear that the police are taking up positions in the Library with tear gas equipment, but our guard on the stairs can hear them in debate with other people who seem to hold some authority and credibility with the police. When we hear that, we get even braver because we figure the mucky-mucks have come to protect their cultural treasures. And hell, we found those treasures very educational ourselves. The boys found an old manuscript on the Great War, about torture and gas and poison, the comforts and diseases of the trenches. By the time they passed that around we had a new appreciation for the exploitation of working-class youth in our parents' generation.

"Towards suppertime I guess, Evans led a delegation to negotiate with

City Hall for a week's worth of relief. He probably knew he wouldn't get that much. Meanwhile Foster, the Chief of Police, arrives at the barricade gate with Oscar Salonen, leader of the longshoremen and the Waterfront Workers Association. They've got some policemen behind them halfway up the stairs whose heads barely show over the top stairs, but clearly they've been told to stay put and not reveal weapons. Oscar's along, no doubt to give Colonel Foster more credibility and to help him negotiate us out of there.

"Foster could sound extremely reasonable, if a bit patronizing, when he wanted the boys to feel he was really on their side. He explained all the old problems that prevented them from feeding us and dealing with this federal issue, how his hands were tied and how the Mayor and public really were demanding that public property and citizens be protected from illegal threats like this, and that he realized that this was not the act of the rank-and-file unemployed boys and that he didn't intend to charge them or hold them responsible. He inferred that the leadership was duping us all, but he had the sense not to insult us in so many words. Nevertheless, he had orders to remove them, and so he wanted to give us a chance to come out in an orderly manner, without any harassment from the police, and he would see what he could do to discuss our problems with the Mayor.

"He concludes with, 'So I want to know if you are going to come out peacefully now.'

"Doc Savage, of course, realizes that this must be an attempt to circumvent Slim's negotiation with McGeer so he cuts to the chase and asks, 'Are we guaranteed to get relief?' Foster says that he has no authority to offer that right now before talking to the Mayor, so Doc replies immediately, 'Then we're not moving.'

"Now Doc's a mere twenty-three-year-old kid at that time and he's facing a seasoned Great War veteran with a hell of a lot of police and negotiating experience, so Foster, who started by talking to the young men, shifts gears and talks past Doc to ask how many Great War vets are in there. Liversedge and Black and a few others call out or raise their hands, and Foster begins to appeal to them as fellow vets to take a responsible leadership role with these young men who haven't had to face gas or don't realize that they might not be acting in their own interest. He was not too subtly suggesting that we were being manipulated and could possibly face gas ourselves.

"However, he steered away from any kinds of direct threats, then, and appealed to us that the traffic was snarled for blocks in every direction, and that people trying to get home on a Friday night for supper could get out of hand and start fighting with the crowd. He claimed that he was entirely with us, but that we shouldn't be contributing to lawlessness or violence, even accidentally. Liversedge and company replied in the same tone, that he must understand that if we left now the boys would starve, and that we had the right to do what ever it took, within reason, to feed ourselves.

"So with that the Colonel turns to his ace-in-the-hole and asks Oscar Salonen to speak to us. Oscar says, 'Well, Chief, I'll help you in anyway possible, but it's pretty clear right now that the expedient solution here is the same one as the morally right solution. And that is to secure a promise from the Mayor to provide some relief for a limited time. Hell, if they don't get fed soon, my own longshoreman would down tools and walk in sympathy for them. With or without my permission. They'd walk out before they'd allowed these boys to go hungry.'

"We cheered him. A bit deflated, Colonel Foster admitted that he was having problems finding the Mayor, which could have explained why we hadn't heard back from our negotiating committee. Anyway we appreciated Oscar surprising us with his solidarity, and, sure enough, Foster finds the Mayor, later that evening apparently, at the Vancouver Yacht Club, and gets him back to City Hall to meet with the strikers' delegation and with Foster. Apparently Foster was finally convinced by Oscar's simple analysis of his options, knowing the rich would not tolerate damage to their Museum. So the delegation had the privilege of hearing the Chief of Police inform the Mayor that he didn't really have any options, the crowds having now swelled to beyond what anyone could count. The figure 30,000 has been thrown around, but there is no objective way of saying anything other than that downtown Vancouver was in peaceful chaos. I think the commuters and shoppers all just decided to stay, knowing the infamous Relief Camp Union boys had finally called the city's bluff out of desperation.

"So sure enough, about 8 p.m. Foster returned with McGeer's capitulation and the authority to negotiate a few days relief. We were ecstatic and asked for a week's relief, but I guess Foster convinced Slim that he didn't have that much funds to bargain with, and we finally voted to accept housing and food to take us through the weekend and probably a couple of meals into Monday. We got this in an exchange for coming out quietly without demonstrating, marching straight home, etcetera. We agreed that Foster should be present with the curator when we vacated the premises, to witness the good repair and condition of the Museum. We offered a clean-up crew, because the crowd had sent up a lot of tobacco and cigarettes along with the food, but the curator decided he'd have his own people sweep up. He just wanted us out as quickly as possible.

"So we sent Brodie back out on the window-ledge to finish his Guinness-Book-of-Records speech by announcing the victory and thanking the crowd for their support. He asked them to disperse quietly as soon as they saw our men safely clear of the police lines. For our part, as we went through the gate and out the doors in formation, we finally believed what Brodie had been telling us about the crowds. And the cheer that went up that Friday evening, as they saw us emerge, would stay with us through the rest of our lives."

Matt paused for some tea, but his face was alive with the story. It was like some myth where the hero grows stronger as the battle progresses. Almost everyone had taken a bathroom break except Matt.

"Hell, that was some demonstration, no matter how quietly and orderly we left. It was like the sun had stood still for us, at Slim's command for that one Friday evening, at least in downtown Vancouver, until we finally won a clear victory. Just one little battle of a much larger war, but it felt sweet. We sure as hell needed the morale boost, and, by God, we packed two days worth of deserts and sandwiches with us out of there, thanks to the folks downtown. We marched out hardly an arm's-length from the police line, but not a single careless word was thrown out from either side, as far as I know. We couldn't help cheering the other divisions and they cheered us and we marched off to our respective halls, to collect our meal tickets, which was especially great for the other divisions who hadn't dined as sumptuously as Division Three. We headed back later to Victory Square, high enough that a few more speeches couldn't dampen our enthusiasm.

"Well now, I've missed a lot of important events, I'm sure," He shuffled through his large print notes. "That's what I brought this old journal along for, but I can barely read the damn headings anymore, let alone the script, no matter how bold the print is. But I should tell you just a little bit about that Mothers' Council."

He really didn't look like he was following those notes. He was following some inner film screen, I suspect.

"Before we occupied the Museum, these women threw a Mother's Day picnic and march for the boys. In fact they even ran a tag day fund-raiser for us before that. The week of Mother's Day they encouraged every sympathetic family to take a boy home to house and feed them for a few days.

"Then on Mother's Day (this was the second picnic they'd put on for us), they had between five and seven thousand mothers in Stanley Park and some of them formed this huge heart-shaped wall around some 1500-plus strikers, holding up these massive four- or five-foot individual-letter placards forming a huge banner across this human sea of a heart, reading "Mothers Abolish Relief Camps," or something like that. There were more mothers wanting to take a boy home that day than there were boys to be taken. It sort of reminded every one of us that while our immediate goal was work and wages, this was merely a means of attaining our rights to have a family and home some day, too. Like that line from the song, 'Bread and Roses' — 'Yes it's bread we fight for, but we fight for roses too.'

"We couldn't have managed a two-month strike in Vancouver without the people's active support like this. The likes of the Provincial Parent Teachers Association and the Vancouver Ministerial Association came out publicly in support of the strikers, just to show you where your average progressive white-collar citizens were on this red-scare issue. Big business, however, was another matter. They organized a Citizens Coalition to help the police, to lobby the Mayor and to spread propaganda. Well they were anything but your average citizens. These were the forerunners of today's Pattisons and Bentalls, the big money that ruled the city, but, in those days, supply and demand included bare-knuckled brutality to weight the balances. Anyway, by the end of May, this so-called Citizens Coalition got stronger and more effective, pouring resources into finding evidence to arrest the leadership. Smokey Cumber was the only major leader for whom they managed to trump up charges. That was just before we voted to take the Trek to Ottawa."

"Matt," I ventured when he paused for more tea, "one thing you forgot to mention to the folks here is about your meeting with the Governor General. You're being too modest here."

"Oh, it's not modesty. I just have a hard time putting hundreds of events in any kind of decent order. Well that happened in the first few days of the strike, if I recall and it wasn't much to speak of. But Jesus Murphy, Paul, you really do your homework. Where did you read about that? I can't remember that in any of the written accounts of the Trek."

"I read about it in my research."

"Yeah? Well it wasn't like they extended us a gracious invitation to meet his Lordship you know. I just found out that he was going to be passing through town, and we managed to talk his staff into forwarding our request for a short interview at the CN station. The Governor General was Lord Bessborough, and he had his own private railway car there. This wasn't like these days when the PM deigns to appoint some progressive leftist home-grown Canadian who can be totally neutralized by the honour. Those days I think the King still had a say in choosing the Governor General. Could be wrong on that. Don't remember that kind of history much anymore. I just remember this elegantly dressed English earl that had a reputation in cultural circles for his sympathy for the "downtrodden," as they called us. I believe he requested to take a symbolic 10 percent reduction in salary at the height of the Depression to show where his heart was, and, though that 10 percent could have fed us all for weeks, that gesture is what made me think he might grant us a hearing.

"Anyway I walked up and down the station platform, explaining our situation and the hopeless conditions, and he listened responsively. Sympathized. Made me feel as comfortable as could be expected for a young prairie boy with a blue-blooded lord responding to me with the perfect King's English like an old-fashioned Shakespearean actor, which I believe he was, as well. He promised to take my concerns to Prime Minister Bennett and I'm sure he did, and I'm sure Bennett offered him some sherry and tried to set the younger man straight, all the time envying the man's class and bloodlines. Well, they're both buried in exclusive graveyards in England and here we are on the Canadian prairies, still trying to figure out how not to be second-class colonials, and how to save enough money to pay for our own six feet of prairie sod."

"Tell us about how you decided to take the strike to Ottawa."

"Well, there's a few different versions of that one going around. As I recall, we were pretty discouraged toward the end of May, especially after Doctor Lyle Telford, leader of the B.C. CCF seemed to turn on us. He was an out of touch academic, and one night he spoke on the CCF regular radio broadcast, saying that the good boys of the RCW Union were in danger of being led into violence by communist agitators. Well, we were used to right-wing crap from the media and from the so-called Citizens Coalition, but from the leader of the CCF? This was discouraging, even though everyone knew the rank-and-file CCF were in support of the uUnion, and its leadership. And no one who had seen us in any of our well-disciplined marches and actions could seriously think we were a violent threat. Anyone who cared to check out our public meetings could have witnessed our democratic decision-making process.

"Anyway, the strike had gone on for two months and some of the boys were deserting and heading east on the freights, alone or in pairs, probably looking for summer work. So we had a mass meeting in the Avenue Theatre to vote on a proposition to continue the strike or shut it down. About three-quarters of the men voted to continue so the Strike Committee met that night to figure out what to do with a slip in enthusiasm like that. Stan Lowe, provincial organizer for the Young Communist League, which had helped work the streets for us, says that he came up with the suggestion that we join the unemployed and go east to Ottawa on the freights. Tellier vouches for that story, but he was a pretty good friend of Stan's. When Evans spoke as a witness at the Regina Riot Inquiry, her said that he had made the suggestion to head on to Ottawa at the mass meeting of the strikers. Others remember someone from Division One floating the idea. We've been debating it ever since.

"The way I remember it is closer to Ronnie Liversedge's version. Slim was up front with the chair of the Strike Committee reviewing the decisions of the earlier mass meeting and the problems arising. This note of despera-tion comes into his voice, and his fist slams into his hand, 'Boys, we've got to come up with something radical and militant or we're gonna lose this thing.' Some of the boys respond, not even paying attention to the chair after that outburst, protesting that they've been damned militant for the last two months.

"Then another member of the Strike Committee spoke out from the floor, again without recognition from the chair. None of us can agree who it was, and the minutes of the meeting disappeared into police vaults, when they raided our office later. But the guy simply said something like, 'Look, fellas, we might be coming to a dead end here in Vancouver, but they keep telling us that only Ottawa can address our demands, so what the hell — *let's all go to Ottawa*, lay it on their table directly. Ride the rails to visit Bennett.'

"Well there's this moment of silence. Like we're digesting how 1800 men are going to go to Ottawa. And if they'll agree to go? And how we'd eat? And whether the harness bulls will fight us at the station, whether the police will be lining the tracks to arrest us all? But we know they can't feed us all in prison. Nor arrest us all without a Vancouver citizens' mutiny. All these thoughts are rampaging through our minds, when Slim stands to his feet and shouts out like he's had a Damascus Road conversion, 'I second the motion. Let's take it to Ottawa!' Well it hadn't really been a motion, but it sure as hell was now!

"You know, just like that the old electricity starts pouring back into us, like the day we took the Museum. People start shouting out suggestions of how it can be done and how it could grow. We started catching this vision, not that we had any illusions about riding the freights. We were mostly all veterans of that racket. But we were screwing up our courage for the effort of organization and discipline that this would inevitably entail. And before long, the whole Strike Committee was energized."

By this time Matt's body was moving like an evangelist. His fist would pump the air at emotional points. We couldn't believe he was still standing. We wanted to offer him a break but one couldn't stop him now, so we just rode with his energy.

"We knew already how our vote was going to go, and we knew we'd have to sell this thing at the divisional meetings in the morning, so we talked it out a little longer till we had the rudiments of a plan and then the chair called the question.

"Well, it was more of a voice vote with fists in the air, and I think it might well have been unanimous. 'On to Ottawa' was shouted here and there on the floor as soon as the vote was called. Because of the huge organizing job ahead, we decided to elect a single leader of the Trek to direct the organizing and the strategy. I think Slim was the only nomination. Hey folks, we knew damned well who to call on when the organizing looked overwhelming. It wouldn't be the last time we expressed those sentiments for Slim Evans either.

"Well, the next day the divisions endorsed the On-to-Ottawa Trek, with Slim as the leader, and there wasn't much debate on it. I guess we were just tired of beating our heads against the wall, with Jeremiah Jesus McGeer and Premier Patullo and their protestations of sympathy, and their hundred or so telegrams back and forth to R.B. Bennett and company there in Ottawa.

Now we had a message that Western Union couldn't handle. And we were going to deliver it in person — every last man-jack of us.

"Well, there you go, folks. That's how it happened. But I think these old kidneys are going to have to take break and then maybe you have some questions."

The audience was laughing and standing to clap at the same time. Almost everyone had relieved their kidneys long ago, and we were all wondering where that tea of his was going. More than that, we just stood and kept clapping, responding to the energy of this old man, riding the magic with him through the portal to the spring of 1935. Finally, I helped him to the men's room, and when Matt came back, nobody had left.

He sat with us as we pulled the three tables together. Almost everyone ordered one last round except for Charles who said his second beer would do him fine. It turned into a rather lively Q&A session partially related to how many beers Tom, Cam and Sammy had consumed. Sammy ended up next to Matt with Daniella on the opposite side, looking like she wanted to protect Matt from the riggers, the rounders and the musicians.

That was not a night we'll soon forget: the miracle of a blind old man in some kind of time warp straightening up, energizing, recovering the grace and poise of that young Matt Shaw at Maple Leaf Gardens, galvanizing us all behind the Trekkers.

For most there around that table it was the last time they saw Matt Shaw, so that is how we remember him.

8

"WADE IN THE WATER, CHILDREN"

CHARLES ON BIBLE CAMP, SAWDUST TRAILS AND SEX

I DO NOT WISH TO LEAVE THE impression that every Tuesday night at BJ's was as organized and formal for four whole years as our last night with Matt Shaw. Summers tended to see Daniella and I missing most of the Tuesday nights, and some years in January and February the Rev (Charles) would make it back to Trinidad, where he still had relatives that wanted to see him. Tom was a member of so many different bands since his original debut with the Swan City Swell Fellows that we never could figure out when he would be on the road or recovering from some weekend gig. Cam was usually around due to his responsibilities as sound man for the weekends, not to mention the occasional Thursday or Sunday. Because he got a beer or two on the house those nights he tended to think that, in a perfect world, that should happen every night. So perhaps he and Sammy were the most regularly there at BJ's on Tuesday nights, but who's counting.

So the other Tuesdays tended to be a hodgepodge of personal stories, second-hand histories of grandparents and scatter-gun political debates when Ottawa was annoying any of us more than usual. These were not recorded of course, so the discussion that I would like to recreate here is somewhat in debate. I think it was early August 1997; others think mid- to late July. Daniella was the most impressed with the evening and kept asking me when I was going to "write it up." She was very aware that I often used Tuesday Club discourse as fodder for the journal.

"We didn't record it, so you need to recreate it, Paul. It's just the kind of history that Albertans ignore — history integral to the social fabric and mores of society, and it ought to be a part of your journal," Daniella said confidently, determined to teach history to a trained historian. For example, she could see the direct historical relevance of my youthful summer Bible Camp experiences to the prairie-fire Summer of 1935. Finally I wrote it, my version of a hot August night. At first I only let Charles read it. Of course, Daniella wanted to read it, too.

"We were all there that night," she argued. "You can't take back any of those confessions. They're all history."

"It isn't all history; part of it is creative writing," I countered. I made excuses that it wasn't revised yet, but she started asking me every Tuesday night to bring my journal the next time to read the story. I waited until Sammy was doing fourteen days straight at the start of September, in a camp near Zama City, which is like the Canadian gulags, six hours north. That's how far away he needed to be before I felt safe enough to read that story at the Tuesday Club. Go figure, because mostly of late I needed to know that he was in the audience. I suppose he can listen to the tape. I also hoped that my creative and frank descriptions of my other friends in the audience wouldn't embarrass anyone besides me, but here's the story.

"This train am bound for glory, this train." I was literally singing it. "Ain't carrying nothin' but the righteous and the holy. This train am bound for glory-land." Oh yeah, that was one of them. We clapped... We stomped... We rocked... The guitarist couldn't decide whether he was Clapton or Hendrix, but we didn't care, because we were just following the drummer anyway. It was two-four time like an old steam engine building, twelve-bar blues with half a dozen subtle licks between each beat."

I was in the middle of explaining to Daniella what our summer church camp programs were like in the early seventies. Daniella was in charge of youth ministries along with just about anything else she wished to write into her job description. The boys in the bar were already taking odds on how long she would last, the common wisdom being that the liberals in the church had given her just enough rope for the conservatives to lynch her. Or burn her at the stake.

Here she was in BJ's Bar and Cue Club, on assignment of course, having a lemonade while the boys knocked back their beers. Not that she wouldn't have a beer when she wasn't working, but tonight she was here to seek out the wisdom and counsel of Charles Quamina. After all, Charles, the Rev, was a former "man of the cloth," Pentecostal version, who had quit the ministry years ago, backing away from strict fundamentalism and from many dogmas of his old faith. But Daniella was no fundamentalist either. She was particularly interested in Rev's experience in running youth camps, because she was to be the director of a United Church youth camp during the summer. To be polite, she claimed to want my advice also, since I had spent three or four weeks every summer of my youth, in such camps. I probably shouldn't admit it, but I have also done a bit of teaching, programming and even directing of these camps once when I was young, but I am far from that kind of head-space now.

Ironically it was Charles, rather than Daniella, whom we titled "the Rev." Charles had left the church in the early seventies. Now his crisis of faith and his past problems with alcohol were reason enough for my father to shake his head and feel deeply hurt whenever I mentioned Charles. I felt just the opposite about him. The Rev had joined AA for a while, and indeed was no longer an alcohol abuser, but he had broken off his relation with AA. I guess he was developing a severe reaction to dogmas, starting with the some of the ones he'd been preaching for years; this aversion to any quick prescriptive answers spoiled his ability to live with even the healthier dogmas of organizations like AA. Matching pace with the cultural metamorphosis of the late sixties and seventies, Charles morphed into a veritable Renaissance man. When Daniella first met him, he was doing a presentation to AA, challenging some of its basic tenets in addressing substance abuse. He and Daniella developed quite a friendship; fortunately he introduced her to me as well. We've managed to enjoy some stimulating late-night philosophical rambles that are always just about to clarify the state of the world. But no one ever quite records those bar-room Socratic milestones and philosophic breakthroughs; and in the morning, they're always gone with the mists, fleeing the merciless routine sunshine on main street.

Tom and Cam are in their mid-forties like me, and because they came of age in the late sixties and early seventies, they are forever marked by the musical and political explosions of that era. Tom is just one of several Grande Prairie musicians from that cultural scene who refuse to grow old. They still hit the circuit with a new band every few years, and, like Mick Jagger, the stage turns them into energetic ageless prophets of our revolution, each time the lights hit them and the amperage rises. Children suckled on that heady music can't help dabbling in philosophy and history, just like Charles and I can't help dabbling in the multiple music genres that were honed in that late sixties/early seventies counterculture. So we thought we made a good foursome to educate the younger Daniella into the boomers' revolution.

The guys in our circle were self-appointed guardians of this woman. She got a kick out of that. We were all quite a bit older than the crowd that made this bar scene regularly on the weekends, so we appreciated Daniella's attention. This particular Tuesday, Cam and Tom were politely interested in our discussion of summer Bible camps as long as they had a connection to the early seventies invasion of gospel rock, which shook the church's status quo to its fundamentalist foundations. Cam and Tom had eclectic music tastes and knowledge of popular music history unparalleled in my experience. So the gospel rock topic seemed a good enough tangent to keep their interests in our broader summer church camp discussion. Cam and Tom found the whole notion of church camps a bit foreign and quaint, since both were of northern Ontario origins. Daniella found our knowledge of gospel and popular music interesting, not to mention our forays into guerrilla drama, drama sports and other camp activities. So the five of us were happy reminiscing and brainstorming.

Of course, a major feature of those camps was the evangelical drama of the "sawdust trail revivals." Now, I realize the connections between the "sawdust trails" of Bible Belt Alberta and the populist politics of Bible Bill Aberhart and Ernest Manning, which were fanning into wildfire across Alberta about the same time as the On-to-Ottawa Trek rolled through in the summer of 1935. Sometimes a prairie fire can meet the smoky fuel-starved wake of another prairie fire and gutter like a faltering candle. In this case the two fires passed each other, virtually unheeded, in the heat of the Great Depression and did not compete for the same tinder-dry prairie grass, or the minds of average Albertans, for some time to come. But the ideologies that fuelled those two fires in the summer of '35 are still the dominant ideologies that divide Alberta and Saskatchewan to this day, not just the provinces but the people who call them home.

Of course, I felt obligated to explain to my younger friends that, in the fundamentalist summer camps, with their sawdust-trail tradition, these in-novations like gospel rock music and forays into drama sports were mostly attempts to sugar-coat some fairly grim theological medicine — grim by most standards. For a certain female United Church minister, however, music and the arts were not merely means to a doctrinal end. To her, they were part of the apex of creation and creativity. So this was bound to be one weird conversation with non-convergent points of view and tangential themes — like most bar room conversations, I suppose.

So Charles was in charge of holding the story line together. He would have made a great historian, the way he imposed order on free-wheeling anecdotal narrative.

"You know this gospel music liberation," he said, "was discovered by the white kids, long after we Black Southern Baptist and Black Pentecostals had shaken the chains off the hymn book. We made the Blackwood Brothers and the Oakridge Boys sound like conservative white barbershop crooners. I suppose it was the Edwin Hawkin's Singers and Andre Crouch and the Disciples that kicked things off commercially in Contemporary Black Gospel music by '69."

That sparked a response in me. "Oh yeah! '69 on the sawdust trails of summer Bible camp. My first exposure to live gospel rock. Some wild memories, there."

"At Bible camp?" Tom raised his eyebrows.

"Yeah. Well, you see the 'less conservative wing' of the Evangelicals and Pentecostals had made the mistake of opening the door to 'gospel rock' around '69, '70, '71. That's about the time, wasn't it, Charles?"

"Something like that."

"Anything to re-ignite the fires of old-fashioned evangelistic zeal in Christian summer camp programs. Tom and Cam with their eastern roots might not be familiar with our Bible Belt summer church camps, Charles. How would you describe them?"

"Kinda like missionary boot camps, I suppose. The evening tent or tabernacle service was the core of the program. They took their inspiration from the travelling evangelist tent meetings that used to roam the heartland of America and Canada during the summers."

"Oh hell." This was Tom. "You guys out west didn't have a corner on Bible camp and sawdust-trail tent meetings. They go back generations in Ontario, too. My grandfather used to tell me about them. But we Dogans weren't quite so afflicted with that 'born again' evangelism stuff. We were just busy trying to ignore Vatican II."

"I guess I've heard of these camp meetings. But… well, they sound bizarre and intriguing at the same time." Daniella knew how to encourage us.

"They were both, Daniella," the Rev started slowly. "As I was saying, our camp meetings were a kind of homage to the circus-tent sawdust-trail of healings, testimony, tongues and deliverance, not to mention the mobile evangelism of the likes of Billy Sunday, Amy Semple McPherson, Oral Roberts, and a whole host of forgotten mesmerizers. The evangelists they brought in were people from far away who wouldn't be around to take responsibility for the long-term effects of their meetings. They probably saw themselves as Jehovah's shock troops. Front-line assault troops for the Kingdom of God."

"You're right, now that I think of it, Rev," I said. "All of them that I remember were very confident that they were at the cutting edge of what God was doing. When they were behind that pulpit and microphone, they could make your average U.S. marine sergeant look shy in comparison."

"It strikes me," Charles said, "that hitting the sawdust trail once or twice in one's past life could potentially help one understand Alberta political history. Bible Bill, Ernest Manning, Preston, Stockwell — all influenced by this tradition."

"Wow. The education I've been deprived of!" Cam chuckled.

"How did this term, 'sawdust trail,' come about?" Daniella asked.

"Well you see," Charles explained, "In the big circus tents where they held their meetings back then you'd have to bring in truckloads of sawdust or wood chips to spread over the sod or else the people's boots would have churned it into mud. Or, if it was dry, the sod would be worn down into hardpan dirt, so it could get pretty dusty in a tent with all those feet. After a couple of weeks or so, that acre would be ruined for pasture, or whatever. Also, there'd be a makeshift altar in front of the temporary stage, just a couple of long two-by-sixes or four-by-fours about two feet off the ground on short posts stretching the length of the stage where people could kneel and pray when they came forward during altar calls. You couldn't have them kneeling in sod full of ants and flees and hoppers, so sawdust and chips were more hygienic and comfortable. Probably helped the acoustics, too, and kept the dust down inside a tent when it was dry, which it usually was on the prairies in the dust bowl during the Depression. I suppose, in a literal way, the sawdust trail was that aisle down to the altar. So, you see, if you responded to one of those Billy Graham type altar calls, you were hitting the sawdust trail.

"Ah, the actual trail to the altar," Daniella said.

"Even some of the semi-permanent 'tabernacles' that were framed — you know, kind of thrown together at summer camps with those side walls that could be lifted outward and propped up by two-by-four studs on hinges, so that you could accommodate overflow crowds — even in those, many of them used sawdust on the floor and aisles, rather than invest in expensive concrete. Less ants and flies with the sawdust, you see."

"My, my, the things we missed out on, Tom," Cam said as he ordered another round, including Tom and me. Daniella was staying with lemonade, and Charles was nursing that first beer.

"You betcha." I said. "Can't you just imagine us singing and dancing in the sawdust back there at the dawn of gospel rock: 'Euuueeeee, ride me high; tomorrow's the day me Lord's a gonna come. Euuueeee, fly me high, up into the easy chair.' Apologies to Dylan, but if the Second Coming was at hand, then copyright was not an issue, not if it's sung in the name of the Lord. Oh yeah, by the late sixties, early seventies, even us white honkies were clapping, rocking, moving to rhythm."

Charles intervened again, trying to put order into my nostalgia.

"You see," he began, "the greening of America had mutated somewhat, by the beginning of the seventies. Moved from the Beats of Frisco's City Lights, from Greenwich Village, from Kerouac and Ginsberg, to flower power, to Black Power..."

"Yeah, we were around in those days," Cam said. "'Black Day in July,' 'Motor City Burning,' 'Watts in ashes.'"

"Electric Kool-Aid Acid" Tom joined in, "starts replacing A&W root beer."

"See, I'm younger than you guys," Daniella said. "I can remember the acid, but the root beer generation I only know from watching *American Graffiti*."

"That's true," Tom laughed. "According to my history of music, root beer disappeared when Woody Guthrie's son opened Alice's Restaurant and 'the good old boys drinking whiskey and rye' 'in their Chevy by the levee' had to decide whether they'd head to Viet Nam, or burn their draft cards, or head north on the underground railway to Canada."

"Well, what I meant to say," Charles said, "was that in all those counterculture mutations from hippies, to yippies, to Black Power, one of the strangest was called Jesus Power, or Jesus People, if you recall."

"Right! I interrupted you back there, Rev," Tom said. "Sorry about that! Sure, the Jesus Freaks, hard to forget them."

"Well they had quite the effect on gospel music and the music the youth were listening to at summer camps," Charles said. "I mean rock was getting harder, edgier, acid-laced and metal-laced. Jimi Hendrix plays 'Star Spangled Banner' on his upside-down guitar, and the rocket's red glare sounds like incoming mortar and live machine gun fire in the Mekong Delta. And that had its effect on gospel music."

"So barber-shop harmonies were definitely under siege," Daniella laughed.

"You betcha," Charles said.

The Rev was stirring memories again, but I could tell he was struggling to put it into a narrative. I decided I'd try his orderly route for a bit.

"Okay," I said, "so you're saying there was a countercultural progression from the Beats, to the hippies, to the yippies, to the Jesus Freaks? It's hard to imagine the Jesus People being part of that same counter-culture. I can't remember anything all that unique in their music though — mostly just gospel words put to rock-music styles. Was there anything exciting and original in the gospel rock of that era, Charles?"

"Well that's a difficult call. No culture is one single pure tradition, and neither was gospel rock. We certainly didn't have any Canadian gospel music of note, but then we didn't have much memorable Canadian music at all back then, did we?" said Charles.

"Now, wait a minute," Cam said. "Bruce Cockburn was not only original, some of his stuff could almost have qualified for gospel-folk or gospel folk-rock in his early days."

"But wasn't Cockburn still a punk guitar picker in Toronto's alleys in '69?" Tom said, "I can't quite remember when he hit the scene."

"I remember him singing 'Yankee Go Home, you've drunk too much,' I said, "and I kept thinking everybody understands this song, except Canadians."

"Trust Paul to find us a political history lesson in innocent folk-rock," Cam chuckled.

"Innocent?" Tom said, "'If I Had a Rocket Launcher' wasn't all that innocent, nor Christian for that matter. 'Burn Baby Burn' wasn't either. I think he's firmly in the folk-rock protest genre. His music itself had few gospel roots. The occasional lyrics maybe."

"True. But we can't let Charles get away with this slur on Canadian music culture," Cam said. "So we back up a bit. Don Messer's Islanders, they did some gospel. Snowbird, what's her name? Help me out here, in defence of Canadian culture."

"Way back then. Let's see. Stompin Tom's 'Sudbury Saturday Night,' to Gordie Lightfoot's 'In the Early Morning Rain,' where a few good men come home (permanently) from the forest. But it sure as hell ain't gospel."

"And after all, the real Canadian cultural music scene was the organist in Maple Leaf Gardens, during *Hockey Night in Canada*," Daniella said. "Just kidding, Cam."

"I guess I wasn't paying attention to much beyond the Afro-American scene back then," grinned Charles. "My apologies Cam. I was into Marvin Gaye and Edwin Hawkins and Andre Crouch. All south of the border."

"But you've got a point hidden there," I said. "We church kids were so starved for something exciting in music, way up here in the frozen north, that any kind of cheap rock-oriented gospel music was going to seem exciting to us. There was probably nothing original or terribly authentic about most white gospel rock at the time; it certainly wasn't in the league of Marvin Gaye or Edwin Hawkins or André Crouch. Much of it was derivative, sentimental American pop, but we loved it in 1969 because it was a crack in the wall of evangelical Puritanism, and, Lord knows, we needed that crack. I mean, our teenage hormones were evolved the same as everyone else's, whether we were born into right-wing fundamentalist families or not."

"So there's a historical topic worthy of pursuit," Cam said. "The history of teenage hormones in summer Bible camps."

"Well, it's certainly part of my cultural history," said Charles. "Oh yeah. We raised our hands, we swayed to the rhythm, danced to the beat. Oh, and we felt the power of the 'Holy Spirit' as the band finally downshifted brutally from rhythm and blues to an eyes-closed, hands-raised, slow waltz, 'Holy holy... holy holy'... and Lord God Almighty, we *were* holy, weren't we? Wholly immersed anyway. Oh, we'd be pumped higher than a cocaine rush, those shivers of ecstasy could only be the real thing, surely. And for me back then, a woman's body as she clapped and swayed to gospel music was as sexy as it could get with her clothes still on. Forgive me, Daniella. But that is the way I felt, probably pretty normal feelings."

"Hey, men don't have a corner on that. I feel pretty sexy myself when that music is playing." The guys didn't respond to that but I'm sure they all took note.

"Then the worship leader," Charles continued, "would give some directions, like perhaps 'Just the band now'; then we would be enraptured by the music, hands raised, till someone started singing out in tongues or speaking like an Old Testament prophet in tongues. That took courage, you know, to babble something that sounded like words but wasn't, so you can imagine the electricity running through the audience, because then the rule was that someone had to come up with an interpretation. Well, there was only a handful ever that could muster the courage to ad lib an interpretation of tongues. It had to sound like the King James version of Isaiah or Zachariah and it was to be in first-person-Jehovah preferably. If there was no interpretation, then the person who spoke or sang in tongues would be disgraced as maybe not really having been inspired. So the babbler or the singer in tongues either had to be ready with a Bible verse from the prophets or trust the worship leader to have something ready for an interpretation. It was always something fairly general, like 'If my people who are called by my name will humble themselves and pray, then will I hear from heaven and heal their land' — something that couldn't really be contradicted, or that didn't need verification."

"So you no longer…" Daniella hesitated. "I mean, you now feel that it was all bogus, just a game of emotion with a few established rules… but no, quote, 'messages from God'?"

"Ah well, I didn't really mean to get into that. I wanted to talk about the role of gospel music in all this. But is glossalia really other languages? Definitely not. These things can be verified now with tape recorders and language experts. But Saint Paul said, 'Though I speak with the tongues of men or of angels…' Ah ha, you see, one can always claim it was a language of the angels. But that's not really the point: tongues, you see, is not an attempt to deceive anyone so much as it is a communication of emotion beyond the logic of language, much like worship music or rock music for that matter. I really wanted to point out the strange powers of music. You've probably heard jazz singers do something similar to singing in tongues when they do scat? First Nations pow wows often include chanting that isn't actually Cree or formalized language. There is a certain psychological release in speaking or singing without having to articulate the meaning in the logic of words."

"I would never have thought of comparing the two," said Tom.

"Well," Charles continued, "the colours of the emotion, the colours of a harmonica or of a lead guitar can communicate powerfully without words. You can express anguish, awe, ecstasy, joy or threat with the blues harp or with tongues — the audience knows these colours of meaning. In fact the 'prophet' who interpreted often tailored his or her message to those emotional colours, if you know what I mean. In rock 'n roll and blues it's like that too. Actual words take a back seat to other aspects of the language of emotion. Did you have messages in tongues at your camp meetings, Paul? Probably not in the evangelical and Baptist camps, right?"

"Well some of the folks were into the tongues, but it was usually confined to small worship groups, like the ones Keegstra and Stockwell Day attended. And in my father's denomination, if they were 'charismatics,' they were usually not part of the organized church program, though some of the evangelical and Baptist churches were more tolerant of them than others. But, you know, Daniella, the basic role of music in the camp meetings was the same. The worship band would lift the beat into some lively praise, with soul and rock roots. The drummer and the guitarist would take it up a tempo or three. Maybe something like, 'Every time I… feel the Spirit… movin in my heart, I will pray-ay. River Jordan... is chilly and cold... Chills the body... but not the Soul.' Then, after some lively syncopated hand clapping jive, like 'Come let us SING... till the POWER... of the LORD... Comes down.' Then eventually the band shifts to slower three-four time or two-four time, something like Charles was mentioning — the worship waltz, basically. By then the speaker didn't really need the skill of Billy Sunday, or Billy Graham, or even Tommy Douglas. He just needed a microphone that he could whisper up close to, an amplifier that would fill the charged air above our heads and a pulpit with a Bible and some ability to speak and to motivate. Oh, and then we hit the sawdust trail alright, usually to the strains of 'Just as I am, without one plea, but that thy blood, was shed for me... oh Lamb of God, I come. I come.' Baptized again in hot tears. It wasn't rock 'n roll then. It was the sweet guilt of the last waltz — whether it was for salvation, or assurance of salvation a second or third time, or sanctification, or Spirit baptism, depending on the theology of your denomination or the background of the speaker. But it really all depended on the potency of the wine of that emotional experience, and music was definitely the key."

"So did the sawdust trail change your lives? Make you altruistic in the true Christian tradition? Both of you guys are 'people' persons who care about the world. If the sawdust trail helped make you into what you are, maybe we shouldn't be so critical of it. It's not my thing, but didn't it change you?"

"Well, it made us testify to a change," said Charles.

"Yes it did that," I said. "And it made us sing till the power of the Lord came down, and anything that makes you sing can't be all bad, I suppose. But listen to the words and you get a mixed message. For example, I remember moving and swaying to that one. You know it of course Rev. Maybe you too, Daniella. 'Lift up your hands, don't be afraid, Come, let us sing till the power of the Lord... comes down.' Then, like Jim Casey in the *Grapes of Wrath*, we'd leave that tent or tabernacle, hopped up on hormones, music and rhetoric. Then we'd meet in the dark spruce groves, after the chapel's altar was cleared and the tears had dried. As a poet might say, 'the fireside embers glowed like dark cherry wine, and so did we.'"

"Oh-oh. This is the part I want to hear about," Daniella said. "And yet I'm scared to hear about it because I'm the director now and feel partially responsible for what these kids get into when they're at summer camp."

"Well the truth is — correct me if I'm wrong here, Rev, if it was different in your experience — we met, still too high to return to the bunkhouse dorms, and she'd throw her arms around you, to let you know she wasn't embarrassed by your tears at the altar, or you'd ease her mind about her doubts about her singing in tongues. Your arms would let her know those tongues were Spirit-born fire."

"Oooh, I love this part," Tom said.

"And often our tongues caught fire again, there after midnight. There on some straw bales hauled in for afternoon archery practice. No yard lights to illumine the fugitive campers to the patrolling guardians of decency and virginity. Then, what can I say? Those jacket buttons open naturally to the chilly wilderness air. Does that bring back any memories for you, Rev, or were your hot flashes strictly in the worship services?"

"Now, I'm too old for those stories, Paul, and I've given up on public confession. But sure, I've been both the young man rolling in the hay, and, after I was ordained, I became the patrolling guardian of decency and virginity as you called it."

"Because, as you know, Daniella, warm breasts and hot tongues can do marvellous things to old-fashioned guilt," I said. Maybe I had a beer too many. Charles was still on his first.

"What exactly is that supposed to mean — 'as you know, Daniella'?" She said, pretending affront.

"Well I wasn't suggesting any specific experience, or lack thereof, on your part. It's just that sublimated guilt is notoriously more erotic than Hugh Hefner could ever understand. And no denim jeans, nor mother's warnings, for that matter, were armour enough to stop that hot driven flesh from rising in temperature. Not that most of us got as far as consummating anything, at least not in what we would now consider a satisfying way."

"So what are you trying to say here, Paul? 'O, lambs of God, we come… fully clothed'? Spell it out while you're at it!" Daniella said.

Cam and Tom started laughing, almost losing it, when she said that. They'd have hardly flinched, if I had said it. I admit… I was delighted by her attention to my early sexual awakenings.

"Don't worry," she said, "you won't embarrass me, just because I'm female or clergy. So did you lose your virginity at a summer Bible camp, Paul? I've got to know if I'm supposed to have a session on abstinence, or safe sex, or what, on opening night?"

"I didn't lose my virginity there, but I definitely ached to lose it, whether I could have admitted that or not. Well, you see, the dorms were full with other sleeping campers and the cars were locked because the adults weren't naive, and total nudity in the chilly air, under the foothills stars, on the prickly straw was not always such a turn-on. So we often settled for a loosened bra, a few opened buttons or the sweet retreat of a Levis jean's zipper. We were frightened, inhibited, fascinated and enthralled. Tongues of fire, you know. What about you Rev?"

"Well, I said I wasn't going to confess, but I suppose it's for a good cause. I did lose my virginity at a summer Bible camp. I know of a few others that did, too. Don't ask me how to handle that part of summer camp,

Daniella. It's like King Canute standing in front of the advancing tide and commanding it to stop. What can I say? I felt guilty, sometimes, but loved the summer camps for the whole emotional roller coaster. Music, spirituality, sexuality. Of that holy trinity, it was the music that was most liberating and least inhibited. The worship appeared uninhibited to a non-charismatic, but it followed certain traditions and patterns of expected behaviour. The sex, Paul covered that pretty well. Us old farts still can't talk openly about it like the next generation seem to. But the music, now — that became less and less inhibited, as gospel rock and contemporary gospel evolved. In some ways that was almost as exciting a memory as the girlfriends. It's the one joy of my religious years that is still there in me when I hear good gospel soul or certain Black gospel music. It could almost move me to hit the sawdust trail all over again. I am often appalled at the message of the lyrics now, if I pay close attention, but mainly I forget about the literal message and respond to that primordial urge. I think it's the same urge that the pow wow singer and drummer and dancer are responding to. You know what I mean?"

"I know exactly what you mean, Rev." I said. "I don't go to church anymore, but when I hear the Montreal Gospel Choir or Edwin Hawkins, something happens. CBC played an old cut of André Crouch and the Disciples the other day doing 'Wade in the Water,' a traditional spiritual. Any of you guys heard that one?"

"Now let me see," Charles hummed a bit. "Wade in the water, wade in the water, children, God's gonna trouble… the water." He mumbled it very softly.

"That's it! I heard that song and I thought of those Bible camps. And I thought of the Boss's song there, 'Down to the River'… 'we went down to the river, down to the river of Love…' That's what I thought of. Baptized into the wonders, the deceits, the urgencies of human emotion. I know the 'Wade in the Water' metaphor refers to the healing pool of Siloam in the New Testament, but for me that 'troubled' healing water was the spiritual and sexual high of summer camps. What did Cohen say? 'She lets the river answer that you've always been her lover.'

"What did you mean by 'the deceits'?" Daniella asked.

"Deceits? Oh yeah. No nostalgia can cover that up. You have to remember the ideals we'd been schooled in: no sex without the commitment of long term love — remember — without the commitment of holy matrimony, a doctrine quite foreign to a sixteen-year-old body. So all our relationships were fast-forwarded at warp speed, and a huge amount of self-deception and role playing became necessary. Two weeks of summer camp could not stimulate prodigious progress toward, quote, 'a long-term relationship,' so one faked the intensity of the commitment. Initial introduction, one furtive eye contact, two sentences (one each), a laugh or a giggle, accidental or casual touch, then a hand held that first evening, and *voilà* — warp drive. 'Miles to go before we sleep,' but such short hours to cover those miles. Entire life stories… entire faith in the truth of the moment… that first evening. And mature love by midnight."

"And both genders participated in this self-deception?"

"I think so… no, I know so. Similar to the bar scene, right? You see, there were things happening to us… how to explain… unseen dialectics of fear and fascination. Generating the 'force that through the green fuse drives the flower.' Know what I mean?"

"God, the man's a poet. Forget about history, Paul," Tom said.

"Dylan Thomas, right?" That was Cam.

I nodded, "Excuse the poetry. Occupational hazard. I taught that stuff before I ever taught history. Good thing Sammy's not here. Anyway, during those two or three days of heaven, we forced a lifetime's complexity of intimate understanding through that green fuse. The whole world's soul contracted, and driven into the lenses of our eyes, with time so short. My apologies to John Donne and any other poets I butcher."

"Hey don't apologize on our account," said Tom. "We didn't catch where the allusions started or stopped, anyway. Let alone which poet."

"Speak for yourself, cretin," said Cam. "Me, I'm still working on deciphering them. Donne's 'Cannonization,' right? How's that for a northern Alberta, red-neck bar. Give this man another beer. I'm enjoying this."

"You're right, and I'm sorry. I get carried away toasting young love, especially my own. But what I was trying to say was that the fear often won out. Even in the frenzy of that fascinating dialectic, we'd begin to see the imminent possible end of that 'lifelong commitment.' The tragic insurmountable barriers. We'd start to blame it on destiny or providence."

"God's mysterious plan," Charles smiled.

"That's right," I said. "All those beliefs were stacked against us, making simple sexual attraction unfathomably complex. Well, we'd come up with some corny explanation of star-crossed love, this having mutated out of our recent breathless passion. What I'm trying to say is that 'breaking up is hard to do,' but, with practice, we could manage it; three times in two weeks was not unthinkable."

Cam and Tom were cracking up; I'm not sure if it was my unfortunate diction after two beers, or my confession.

"You're sure this wasn't just you playing an immature Casanova?" Daniella laughed.

"You see! She sure as hell has got you pegged!" Cam said.

"I'm still trying to follow how he got from 'mutating breathless passion' to 'breaking up is hard to do,'" complained Tom.

"Sorry, Tom, but yes, of course I was just an immature young man…

hardly Casanova though. That's way too exaggerated a description of my limited charms, then or now. But that's not the point. All the relationships that I can remember during those camp weeks seemed fast-tracked, hothouse grown if you will. Just like the supposed spiritual progress we were suddenly making. But I think it was the sawdust trail environment. Even the adults believed in it, or tolerated that hothouse magic for a few weeks."

"You've hit the nail on the head, Paul," Charles said. "Hothouse magic, and self-deception. Both on the spiritual progress and on the sexual thing. Only, hothouse tomatoes are a lot more authentic than most of the progress that we made at those summer camps. Maybe there were exceptions, but Paul's right about it in general, there."

I liked it when the Rev backed me up on those things. I had a feeling he had more credibility and authority with Daniella on these matters than I did.

"Yeah, there might have been exceptions. I'm sure there were. But I always felt that the luckiest relationships were the ones starting late in the cycle, with camp almost over. Then often one could part with the expectations of letters, long-distance love and the unspoken fantasies that would hold body and soul together in the depth of those dark lost years called 'high school.' Funny how dates, relationships, escorts to the dances were so much harder to come by during the school year. At least for me. These were the 'horrifyingly secular, innocence-sucking public schools,' supposedly. The long-haired years. Our elders thought the schools were flooded with mores that would entrap us in sex, drugs and rock 'n roll. Probably attacking in the reverse order. Yet for me and others raised on the hothouse Bible camp sexuality, school was a sterile, inhibiting, disappointing atmosphere compared to the sawdust trail at summer church camps."

"So Paul, you're telling us that you almost scored at church camp but not at high school. Is this some kind of significant pattern in the lives of young evangelicals? You got a point here that's coming through foggily, but I've had too many beers to sort out the subtleties. So lay it on us clearly now."

That was Cam, and I realized finally that this was a story more for Daniella and Charles, but I couldn't give up on it. I suppose I was exploring my adolescent identity to some extent.

"Well, yes. What I'm trying to say is that out of that almighty trinity of sex, drugs and rock 'n roll, high school scored a slim victory over church camps in the drugs column. And that's only if one counts mickeys of rum on basketball trips as drugs. But as for sex and rock 'n roll, summer Bible camps in the early seventies won hands down. In fact, I recall one of the steamiest guitar solos in the history of rock 'n roll guitarists, at youth Bible camp, right up there with that Clapton solo that anchors 'In the Presence of the Lord.'"

"Derek and the Dominoes…" Tom said, and I nodded.

"It was right up there with Jimi Hendrix's rendition of the 'Star Spangled Banner.' Okay I'm exaggerating the quality a bit, but you get the point. In fact, in this case the concept was borrowed directly from Hendrix, by some of my friends in this makeshift gospel rock band. I suppose we were their foot-stomping, hand-clapping, hip-swaying groupies. They were massacring that hymn called 'Hold the Fort' that Matt Shaw mentioned. Anyone who could introduce syncopated rhythm into that staid old military hymn, deserves musical credits. They had new lyrics, new stanzas and a new refrain that smoked your socks. 'Ho, my comrades… rat at tat boom… see the signal… tsh tshtsh bop… waving in the sky…' The lyrics were helped out by miniature drum solos, sort of building from a conventional Shilo drummer boy, to funky hip-teasing Caribbean riffs, to rock spastic. And a bass guitar solo that Jack Bruce would have envied, with its military automatic fire mixed with artillery. Tom, you would have been proud of him. Then he would knock it back to soothing swing, for a couple of bars, then back to artillery. Then came our infamous guitarist with the red scarf around his head, a white-trash version of Hendrix, and like the 'Star Spangled Banner,' that Charles mentioned, he brought us into the combat zone, with missiles and tracers humming overhead, and staccato machine-gun fire. Then distortion, amps cranked. Armageddon throbbing. Then there was the finale of the hydrogen bomb to cleanse the planet. Then the song mellowed, mutating from the classic hymn into Larry Norman's 'I Wish We'd All Been Ready.'"

"I've seen that one in one of those contemporary hymn books," Daniella said.

"Well, I'm sure Rev's heard it, but if you've never had the dubious privilege of hearing this gospel folk-rock classic, then you're not a veteran of the Jesus People era," I said.

"That's the acid test?" Tom teased.

"That's the acid test," I laughed. "It's all about the Rapture, describing the bleak harrowing world of the Apocalypse's Four Horseman, a blood-red sun, the days grown cold… 'A piece of bread could buy a bag of gold, I wish we'd all been ready.' Larry Norman had long bleached-blonde hair, and a compelling personality, and that song of his became an all-purpose classic; his answer to Vietnam, drugs, youth alienation, you name it. So you see how our upstart Jesus-rock band, named Surely Goodness, merged that conservative old hymn…"

"A Jesus-rock band named Surely Goodness, with a guitarist who thought he was Hendrix? This is as weird as my own screwed-up youth," said Tom.

"Yup. Surely Goodness! Merging this rock version of a hymn, 'Ho my comrades see God's signals waving in the sky…' And then, 'Hold the fort, for I am coming, Jesus signals still…' Merging that right into 'I wish we'd all been ready…' Because after all, most of them believed that 'the elect' were going to be raptured before all hell broke loose. Sure, the atomic arsenals would probably wipe out those not counted in the elect, the less privileged, those who never got around to praying the sinner's prayer, or who simply couldn't concentrate enough to memorize it. That didn't seem to bother us, like it should have. Wiped out… through a Seven Year Tribulation, perhaps a nuclear winter we thought. Well, Larry Norman and the prophets warned them, right? So their hell on earth ends with a whimper, just before the eternal flames of Gehenna greet them all for their eternal death sentence."

"Hell, fire and brimstone as they say," Cam said.

"I guess capital punishment wasn't good enough, wasn't sufficient justice for those who had the wrong theology. For those who failed to pray the sinner's prayer, for those confused as to God's plan for their lives — I mean for these poor folks a swift execution was far too lenient, I guess. The eternal flames of hell for those with the wrong salvation formula, didn't seem to contradict 'God is Love,' back then for us. Not if you turned up the music enough."

They were all kind of staring at me now, some in fascination, some in horror, perhaps. But I just continued the great confession, and it wasn't just the beer I had consumed either.

"We were all taught to believe in that Rapture, though there were differing versions of the belief. We learned to argue the pros and cons of a mid-tribulation, as opposed to the more loving and safe pre-trib Rapture, or the unthinkably Old Testament post-tribulation Rapture. Pre-tribulation Rapture was and still is by far the most popular theology. One can understand why. But you know, while we believed in the Rapture with our heads, our bodies and souls seemed to ignore the belief most of our waking lives."

"That's the point!" Charles said.

"I mean, we did not stock up on food and guns like Posse Comitatus and the right-wing American Paramilitary Militias."

I must have sounded like the Ancient Mariner in trance-like confession, but somehow I couldn't stop until the tale was told.

"Because we'd learned that the belief in the Second Coming and God's pre-emptive strike with the Rapture didn't have to interfere with our careers or weekday routine, nor our weekend leisure really. In fact, a strong belief in the Rapture kind of frees one up from a lot of concerns about nuclear war, degrading environment, global warming, inner city social problems, exploitive low-wage economies and a host of troublesome distractions to faith."

"Aye, there's the rub!" said Charles.

"I see, now," Daniella said. "That's where you were headed all this time."

"I'm not sure where I was headed all this time," I said. "Just sort of confession, you know."

"Well, I'm glad I'm not the priest that has to hear your confessions, Paul.

It might drive me to drinking," Tom said.

"I don't know, Paul," Daniella said. "I started this little chat to get some ideas on youth camp programs, but you old jaded backsliders have made me feel like I'm about to lead a right-wing Nazi youth camp. I'm feeling guilty just being associated with this crazy tradition of Bible camps. Don't get me wrong, Paul. I found your story of camp very moving and credible, even in its craziness. Still, you guys as my elders have a responsibility to give me something positive here to go home with. And don't just tell me to secretly distribute condoms. I think that would still get me fired."

"Paul, an elder? Sure am glad you're not including me in that," Tom said.

"Well, Daniella," the Rev drawled, "neither Paul nor I could run a summer church camp anymore, you see, so we kind of envy you, because there's a lot of nostalgia there for us, still. In spite of everything Paul and I said about the deception, there was something alive and vital there which we miss."

"That's right," I said, kind of anxious to atone for the spiel. "And you're fortunate because at least in your denomination you don't feel obligated to have a body count after the altar calls. You can concentrate on just celebrating good music and... well... the virility, shall we say, of youth, and of the new music. Maybe you could help them learn to respect each other's emotions and inhibitions. That would be something. Maybe even help them learn to respect those with a lack of inhibitions, too. I'm not thinking of sex, exclusively, there, with that last comment."

"Sure, you always think of sex, Paul," Cam said. "You were an English professor before you were a history professor, for God's sake. That means you were trained to find sex in everything."

"That's true, I do find sex in everything. Some kind of Creation principle, I think."

"You think I can teach them that principle the first night at camp? And thus somehow save them from the exploitive sex that their parents so fear?"

"Nope," said Cam.

"Not unless you're a teacher on par with Jesus Christ," said Tom.

"He never taught about sex, did he? Or did I miss that part?" Cam said.

"Thanks a lot, guys. You're a terrific encouragement," Daniella said.

"I hear you, Daniella. We haven't exactly been loaded with suggestions for summer camp programs. We'll have to make it another night for that, with a few less pagans around," I said.

"Well, these pagans never fail to illuminate me on the history of something. I think I should just record every conversation I get into here in BJ's and file them in my own archives under 'BJ's History Lessons and other BS,'" Daniella said.

"And when your nosy board members check out your tape library, I can just imagine them wanting to borrow 'History 101—BJ's Bar & Cue Club.'"

"And the other thing you want to try is a unit on peace and justice," Charles said. "Tell them about King, and Gandhi, and Mandella. But get them thinking about the current social-justice issues surrounding them, too. Environment, globalization — that is the kind of religion they're going to need to survive. And if you can do it through rock 'n roll, or rap, or music appreciation, all the better."

It might have been at this point, but at some point in the evening Cam's cryptic remark made everything else seem repetitive, "Hell, if it gets them voting something else than Conservative, I'd suspend my suspicions of church camps in general."

"End of story, folks." I closed the journal.

'I love it, Paul," smiled Daniella. "I didn't remember half of that."

"That's because he invented half of it," said Cam. "He's morphing from a history prof to a novelist."

9

LOAVES AND FISHES

DOC SAVAGE ON THE TREK
FROM VANCOUVER TO GOLDEN

DOC SAVAGE WAS DELIGHTED THAT his old friend Matt Shaw had addressed our Tuesday Club, so we managed to talk Doc into coming back to Grande Prairie in mid-September of 1997. The two of them had been reunited in Regina in 1995 for the sixtieth anniversary of the Trek celebrated by the Saskatchewan Federation of Labour. Doc's gracious granddaughter was willing to drive him all the way from Quesnel, B.C., to Grande Prairie, so that sealed the deal. I hope I have a grandchild like Daniella when I'm Doc's age.

So there we were at BJ's and Daniella had just made the "portable pulpit" comfortable for her eighty-six-year-old grandfather. Cam turned on the tape recorder, while I welcomed him back, shook his hand and rested a welcoming hand on his shoulder, feeling the bones beneath a spare frame that moved a bit slower this time, despite the enthusiasm of his smile. The audience politely applauded as he moved to the lectern, acknowledging a glass of apple juice that Daniella set beside him. Then I sat down between Daniella and Charles. As she sat down, she put her hand on my arm momentarily to communicate her anticipation.

"Great to be back here," Doc began, "standing in the same place as my old comrade Matt Shaw. Paul tells me that he covered the Vancouver protests of April and May right up to our decision to take the Trek on to Ottawa. Well it was June 3rd that we mounted the box-cars, my notes say, two months exactly after we walked out of the relief camps and converged on Vancouver. If anyone had told us back then about all the marches, rallies, tag days and occupations that we were about to organize, we would have thought they were dreaming in technicolor. Two months later we were organized and ready not just for another march, but for a Trek across the continent to chat with the Prime Minister and his cabinet.

"I recall we had a Route Committee that was in charge of knowing the train schedules and deciding the time lines, where we would stop, when we would leave, etcetera. They had planned for two full divisions to leave that night on the 10 p.m. CPR freight below Gore Avenue, and approximately half a division to leave about an hour after midnight on the next eastbound

CNR freight. Then Division Two, I believe, was leaving on the evening CPR freight. We only had three full divisions and another half a division starting out on the On-to-Ottawa Trek. That's what we were calling it by then.

"You see, quite a number had left the strike in the last couple of weeks in Vancouver, most headed east looking for spring work on farms or construction, but most of the desertion came from those who had family or girlfriends or something going for them in Vancouver. Then, of course, many of us fully expected to be stopped by the police, either in the Vancouver rail yards or in some isolated place in the Rockies where public support couldn't rescue us. So some of those who voted against the On-to-Ottawa venture probably decided it was warmer and safer in Vancouver. We didn't call for solidarity on such a decision to ride the rails because the Trek was going to be difficult enough without having to deal with guys that really didn't want to be there.

"Nevertheless, the press accounts were unanimous in underestimating the numbers because they never bothered to find out about all three departures. I'm just making the point that those academics who study history by looking up archived press reports don't realize that they are really studying not only pulp journalism, but in many cases, pulp fiction. We knew the exact numbers because we had card committees that reported if someone joined or left a division. We needed that information for discipline and to watch for stool pigeons, fifth columns and the like. We were just a few bodies, under 1400, who began that Trek, but it was destined to grow. Foster, our old Chief of Police in Vancouver, had the departing Trekkers counted almost as accurately as our Card Committee, because he apparently reported almost the exact numbers and times of departure to McGeer, although he didn't bother to correct erroneous press statements, naturally.

"Anyway, this Route Committee was something else. They discovered that the CPR was planning on sending the 10:15 p.m. freight ninety minutes early to foil us, but we were there in plenty of time so they didn't bother leaving that early. So there we were in the yards, in formation, singing our union songs, laughing, cheering, saying good-byes. Hundreds of people, including many from the Mothers' Council, lined the tracks passing parcels of sandwiches and other goodies to the boys. Matt Shaw swung up on top of a boxcar and addressed the crowd briefly, thanking them, especially that Mothers' Council, for their wonderful support throughout the Vancouver Strike. This was the end of an important two months in which the Relief Camp Workers Union came into its own, shall we say. The values of discipline, solidarity and organization forged in April and May were the keys to our survival on the rails and in Regina.

"So Cosgrove, the Trek Marshall, gave the signal with his arm and that traditional bellow, and we division captains had one twelve-man platoon beside almost every one of those ninety freight cars. We'd rehearsed it well, veteran riders teaching the novices ahead of time, so we looked damned efficient as we swung up those ladders in one massive human wave. A lot of the groups were singing — pop songs, World War I songs that everyone associated with boys leaving for the front. Besides our lungs, we had a few harmonicas and Comrade Marsh's concertina accordion in Division One, a long way down from me. One squad sang a parody of 'Bow Down to Washington,' a University of Washington cheerleading song. As the engine lumbered into motion, one of my boys yelled out, 'Good-bye Vancouver; you treated us right!' We all cried, 'Hear, Hear!' to that. One lad further down stood up and gave us a solo rendition of 'There's a Long, Long Trail.' That proved prophetic, especially for the first leg of our journey to Kamloops.

"Years later, I read a newspaper clipping that someone back in Vancouver had saved in an Ottawa Trek scrapbook they put together. In it, a *Vancouver Province* reporter recorded some comments he claimed to have overheard from the crowd. He said many shook their heads at some of the boys who were too lightly dressed for mountain nights on top of a freight car. He heard one woman say that the last time she saw her own son was from the same spot as he made his way towards the trenches of France. She never saw him again. Her companion had seen her son off there too, but he was lucky enough to come home with a war wound. A third companion was quoted as suggesting that our boys were off to a different kind of war, one that took a lot of courage and vision as well. I always wondered if that reporter wasn't a closet creative writer, coming up with a scene like that.

"Anyway, no confrontations at all in leaving. We even risked a few jokes

Trekkers board the train in Vancouver, June 3, 1935. Saskatchewan Federation of Labour document.

RCWU members mounting train at the start of the On-to-Ottawa Trek, Vancouver, June 3, 1935.
Library and Archives of Canada, Ottawa. C-029399.

and banter with the police officers who were assigned to see us out of town. Maybe Jeremiah Jesus McGeer had sent out the word — 'good riddance to bad rubbish.' No doubt that's what he thought of us."

I noticed Sammy whip his cap off, shake his head grinning, "Jeremiah Jesus!" he said under his breath.

"But by God," Doc continued, "we had left our mark on the social consciousness and class consciousness of many in Vancouver. The day after we left, the longshoremen struck the waterfront, and it was to be a long and bitter strike. We even discussed heading back to help them, but we were committed to this Trek by then.

"Now riding the rods is and always was illegal. Some hobos would reach the top rung of the boxcar's ladder only to see the head of a CPR harness bull, with his club descending on the hobo's defenceless fingers, and sometimes they fell from those ladders and never lived to describe that horror; certainly the police and press and public weren't interested in hearing about it — if they lived or not. We all knew this, but felt a bit of safety in our numbers. So it was a touch ironic when we met our first harness bull willing to enforce the trespassing act in Hope, just where the Fraser Valley begins to narrow some."

"Maybe you'd better explain a CPR harness bull, Doc," I suggested, glancing at Sammy, who was slouched forward, arms on knees like he was watching the Stanley Cup finals.

"Railway security cops. They had all these belts, and weapons and straps attached… made them look like they were in harness, I guess. No morals. No training. No guts, as a rule, if they're not in a gang. But this single, lonely harness bull stood his ground there late at night as we braked to a stop in the yards. And when the squealing brakes let off, he bellowed out his challenge, as if he were backed up by a corps of panzer tanks, 'Get down from those cars boys; you're trespassing on CPR property.' Well, we all had been schooled in non-violent protest for the last months and we were sworn to avoid anything but positive peaceful non-confrontation on the Trek. Besides we were planning to get down to stretch our legs anyway. We climbed down, milled around a bit, and the bull couldn't quite decide if he should start arresting or herding us, a hundred at a crack. Perhaps he hadn't thought that far. A few minutes later the locomotive was steaming and the brakes released, and I ordered the boys to mount up. They climbed back up and waved good bye to Hope's fearless harness bull; a few of the boys complimented him on the great job he was doing. I'm sure he appreciated that.

"Anyway, some of the boys without decent jackets and blankets damn near froze to death that night through Hell's Gate Canyon. That is a slow, miserable section of the line, and it felt more like March than June. There wasn't a hell of a lot of food left by the time we hit Kamloops about noon the next day. We were all stiff, grimy and dog-tired. Some were chilled badly. Morale was lower than a relief camp bunkhouse in January. Now, Slim Evans had hopped a freight a couple of days earlier to organize our reception in Kamloops and Golden, the two major stops planned before Calgary. He had even wired his contacts before he left Vancouver. Well, his connections in Kamloops let us down badly. Apparently, Morris Rush was out of town, and the alternates, the people he should have been able to trust most to get things done, didn't come through for us. No welcoming committee, no grub, not even a coffee, or a glass of water 'in the Master's name,' as they say.

"Some men started grumbling, some talked of leaving, maybe heading off on their own for better foraging. The radio was telling us about the longshoreman's strike back in Vancouver, and some thought we'd be better off helping them. Some said we'd never make Calgary at this rate.

"Hey listen! These guys had been hungry, tired, sleeping on their rolls on hard meeting-hall floors for two months. Fighting for survival and dignity. Don't be too hard on them till you've ridden the rails a few nights in their shoes, in their company, in their desperation, if you're hearing me, gentlemen."

By this time, Doc was taking it to us. Though he had looked frail when he rose to the pulpit, now the veteran campaigner was coming through. His body rocked to the rhythm of stories that he had told a hundred times before.

"What I mean to say is I'm not condoning the break in solidarity, but I'm not about to criticize those boys, if you get my drift. Not many of them over thirty; most younger than I was. I was twenty-three, twenty-four, and God damn it, I didn't know what to say to them.

"Now, I got to tell you folks, what happened next to turn the tide for our morale has been a matter of some controversy among my surviving and no-longer-surviving comrades in Division Three. Ronnie Liversedge was secretary of Division Three, and we were always in close contact, so you'd think we could agree on what happened next. Well, Ronnie was always a great storyteller, and of course he wrote a fine book on the Trek, which elaborates on the oral accounts that he was called upon to give, back in Vancouver and various centres, starting in the thirties when this was still fresh in people's minds. He and Gerry Tellier remembered this event quite differently than I remember it. Somewhere along the way I stopped trying to correct their version, but I and the others heard it enough that any of us can tell it ourselves, almost as colourfully as Ronnie's live performances of it. It's become the more celebrated version of events, so I'll tell you Ronnie's version first without comment, and then maybe I'll tell you what I remember.

"Ronnie would start by describing our bedraggled condition and the disappointment at our lack of reception upon dismounting in Kamloops. Then he'd say something like this: 'Let me read it to you from my book, *Recollections of the On to Ottawa Trek*.'

So you see it was times like this that we were glad Arthur Evans was our leader, because Arthur knew what shape we were in and he knew it was up to him right then. No speech or rhetoric that night. Slim was a straight shooter when he dealt with working men. Not an ounce of bullshit in the man if you know what I mean.

He asked us politely if we'd listen to him for a minute or two. "Look guys," he says," I think I can promise you that we've seen the worst leg of the Trek. Kamloops here is the first stop and the media is still warming up to the story. They haven't caught a vision for what we're doing yet. But they will by God. They will. They can't ignore this size of a delegation on the way to Parliament Hill."

He said, "Our people didn't come through for us here, but we can fix that," he assured us. And he guaranteed us the folk in Golden would be there for us in spades. Then we'd hit Calgary, together and strong. Four days rest. We'd stage a tag day. We'd force relief from the Mayor, and take in reinforcements from Calgary and Edmonton. You see, Gerry Tellier and his brother were chosen to head north to Edmonton on the CNR to recruit the unemployed there, to bring them down to meet us in Calgary.

Slim said we'd be refreshed, strengthened, and under a strong prairie sun. Then he got serious and personal. He promised that every damned one of us would eat, and eat well for supper there in Kamloops, and that if we all pulled our weight with the organizing, we'd pull not only supplies from this town, but a crowd for an evening meeting and enough money for not only sufficient food but a decent smoke to boot, for anyone that cared to indulge.

"So now," he says, "in a minute I'm going to ask for volunteers to fan out in organized groups to visit everyone from City Hall, to the CCF, to the Unemployed Office, to the smallest church. But first we got a question to settle here. We want to know who is for packing it in, and who's for continuing the Trek. It's your call."

He called for a show of hands, and what do you know. Every hand was with Slim. If he said we could do it, by God we were ready to prove him right.

"Well, there you go. That's the way Ronnie remembered it, and I heard him tell that story several times back in Vancouver in the late thirties. Still I can't tell it quite as convincingly and dramatically as he told it. I can almost remember it that way myself, if I don't give my head a shake. First time or two I heard him tell it, I tried to correct him, but the next time he'd tell it he'd forget that I'd corrected him the last time. Finally we agreed to remember it differently, I guess. Anyway, the truth of the matter is that I don't remember Slim Evans being there in Kamloops when we arrived. Not even the next day, as I recall. I am pretty damned sure he waited for us in Golden, but I've heard Ronnie's version and Gerry Tellier's version often enough and I suppose one ought to give them the time of day on this issue sooner than the mixed-up reporters' and historians' versions. Sometimes I can almost believe that Slim made that speech, almost hear him saying those lines, but what I do remember is that Jack Cosgrove was fairly annoyed that the advanced party had failed us. Seems to me he wired Evans in Golden; well I'm sure he wired Golden anyway a bit later to tell them we wouldn't be staying the extra day in Kamloops, but would leave on the seaboard freight the very next day when our last division arrived.

"First thing, as I remember it, was he called the captains and chairmen and secretaries of our two divisions there and told them to gather the boys for a meeting in the park, down by the river. He told us that we were going to get us some food and support here, but he needed us to stick together, keep the discipline, and stay on side till he had a few minutes with the boys. So we marshalled the boys, did our jobs and Jack Cosgrove, an ex-noncom officer from World War I, gave us a matter-of-fact speech, some of which was similar to the one described by Ronnie. He asked Matt Shaw if he thought he could contact the unemployed offices, the Young Communist League, the CCF and a sympathetic printer to help advertise an evening meeting? Shaw answered with this incredible optimism as if it were just another routine day on the job in Vancouver, where he'd done this scores of times in the last few months. Jack told us that we were going to hold a tag day even though we'd got a cable that Mayor Moffat wasn't granting permission. Cosgrove did warn us that we'd all have to volunteer for immediate committee work to scrape together a good meal and some basic supplies. I don't recall, getting to vote on allegiance to the Trek. Jack was still too much of a World War I sergeant to be that democratic. But his rough confidence did inspire 'volunteers,' so-to-speak, and it also inspired a renewed sense of purpose.

"That's the way I remember it. I think Ronnie and Gerry were remembering part of Slim's speech to us in Golden mixed with part of Jack's instructions in Kamloops. Both were tall, and Jack and Slim both had deep voices, wore working man's overalls and had that authority in their voice, so maybe time did a number on Ronnie's memory. I'm sure it's done a number on my memory from time to time, wiping a bloody lot of important memories out too, you can bet. So anybody like Ronnie that tries honestly to keep alive the memory of what those boys did, well, hell's bells, I'm just glad they've spoken up or written it down.

"So there we were. We were all assigned our missions and we fanned out. Found a few contacts from the Young Communist League and that paid off, because they knew where to go and who to see, and they didn't waste time debating or thinking about it. Some of them joined Gerry and his brother Louis Tellier on their recruiting trip to Edmonton. Those two characters, by the way, went by the aliases of Gerry Winters and Louis Summers, if you can believe it.

"Well, we got our food. We got our crowd. We even managed to collect a bit of cash before the evening was over. We didn't get along with Mayor Moffat very well, so we declined his offer to sleep on the cement floors of an abandoned hospital. Looked more like a prison than a hospital, and I guess we preferred Riverside Park out in the open and nearer the freight cars in case the police tried anything funny. So Matt Shaw and a couple of others spoke to the crowd that night and we even began to change our minds about the social consciousness of Kamloops. Matt's voice, you know, would rise somehow like a young man full of hope and confidence. There is something infectious about Matt when he gets in front of a crowd. I hear he's been in the hospital now in Regina. But back then he'd hold that head of his high, and that voice, well you'd start feeling that lofty idealism, like he was calling up to some huge flock of greater Canada greys on that prairie flyway that he was born under. And, by God, sometimes when he'd get wound up, I'd get that shiver running down my hair roots, that same shiver a guy gets when the Canada greys honk over head for the first time after a prairie winter. I guess that's why we called upon him so often to do the speaking. It was good to see him again, there in Regina. The Saskatchewan Federation of Labour had the two of us there for the sixtieth anniversary of the Trek in July of '95. I'd like to see him again, you know, if you ever bring him up this way again."

Doc paused for a bit of his apple juice, and I noticed Sammy cock his head, as if something was bothering him; he chose that moment to signal the waitress who had been at the doorway for the last half a minute, to bring him something stronger than an apple juice.

"Anyhow, the men were finally bunking down, hunkering down into our rolls and blankets, under the stars in the park, though it hadn't cooled off so badly yet. And I was off meeting with Jack Cosgrove and Red Walsh, so I didn't hear the start of this, but I've heard Ronnie tell it a time or three. Down in the middle of Division One comes the tentative wail of a home-sick accordion. Then a bit of an intro and a fancy riff or two. Then the full musical lungs of Comrade Marsh's concertina, that would not be denied, and a rich baritone voice that carried on the night air those words that had echoed between the bricks in downtown Vancouver. 'Ho my comrades,' … little fancy run in there as he takes his time building to it. 'See the signal,' a pause to build the tension, 'Waving in the sky… Reinforcements… Now appearing…' Then he belts it out: 'VICTORY IS NIGH.' Damn near his whole division was with him by the time he hit the chorus. And before he was through repeating the chorus, even I could hear them through an open window. We paused in our meeting, two blocks away from the park, to listen to more than four hundred voices.

"Well, sure enough, after that rough ride to Kamloops, if it wasn't the God-damned Hobo Jungle Choir. And, by God, I'd prefer to hear them again any day to that Mormon Tabernacle stuff. They hit the chorus with some sort of syncopation."

Doc's left fist punctuated the rhythms now. 'Hold the fort — For we are coming — Union men be strong — Side by side we'll — Battle onward — Victory will come!' Some of them did a few World War I songs after that but 'Hold the Fort' is the one we'll all remember.

"Well, friends, it was like the Great Divide was behind us and the Little Engine That Could was no longer struggling with 'I think I can, I hope I can' but was running with 'I thought I could, I know I can.' That darn hymn became the anthem of the Trek. We sang it in every parade at every stop. For one ringing month in the middle of the Great Depression, this hymn replaced both the 'Internationale' and 'Bread and Roses' as the number one anthem of the revolution. The press started mentioning it. Hell, they could hear us singing it in Ottawa before we even hit Regina, and we didn't even have CBC Television to cover it back then.

"The next morning wasn't rushed, and the sun warmed us quickly. Some Kamloops folks inspired by the last night's meeting had coffee and food prepared for us. Some of us managed to wash up in the park pool, because the Thompson River by the park there where we slept is pretty damn cold and running fairly high that time of year. A few of the boys were even suspected of shaving though some of us were so young we hardly needed to. We enjoyed that day, and those that weren't involved in the leadership and organization caught up on some rest. We also had a clean-up crew scour the grounds before leaving.

"The two hundred Trekkers that left Vancouver at 1 a.m. caught up to us that first evening while the three hundred and fifty from Division Two caught up to us just a bit after noon the second day, slightly more than twenty-four hours after the main group arrived, on that same daily seaboard freight. A few more unemployed and former relief camp workers joined us at Kamloops; the papers claimed sixty more signed on, but Division Four wasn't fully manned and fully reorganized till we got our reinforcements in Calgary.

"There was a *Toronto Daily Star* reporter by the name of Kingsbury who had joined the Trek in Vancouver. He had promised to just report the facts, and he didn't do too bad a job at that, though they pulled him from the story by the time we hit Regina. He reported that a couple of young women, sisters in fact, climbed onto the boxcars with the Trekkers when we left Kamloops. I certainly didn't know about it then, but I heard about it later and took action. Kingsbury even reported their names, though fortunately for their family's sake, no one out west got the *Toronto Daily Star* in those days. The youngest was nineteen, so at least they weren't juveniles.

"We held a disciplinary meeting in Calgary for the Trekkers who were hanging out with them though they claimed that nothing had happened, whatever that meant. A couple of guys were booted off the Trek over it; we won't mention names. One of them might have rejoined at Medicine Hat. I'm fairly certain that the girls stayed in Calgary. We certainly made it clear to the men that this sort of thing would be used as ammunition against us. We soon heard how the dailies were inventing news about us day-by-day, filling columns with second- and third-hand reports, not even bothering to interview us, some calling us 'bums, riffraff, rabble and Bolshevik-led,' and even when they were trying to be polite they emphasized 'many European born.'"

Doc paused, and Charles was shaking his head. He took all bigotry personally; I learned that proper response from him, I think.

"But some of the more responsible papers," Doc continued, "reported on our discipline and good behaviour — we needed to reinforce that in the public mind if we were to have a successful Trek; so we came down hard on any drinking, fighting or disturbance of any kind. You were out of the Trek, just like that. You see the girls weren't the only ones trying to join the Trek on the sly. We had paid police informants in our ranks, some of whom we never discovered until after the damage was done. For example, we were fortunate to have a short stop in Revelstoke and you can imagine now, with all the divisions together, a full 1450 men could strain the capacity of Revelstoke's cafes to serve such a crew. The CPR harness bulls for which

Revelstoke was infamous were noticeably absent, and the engineer agreed to start the departure a little later than usual so the men could all be served. This cooperation on the part of the CPR seemed too good to be true.

"Anyway it seems a couple of Trekkers had smuggled liquor with them from Kamloops and one of them carelessly broke some dishes in a restaurant in Revelstoke. We brought this up at Golden (our next stop) with the division leaders, along with Evans and Cosgrove. We were all for expulsion, but decided to let the Trekkers vote at the general meeting on the appropriate discipline to keep the solidarity. We wanted to encourage the men to be committed to the discipline they were endorsing and enforcing. The men voted to expel the two Trekkers for drinking and sent a cheque to reimburse the café owners. Much later, in evidence from the Regina Riot Inquiry, we learned that one of those men was a paid RCMP informant. Paid to tarnish our reputation as well, I'm sure, since the papers all jumped on the incident.

"Well, ever since Jack Cosgrove decided to cancel one of our days of rest in Kamloops, I had been nervous about stopping in Golden. Nobody could remember much of anything in Golden, and, if Revelstoke had a hard time handling a coffee-break for this many, how was Golden going to support a twenty-four-hour stop. Food, sleep, bathing and laundry were all serious organizational problems. In Kamloops, Slim's advance-party preparations had fallen through, and now he had twenty-four hours less to complete a seemingly impossible task.

"When we left Revelstoke it was well after midnight, and the trains were slow heading up the grade through the Rogers Pass. There was no Trans-Canada highway in those days through there, no possibility of a stop. The cold bites through blankets at that altitude even if you're inside a boxcar. Most of us were on top and freezing, not getting a hell of a lot of sleep.

"So dawn was just breaking ahead of us when the engine whistle started announcing the road crossings near Golden. When it stopped, we dismounted sleepily, but Slim Evans was right there directing Cosgrove the way to march once we got the boys assembled. Well, they took us on a fair march, but it was a beautiful tourist camping park along the Kicking Horse River, just before it flows into the Columbia. Slim told us along the march that they had some hot stew waiting for us, but when we got there we couldn't believe our eyes. There was this sturdy, older lady... (I wouldn't agree with Ronnie's description of a little, old white-haired lady); she was strong and capable, and she didn't need a megaphone when she summoned us all to her feast. I say 'her feast' because she clearly presided over the spread there: not just over her gigantic bubbling cauldron of stew that she was stirring, but over the whole scene with half a dozen other huge rendering vats, or reduction pots, or wash boilers, or oversize canning canisters. I don't think pots exist in those sizes any more. They had at least one of those old-style tin washtubs full of stew over one fire, and they had these long tables covered with loaves of bread, plates, mugs, utensils, coffee, and a few other motherly women ready to direct the boys into queues.

To our tired, hungry eyes, there couldn't have been a more welcoming sight. The sun was up and we'd warmed up from walking, but we were hungry and there was the earth-mother, Ramona Sorley, standing over her bubbling cauldron of stew, beckoning us to their Golden welcome, taking charge of us as if she had decided to adopt 1500 bedraggled young sojourners from the CPR boxcars. The story has been told and retold by every Trekker living and dead, and I imagine it's gotten more idyllic with the years of retelling, but it will remain a highlight of our Trek that deserves the honour of retelling as long as there's a voice left to tell it."

Doc reached for the juice, and Daniella glanced my way, eyes dancing as if to say, "One voice sure as hell hadn't been silenced yet."

"But I've got to tell you, gentlemen, moments like that don't just happen. Hospitality is generally damned hard work, and hospitality for 1500 takes more than good intentions, more than even a sincere belief in community cooperation, or Christian compassion, or workers' solidarity. It takes that... plus damn hard work! People skills, solid contacts and organization. Slim Evans had been there to rally Golden, and his signature attention to detail and his ability to inspire service were evident there. We didn't know the details at the time, but he'd been there for less than a day and a half. He had wired ahead to Ramona Sorley and she had already contacted the local CCF members and formed a committee and started to collect food.

"Now Ramona was dismissed by some writers later as a commnist. Well I've been dismissed with the same label my whole life, but it points to the fact that sometimes in small town Canada, those vilified communists, along with the CCF 'socialists,' and the, quote, 'misguided' social-gospel Christians, didn't seem to have the luxury of factions and separate fronts that the left and the union movements were noted for. In the crunch, CCFers didn't need to fight with communists over who had the best interests of the workers at heart. Anyhow, I guess I'm getting sidetracked there. What happened, according to Ramona, is that this committee had called a mass meeting for Evans that turned out almost 200 people, largely women whose husbands were all up the road working on the Big Bend Highway or in camps nearby. Now that means most of the families in the whole area were represented, and you can bet they weren't all CCF, much less communists. You see what I'm saying about community cooperation and organizational skills?

"I guess they decided they didn't have time to bake sufficient loaves of bread for that many and collect food at the same time, so they wired bakeries in Calgary for 800 loaves of bread, while they came up with wheelbarrow loads of potatoes, carrots, turnips, four cords of wood for the fires and a few quarters of beef, I would guess, considering how much meat was in that stew. They had butter and eggs, things you couldn't exactly stock up on either. Coffee, cream, sugar. And where did they find all those cups and dishes and utensils in that little community? They obviously had a few washtubs left because someone had even arranged to take some of the men's laundry, if they had a change of clothes, and to bring it back to them by evening. You can't get that kind of service at a four-star hotel most of the time.

"So you can't help but see Slim's ability to organize and bring out the best in people. Not to take a bit of credit away from the fabulous people of Golden. Ramona and her family were Slim's friends, but she sure must have had a lot of friends herself in that town. I've often wondered if Slim's friend Morris Rush had been home in Kamloops, whether things might have been different there, too. Slim and Ramona also talked the city clerk out of making them sleep in the local hobo jungle and into allowing them to use that beautiful park for both eating and sleeping. Most of us even managed to baptize our sooty bodies in that freezing cold Kicking Horse River.

"Well, we had a public meeting there that night for Trekkers and citizens, where Cosgrove, Walsh, Shaw and Evans all emphasized the need for discipline and cohesiveness if we were going to win public support. We learned that every news broadcast and all the papers were following our progress. That's where we voted to eject the pair who were drinking. One of them, I think I mentioned, we found was employed by the RCMP — he was even reported to have advocated acts of violence.

"The shocker at that meeting came when Evans revealed that he had been ordered to return to his duties with the B.C. Workers Unity League in Vancouver. Apparently they had only given him leave to make preparations in Kamloops and Golden, thinking I suppose that he had lots of organizational work left to do in B.C. The Strike Committee chose George Black to fill the place of Evans. Black was not well-known, but he had been an active member of the Workers Ex-Servicemen's League — a veteran like Jack Cosgrove. He had worked hard on the Strike Committee and we knew he and Cosgrove would make a good team. The Strategy Committee had no hesitation recommending him to the men.

"All the boys seemed to accept the change when they realized that Evans had no real choice in the matter and that he wasn't leaving willingly. Black, no doubt, recognized Arthur Evans' incredible organizational efforts and inspirational abilities, because one of the first things he did when we reached Calgary was to wire the Workers Unity League in Vancouver that the On-to-Ottawa Trek needed Art's leadership and that they should give him leave to finish the job they had assigned to him — this protest movement that he had done so much to inspire and organize. Fortunately, the League's executive saw his point, changed their minds about Evans' duties, and allowed him to return to lead the Trek. I don't think they paid him for that leave, though I don't recall that for sure. I do know that the records show that the Communist Party brass down east and back in Vancouver were dubious about the Trek and in private were very guarded in their support of its practicality. Tom McEwan, Party Secretary, later accused Evans of leading the boys into a bloodbath. Yet the right-wing press, the RCMP and the Prime Minister were all convinced that the Kremlin itself was sending orders through Tim Buck to Art Evans. Nevertheless, without the rank-and-file members of that party, and without Arthur Evans and the Workers Unity League, we wouldn't have got to Vancouver, much less to Regina or Ottawa."

When he paused Sammy spoke up, "Want a cold beer, Doc, instead of that damn warm apple juice?" Doc looked at him like he was trying to remember where he was.

"I'm okay with the juice for now, but hold that thought, Sam," Doc said as though he were getting feedback from a graduate seminar. Cam cracked a smile. Doc was a natural with a lectern.

"I also recall that Art Evans was up before sunrise after that meeting in Golden, still organizing, making sure one division did a clean sweep of the park to gather and burn all litter before marching off to join the others at the rail yards to catch that same daily seaboard freight about an hour after dawn.

"The engineer delayed his departure for us till we were all organized and mounted; normally they'd only stop fifteen minutes or less to add an extra engine to help pull the train up the steep grades just east of Golden. They waited an extra half-hour this time, so we got the distinct impression the CPR officials were cooperating with us for some reason. For example, there were more open boxcars, meaning not so many of the men had to ride on top, and two of the RCMP constables from Revelstoke who had come up to join the three local constables, approached Cosgrove and Black, along with some of the CPR personnel, to warn us about the Connaught tunnel ahead. If anyone rode on top of the cars through that six-mile tunnel, you had to keep yourself flat on the roof of the car and breathe through a handkerchief or something, because the build-up of warm sulphurous smoke was suffocating. If anyone panicked in the dark on the roof of those cars, in the middle of the tunnel, it could easily mean horror and death. Some experienced riders used to drop off as they approached that tunnel from the west, then follow a footpath over the top while the freight curled its way slowly in a huge loop to the east exit. A single healthy man with a light load could beat the train to the east exit. But with 1500, though, it would be chaos.

"So here we have the RCMP and the CPR officials coaching us on our safety, helping us make it a successful Trek, yet Prime Minister Bennett claimed publicly, just three days later, that he had received a letter from the

CPR, complaining of our trespassing and requesting that he uphold the law by stopping us from riding. And this was dated the day after they were so helpful to us in Golden. We all suspected, and evidence later emerged, that Bennett had pointedly 'requested' both railways to send him such a letter. He had been advised earlier that we would never make it through B.C. without most of us abandoning the Trek. That assessment came from an RCMP informant. So, when we made it to Calgary with more men than in Vancouver, and were met with reinforcements from Alberta, with the press reporting more reinforcements waiting at stops along the way, well then, Bennett started feeling his yellow streak, started planning his goon strategy.

"But I'm getting ahead of myself. Where was I? The tunnel. That tunnel was as bad as they said; worse probably, but the men knew what to expect; thanks to their warning, no one panicked, though many thought they'd throw up or suffocate. After that tunnel, the mountain air and sunshine felt like a reprieve from hell's belly to paradise. We were going to hit Calgary in fine spirits. We were ready for Calgary, then. Calgary was the home town of Prime Minister Robert Bedford 'Iron Heels' Bennett. Jack Cosgrove's hometown too. He told us that, as a boy, he used to deliver Bennett's newspaper, when Bennett was a millionaire Calgary lawyer. I can still remember Cosgrove's mother out there waving to us when we left Calgary.

"But the more I think of it, the more I believe we were ready to take on Calgary and Bennett himself because of that miracle in Golden. Not the kind of miracle they taught in Sunday school of course. Just some good people, with community cooperation, that inspired us body and soul, kept us together. I guess I don't believe in the kinds of miracles that they were teaching about in Bible Bill Aberhart's Prophetic Bible Institute in Calgary there. Or on his *Back to the Bible Hour* radio show. Well… except maybe for one miracle that's always intrigued me since that day. I think I believe in the miracle of the loaves and the fishes.

"You see, gentlemen, as that train of ours descended from Banff to Calgary, we were heading into a province that was going absolutely wacky, swallowing Bible Bill's version of the loaves and fishes. Through his *Back to the Bible Hour*, he had hundreds of thousands of gullible Albertans ready to sweep him into power; they believed their new prophet could feed the multitudes, create loaves and fishes for everyone out of nothing, to the tune of twenty-five dollars per month per family. Money that was to be created miraculously out of the crumbs of debt and Depression desperation. Most Alberta folks believed in the Aberhart version of loaves and fishes completely. They voted in droves for his supernatural Social Credit Revolution. Bible Bill was swept to power, I think it was a mere two months after our little On-to-Ottawa miracle hit Calgary.

"What I'm trying to say is that I could never swallow Social Credit's version of economic miracles, but I do believe in the miracle of feeding the multitude there that we witnessed in Golden. When that saintly woman, Ramona Sorley, pointed her ladle to the loaves lining those tables, and the beef stew bubbling in those cauldrons, and ordered the men to come and be served, I believe we Trekkers witnessed the real New Testament miracle of feeding the multitude. Arthur Evans was no Jesus Christ, and Ramona Sorley was probably no saint, but they had that common touch with the good people of Golden, and they in turn touched 1500 young unemployed Trekkers in a way that none of us could ever fully explain. But we've all told the story ever since.

"Many of the Trekkers later talked about hugging Mrs. Sorley before climbing on that train. Ronnie Liversedge remembered us hugging all the women of Golden who served us that day. I can't say as how many of the boys got hugs there in Golden, but I think I understand how one man in carpenter overalls, matched with one woman with faith in youth and humanity, could produce the kind of miracle a working man can appreciate. Like I said before, we'll be telling the story of the stew and dumplings in Golden till every one of us is dead and buried, which isn't all that far away now. I just hope to hell someone will tell it after I'm dead and gone too, and I don't really give a damn whether they throw in a few extra hugs, or a few extra loaves and fishes for that matter, you understand what I'm saying?

"Because I'm here to tell you there was hot beef stew for every man-jack of us, and for the women and children who joined us there. There was real bread and butter, enough for all of us and more; I sliced some and distributed some myself. And, by God, when we appointed Perry Hilton to head up our new food committee there, he managed to take a heap of leftover food onto the train with us the next day. It damn near fed us all the way to Calgary.

"So I believe in the loaves and fishes miracle, gentlemen, because I was there. And what's more, I'll swear on a stack of Bibles, it wasn't fishes at all; it was God-damned mouth-watering beef stew, and plenty of it. Thank you, folks."

Doc Savage was finished his formal presentation, and we all gave him a standing ovation, which silenced the bar patrons in the main lounge in the next room for a whole five seconds. Doc joined our table and Cam and Tom moved their table, as was our custom, to join up with ours, peanuts and pretzel odours and jug of draft included. Sammy made sure Doc had that cold beer he promised, but he remained quiet, not asking any of his usual questions. Tom, on the other hand, was more voluble than he'd ever been at the Tuesday Club. He was telling us of their decision (Cam was in on it) to convert some of my Tuesday Night tapes into a professional CD.

Tom had ideas on adding music tracks, "Utah Philips would fit right in. Billy Bragg. Pete Seeger. Maria Dunn, closer to home…" And on he went.

Cam and Tom kept arguing about the title.

"The BJ's Motley Crew History Club," suggested Cam.

"The BJ's Tuesday Night Sessions," offered Tom.

"What about 'The BJ's I-Am-Canadian Club?'" quipped Cam.

"That's mixing beer and whiskey, Cam," Tom complained.

Finally Daniella joined in, once she saw that the topic couldn't be avoided. "Well, since we just asked Charles here to tell us a little bit about Bible Bill next Tuesday, and Paul already told us about the Reverend Tommy Douglas, and well… since we introduced this portable pulpit into BJ's, maybe we should call it 'BJ's Pub, Pulpit, and Prairie Fire.'" We all considered that for a moment.

"Probably be a shady day in hell before we could upgrade BJ's from a bar to a pub," said Cam, leaning back in his chair.

"And I'm not sure we should be mixing religion with anything as sacred as history, or even music," said Tom, winking at Daniella and nudging Charles the Rev with a chuckle. He must have been thinking of last week's Bible camp session.

Doc just smiled and relaxed with a beer next to Daniella. He had reached the next generation, and it showed on his face. I thought he'd live to be a hundred if we found him a circuit of pulpits. Or pubs for that matter.

10

BIBLE BILL AND THE MAJOR

CHARLES ON ABERHART AND SOCIAL CREDIT

T HE NEXT TUESDAY NIGHT IN late September 1997, Doc was off visiting Daniella's sister in Calgary, with the promise to be back the following Tuesday before Daniella drove him back to Quesnel. Charles was the speaker for the evening, but we were having trouble getting the Right Reverend Charles Quamina to take up his position behind the lectern. Maybe he had sworn off pulpits forever, so he felt we could do just fine sitting where we were around a couple of tables informally. He kept insisting that he would need my help anyway.

"So Rev," Sammy said, from across he table, "you were raised here in Alberta, weren't you? What the hell was that old coot going on about last week with that stuff about Social Credit miracles and Bible Bill?"

"First of all, Samuel, Doc Savage is not an old coot," Charles said, glancing at Daniella. Charles tended to call him Samuel when he expected more mature behaviour from him. "Doc may be pushing ninety, but he's a walking gold mine of Canadian history. A veteran of…"

"I know, I know, I was here. I heard the Doc. I didn't mean nothing by it, Daniella." He turned from Charles to her. "For me it's a sort of term of endearment, if ya will. He's a fascinating man. I just don't know enough about history to follow some of this shit. Social Credit miracles? What is that? Socreds around here are just a bunch of religious wackos that can't decide whether Wiebo Ludwig is one of them or not, or whether it's legal or not for the friggin' feds to collect income tax, for Christ' sake. So what's this stuff about Social Credit miracles and feeding multitudes back in the thirties. They sure as hell couldn't have been as wacked out then as they are now, 'cause how the hell'd they ever get elected?"

"And that's your second unforgivable insult, that you should think I'm old enough to personally remember Bible Bill and the birth of Social Credit," Charles said, with a forgiving smile.

"Rev, you remember everything. If you weren't there, you read about it," Sammy turned to Daniella for support, leaning towards her from the little round table pulled next to our own. "I'll bet you he remembers this Bible Bill character, 'cause the Rev was a Bible-thumper himself once long ago, rumour has it."

"Sammy, you've got all the finesse of a bull in a china shop," Cam said, kicking Sammy's chair lightly with the sole of his boot. "There's a difference between a clergyman and a Bible thumper. Just because he was a man of the cloth many years ago doesn't mean he was a Bible thumper."

"That's okay, Cam. Truth be known, Sammy's probably accurate. I was probably more of a Bible thumper than a man of the cloth and collar. We didn't wear any robes or collars in the Apostolic churches. Paul's dad and I were pastors together in Leader, Saskatchewan, when Paul was a kid. The worst of the matter is that I actually do remember Bible Bill and the Social Credit landslide."

"What did I tell you!"

"I just don't like the fact that Sammy here was so sure I'd remember," Charles laughed. "I was about sixteen when Aberhart became premier."

"Jeez, even I didn't think you were that old, Rev. You don't look a year beyond seventy. I just thought maybe you'd have heard about it from your old man or something."

"Actually Sammy," I chimed in, from the far end between Daniella and Charles, "you couldn't have asked the question of anybody more qualified to answer it, truth be known. Back in the fifties Charles was into that party and their history in a big way. I recall a few discussions between my father and this guy." I rested my hand on his shoulder.

"Yes, I'm ashamed to admit it, but it took a while for me to see the light. And you, Paul, are not supposed to reveal my deep dark secrets."

"Sorry Rev."

"Well, Samuel, truth is I recall way too much about Bible Bill and his lead disciple Ernest Manning. On the other hand, I don't recall hearing much about the Ottawa Trek at that same time. We weren't living anywhere near the CPR main line. We were living up in Amber Valley until that August when my parents sent me to Prairie Bible Institute in Three Hills for high school. But I do recall hearing about the Regina Riot. However, Aberhart's election that August, that was big news even for a teenager. Around Three Hills everybody, I mean everybody, used to find somebody with a radio on Sunday afternoons and listen to Aberhart's *Back to the Bible Hour* broadcast. My host family had a radio in the kitchen — a big old-fashioned kitchen with a table that sat ten easily without even putting the middle boards in. So they had their friends and neighbours come over after lunch every Sunday for more than a year before that election. I only witnessed one of those Sundays before the election itself near the end of August."

"Wait a minute Rev." Sammy pushed back his chair a bit to face Charles more directly; he pushed his cap brim higher and shook his head. "You can't tell me everyone went to church, even back then. And now you're telling me they all trooped off to the neighbours to listen to some more preaching after

William (Bible Bill) Aberhart broadcasting from CFRN, Calgary, 1930s. Glenbow Museum Archives, Calgary. NA-2771-2.

lunch? For me that's tough to chew." He pulls the ball-cap peak back into place.

"Oh, not everyone went to church back then, but these weren't just church people coming over to listen to Aberhart. There were folks listening to his broadcasts regularly that would never darken the doorway of a church. Wasn't always like that though, they tell me. They used to have occasional visitors for the broadcast, before he went Social Credit, but not nearly as regular or as crowded as those two years before he was elected, when he started talking about Major Douglas and how economics fit into the gospel."

"Major Douglas. So this is the cat that brought medicare to Saskabush."

"Wrong Douglas, Sammy!" Tom chimed in from his side of the table.

"That was Tommy Douglas," said Charles, "Premier of Saskatchewan. That was later. We're talking about Major Clifford Douglas, an eccentric Scottish engineer. Inventor of social credit economic theory, which was all the rage in Britain, back then."

"So how did this Limey get mixed up with Alberta politics?" Sammy poured some draft.

"Let him tell the story, Sammy. He'll get to all that." I reached for my traditional ale.

"All right, all right. I'm just participating, man. First you guys accuse me of general ignorance. Then when I attempt to educate myself on the friggin' history of my province, you tell me to shut up and not ask questions." Sammy had a glass in one hand and a palm outstretched to us, pleading innocence to all charges.

"You go right ahead and ask your questions, Sam," said Charles. "Just don't accuse me of being an old coot if I attempt to answer the question."

"And if you wait five extra seconds before asking, he'll often get to the explanation without you prompting him," said Cam, foil drawn in gleeful challenge.

"All right, so I won't interrupt," Sammy snatched the peanut bowl from Cam's side of the table, "as long as he can explain why these kooks are huddled around the kitchen table listening to a Bible broadcast if they weren't religious."

"Well, they weren't all kooks," Charles explained. "Some of us were religious, some weren't. But Aberhart had been doing a series on prophecy and the end times for as long as anyone could remember, and that seemed to be intriguing to more people than just regular salvation theology, you see. Then all of sudden he gets talking about how social credit philosophy was like some kind of God-led revolution that would bring down the banks and the powerful and give justice to the weak and downtrodden. Well, there was a hell of a lot of weak and downtrodden at the height of the Depression, you see."

"Give us a short primer on the actual social credit theory, Rev," Cam said.

"If you'd a given him another five seconds he'd a got to that, Cam!" Sammy's eyes lit up with mischief.

"All right guys," Daniella chimed in. "I've got the tape running here and Charles has got a story here well worth recording, so let's hear from the Rev."

"My lord, Reverend Arthur," Charles grinned, "do I get my voice immortalized in the archives like Doc Savage and Matt Shaw? Kind of ironic you know. Just when I find a way to that illusive immortality, I have to admit that I'm not the definitive expert on the subject at hand, as Paul suggests. I mean, to a sixteen-year-old, this social credit sounded pretty good to me, with all those war vets and farmers around the table excited about it. Twenty-five bucks a month for the family might mean that guys like me wouldn't have to work after school. Many of us had to quit school. I was luckier.

"I think the Socred doctrine was a bit vague to everyone. I remember them talking about the *Yellow Book* or the *Yellow Pamphlet*. It was written and distributed by Aberhart and the Prophetic Bible Institute. They deferred to its authority like the young radicals in the sixties would to Mao's *Red Book*. I think the *Yellow Book* was called *The Douglas System of Economics*. I read up on some of this later. As I recollect, it emphasized that everybody's labour and social contributions had a value that the state, and therefore the banks, must honour. Any government recognizing social credit principles would therefore be obliged to honour that value with credit. It proposed credit certificates (he used $25 a month per adult as an example), and this scrip could be exchanged for essentials such as food and shelter.

"Other notorious points included the state claiming the savings of the rich when they died. In fact all bank savings accounts were to be exchanged, once operational, for provincial government bonds! You'd only get interest through scrip instead of actual money. The plan was that with the government able to access that kind of money, the government could implement all kinds of great programs — no one would go homeless or hungry and the work week could be reduced to sixteen hours a week. At least he didn't include Colonel Douglas's addiction to the international Zionist banking conspiracy theory."

"Jesus Christ. They sound just as wacko then as they are now!" Sammy said, forgetting to censor his language for Daniella.

"Well, Sam, I'm just remembering the more spectacular aspects of it, I suppose, but you have to remember that people were desperate — losing their farms, losing jobs, young guys joining the hobos, riding the rods. They were ready for a messiah. They needed some hope and the *Back to the Bible Hour* was suddenly giving them hope for a utopia or the Kingdom of God right here on earth, rather than the old message about pie in the sky when you die. Mostly they understood that $25 a month would mean a measure of basic economic security, and that was a heck of a lot more back then than Ralph Klein's paltry $300 rebate bribes to buy his last election."

"So was this stuff broadcast on CBC? Was it all over Alberta?"

"No it was CFCN Calgary and it reached most of southern and central Alberta but I don't know how far north of Red Deer it got. I don't think it got to Amber Valley. But I think it might have been syndicated later and other radio stations across the prairies picked it up. Anyway Prairie Bible Institute was the very buckle of the Bible Belt there between Red Deer and Calgary, and that area of middle Alberta was where Aberhart and Manning held the most meetings and created all the initial excitement. The crazy thing about this all was that the real social credit devotees, the purists, like Bill Irvine, couldn't stand Aberhart. They thought he was a fraud who was just using the name social credit to boost his radio ratings. Major Douglas actually agreed with that sentiment, but never denounced him publicly.

"Perhaps they should have guessed that what started out as social credit study clubs, and a massive radio fan club, was really headed towards a political party. You see, to begin with there were social credit advocates in every political party even before Aberhart jumped on the bandwagon. It was a definite political movement in England by then, and it had devotees and allies south of the border, too.

"Apparently the election was still almost a year away when the radio broadcasts started including the *Man From Mars* skits. It featured caricatured political types like C.C. Heifer (CCFer, you know), and there were ridiculous UFA defenders, and Kant B. Dunn. Kant with a K, and Dunn — D-u-n-n. Can't-be-done was the apologist for the banking establishments I think. It was a riot. The Christian social credit theme in all of them was heavy-handed, but it surely was popular.

"By then it was clear to the media that this was a political campaign, but the UFA government was divided as to whether they should try to co-opt the social credit movement or treat it as opposition."

"And UFA stands for United Farmers of Alberta, a fairly progressive government for the time," I added.

"Yes, thanks Paul," he rested his hand on my forearm for a second. "They actually paid Major Douglas to come to Alberta for a tour in the highly publicized role as economic advisor to the government. But it didn't help them any when folks found out what the government paid him. I guess he had a rather lavish expense account. So, by spring of '35, I think it must have been about the same time as the relief camp workers struck Vancouver, Social Credit held their founding convention as a political party, though everybody knew they were going to run candidates by then. I don't remember all this but I've read a lot about it since. Apparently Aberhart insisted that the convention give him a say in who the candidates would be for each riding. He just couldn't understand this democratic dogma about having constituency members nominate their candidate. So they compromised with the boss and named a committee chaired by Aberhart to have the power to appoint the candidates, out of a list of four selected by party members in each constituency. So all four candidates would campaign for the party, and at the last minute of the nomination deadline, Aberhart himself appointed the candidates."

"Bullshit?! You gotta be shittin us, Rev? He *appointed* his candidates?" Sammy said as he removed his cap, ran his hand through his hair and stared across the tables to Charles.

"It's not bullshit, Sammy. It's historical fact. The papers howled." Charles reached for the peanuts and water, seemingly quite comfortable with the feedback.

"Nobody could get away with that. Jesus H. Christ couldn't get elected pulling a stunt like that," Sammy said.

"Jesus H. Christ didn't have a whole lot of opportunity to reveal his hand on his preferred electoral politics, here in Alberta," Cam deadpanned; but a good poker player could probably tell that he enjoyed interactive lectures as much as Sammy. I needed both of them in my first-year classes.

"Well, Aberhart did it," Charles responded, "and in Christ's name, too. The papers called him a tyrant, a dictator and an autocrat, but he calmly went on the air and called for Social Credit supporters to boycott those papers that were spreading lies against the movement. He forced some papers right out of business in our area. I remember being told of some once-respected community leaders standing up at meetings and begging the folks to think logically about where the money would come from to give everyone $25 a month, since the government was too broke to meet its payroll and the provincial economy was a basket case — down the tubes, bankrupt. Well, people would shout those voices down, denounce them as pawns of the either the government or the Antichrist. Many sober citizens and potential voices of reason were humiliated in those mobs, as I recall. I think my host family in Three Hills and I were thrilled to see them shot down, I'm ashamed to say. These were the first political meetings I'd ever been to. We were so caught up in the frenzy of the moment, the energy of that radio-led revolution. But then I was only sixteen, taking my lead from men in their prime, who sat around our table and travelled miles to a campaign event. We could feel the landslide coming, and, to many an impoverished Albertan, this was a way of striking back at the injustice of the Depression and our own helplessness. They estimated that 300,000 Albertans tuned in to the broadcast each Sunday."

"Jesus," Sammy breathed.

"From Radio Calgary to the king's throne, just like King Ralph," Tom said as he passed the pretzels to Charles again.

"His Highness, DeKleiness," said Cam. "from CFCN radio, saying, 'Send those creeps and bums back east where they came from.'"

We laughed. This lecture was going down just fine without the pulpit.

"One reporter," Charles continued, after a sip of warm beer, "did actually ask Aberhart to respond to accusations about his autocratic style and personal ambition. Apparently he chuckled and said something like, 'Oh, I'm getting on in years. I can't be ambitious, at my age. It's just that the Spirit of Christ has gripped me. He's asking me to do my part to feed, and clothe, and shelter starving people. If that is what you call a dictator, then I guess I am.'

"I suppose it didn't hurt Bible Bill's cause any that Premier Brownlee had been charged in a scandal, accused of an affair with a young secretary, and he finally had to resign in July of 1934. He didn't have the Teflon charm of Bill Clinton or Jack Kennedy to mask his faults. People were hurting and indignant. Bible Bill was quite vicious in his attacks on political opponents too. When the UFA tried to get him to cooperate on a social credit program, he announced that he 'would not cooperate with the devil.' And Albertans 'would not be bullied and buffaloed.' He wasn't above using the prophet's ultimate weapon: 'God would open the Red Sea and swallow the corrupt and the fornicators.' I think the UFA replaced Brownlee about a year before they had to call an election, but by then they were caught in a Red Sea tidal wave.

"Come the election, the ruling UFA government didn't win a single seat. Polling wasn't as common then as it is now, you know, so many of the papers and radios were still predicting a minority or majority Liberal win. But the voter turnout was incredible, something like 80 percent, as I recall. The Liberals only elected five members, the Conservatives a couple — all the rest were Social Credit, many by a landslide, especially in our area. Very much like Ralph Klein's landslides. Same kind of personality focused election. Many voters determined to ignore facts, issues, logic. They were voting for the strong man. It was only about 55 percent for Social Credit but they had fifty-six seats to a total opposition of seven. 'Course one can't really compare the Depression to oil-rich Alberta, today, but that first-past-the-post curse made it always seem like a landslide of lemmings; yet we've always had around half of the province that was never fooled by these characters.

"Anyway, that's what was happening in Calgary when the On-to-Ottawa Trek reached town. It was about a month prior to the election call, but the campaign was on regardless, and people were smelling change in the wind. I don't think many people thought of the 'Ottawa Trek' as being left-wing and the Social Credit being right-wing as we would today. They just saw an awful lot of people hurting, and national and provincial governments that seemed to have their heads in the sand. So a little over two months after the 'Ottawa Trek' passed through, we elected Aberhart in this landslide. I wasn't voting yet; I had just turned sixteen, but I felt part of it.

"I guess we saw Aberhart as this giant prophet-like character standing up to the banks and the Eastern establishment, yet he was barely in power a month when he signed up an Eastern high-finance banker to be his financial adviser. Bible Bill himself was rabidly anticommunist and antisocialist. He viewed the UFA as godless socialists, as allies of the CCF socialists. He viewed all leftists as pawns of the Antichrist. Some said he had once predicted that the world would end in 1934. Of course his world was just beginning in '34."

"Did you ever meet this Bible Bill, Rev? What did he look like?" Tom leaned his chair back, taking the bowl of pretzels from the table with him. Cam immediately reached over for a handful.

"Oh, yes, he spoke in Three Hills several times, and my family sometimes travelled to hear him in Trochu or Torrington or Beiseker. He was a huge man. Six-foot-four, 260 pounds easily. He had this huge square head that came right out of his massive shoulders like a bulldog. Bald as the proverbial billiard ball, but square. They would sometimes call the German immigrants "Square-Heads," you know — disparagingly, I suppose. The cartoonists had a field-day caricaturing his features as well as his beliefs.

"I remember one cartoon that I saw in a collection years later when I could appreciate it more fully. It showed Aberhart off to Ottawa, cap in hand, after finding out the Alberta coffers were empty and people were demanding their $25 per month. Aberhart is walking towards Ottawa with an empty treasury chest dangling from one of those hobo sticks over his shoulder. Above his head the thought-cloud has the bells pealing in the Peace Tower on Parliament Hill 'ding dong' as he fantasizes getting $18 million relief from Prime Minister Bennett. In the background is the naive Alberta citizen pointing to a pair of huge boots with Social Credit written on them, and the Joe Average Albertan queries, 'But Bill, why don't you use your seven-league boots?' You see, obviously many in the press and the rest of Canada understood that these Social Credit folks were living in a fantasy world. I mean, Prime Minister Bennett had a federal election upon him, which he wasn't going to win — Social Credit was going to take seats from him and he certainly didn't intend to aid their cause."

"Excuse me, Rev. Seven-league boots?" Sammy eyes squinted.

"From a fairy tale about magic boots that helped you cover seven leagues with one stride. That's all I remember. Anyway, I guess all the historians agree that Bible Bill was one of the most disastrous and incompetent premiers in Canadian history. His own party members and caucus turned on him in the first two years, especially. It was vicious. The Douglasites led the charge and eventually this faction took over the lead in government policy. But Aberhart stubbornly refused to relinquish his unpopular leadership. So they introduced this $25 dollar credit voucher called 'scrip.' This was after the Supreme Court ruled their first hair-brained money-printing scheme as *ultra vires*. That's Latin for 'ain't your jurisdiction, buddy.'

"So the new scrip was complicated by the fact that you had to renew its value by sticking another one cent stamp on the certificate each week to keep it valid. The provincial treasury promised to redeem it after two years if you had all 104 stamps attached. Some damn thing like that. His lawyers figured that would skirt the issue of federal jurisdiction over currency. It was a royal pain in the ass. The stamps would fall off after a while and then nobody in their right mind would accept them. Well everybody but the most die-hard Socreds started calling it 'funny money' and the Socred MPs in Ottawa were called 'scrip-tease artists.' No financial institute and increasingly few stores on main street would accept the stuff, except for the army-navy store in Edmonton."

"I been there," said Sammy. "White Avenue?"

"Yes. Still there. Well the government certainly wouldn't let you pay them with scrip, yet they tried to use it to partially meet their payroll problems.

"Well, 'funny money' became the national joke; cartoonists went wild. Newspapers poked fun at Aberhart and gullible Albertans. I remember this news rag out of Calgary called *The Rebel* that openly scoffed and mocked Aberhart as a charlatan and shyster of low I.Q. Aberhart responded by threatening to put controls on the press, suggesting that, if we had to license professionals like lawyers and pharmacists, why shouldn't we license newspapers as well, once they'd proved their competence and credibility? People actually cheered that speech.

"But somehow, between funny money and World War II, Albertans managed to screw up enough hope, mixed with desperation, to re-elect Social Credit in '39. I think they got 43 percent of the vote — something like that — though nobody you met on the street would admit that they voted for them. I still wasn't twenty-one, so I couldn't vote, but I don't recall whether I was still a gullible supporter in those years or not. Twenty-year-olds had other things to think about at the outbreak of the war, and I was in college preparing to become a preacher. I've thought and studied a lot about it since.

"Anyway, Aberhart kicked the bucket before his next term was over, and his young protégé, Ernest Manning, father of Preston Manning, inherited the mantle, not at a leadership convention, I believe, like other parties, but by the 'laying-on of hands,' as we used to call it, by the caucus members. It came from the New Testament practice of the apostles transferring God-given authority by laying their hands collectively on their chosen ones. It's still practised in some churches in Alberta today. Manning continued to be the voice of *Back to the Bible Hour*, a widely syndicated radio program inherited from Bible Bill. It continued all through his long tenure as premier. Some of you probably remember it from the mid-sixties. You might be surprised how much of those sawdust trail roots you can still find in the parties of Preston Manning, Ralph Klein and Stockwell Day. For every Reform MP that declares Nelson Mandela a dangerous communist and terrorist, there are thousands of members that secretly applaud, and another thousand that wish one of their MPs would speak up on the international Jewish banking conspiracy, like Keegstra did for the Socreds. It's a generational thing, with Stockwell Day Senior a stalwart of the Socred religious right and a supporter of the Western Canada Concept fanatics. There's at least three generations of religious dissent behind the history of Stockwell Day and Preston Manning. It's interesting that the spiritual descendents of Ernest Manning are the strongest critics of Islamic theocracies, where religion and government are merged, yet that is what happened for decades here in Alberta.

"You see, both Paul and I, at least Paul's dad and I, come from families heavily influenced by those same itinerant evangelists, the big-tent revival meetings, the same sawdust trail, fundamentalist, evangelical revolt that Bible Bill was into. It came out of the more extreme right-wing elements of the Methodist blue-collar reformation that swept England and the American heartland, during the early part of the century. In America it mutated into a hundred different independent travelling salvation shows, some less reputable than others, many of which pushed up into the southern prairie provinces and southern Ontario as part of their annual summer tours. I've read that Bible Bill himself was raised a Presbyterian, and wanted to become a Presbyterian minister, till he fell under the spell of one of these born-again gypsy-tent evangelists in rural southern Ontario. When he moved to Calgary, the Presbyterians, the Methodists and the Baptists all got tired of him in turn till he had to create his own Calgary Prophetic Bible Institute and his own denomination. He was into some elements of Pentecostal doctrines and charismatic worship, which didn't endear him to the more conventional evangelicals.

"But you see, radio was the popular medium of entertainment and mass communication back then, and you didn't have fifty cable channels to choose from. CFRN is the channel that came in clearest in Southern Alberta; other than *Hockey Night in Canada*, Aberhart was the most dramatic entertainment on the tube — radio tubes, that is, before transistors. Many a snake-oil charlatan became wealthy by radio evangelism. These men became both wealthy and powerful."

"You're saying this Bible Bill premier was one of your generic snake-oil con-artists?" Tom had pretzel crumbs in his huge beard, but somehow it suited him.

"Well, not exactly. At first he was just a reputable high school principal that the Calgary Public School Board imported from Ontario because of his old-school spare-the-rod-spoil-the-child reputation. This Prophetic Bible Institute was a moonlighting hobby that grew into a full-time business, and then into the Social Credit League in 1934. He was sincere, and dedicated, and..."

"And deluded?" Tom asked as he took the pitcher and offered a glass of draft to Charles beside him.

"Deluded? I think so now, Tom," Charles waved off the beer. "But back then I was persuaded differently, you see. You really have had to experience the sawdust trails to understand that these guys live among us with an entirely different world view. Stockwell Day's six-thousand-year-old planet earth comes right out of the liner notes of the Scofield Reference Bible, King James version naturally, which Aberhart and other radio evangelists popularized in evangelical and Pentecostal circles. The Hebrew Bible certainly doesn't tell you that the earth is only 6000 years old, yet that became part of fundamentalist orthodoxy. And Scofield's version of God-appointed dispensations in world history became the dogma by which one could figure out the future plans of God for planet earth."

"This is bizarre. Sounds like you're suggesting that modern Alberta history is the product of some fringe protestant religious history. Is that a widely accepted theory?" Tom queried.

"Well Tom, it's more like a religious sideshow that became a significant factor in Alberta history. That's fairly well accepted, wouldn't you say, Paul? Sure. But the broader religious influence was not just in Alberta. The mainstream heritage of the Methodist reformation in England strongly influenced all of western Canadian politics you know. Especially in Winnipeg and Saskatchewan. The Methodist social-gospel tradition emphasized street level commitment to the physical and social needs of the downtrodden and the working class. These guys like J.S. Woodsworth were such social revolutionaries that at times they posed more danger to old money and the establishment than did the Communist Party of Canada. For example, Woodsworth, a Methodist minister, was one of the leaders of the Winnipeg General Strike and one of the earliest socialist members of Parliament. He became the first leader of the CCF in 1933. Tommy Douglas came out of that same movement. They say he witnessed the police charge on the strikers in Winnipeg in 1919 from the top of a downtown building. Woodsworth was arrested and charged with sedition for his role in the strike, but he was so popular and respected that the people turned around and immediately elected him to Parliament just after the strike, and he stayed there till he died twenty years later.

"In fact, just about the time that the On-to-Ottawa Trek reached Regina, the Reverend Tommy Douglas was getting nominated in Weyburn, Saskatchewan, to run as a CCF candidate in the party's first federal election. He had accepted a pulpit call from Calvary Baptist in Weyburn when he was fresh out of seminary, though he was far from a mainstream Baptist. So the Baptist Conference Superintendent warned him about his political involvement, saying that he had to make a choice: if he ran for the CCF that fall the Bishop would see to it that he would never get another Baptist pulpit in Canada. Apparently Douglas had resisted the temptation to run up until then. But in response to that ultimatum, as legend has it, he told the good bishop that he had just handed the CCF a candidate.

"So you see, the Methodist prairie fires seemed to be burning in two different directions: social-gospel socialism in Saskatchewan and Manitoba, and Social Credit fundamentalism in Alberta. I don't think the radically different directions were so noticeable back then. All populist prairie fires looked the same to the uninitiated eye. Maybe if I'd grown up around Weyburn, Saskatchewan, instead of Three Hills, Alberta, I'd have heard Tommy Douglas instead of Bible Bill, and who knows how much of my life might have been changed. Perhaps I would have enlisted in the business of saving society rather than saving individual souls. That's environmental determinism for you. I certainly give that more credence now than the divine determinism I once believed in.

"On the other hand, Paul's father grew up around Weyburn, I believe, and he grew up to be an Aberhart and Manning fan, rather than a Tommy Douglas fan. So there you go. That's my stranger-than-fiction account of the Bible and the pulpit in prairie politics."

Well, Charles was officially finished, so he shut his black file folder. I hadn't seen him refer to it more than once, but I'd noticed some numbers on a single page with one word or two after each number. That was the sign of a confident, practised speaker. But since he had never used the lectern, we just naturally slid into an hour or two discussion of the Canadian prairies' mixture of religion and politics. We stayed late, this time, enjoying each other's company and the wellspring of stories that Charles could deliver, if one found the right bucket.

That was a night to hear Charles, but even at home in my den hours later, it made me reflect on the dialectic of religion and politics that figured in my own narrative trek. Charles was right about one thing. My father's family in Weyburn were converts to the fundamentalist tent-revival ministries, too. And that was destined to colour my narratives, forever perhaps. My grandparents quit their traditional Lutheran Church and joined one of the upstart evangelical churches that blossomed from those tent-meeting revival campaigns. Charles was also right about the difficulty at the time for many to distinguish between two populist prairie fires. Some of Dad's brothers and sisters, and even my grandfather, loved to go hear Tommy Douglas speak, either in his Baptist pulpit, or on the campaign trail hustings. Many conservative and religious people had great respect and admiration for Premier Tommy as he took Saskatchewan from the poorest, most backward province in Canada, into the relative affluence and modern conveniences of the latter half of the twentieth century.

Nevertheless my father saw Douglas as a deluded, apostate Baptist minister who had deserted his pulpit and his calling to lead a godless political party. He agreed with the young Opposition MLA who chided the Premier from the floor of the Legislature that it was too bad a Baptist minister had turned into a socialist premier. Douglas smiled and replied that "eighteen years ago I dedicated my life to the Kingdom of God; if I didn't believe I was still doing that, I wouldn't be here today."

However, as a poverty-strapped preacher, my father didn't buy that version of building the Kingdom of God — here and now among us — at least not in the sense that Douglas meant. He looked enviously toward Alberta, always hoping his conference superintendent would reward him with a pulpit in the promised land of Bible-belt Alberta, home of *Back to the Bible Hour* and the Aberhart-Manning dynasty, where the big-tent revival meetings had evolved from fringe into evangelical mainstream and status-quo.

I've read somewhere that on the night of his election in August of 1935, Aberhart began his acceptance speech by thanking the "almighty God for His guidance and direction" in the campaign and promised to submit all future "deliberations to His Divine guidance." Then after asking for their prayers he urged the people of Alberta to remember their theme song, "O God Our Help in Ages Past." Thus one might understand that in my father's house, if the head of the house looked longingly across the border to the green hills of Alberta for inspiration, then so did his household: *As for me and my house, we will serve the Lord,* in the footsteps of Aberhart and Manning. That's the Alberta story for far too many; and I suspect it has the makings of a moral tragedy, but a very different sort of tragedy from the one that climaxed on Dominion Day, 1935, in Regina.

11

THIS TRAIN AM BOUND FOR GLORY

DOC SAVAGE ON THE CALGARY TO REGINA TREK

D OC SAVAGE WAS BACK WITH us in early October 1997, bearing the bad
news that Matt Shaw was in the hospital in Regina and not doing too
well. Our concern for Matt, began to rub off in the way we looked at Doc;
he was planning to visit Daniella's sister in Calgary for the first time in a long
while, agreeing to the one hour flight from Grande Prairie. Perhaps he was
more aware now of his own mortality, as he told us of friends and members
of the Trek who had passed away in the last two years. He had grown close
to Daniella over the last year. Charles and I had been close friends for some
time, but now Daniella was an integral part of our Tuesday Club rendezvous.
Thus the health of her grandfather and our passion for his stories became
critical to our lives. During the informal Tuesday evenings we often spoke
of our bigger dreams for the recording and preserving of the sessions. They
were giving me ideas for research; Charles and I were also taking a closer
interest in Daniella's work and her grandfather's quality of life. This man
walked over twenty kilometres almost daily to pan for gold on a gravel bar
in the Fraser River. He seemed frail and vulnerable to be doing that at his
age, yet he'd been doing it regularly for sixteen years, since his wife had died
in Vancouver.

At BJ's we offered him a chair to sit on, with another stool beside him
for the lectern, because he appeared a bit more stooped than the last time,
but he preferred standing. So Daniella sat down with that glint of concern
accentuated by the first hint of crow's-feet at the corners of her dark eyes.
She had the same thick shock of black hair framing her face that Doc has
in the few surviving photos from 1935.

Doc began with a few introductory remarks about Matt, and about their
exchange of notes over the years, and finally began the Trek narrative where
he had left off two weeks earlier.

"So it was sunny and hot, late afternoon I believe, when that CPR freight
rolled to a stop in Calgary. Slim had sent Bill Hammill ahead to Calgary
with a couple assistants to prepare our reception there. He understood the
importance of preparation, organization and cooperation with city officials.
We were disappointed that the Workers Unity League had yanked Evans from
the Trek; at least that's the way we saw it. But between Hammill's prepara-

tions and George Black's leadership we didn't suffer too much in Calgary. Our morale was high as a result of our experience in Golden, so we were ready to march, to hold a tag day, to demonstrate, whatever it took. This Trek was rolling now; we felt like we were veterans at this kind of thing. Hammill was there to greet us with a photographer from the press and a delegation made up of the CCF, the local Communist Party, the Association for the Unemployed, and some union leaders who led our march to the Exhibition Grounds, which was to be our accommodations, where we were welcomed by coffee and sandwiches.

"Black showed his leadership abilities in planning our strategy for feeding the men for the weekend, and for winning public support in Calgary. Remember, gentlemen, that Calgary was hometown to not only Prime Minister "Iron Heels" Bennett, but also to Bible Bill Aberhart, who was about to rock Canada by sweeping to power with his revival-meeting charisma, selling his 'funny money' like 'Brother Love's Travelling Salvation Show,' leading Alberta backwards toward the Middle Ages. If you study the history of western Canada, the Calgary establishment has never been a bright light for progressive thought. It's generally turned to the far-right fringe of American politics for its ideas.

"I mean, even today they perform gleeful handstands in downtown Calgary when some Yankee clown starts talking continental energy policy. Meaning 'what's ours is theirs' by law — not just by custom. This is a town that claims down-home Calgary hospitality as a trademark and nobody wants to tell them that the rest of the world laughs at the irony. Klein tells the world that eastern bums and unemployed riffraff aren't welcome. They offer bus tickets to B.C. to anyone on Alberta social allowance who is tired of starving. You know, many Calgarians supported letting eastern Canadians 'freeze in the dark,' yet they believe they've got a reputation for hospitality. Give your head a shake. Their one moment of historic prestige was the founding convention of the CCF in '32, and that was only because Calgary was a convenient midpoint between Winnipeg and the Vancouver leftists.

"What I'm trying to say is that winning public support in Calgary for the unemployed or for the average working stiff is a hell of a lot harder than winning support in Vancouver, or Golden, or Moose Jaw — or, say, Winnipeg, Regina or Edmonton for that matter. Sure, there are some great socially concerned people living there occasionally, but most of the working folks down there don't even know that they're living their entire miserable lives inside the stuffy pockets of the oil barons, and they're deep pockets, you can bet your bottom loony.

"So where was I before that rant? Yeah, this George Black handled the matter the only way possible, as if he'd been doing this kind of organization as long as Arthur Evans. He met with the Strike Committee, explained that feeding the men was the priority and that three simple tactics were required: a full-blown tag day, a snake-parade downtown (ending wherever the Mayor would be holed up) and thirdly a committee of progressive public supporters to help the negotiations for a couple of days' relief. We had committees to handle all aspects of those plans.

"The public support was going to largely hinge on the abilities of Ronnie Liversedge and Perry Hilton to persuade the diverse membership of the Canadian League Against War and Fascism to march with our cause. This group was one of the most popular and broadest of common fronts against the right-wing agendas of that day, and we had word that they were meeting that same night and that A.A. MacLeod, their national secretary, was to speak. Ronnie tells a great story in his book about that meeting — how they arrived late and how their hand-scrawled note to the chairman about a chance to speak was almost ignored. Hilton insisted that Liversedge do the talking, although Perry Hilton was a giant of a man with a great voice.

"Well, MacLeod finished a long address, and the meeting was about to wrap up with a piper playing the anthem, when Liversedge panicked at their missed opportunity, leaped to his feet and shouted that the chairman had ignored their plea and that he was appealing to the members to decide whether they wished to hear the delegate from the On-to-Ottawa Trek who had just arrived in their fair town. Many shouted to give him the stage, so the chairman and MacLeod, yielded the stage to a shaky Ronnie Liversedge. His voice squeaked and wouldn't work so they graciously handed him a cup of water."

Daniella had chosen that moment to place a glass of water next to the lectern and Doc picked it up, toasted us, and drank, to some general laughter.

"Well, that token water turned the tide," he proclaimed with new vigour, holding the glass high. "Because it didn't take a powerful speech to convince these folks. He concluded by asking the chair to read a resolution from the Trek about choosing a delegation to help them negotiate relief from the Mayor. The chair was not encouraging and told him to read it himself since he had the floor. Well, Ronnie was getting annoyed at the chair and read the resolution with a flourish and challenge. The meeting passed the resolution to elect a delegation. The chair for the evening refused a nomination to lead it, insisting that the Mayor was not going to be convinced by such a delegation."

Doc gripped the edges of the pulpit tightly now and his voice quivered ever so slightly. "This was the last straw for Ronnie. This fellow's rudeness galvanized Ronnie, who told the crowd, in no uncertain terms, that the Trekkers changed the mind of Vancouver's Mayor McGeer by a peaceful occupation of the Museum, and that Calgary City Hall would negotiate when they saw 1500 disciplined but militant marchers backing up the negotiating committee. After that show of courage, someone nominated A.A. MacLeod himself, who also had been hesitant to throw the meeting open to the Trekkers. By then he saw the mood of support, and he answered strongly that he would be honoured to lead it.

"A cup of water and a little opposition had swelled the tide and accomplished our third objective of public support. We were well positioned now to take on City Hall. The next morning we marched to Seventh Avenue and turned toward City Hall with A.A. MacLeod and delegation in the lead, arm-in-arm with Black, Walsh and Cosgrove. We did the snake parade with Comrade Marsh and his accordion pumping out our 'Hold the Fort' anthem. We were in a good mood, but hungry, and we sang it out: 'Ho, my comrades... see the union... banners waving high.' And, by God, we even had banners: 'Relief Camp Workers Union,' 'On To Ottawa!' and 'Abolish Slave Camps.' I can't remember if there were others."

Doc checked his notes, and I glanced around the audience of attentive faces.

"Soon we had crowds packing the sidewalks and blocking the intersections, and pretty soon a legion of women from the Unemployed Association showed up to canvass the crowd with the traditional tin cans. Obviously the Tag Day Committee was on the ball. MacLeod, George Black, Gerry Winters and the delegation from the League found the Relief Commissioner, a Mr. MacKenzie, in the City Hall in the company of his associates and a retired North-West Mounted Police officer, Colonel Saunders.

"We kept the boys in a continuous snake parade around that block so that no traffic could move in or out of the City buildings without crossing that formidable parade line. We started chanting, 'Grant Relief! Grant Relief!' and soon the crowd joined in. It was more entertaining than a Calgary Stampede Parade.

"We have a pretty good record of what went on inside, because the clerk of the office recorded the negotiations. Apparently this Colonel Saunders leapt right in and gave them a lecture on the dangers of communism, calling them hooligans and tramps. Fifty years later, Mayor Klein struck that same deep-south Calgarian note, with his 'eastern bums and riffraff' speech. MacLeod and Black got down to business by criticizing Commissioner MacKenzie's wire to Ottawa, which described us as 'defying authority.' They demanded that he send another wire requesting assistance for the Trekkers, stating that the provincial government was prepared to deliver the relief. MacKenzie argued that he had no authority or mandate to provide assistance to an 'invasion from another province.' George Black retorted that the people who elected his party were out there in the streets. Why shouldn't we check their opinion on the mandate? That was a pointed jab because that government was about to be annihilated at the polls in the coming election. MacKenzie protested that he'd leave office willingly if voted out, but the troublemakers in the street were creating revolution, not democracy, and that the dominion government should handle the situation.

"MacLeod turned out to be a good choice for leading the delegation. He stuck to crafting the wording of the telegrams necessary to get the job done. At one point, Mackenzie was balking at sending the new telegrams with MacLeod's wording. MacLeod looked him hard in the eyes and declared that the commissioner should damned well know that the men outside could go without food for just as long as the commissioner and his officials inside the office there, if they didn't come up with a solution. The inference was that the boys could outlast the commissioner since they had more experience with going hungry than he had. So he made it abundantly clear that they might as well get this telegram sent and the matter concluded, so they could all eat again. And this was the same MacLeod that had previously been a bit leery to let a couple of Trekkers prejudice the order of their League meeting. He'd certainly gotten into the spirit of the fight.

"The officials realized then that they weren't exactly being held hostage, but that they weren't likely to leave very easily, surrounded by that snake-march and the chanting crowd. So when MacLeod declared that he would send the telegram himself on their behalf, the Commissioner's assistant, Edward Kolb, said that nobody but the officials of that department were allowed to send telegrams out of there, but that, if it would end the stalemate, he would call the telegraph office and read the telegram to be sent as worded by MacLeod. So the telegram was sent to Edmonton rather than Ottawa, and MacLeod then insisted that he read the text to the men outside so that they would know that progress was being made. Mackenzie objected that office communications were confidential, but MacLeod ignored him and took the text of the telegram outside, waved it in the air and read it to the cheers of the men.

"Now, Ronnie Liversedge claims that the commissioner tried to leave the building at this point but got tackled by Jack Thomas, leader of Division Two. Unfortunately Jack is no longer with us to comment on that version. I was a ways away from the action that provoked this story, but as near as I can reconstruct it, it was actually Colonel Saunders who left by a side door, accompanied by a couple of women from the League, part of our delegation. Saunders had taken to arguing and lecturing them since MacLeod and Black ignored him. The women weren't about to take his lecture quietly so their argument seemed to be interrupting negotiations.

"It isn't quite clear whether the Colonel was asked to leave or volunteered to leave. Regardless, he only got to the parking lot and into his car when some of the boys from Division Two surrounded the car; by their unwillingness to move, it became clear that nobody was going anywhere until negotiations were complete. One of the women from the League sat on the fender of the Colonel's car to emphasize the futility of trying to move, and some say she continued their argument with that right-winged gentleman from her new vantage point. I would like to have had a tape rolling on that one for the archives."

Doc paused for a sip of his tea, to absolute silence and I noticed all eyes focused on the ancient mariner at the lectern.

"Anyway, it wasn't long after that, Mackenzie received word from Edmonton authorizing money for two meals a day for that day and Sunday, since we were leaving on Monday. It wasn't much money, but MacLeod and Black accepted, knowing that a symbolic victory was the main issue. As the men cheered the news, Black ordered Cosgrove to end the march and the pickets, though they continued helping out with the tag day collection. We got considerably more money from the crowd downtown and the tag day effort in general than we did from the Alberta Government, which I suppose is appropriate in Alberta.

"Well, we had enough for hot meals, plus money for rations to feed the boys for a few miles down the rails. So Sunday we held a public picnic and a rally, but what I remember most about that day was the efforts to reorganize the divisions, because Gerry Tellier and his crew brought in over 300 recruits from Edmonton to join the Trek. This was great for publicity and momentum, but, from an organizational point of view… hey, gentlemen, it takes a long time to teach men the value and necessity of working together and sacrificing your own whims for the sake of solidarity and efficient collective action. So we revamped Division Four, putting in a majority of veteran Trekkers from Vancouver, and spread the new men among all four divisions so that they could learn from the majority. Discipline was a major concern for the division leaders.

"Maybe I can give you a couple of examples. We all had a big laugh when Red Walsh read out a proposal from the unemployed women at the Association office to join the Trek. A couple hundred women on the Trek was a nice fantasy, but it would have been absolute havoc for discipline and the press would have had field day describing us as degenerates, sex-maniacs, rapists and every other form of criminal perversion you can imagine. Most of the men understood this. However, we already had expelled one young man who was taking up with the girls from Kamloops. We gave the other one an ultimatum that the girls stayed in Calgary and that he would be expelled from the Trek as well, if he didn't cooperate fully.

"On Monday when we were marching to the rail yards, there was another incident. You've got to remember, gentlemen, that Canada's eyes were on us, but mainly through the inadequate and often disparaging and distorting lenses of the press. That means arrivals and departures were important opportunities to show discipline, restraint and organization. So when some of the new Alberta boys at the back of my division started acting up, running out of line to hug the female fans that lined our way, the veterans of the Trek knew that something had to be done. Ronnie Liversedge, our division secretary, who used to ride shotgun on the rear of our division, sent word forward to me that he was having trouble with the new boys and needed some help in bringing them into line, literally. I sent Paddy O'Neil back, since I wouldn't have to explain the problem or the solution to a veteran like Paddy. Paddy was from Newfoundland and an ex-sergeant in the British Army.

"I could hear a bit of the excitement, but it was Ronnie who saw it, heard it and told the story several times. Apparently Paddy descended on the wayward boys with a fury: Let me read it from Ronnie's book: '*What da hell's goin on here!*' he roars. '*Have you bastards gone mad? Get back into line there or get the hell off the Trek. Do you think we've spent years building our organization to have you come and wreck it? If we wanted clowns here, then we'll damned well apply to the Ringling Brothers. Now get the hell into that line!*'

"And, by God, they listened to him and shaped up.

"Then Paddy ribbed Liversedge about being too soft on the boys, suggesting his anarchist ideology was fine in theory but the rigours of operational tactics needed something a bit more direct. He told him that you can't always appeal to the people's knowledge of common sense and common cause, since the system they lived under robbed them of such experience. 'We'll teach them!' he said, and Ronnie tells us that the wicked smile on that gargoyle face of his was so ominous that it was absolutely hilarious."

Doc reached for the teapot and poured another cup, hesitated and pulled up the chair beside the lectern to sit down for the rest of his presentation. Daniella bounced up with athletic energy, moving her portable pulpit to the stool beside him so that he could still command the attention of all three tables from his position in front of them. The waitress, who seemed to have been watching for an opportunity, promptly brought Cam, Tom and Sammy another round.

"Thank you so much," Doc said to his granddaughter, while he looked directly at me with those piercing eyes. "Isn't she something?" I just grinned, in silent agreement.

Then he continued, leaning forward in a more intimate manner, "Now you'd have to understand that the older guys, like Liversedge and O'Neil were often the most experienced leftists in the Trek and knew a bit more about the great ideological debates between anarchists and Marxists, so this last comment from O'Neil was a bit of philosophical humour that only students of the First Socialist International might really appreciate. You see, the anarchists, who were to lead the Republican cause in Spain against fascism in the next few years, were noted for their belief that the ends did not justify the means. They didn't believe that you could have a Marxist-Leninist dictatorship of the proletariat using antidemocratic means to lead the masses into an understanding of their common cause and their need for working-class solidarity. They believed that you could only use democratic and ethical means to bring the masses on side.

"Of course nobody these days knows, or gives a damn, about what those strange leftists back in the thirties believed in, or why. Anarchists, to your average citizen today, means some terrorist who throws Molotov cocktails, someone who's out to destroy law and order. Too bad, because we could learn a lot from the European anarchist writers. They were the first to realize that international fascism had to be stopped at any cost. Yet our government still won't recognize the contribution of our MacKenzie-Papineau brigade in Spain. They won't honour them; they won't honour Bethune. Billions of people in other countries around the world honour these Canadians, but our government hides their story."

"Okay. Time-out there, Doc. Excuse the interruption but you gotta give me some more of the dope on this Spanish fascism thing." Sammy was even more brazen with questions when a speaker was seated and not behind the lectern, but he was learning classroom manners. I'm sure he would have had more questions if Doc had been seated with us at the tables.

"Well, okay," Doc replied. "I started to tell you about some discipline problems and the reorganization of Division Four, but I sort of got sidetracked there. But sometime you've got to sidetrack or you miss the significance of where your train is headed. The Mackenzie-Papineau Brigade was one of the International Brigades fighting Franco and the fascists in the Spanish Civil War from 1936 to '39. The Internationals were made up of volunteers coming from all over the world who recognized the threats to democracy from Franco, Mussolini and Hitler. The Mac Pap volunteers were all from Canada. The new leader of Division Four for example, Svend Uden, a solid veteran of the Relief Camp Workers Union and the slave camps, served with the Mac Paps, as did Ronnie. Liversedge in his book tells how the young Spanish republicans admired Svend for the time he stood alone on a bare hill near Albalate, with a mounted machine-gun focusing on a squadron line of incoming Messerchmidt 109s. They were swooping towards him in a single-line dive to take out his position. The screaming of their engines and the rattle of their guns apparently instils pure terror, especially if you are their object. Svend stood his ground, and with that light gun he took out the lead plane, which caused the second one, right on his tail, to crash into the first. And the others veered off to avoid the explosions.

"There are hundreds of stories like that about boys from the Trek who fought that initial war against Franco, Hitler and Mussolini. Paddy O'Neil himself died there in Spain two years later. The giant Charles Sands, who preached Lozofsky to Red Walsh, fell there in Spain. There are some great stories of Charles's work as captain of our Pickets Team in the rail yard in Vancouver. Red Walsh, Tony Martin and Louis Tellier, Gerry's brother, all went to Spain to stop the fascists. The survivors of the Mac Pap Battalion figured that as many as 400 Trekkers ended up in Spain in the Fifteenth International Brigade, which we called the Mackenzie-Papineau Brigade. It was named for the two Canadian leaders of the rebellions in 1835 that were trying to achieve democratic government, a government responsible to the citizens rather than to imperial Britain. I guess the Trek was involved in the same fight, trying to make government responsible to the citizens, rather than just to some corporate or social elite." Doc glanced up at Sammy to see if that answered the question; Sammy was nodding appreciatively.

"Well, getting back to the Trek, we left Calgary that Monday evening and it was a damned good thing that morale was high from our Calgary victories, because it was a rainy cold night travelling across southern Alberta to Medicine Hat. The train stopped several times that night, and the engineer was very good about giving us time to stretch and get back on before he started up again. After a particularly vicious storm squall, he stopped and told Cosgrove and Black not to worry; he would give the men extra time and blow the whistle to warn us when to get back on the cars. So we arrived in Medicine Hat after an all-night ride, tired, shivering, wet and filthy from a hard wind that whipped the soot and steam into our faces.

"It was the morning of June 11 when we dismounted in Medicine Hat and marched to the ballpark not far from the Saskatchewan River. The only reason I remember the date is because we later found out that it was that same morning, while the CPR engineer was being so accommodating, that the Prime Minister claimed that he got requests from the CPR and the CNR to help them stop the dangerous trespassing of these unemployed Trekkers. The correspondence trail suggests that the RCMP Commissioner MacBrien, at the urging of Assistant Commissioner Wood in Regina, informed the PM of a strategy for stopping the Trek in Regina, and that Prime Minister Bennett himself requested letters from the CPR and CNR asking for police assistance to stop unlawful travel, so that it would look like an initiative from the railways. These letters were not supplied until June 12, but Assistant Commissioner Wood already had word on June 11 from Commissioner MacBrien of the detailed strategy for stopping the Trek in Regina. So there was no question as to whether or not the CPR and CNR had a choice in the matter. By June 11 the decision had been made, and the order to stop us in Regina was issued June 12, the day we left Medicine Hat.

"You've got to remember, gentlemen, that Bennett's initial reconnaissance reports from undercover RCMP suggested that the men would never

Trekkers disembark at Medicine Hat, June 11, 1935.
Provincial Archives of Alberta, Edmonton. A5149.

stick together long enough to make it out of B.C. Also, Bennett wouldn't have wanted the police action in his home riding of Calgary. The reinforcements from Edmonton and the rumour of greater reinforcements waiting along the way, especially in Winnipeg, no doubt scared Bennett. He remembered the 1919 Winnipeg General Strike and he knew of the potential labour solidarity in Winnipeg if he allowed us to get that far.

"Regina of course had the RCMP training academy, so it was quite easy to supplement the force in Regina. Besides, Premier Gardiner was a Liberal — why not dump this mess on a Liberal premier? The RCMP were supposed to be under provincial control in Saskatchewan; that was the agreement at the time. But Assistant Commissioner Wood didn't discuss his plans with the Saskatchewan Premier or with the provincial Attorney General, who had line authority over him, according to the provincial agreement with the RCMP. Wood communicated directly with the Commissioner and federal head of the RCMP. Neither of them informed Gardiner of the plan to halt us in Regina until it was *fait accompli*.

"Gardiner protested to MacBrien immediately that the RCMP could not act without his authority in the matter. His Attorney General ordered Wood not to act without his authority. But Bennett and the RCMP just ignored the protests of the Saskatchewan Government, as they would throughout the events that were about to unfold there in the next weeks. Interestingly enough, Commissioner MacBrien on June 8th was still forbidding Colonel Wood, in Regina, to act without the permission of the province. That all changed between June 8th and June 11th. We didn't find out about the plan to stop us until we were in Swift Current or Moose Jaw, but by June 11th, when we were still in Medicine Hat, the PM had decided to stop us."

Doc stopped briefly to glance at some notes beside him on the lectern. I noticed Sammy pour another draft.

"The other event I remember about Medicine Hat was the return of Arthur Evans. This was George Black's coup. From Calgary he had sent cables out to Medicine Hat and points east to help prepare the ground for his advance party organizers, but he also sent a cable back to Vancouver to the Workers Unity League executive, begging them to reconsider their decision on Art Evans' work assignment. Give credit to George; he knew that organizing something this big was a formidable task and that there was one man who was better than anyone else at organizing a militant non-violent protest on this scale. I don't know what he said in that cable, but the Workers Unity League was moved by his plea; they sent Slim Evans back to us to lead the Trek.

"He just appeared that night of June 11th out of the dark approaching a fire where Steve Brodie and company were peeling potatoes, preparing for the next day's meal. Hell, it was probably after midnight because many were rolled up in their blankets already, inside the civic arena where we were bunking down. Somebody stared out into the dark and said, 'Well, I'll be damned. Here's Slim.' Brody says that he looked like a walking skeleton, bone-weary, staggering from weakness, with a soot-blackened face. He was wearing his traditional carpenter's overalls over his suit, so the boys knew he had a story to tell.

"'Steve, for God's sake, pour me a mug of that coffee,' Slim says, 'to save a dying traveller.'

"Well, Steve got him his mug in exchange for the story of why he was riding the tender instead of the cushions. I mean, everyone thought he'd be sent as a passenger on a through-train to ensure that he'd catch us as soon as possible, if he were allowed to join us again. It turns out that he started out with a ticket to Medicine Hat on the cushions but that a couple of plain-clothes cops got on at Calgary or possibly earlier. At least Slim was sure they were cops from the way they kept glancing slyly his way. He had been under surveillance so many years of his life by then that he got used to knowing what to look for. He suspected strongly that they had orders to arrest him as soon as they had evidence that he was attempting to rejoin the Trek, so at one of the station stops, either at Bassano or Brooks, he went in to the station restaurant and ordered a sandwich and coffee, knowing that they were watching. Then he slipped out the side door, hurried through town and got to the Hobo Jungle, where the bums would camp out, and hop onto a freight car before the engine had achieved a faster speed. So he hopped the tender of his own passenger train and pulled the overalls over his suit to protect himself from the wind and the smoke. We were damned glad to have him back in any sort of condition at all.

"Slim respected the job George Black had done, so the next day he made it clear that George and he would share the responsibilities, though everyone understood that Slim Evans was the man the Trekkers had chosen, if you know what I mean. He and Black and Cosgrove rode the tender when we left Medicine Hat; they might have got a bit dirty there, but it was a great position to oversee eighteen or nineteen hundred men. Yes, we were taking in more men at every stop now.

"At Medicine Hat the Divisional Freight Superintendent ordered the freight train to pull up right next to the passenger train at the loading platform so it would be easier for us to mount. Obviously the CPR hadn't told him that we were unwelcome trespassers. In fact that kind of courtesy was typical of the CPR engineers all along the line from Vancouver to Regina. We stopped at Swift Current where a local delegation welcomed us and assured us that we could leave our baggage on the train and come for a quick meal at the restaurants; the CPR had promised the freight would not leave until we were back on board. How's that for a company supposedly petitioning the Prime

Minister for police protection from trespassers? Apparently the provincial government had offered Swift Current the money to feed them since the town had gone into receivership. This part of Saskatchewan was about as desperate as it got during the Depression. But they were good to us, and it was the first provincial government that volunteered anything for us.

"Also the press reports in Saskatchewan were increasingly positive, noting our discipline, our organization and our grit. By Moose Jaw we had heard the news that the Prime Minister and the RCMP planned to halt the Trek in Regina. That made Moose Jaw a rather exciting stop. We had a huge welcome from crowds at the station, in automobiles, and all along our march to the park where we were camping. We were into town by evening and Slim Evans addressed us that night, encouraging us to avoid any provocative behaviour and to maintain discipline. He left for Regina late that night on a freight to meet with the Citizen's Emergency Committee in the morning. They sent a delegation with him to a hastily arranged meeting with Premier Gardiner.

"Well folks, you can see that our reception in Saskatchewan was an entirely different kind of affair, compared to our receptions in Calgary and our treatment from officials in Vancouver and Victoria. Slim returned by bus that same day to meet us and address a public meeting the second evening in Moose Jaw. He reported that Premier Gardiner had promised to house us and feed us in the stadium at the Exhibition Grounds, that they would get two meals a day from provincial funds for the two or three days in Regina, and that they had arranged to feed them a meal in Broadview, east of Regina. He also declared that the Premier had promised that they would not be harassed by police in Saskatchewan. I guess it was obvious that Premier Gardiner still thought that the RCMP plan to stop us in Regina was subject to his veto. Nevertheless, Gardiner's support and Saskatchewan's welcome made our speakers unusually bold at the public rally the second night in Moose Jaw. Moose Jaw was just a little town back then, but we had about 3000 people in that crowd including the Trekkers.

"I guess the crowd was inspiring too, because I recall Paddy O'Neil thundering out, 'I'm here to tell the police that they better keep their hands off the relief camp strikers. We are going through with this march even if we have to finish it in our stocking feet.'

"Matt Shaw was in fine form that night too. I remember the papers reporting his more sensational statements, like 'They call us agitators, you know, but what do they know about being condemned to a living hell for four years?' They also reported that he threatened that we would not take an attack lying down, but I don't recall him using that tone of threat. We were warned against using such threats.

"I do recall him saying something like, 'In Vancouver McGeer read the *Riot Act* to us in Victory Square. when he should have been reading it to the money changers in the temple.' Then he went on about the collaboration of the governments with those who made huge profits from the slave labour of the relief camp system. He said the relief camps were run by a 'broken-down Major and a skinner Colonel, and that if the workers of Canada were organized into one large organization, they would not have to accept relief doled out by pot-bellied political heelers.'

"Oh yes! He was rolling and we were in high gear. Our old CPR freight train might not have been bound for glory exactly, but, by God, we were bound for Regina at least. And those last three days, as well as the history of those last three months, and, I suppose, the last three years as a struggling union, had kind of prepared us for what we were to face in Regina, you see. Then of course there was Slim Evans, acting as the father figure, warning the men in the last few hours before leaving Moose Jaw that our discipline would be more important than ever, warning that under no circumstances should we allow ourselves to be provoked by police or by anyone else. Then he was off again to Regina to help his advance committee for our arrival. The man was back and forth like a whirling dervish. There were times when we wondered if he slept at all and what drove him to put in that impossible effort.

"Anyway, we caught up to him about 6 a.m. on June 14th. There he was, along with maybe two hundred unemployed men from Regina, one city police officer and a handful of CPR bulls. Not a lot of people are up and around at 6 a.m. in Regina or any other city, but there they were, the unemployed welcoming the unemployed. A few reporters and photographers were there, of course, because we were now the lead story every day in every paper and news broadcast. A newspaper reporter even decided that Cosgrove must be the leader since he was marshalling the men. I guess they saw him verbally chastise some of the new Moose Jaw recruits for dismounting before the orders were given. Cosgrove explained that the Strike Committee of about eighty men was the authority for the Trek. Then he told them to move out of the way because they were impeding progress.

"Well you can't blame him. We caught that freight from Moose Jaw at 5 a.m. so we were dog-tired, and, as we marshalled our ranks, those of us who didn't know Regina found out that we had a fair bit of a walk to reach the Exhibition Grounds. We even managed our 'Hold the Fort' anthem, which must have been a strange wake-up alarm for some of the residents along the way. But, by God, we were in Regina and the eyes of all Canada were on us, now that they had sworn not to let us leave. I was feeling that whatever happened now, we could still know that we'd made the right decisions, that people were forced to look at us, and therefore at themselves and their country. The governments at all levels were now forced not only to acknowledge our existence, but to reckon with our determination to have our hearing on

our terms. We might have been dog-tired, but, gentlemen, our train had arrived in Regina and we were feeling good about ourselves… You know what
I'm saying? We'd arrived, by God. Not in Ottawa, you understand, but at
the centre of our nation's attention, and we were about to stay there for a
while."

Well, Doc sort of shuffled some of his notes and files together, not
that he'd paid attention to them much, and then he continued in a quieter
voice.

"Well that is about all I can manage for one evening." His posture stooped
ever so slightly, but then his voice strengthened a bit. "But I think I could use
a beer now."

Daniella got up to help him as he stood up, and Sammy grabbed him
a spare chair and placed it beside Daniella's when it became clear he was
headed for our table. That was penance for once calling him an "old coot."
Everyone was clapping. I helped Tom and Sammy bring their little table a
bit closer to ours, while Cam had already hailed a waitress to find out what
kind of beer Doc wanted. His ever-so-slight suggestions of weariness, as he
ended, seemed to galvanize everyone into action. Once we relaxed again,
we had another hour or so of great conversation bounding from the Trek to
Ralph Klein to Jean Chrétien and back again.

Doc was flying to Calgary in the morning, staying overnight with
Daniella's younger sister, then flying back to Grande Prairie. Daniella was
then driving him back to Quesnel the following morning. I was worried
about the Pine Pass in late October and shared my concerns. She laughed
delightedly and patted my arm, thanking me for worrying. Thus I failed to
mention to her that I also worried about getting Doc out here again during
the winter since he didn't like to fly, especially if there were other airport
connections to negotiate. I'm sure Daniella was considering these things. I
was looking at Doc through different eyes, noticing the frailties of his body,
thinking about Matt as well, realizing that BJ's portal to the Tuesday Club
might someday fail to open without eye-witnesses like these two.

12

JERUSALEM TO JERICHO

PAUL ON RIGHT-WING
ALBERTA AND CONSPIRACY THEORY

IN EARLY NOVEMBER, NOT EVEN two weeks after Daniella returned from
Quesnel, Doc phoned Daniella to say that he had received word of Matt
Shaw's death, too late to make it to the funeral. It had taken him a couple of
days to remember that he should phone Daniella. She said that Doc sounded
shaken. We called around the Club regulars, so everyone but Sammy showed
up on the following Tuesday. Tom and Cam were already at the main bar
when Charles, Daniella and I walked in.

Cam saw us first. "Hey Daniella, Paul, Rev." He nodded his head acknowledging each of us, more formal than normal.

"Glad to see you all," Tom said, a bit more subdued than usual.

So I just nodded toward the door that didn't seem so magic to me tonight, and we all straggled into our corner, and pulled our two traditional
small round tables together into their figure eight with me at my usual far
end. Even Charles and Daniella only managed awkward small talk like, "Hey
guys," and "Been here for awhile already?"

So, once we were seated, I stumbled through the inevitable opening
lines: "Well folks, it's obvious that we all got the phone messages one way
or another that Matt Shaw is no longer with us. He suffered an aneurism
some time ago and he passed away late last month. His wife expressed her
appreciation for our interest here in his life and his contribution to history. I
know we were all hoping to get him up here again some time. She said that
he was looking forward to another visit."

"Christ!" Cam said barely above a whisper, like his solar plexus was
constricted. "I know it's been a while now since he was here, but he looked so
healthy and energetic and… well, almost youthful, in a way. I mean, I know
how old he was, but once he got warmed up, I could still see the Matt Shaw
that spoke there in Vancouver and Moose Jaw and Maple Leaf Gardens!"

"I know exactly the look," I said. "When he got rolling one could sense
that time warp happening. Well, there's only Doc Savage left now. Hopefully
he'll be back around Christmas to visit Daniella, if things work out as expected, and we'll try to have him finish off the story with two or three more
sessions. Before we heard about Matt , you remember I also mentioned some

hopeful plans for hearing certain other veterans of the Trek and the riot. Well none of them have worked out. Andy Miller from Rocky Mountain House isn't up to making a trip this distance anymore. He had some of the most vivid descriptions of his involvement at the Regina Riot."

"Time's running out on us all, folks. I feel it a little more each year, myself," Tom philosophized. Daniella turned her face away from us, toward the unlit empty stage for a few seconds. I didn't have to be psychic to figure out who she was thinking about.

"Yes." I said lightly, wanting to avoid turning the evening into a wake. "Anyway, Daniella and Charles and I have been thinking of some ways to supplement our little BJ's History Sessions here, and we came up with a few ideas. I… I know we can never quite replace Matt's live voice, that 'presence' Cam referred to, but we were thinking that if any of you are interested, we could play for you one of the tapes of my interviews with him in Regina. The sound isn't all that great on some of those tapes, but I've got a half decent one of Matt describing those first two weeks in Regina, before they sent him off to Toronto with the Reverend Sam East. That's probably better than any eulogy I could give him. Charles says BJ's isn't the atmosphere for a eulogy, anyway."

"The eulogy," Charles said, "is the one thing I could never do a decent job of, as a minister. Paul's father, on the other hand, had the words and the touch for that. He seemed somehow to relish the catharsis of those standard words of comfort. He never seemed embarrassed by them, like I sometimes was. I mean he believed it thoroughly, when he said that they were 'in a far better place.' Me, I keep thinking Matt Shaw would be in a far better place in front of that microphone over there, with the tape rolling and Sammy interrupting like a volcano in paradise."

"I'm with you on that one Paul," Daniella said. "Where is Sammy, anyway?"

"He's up north tonight," I said. "He was pretty quiet when I told him about Matt. I mentioned that we might do this Matt Shaw recording next week. He said he'd try to make it but it just wasn't the same without Matt."

"Is it my imagination," Tom asked, "or is Sammy acting more civilized of late compared to say a year or so ago when you first started telling us about these geezers from the Trek?"

"Yes, he's actually caught the history bug and really wants to hear these guys," Charles joined in.

"Even before Matt died," I said, "he was developing a different attitude toward Doc and of course he was thoroughly impressed with Matt. Hell, I'm going to need another beer down here, man."

"Holy mother, two beers in the first hour. The professor is turning into a regular drinking man in the face of all this talk of mortality," Tom said, but everyone just looked at the table, unable to lighten up. "Okay, sorry, folks. But I just am used to my buddy Paul sipping one light beer over two or three hours, while I leisurely down the better part of a six-pack."

"Well Tom," I put my hand on his shoulder, "you and I probably see eye-to-eye on a number of issues including eulogies and wakes, including the need for humour in the face of death, but even with a wake to sharpen my thirst, I would never try to match you beer for beer," I said.

"Well, of course, few men can." That was Cam who surely was one of the men who could.

"Anyway, gentlemen, and Daniella, we got this idea for the archives to-night," Charles broke in. One has to understand Charles. He had no time for discussing prodigious drinking feats. He wanted to get into a serious Tuesday night at BJ's, now that Tom and Cam had finally lightened us up a bit.

"Last time we needed a filler," Charles said, "I managed to come up with a story about Bible Bill. What do you say we skip about thirty-five years and get Paul to tell us the story of his radical years in college? I've heard a bit about this Che Paulo Guevera from some perfectly neutral sources, like his father years ago, and a couple of Paul's former flames, again years ago. So why don't you grab that machine over there and throw this tape in, and punch record, and we'll figure out the intros, and wing it from there."

Daniella cut in, "Well, the story of Paul's former flames alone would keep me entertained. Charles can tell us if Paul won't. Let's hear about Paul's flames." She had me smiling.

"No, seriously, Daniella, Paul went to Medicine Hat College and University of Calgary for a few years at the beginning of the seventies. I heard him talking about the political atmosphere in southern Alberta at the time and I also heard a few things from his father. I think he might be able to enlighten us on how that part of Alberta progressed from the days of Bible Bill and Premier Manning. You see, from what I've heard, Paul was a regular long-haired yippie. The Medicine Hat version of Abbie Hoffman. At University of Calgary in the local Campus rag, they called him 'Paulo the Anarchist.' Hair down to his shoulder blades and a Che Guevera head-band. The few times I saw him then, I could never figure out whether he was a Jesus-freak or the northern secret leader of the SDS. Or maybe even the Weathermen."

"I hate to sound like Sammy, Rev, but who's the SDS and the Weathermen?" Daniella asked, the only one of us young enough not to have been there, so to speak.

"Students for a Democratic Society, Daniella. American student leftists. Starting when? Maybe '65 through to the end of Vietnam?" Tom said, one hand partially raised for help.

"Dedicated to *The Greening of America*," said Cam and I couldn't tell if that was irony or nostalgia, but it was good history.

"Many folks figured they were trying to paint America more red than green," said Charles.

"True. And the Weathermen didn't help that perception." I cocked a finger and thumb his way.

"And who's the Weathermen?" Daniella asked again.

"If I recall," Charles said, voice pitched high to begin with, "they were an underground faction splitting from the SDS in about '69, totally disowned by what remained of a badly split SDS, mind you. The Weather Underground believed that a little violence could advance the cause, if planned and executed with appropriate strategy towards a clear political statement. I think they wanted to surpass the Black Panthers for direct action."

"They just gave the FBI an excuse to put regular SDS members under surveillance, or arrest and detain any student protester, even if they hadn't broken any laws," I said.

"Abbie Hoffman, Jerry Rubin types, right?" Cam said, raising his beer with the question.

"So were you an SDS member, Paul?" asked Daniella touching my arm for a second.

"Ha! No. I might have been, if they'd been up here, Daniella. They didn't exist in western Canada to my knowledge. Certainly not at Medicine Hat College or University of Calgary. Charles didn't mean to infer anything like that."

By this time the waitress had brought another pitcher of draft to our cozy circle around the two tiny tables, we hardly paid attention to her.

"Go ahead, Paul," said Charles. "Tell them about the time you tried to lower the flag to half-mast when the college imported a new president from the States. Right-wing Mormon chap I recall."

"That was hardly a successful protest, Rev. Who told you that?"

"Well, tell them about Paulo the Anarchist trying to blow up the Rock of Apathy with gunpowder and a firecracker fuse."

"Come on, Rev. That was just kids playing with matches at 4 a.m. There wasn't any bomb. Little bit of fireworks, not enough for security to even notice. Singed the paint off one side of the rock. They probably thought some homeless guy built a fire there to keep warm."

"Right next to the Student Union Building. Huge Ice Age boulder. Graffiti all over it. If it had blown it would have made the front page."

"Front page of the university student rag maybe. Anyway, no chance of any explosion. We knew less about gunpowder than a couple of dead gophers. Besides we had huge water bags packed against the gunpowder to prevent flying rocks, if something did go wrong."

"He wasn't kidding us? You actually tried to blow up the Rock at U. of C.?"

"No. Not exactly. I'd rather not talk about that. It was just a bit of an immature stunt to singe it, trying to comment on apathy at U. of C. at the height of the student movement in America. We were probably feeling left out of the real action."

"Hang on, Paul. You can't get out of this so easily. How in God's name did you get from a sawdust trail Bible camper and Jesus-rock fan to the Canadian Unabomber in… what? Two or three years, tops?" Daniella's face was glowing with curiosity about this wilder younger me.

"Daniella, I was no Weatherman or Unabomber. I might have looked like one but that's as far as it went. I bet you I didn't know from one day to the next whether I was a Jesus-freak or a leftist activist. I probably thought I could be both. All I know is that I voted David Lewis, NDP, but thought they were misguided moderates and unexciting. Cutting off the corporate-welfare bums was not fast enough for me. And I was even more impatient with Inter-Varsity Christian Fellowship and Campus Crusade for Christ; they were the misguided heart and soul of fundamentalism on campus in those days. I was just an alienated long-haired preacher's kid who had lost his tribe, because his father had encouraged him to be a critical thinker."

"No shit?" Cam looked doubtful.

"Yeah. No kidding! He wanted me to challenge all the premises and not accept the dogmas of modern education. At the same time, he desperately wanted me to get an education. And not just a Bible school or seminary education, though I'm sure he wouldn't have minded that, if I could have done both. But I was majoring in philosophy, so I took critical thinking seriously. However, this seemed to generate more damage to my identity as a Jesus-freak than to my identity as a student radical. All of a sudden I was more interested in Bobby Seal, Huey Newton, Angela Davis and Eldridge Cleaver than I was in the excitement of my boyhood calling to be a 'flying medical missionary to the jungles of Brazil.' You see, the sawdust trail had called me to save those 'pagan savages' at the headwaters of the Amazon, while the hallowed halls of learning were leading me into opposite interests. So philosophy, history and anthropology, not to mention Neruda and Garcia Marquez, were calling me to throw my lot in with the natives of the Amazon, the Sioux at Wounded Knee and the Viet Cong, all of whom were defending themselves, it seemed to me, from white western imperialism, which included the Christian missionaries, that was clear. I seriously considered dropping out of university and joining Dennis Banks and Russell Means at Wounded Knee. Just what they needed: another long-haired honky from Canada. Anyway, that's a very boring personal story of a mixed-up, misspent youth and I'm not proud of it. There just isn't a story there."

"Yeah, but did you inhale?" That was Cam.

After a brief laugh, Daniella sobered up and announced, "There is definitely a story there; it's far from boring and we're going to hear it." She poured me a glass of draft and topped up everyone's glass except for Charles. She turned the pitcher handle to him to give him the choice and he just smiled politely.

"She's right, of course," said Charles. "However, the story I was thinking of was triggered by Paul's reaction to the Medicine Hat section of Doc's On-to-Ottawa story. We were driving home after that session and he was telling me how Matt Shaw's Medicine Hat speech reminded him of another Medicine Hat political meeting in the early seventies. But this was an extreme right-wing fringe political meeting that he attended out of curiosity. Paul, you can't deny that you know a thing or two about those 'conspiracy theory' guys. I don't know where you learned it all, but I think you owe us that story."

"No. I really don't know that much about them. In fact I never really agreed with Charles and Daniella that there was anything in this, for the BJ's Sessions."

"Yeah, but you were outvoted!" Charles said. "It's a story that needs to be told, because I've a hunch it's connected to our Depression era stories. The Trek and the Regina Police Riot changed Regina and Saskatchewan, though Tommy Douglas had a hand in that too, I suppose. But Medicine Hat and Red Deer — not to mention Olds, Didsbury, Three Hills, Hanna — these places weren't affected by the Trek and the thirties labour unrest, like Saskatchewan was. Not even like B.C. and Manitoba. For one thing, their access to accurate media was severely limited. But Paul's got a story about that here, that fills out the larger darker landscape a whole bunch, and Daniella here, not to mention these more jaded fellas across the table, all want to hear that part of the story. Besides, I used to be one of those conspiracy theory kooks, so when you need a hand flushing out the details… Come on Paul. Go for it. We'll roll the tape, and tape's cheap. Just tell us about Walsh and the John Birchers."

"Go for it, Paul. These 'jaded fellas' this side of the table want to hear it too, especially the parts about the Rev being a conspiracy theory kook," Cam said. He respected and liked Charles without ever admitting it aloud to him.

"All right, all right." I gave in because I've had a lot less willing listeners in classrooms over the last decade. But here I had five intelligent motivated listeners close together at two tiny intimate tables and I was in my usual place back to the west wall, perfect to lead a graduate seminar, except that this gig came with beer.

"Let me see," I pondered. "This is a long time ago. You've got to know that many of these evangelical preachers were into this conspiracy theory stuff in Alberta at one time or another through the fifties, sixties, seventies; I can't speak for earlier than that, though the Rev might. Conspiracy theory came out of the Social Credit ranks, especially the Douglasites as they were called — followers of this Major Douglas that Rev was telling us about. He had some very anti-Semitic views about Jewish control of world banking. Actually that Steve Brodie article Matt read suggested that Mayor McGeer out in Vancouver was enthralled with their doctrines, too. Anyway, the radical right in America, like the Klan and the John Birch Society, often reprinted the anti-Semitic literature from Europe, like the stories of the Illuminati, the *Protocols of the Elders of Zion* and popular whispering about the Masons and other secret societies, and they wove these into a complex quasi-historical narrative about the conspiracy of world banking (and its Zionist links) out to 'control the world.'

"Oh yeah. I mean why would the world banks and the IMF have to conspire to control the world when they can do it quite effectively through the use of credit and credit rating systems already? Anyway this was much more sinister than simple control. According to these folks, the Rockefellers and the heirs of the Rothchilds and the big-money Jewish liberals of New York who supposedly owned Chase Manhattan and other banks were part of this secret cabal that has managed to sell arms and aid to both sides of every conflict, most recently the Cold War opponents, and they held the mortgage, so to speak, to both the American and the Russian states, not to mention every European state whose mortgage was worth holding.

"Of course, it's no secret that large money interests and corporations as big as Krupp and Ford have indeed been selling to both sides with impunity come war or peace for a long time. The World Trade Organization now just wants to establish, in trade law, the customary practice and traditional exemptions for big business in as many first world countries as possible. Third-world countries don't really matter to them except as economic colonies to exploit resources. That's why good left-wing folks like Bill Irvine of the CCF in Alberta, and many others, were sometimes taken in by the Social Credit/ Major Douglas ideology. It had just enough superficial facts and a sprinkling of insight into international finance to be damned dangerous in the hands of racists, bigots and Apocalypse-conscious Christians. And sometimes those were the same people."

My friends were all nodding in agreement, a good sign that they were with me, so I pressed on. "Unfortunate but true. The Christian connection came through this belief that the Second Coming and the Mark of the Beast were near at hand and that the Bible asked us to 'watch' — watch out for the signs of the Antichrist, the Beast. Well the world-banking conspiracy fit into this remarkably well, since Saint John's metaphor about the Mark of the Beast seemed to fit a rather literal description of the banking system's growing control over people and governments, through credit. At least it seemed that way to those who refused to read about the beasts of Revelation in the context of the pre-Christian Roman Empire in which it was written.

"So, you see, the Social Credit landslide in 1935 and their dominance in Alberta was seen by many fundamentalists as a strike against the Antichrist and the Mark of the Beast. Oh yes. It was as if Aberhart's Prophetic Bible Institute had delayed Armageddon, and like Gideon's Band, held the Powers of Darkness at bay. On the other hand, the Ottawa Trek was just an Apocalyptic sign of the end times to many in this province.

"Well, apparently Premier Ernest Manning, Preston Manning's father, tried to reign in the influence of the Douglasites in the Social Credit Party. But literature poured in to southern Alberta through the right-wing underground. Newsletters from organizations fronting for the John Birch Society, and books like *None Dare Call It Conspiracy* and *None Dare Call Iit Treason* swept through the province. Fundamentalist Christians 'watching' for the Second Coming, as well as social credit purists, who still followed Major Douglas's philosophy, ate up this literature like food for a hungry soul. I guess it made them feel like they had an inside track on where the world was headed, in a very confusing time when technology and social mores were changing society and people's lives. These were the books and this was the literature which influenced Keegstra and Zundel."

When I paused the lecture, Cam said, "I can't believe he's finished two beer already."

I laughed, "I should probably be drinking coffee if I want to remember all this stuff."

"I heard somewhere that Stock Day was into the same Bible-study group as Keegstra, way back when. Is that true?" Daniella asked.

"I heard it, but I don't know the source. I know that he grew up right in the centre of those influences. Same area of the province. His father lives up here now, and this was a hotbed for Social Credit and conspiracy theory. Their literature basically suggests that the Trilateral Commission and the International Monetary Fund were part of a world-banking conspiracy where power was held by the heirs of the Rothchilds' banking empire and other 'sinister' Jewish interests. The literature to support this crap was actually passed out on Henry Ford's factory floors even though that particular tract was proved to be a fraud."

"I heard that Henry Ford did a booming business with the Nazi Germany," Cam said.

"I think that part is true. Actually, the notion that Jewish bankers were in a conspiracy against the Christian world was widespread in Europe, but was certainly popularized and went mainstream with the rise of the Nazis in Germany, the same time as the conspiracy theory became popular in

America and Canada. Jeez, I think I'm giving a lecture here instead of telling the story the Rev requested."

"Paul, just before you go on to something else… Who wrote these conspiracy books, and what were the titles again? I'd like to check them out, in
the library, maybe."

"I don't think you'll find them in a library, Daniella. If I recall, they were
written by neo-cons like John Stormer in the mid-sixties for *None Dare Call
It Treason*, and Gary Allen published *None Dare Call It Conspiracy* in 1971. It
was mainly underground distribution and the libraries won't stock them as
a rule; there are some things libraries won't touch. I've only read the later
one and I don't know where you can get them anymore except if you ask to
borrow a copy from an old time Socred hardliner. Some of them still have
their copies, if they trust you enough to lend them out. They're collectors'
items now, sort of like Nazi memorabilia."

"Tell us about Walsh in Medicine Hat, Paul," Charles said with a knowing smile.

"Right. Sidetracked! The best storytellers, you know, drive you crazy
sidetracking. Tangent running. If you get a prize for circling the story, spying
on it, 'laying siege to it,' as O'Hagan says, but never attacking it, then I'm
in the running, here. Walsh… I don't recall his first name. This isn't Red
Walsh, of the On-to-Ottawa Trek. Patrick Walsh, I think it was. He claimed
to be an ex-RCMP intelligence officer, if I recall. He took to the lecture circuit in the sixties and early seventies spreading his far-right gospel in towns
that had an audience for this stuff. Actually he was connected with several
fascist spokespersons long before my day and apparently he was a witness
for the House Committee on Un-American Activity, the heart and soul of
McCarthyism. I remember my father had quoted Walsh about Mr. Trudeau's
'sinister' background.

"So Walsh breezed into town in Medicine Hat in '71 or early '72 — I
might have heard about it through our political science instructor — I can't
recall, exactly, but I remember I noticed my instructor there at the public
meeting. I guess they weren't all conspiracy kooks there. Maybe some were
just visiting the side show, like the professor and me. So Walsh is introduced
and he starts things off with 'O Canada' or 'God Save Our Gracious Queen.'
I think they started with one and ended with the other. We sang and then he
asked us to bow our heads and he opened this political meeting with prayer
that the Good Lord would continue to protect our great land, and that He
would sharpen our perceptions and make us eternally vigilant against the
forces that threatened our peace and democracy. I've heard that most Social
Credit League meetings used to start that way, as well as Bible Bill's political
rallies.

"I don't remember the actual text of his speech, nor even his central point other than that Canada, even more so than America, was at deep risk from forces in high places. Like the Prime Minister. His thesis there was that Trudeau was not only a communist, but an insider on the Trilateral Commission and the IMF, central villains in the conspiracy to control the world. I believe he explained that your run-of-the-mill communist and your run-of-the-mill banker weren't aware that the higher powers in both of their organizations were in cahoots with the Rockefellers and Rothchilds to rule the world. This would happen through the sinister control of credit and banking, first. Second, the United Nations. Third, education and propaganda (media control), and eventually military control. I don't recall *all* his evidence for these claims, but some big scores were the fact that he had documented evidence that Trudeau used to be an NDP member and had once tried to row to Cuba in an open boat. He was a friend of Mao Tse Tung, went to meetings in New York for the Trilateral Commission, and there you can see the pattern. Something like that. Also René Lévesque only appeared to be Trudeau's opponent but was really leading those beguiled dupes in Quebec toward the forces of world domination. And of course some of the top 'liberal' capitalists in America only appeared to be opponents of the 'Iron Curtain' nations.

"Now, the Soviets, those Rockefeller Democrats, the World Bank and the International Monetary Fund were really all controlled by this secret society that had been around for a hell of a long time in Europe. The European Economic Union was supposedly its front, and their huge central computer in Brussels was the heart and brain of the Beast. It would force a single currency not only on Europe but on the world, and eventually control all credit and trade."

"Sounds a heck of a lot like the World Trade Organization's actual five-point plan." Daniella followed these issues with a passion, which she shared with us on many a Tuesday night.

"Perhaps, but the WTO doesn't stand accused of supporting Zionist control and secret societies that want control of the world. They just want to make sure governments don't interfere with their right to rob and plunder the world in the name of free trade."

"Wasn't that my point?"

"Right," I nodded. "Anyway Walsh goes on about the long history of secret societies that have led to our present world danger, from the *Protocols of the Elders of Zion* to the Illuminati to the Masons to the Kennedys and Rockefellers to New York Jewish money (Chase Manhattan Bank always got thrown in there), to Trudeau and Lévesque. And 'did you know that the Royal Bank symbol came from the symbol of the Rothschild's secret seal?' Well, you could tell by the grunts and the wagging heads that the evidence was seen as overwhelming, and that many of the good folks at the meeting were excited and grateful for this latter-day prophet who fearlessly stood in the path of the Beast. Many had always suspected those 'frogs' and 'Jews' anyway. Nobody said that aloud of course. Then he pointed out all the literature available; I believe he even admitted that much of it came from the John Birch Society, and he had *None Dare Call It Conspiracy, Protocols of the Elders of Zion*, an earlier version of *Hoax of the Twentieth Century, The Talmud Unmasked, None Dare Call It Treason* and a host of curious books about Posse Comitatus and the beginnings of the Militia movements state-side. Many of these books and pamphlets are still available through Walsh's secretive organization called the Canadian League of Rights; some are now legally classified as hate literature."

I reached for a beer and noticed that all eyes were following my lips and then my hands, so this was a good sign.

"Well, I could see my political science prof slouching deeper and deeper into his chair as if the entertainment was turning into a horror show, or maybe he was thinking that someone would mistake him for a believer or a compatriot. Anyway, I couldn't sit through it without saying something, although speaking up for the Antichrist in this room of zealots had me quivering a bit. I raised my hand and was rehearsing my speech, imagining the rhetorical flourishes necessary to crack this crowd, when Walsh recognized my hand. I asked if he would allow me to say something. He was a bit hesitant but agreed.

"I said something like the following. You'll have to excuse me if it wasn't a brilliant answer; it was all I could think of to jog this mob's conscience, and I was shaking from nervousness. I said, 'Mr. Walsh, you started this meeting with prayer so I think you might appreciate a certain applicable parable that I recall from the gospels.

"'A certain man went down from Quebec City to Ottawa and fell among thieves, who stripped him of his clothing, robbed him and wounded him, attacking even his identity as a Québécois person, and they left him there by the side of the road half-dead, caring not whether he recovered or died. And by chance there came a famous conservative prime minister who the wounded man thought might help him, but he passed him by on the far side of the road. And likewise a Toronto financier, and a fundamentalist minister came and looked on him and passed by on the other side.

"'But a certain Québécois journalist and chain-smoking politician, as he journeyed, came where he was. And when he saw him he had compassion on him. And he went to him and bound up his wounds, pouring in oil and wine, and took him in his own car and brought him to a hotel room, took out a cheque and wrote it out to the innkeeper, saying whatever it costs above this I will pay when I come again. And he signed that cheque — René Lévesque. So I ask you, Mr. Walsh, which of these four men do you think was neighbour to the Québécois man who fell among thieves?'

"Well, I couldn't believe he had listened in patience through the whole parable because I stumbled a few times and my voice was not all that confident, especially when I started.

"But he just laughed and said, 'Well, young man, all I can say is that I think you've got your good guys and bad guys mixed up.'

"I can't remember what else he said, because I was so relieved that the eyes of the crowd had finally turned back to him; but I'll never forget his 'good guys, bad guys' comment. His was an exciting world of good guys and bad guys, and I don't think I converted anyone that day. I believe my political science prof gave me an 'A' in his course, though I don't think he ever mentioned my parable. He probably figured that if I failed to escape Medicine Hat without being stoned, that he didn't want to be seen as contributing to the assault. No, not that kind of stoned, Cam."

Daniella was shaking her head, "So this is a good news story, Paul. Alberta seems to have progressed in the last thirty years from those days, right."

"Daniella, I can hear your irony, I think, but, just in case there's any question, I can introduce you to folks in this community today who go to secret meetings of the Canadian League of Rights, and one man who goes on speaking tours at their expense. The Social Credit movement always had many members with ties with this group. National Social Credit Leader Robert Thompson in the early sixties was a fan of Walsh and his mentor and wrote memos supporting them."

"Wow," she responded. "Sammy wasn't far off when he branded them wackos."

"It's almost a fair term for some of their hard-core die-hards," Charles admitted.

Well we talked late into the night about the roots of racism and bigotry in Alberta. Now and then we would remind ourselves that there were other pockets of darkness in rural southern Ontario, parts of the B.C. interior, parts of rural Quebec, even dark corners of progressive Saskatchewan that had their share of bigots. But we kept on coming back to our beloved Alberta Bible Belt. It felt good to have shared, sort of like truth and reconciliation.

13

DEAD MEN WALKING THE TALK

MATT SHAW ON REVEREND SAM EAST AND REGINA

THE NEXT TUESDAY IN NOVEMBER we were at BJ's again to listen to a tape from my last two summers of research. It was Matt Shaw delivering a polished interview about the Trekkers' first two weeks in Regina before the riot. That was a hot June, but here it was snowing outside and we had our coats over chairs, gloves and tuques thrown all over the tables, and brownish water puddles around our boots, from the melting snow

"All right, tape rolling!" I said.

"As in *Dead Man Walking*. Or at least talking," Cam said with his irrepressible morbid humour.

"Jesus Christ, Cam," Sammy whipped off his cap. "The man came all the way from Regina to speak to us in the flesh, and you can joke about his death? And you guys accuse me of insensitivity."

"Okay, let me pause this for a moment. You got to admit, Cam," I said with a chuckle, "that when you stoop enough to need sensitivity lessons from Sammy, your humour's hit a new low. On the other hand, Sammy, I think some people just deal with death through humour because at least it's one strategy, and we haven't got a whole bunch of better strategies to choose from. We were discussing that last Tuesday."

"I'm just saying…"

"Now hang on, Sammy, let me finish. I just wanted to say that I appreciated your reaction here. Matt was just too healthy and had too much spirit left for us to take his death in stride. And I appreciate what you said."

"Thank you. You see that, you potheads, the professor appreciates me," Sammy could morph from aggression to self-deprecation within seconds.

"I'm glad," Cam said, "because everybody needs somebody to appreciate them, and…"

"Okay, enough already, guys. If we're going to listen to the tape, I don't want to have to stop it this time. I was going to say further that Sammy might have been surprised to hear Cam express our exact same feelings about Matt the other day when he wasn't here. I guess, sometimes we just deal with the grim reaper through grim humour because sometimes that seems like the only effective weapon left. You know what I mean? So we all feel the same about Matt. There just aren't a lot of men from those days left who can tell it the way he did. So this tape is actually my attempt to mark his death appropriately, finally, and I know that goes for everyone here because no one would sit in the corner of a bar listening to a tape of some old guy talking about the thirties unless they were serious about paying tribute to him too. So I appreciate every one of you showing up tonight. Here we go again. Tape rolling. Matt Shaw talking on the first weeks of the Trek in Regina."

Matt's voice came on with a bit of distortion from the ghetto blaster boom box, and I couldn't help thinking about Albertans getting together around their tube radios on Sunday afternoons in 1935.

"Well Regina's my home now, so I have visited these spots many times since, but my eyesight's been going for some years now, and many of the buildings and streets have changed since '35. The old fire hall is still there on Market Square. The city police garage station next to it has been renovated and expanded, and they built that huge Regina police building right on top of where the meeting took place July 1st, right on top of where the police charged the crowd. It's like they wanted the foundation of law and order in Regina built on the footings of their vicious assault. Oh, they put a little monument to the event in front of the entrance, emphasizing the police officer that died, but they don't mention the Trekkers that died, or the Trekkers that disappeared, and they kind of gloss over the citizens and Trekkers that got shot down in the streets downtown. Nor do they attempt to explain how a police charge on a peaceful crowd could be universally described in the press as a riot and in the history books as the Regina Riot. If they called it the Regina Police Riot that would be closer to the truth, except that few riots have ever been planned so painstakingly by the police as this one, at least not in Canada.

"Of course, somehow we're getting ahead of ourselves. You wanted to hear first about the weeks leading up to the police action. Did I describe for you the pavilions where they housed us? Well, sure I can do it again for the tape. At about six in the morning, we marched from the railway yards near the centre of downtown Regina, back towards what was then the western outskirts of town, to the Exhibition Grounds. That's just a couple of blocks west of today's Football Stadium and just off the new freeway that runs north and south there. You've been there no doubt. Well, these pavilions were used to house the livestock during the agricultural fairs in summer. So in mid-June they were still clean, but where the makeshift pens would stand in July, they had spread out fresh straw, apparently for our comfort when we bunked down. Now the boys were welcomed on behalf of the town by a city police officer and shown their beds. Well, there were a few imitation sheep and cattle lowing sounds here and there when we saw our quarters, but I think we all realized that Saskatchewan folk were practical, and straw is one of the more sanitary ways of cushioning and protecting bedrolls. Two thousand plus mattresses were hard to come by."

"Two thousand?" Daniella nudged me, whispering over the tape. "How did they get to two thousand?"

I paused the tape for a minute. "Three hundred or so joined in Calgary. Another hundred joined through Alberta, I believe, and more joined at Swift Current, Moose Jaw and Regina. Not sure of the numbers at the moment," I said. Cam took the opportunity to flash three fingers at a waitress he addressed as Stacy. Another round was on the way to that table. I started the tape again.

"We were also directed to coffee, sandwiches, latrines, basic laundry equipment, most of the comforts of home for the homeless. Then a bit of a surprise that early in the morning, a choral choir from the CCF Youth assembled and sang the "La Marseillaise" for the boys, changing some of the words to a welcome for the heroic relief camp workers, which made quite a hit with the boys.

"Overall, we felt extremely welcome in Regina, and that feeling just increased as the days turned into weeks. Some of the boys grabbed a quick nap that first morning while the Strike Committee met with newly formed Regina Citizen's Emergency Committee. These folks, like the Action Committee in Vancouver, were made up of representatives from more than thirty supportive organizations. They arranged for rallies, press releases, meal ticket distribution initially, meetings with appropriate government officials and even entertainment for the men. They kept up their activities all through our time in Regina. At first everyone thought we'd leave as planned on Monday, regardless of the federal government's threats to enforce no trespassing on the rails. I think that might have been because Premier Gardiner didn't seem to believe that the federal government was prepared to overrule his authority over the RCMP. So this group remained active a lot longer than they had planned. I tell you, Paul, these people made us proud once again to be Canadian."

The club members all glanced at me, realizing again that I was with him in Regina. It seemed a long time ago for some reason, but the voice kept talking.

"I remember they managed to deliver donated socks, boots and clothes from merchants and citizens that weekend. So later that first morning we marched downtown, much to the Regina folks' delight. This was the first we realized how broad-based our support was in this town. They handed out meal tickets to each Trekker at the Unity Centre. That was just a few yards beyond Market Square, where the police action started a couple of weeks later. The Unity Centre was the quarters for the Unemployed Association and other affiliated groups. We were given office space there later, when it was clear we weren't leaving town quickly. The provincial government was providing food vouchers, which the men could redeem at any restaurant in the downtown area. So we all broke up for lunch and felt free to explore the downtown area in small groups. That was an extraordinary feeling. We felt trusted and free to mingle and meet the Regina folk. We began a love affair with that town right there and then, and the restaurant owners loved to see us coming.

"That night George Black chaired a rally at the Exhibition Grounds and we all attended. There were thousands there, more than twice as many citizens as Trekkers and, remember, Regina was less than a tenth the size of Vancouver at the time. Black started things off by giving a history and rationale for the strike and ended with a plea to the citizens to support us, so that on Monday or Tuesday when we boarded the freight to leave, Bennett's forces would not be able to stop us. I suppose the most paranoid of the right-wing media read danger in that statement, but that bunch could read incitement to violence in just about any rousing call for action or support. Reverend John Mutch, president of the Ministerial Association, spoke, and he surprised us with a plea to stay in Regina till the Prime Minister or his deputies could meet with us here, as if it were just a matter of saving money or time. No one bothered to respond to that suggestion, and he received only a smattering of applause when he was finished.

"Apparently, Assistant Commissioner Wood, head honcho for the RCMP in Saskatchewan, saw an opportunity there; we found out years later that he spoke with this influential United Church minister that night, revealing the 'criminal records' of Slim Evans and myself. He embellished that with sinister tales of agitation and revolutionary intent. The record in my case was fraud — for obtaining a meal in a Vancouver restaurant and then refusing to pay. We did this as mass protest in the first month of the strike. We called the protest Operation Pork-Chop Bandit. We'd all go order meals and, after eating, ask for the owner to call the police because we couldn't pay. One of the owners kicked us out and refused to call the police, so we were fairly stuffed when we finally found an owner to cooperate and phone the police. We would do this in one police precinct in sufficient numbers so that we would fill the local cells and overwhelm their capacity for processing the charges. Then they would often give up and kick us all out on the street rather than feeding us for the days it took to administer justice against us. It was good publicity for the fact that men needed to eat, regardless of the government's regulations on relief or their excuses about the economy. I'm sure the good Colonel Wood failed to include those details in his propaganda.

"So apparently Wood told Mutch that Evans was a convicted thief and mentioned the three-year sentence he received. It wasn't for theft, of course; it was the fraudulent conversion charge brought by the American United Mine Workers Union, with the cooperation of the RCMP. Evans had helped

Rally for the Trekkers in Regina, June 1935. Saskatchewan Archives Board, Regina. R-21749-2.

his fellow Drumheller miners teach their reactionary American head office to honour the local strike votes. As their treasurer, he basically had followed the vote of his Local in using 60 percent of the union dues to provide relief for striking miners, instead of sending it to the head office in Indianapolis. He only served about a month for that travesty of justice because most of the miners in the valley and a host of legal folks across the country signed a petition warning the Attorney General to let him out."

Tom slipped from his seat to go to the men's room, but signalled to let the tape run.

"I'm sure Colonel Wood embellished Slim's Section 98 frame-up to the gullible Reverend as well. Anyway, the Right Reverend spoke to a crowded congregation on Sunday, no longer emphasizing Christian justice or even charity toward us, but emphasizing the sinister leadership and the threat to the dominion. Talk about critical thinking. I guess the papers reported that two female members of the congregation got up and walked out in disgust at the clergyman's sell-out to right-wing propaganda. Well, I don't recall much about Reverend Mutch. I do recall that M.J. Coldwell himself spoke following Mutch at the rally that first night. I'm sure you know that Coldwell was one of the key leaders and founders and an elder statesman of the CCF along with J.S. Woodsworth. He apparently appealed to Woodsworth on our behalf to defend us in Parliament rather than falling into this red-baiting hysteria about communist influences. And Woodsworth apparently did mellow in his opinions of us, defending our cause several times in Parliament. Coldwell encouraged us. He suggested that if we kept up the good fight then no power could stand in the way of the justice of our march. Now Art Evans finished things off that evening with a little more dramatic force than Coldwell, his big ringing baritone bringing us to our feet when he said something to the effect that there were not enough Cossacks in the entire dominion to stop us if the workers of Canada united in this message to Bennett: 'Hands off the relief camp strikers.' He liked calling the police 'Cossacks.' He had faced enough of their military brutality to know it wasn't an exaggeration. He had taken a couple of bullets in the leg from the National Guard once in Ludlow, Colorado. You might have heard of the Ludlow Massacre in the coal miners' tent city. 1914, I believe.

"Well we had a very successful tag day the next day and a public picnic at the Exhibition Grounds on Sunday. We had never seen this level of community support. Again it seemed more pervasive and general than even in Vancouver. Many of these folks had no doubt been hit harder by the Depression than most in Canada, yet they were there for us. And most active in this Citizen's Emergency Committee was the indomitable Reverend Samuel East. This man made the Trek his public and personal crusade. He publicly tore into the Reverend Mutch for falling for the red-scare tactics. For 'making impotent true justice' were his words. I got to know and admire the man those weeks, especially when they sent the two of us out to rally support in Toronto. We actually left together on the train for Toronto just before the meeting started where the police attacked the crowd at Market Square. I suppose the death and mayhem in Regina assured us a huge audience at Maple Leaf Gardens a couple of days later.

"I'll be telling you more about Reverend Sam East, you can bet. He even won over the grudging trust and admiration of Slim Evans, and Art wasn't known to look to the clergy for help too often. But, I recall one of Sam's eloquent speeches where he paraphrased Roosevelt, saying that 'we looked forward to the day in Canada when the money-changers will have fled the temple and we can proceed to restore it to its ancient truths.'"

Tom returned and Cam cuffed him on the arm.

"Getting back to that Sunday, I think it was that afternoon at the Strike Committee meeting, while most of the boys were at the picnic, that we had an interesting encounter with the press. I've kept this photocopy of Steve Brodie's account, because Steve was one of the best at capturing the significant moments in his anecdotes. This kid that was helping out on picket duty comes bursting into our meeting and Arthur pauses and asks him what was wrong.

"He says, 'Mr. Evans, there's half a dozen cars out there loaded with reporters. I don't know what they're up to, but they're asking if they can see you guys.'

"Arthur treats the kid as if he'd just made an important motion to the committee. He says, 'Well, what's the consensus of the committee? Shall we take a break and invite these folk in? See what the fuss is?'

"We voted to see them, so Arthur asked the boy if he'd escort the reporters in to see us. So there was a small crowd of them from the two local dailies and the radios and national media from Ottawa and Toronto. Art thanked the boy first, then turned to the national reporters, some of whom he knew, I guess.

"He says, 'So, what's all the excitement, boys?' They were all carrying fresh copies of the *Regina Star*, a particularly conservative daily, and one of them handed a copy to Slim, pointing at this huge bold headline and asking him for a reaction. 'Plot to Kidnap Prime Minister Bared,' it blared. Apparently some RCMP operatives — 'stoolies' or stool pigeons, we called them — had tried to justify his existence by inventing or imagining this story to his superiors in Ottawa, who took it seriously. Or perhaps they just needed some hot propaganda to justify the moves they were about to make. So the slavish press runs with a story that they didn't bother to check out.

"So now the scavengers were swarming, attracted to sensationalism like crows to a carcass. They wanted a statement from Evans, so he paused very deliberately after reading a bit and gave them all a withering once-over.

"'Well now, I think we can deal with this directly,' he said to the Strike Committee. Then he turned to the reporters, "'So sharpen your pencils and prepare for the Strike Committee's comments on this bit of sensationalism.'

"Then he turned to one of the Ottawa correspondents he recognized. 'You're a senior commentator here; why don't you read this aloud for all those here who aren't up on the latest news.'

"So, with a great flourish, the reporter played along with Art and read it with all due seriousness: the kidnapping plot, what the PM's office said, what the Attorney General said, what the Leader of the Opposition said. When he finished he paused and peered over his glasses, completely into the delicious role that Arthur had handed to him.

"'Well,' he said, 'what have you to say to this?'

"Evans paused dramatically, 'Well, sir, maybe you could help us with this one. Tell me, what would we feed that glutinous big bastard supposing we did kidnap him?' He paused, as if for a serious answer."

We at BJ's were certainly chuckling.

"'Is that all you've got to say?' another reporter asked.

"'You see, we're having trouble feeding ourselves, let alone fat millionaire lickspittle capitalists like Bennett. I realize some of you are fairly green at this yet, but surely you know your history that the politics of assassination and kidnapping outlived its usefulness by 1910 or earlier, because you decapitate one bloated capitalist and a dozen spring up to take his place. And you only give them the excuse they need to use the Iron Heel. We've learned that well.

So don't be so damned absurd and naive. Now get the hell out of here so we can proceed with the orderly business of a very orderly march across the country.'

"He had the boy show them the exit, and waved off any further comments with disdain. Some of the Strike Committee were hooting and laughing at them. Evans always wanted to make sure that the workers in a strike, or in some political action with him, knew that they didn't have to feel inferior or intimidated by the establishment or their 'lap dogs,' as he called these poor reporters, who were willing to sell their souls to hold their jobs.

"So Monday came and it was uncertain yet whether we would attempt to leave that night. Prime Minister Bennett had sent out two of his cabinet ministers, Manion and Weir, who met with Gardiner early on Monday; apparently Gardiner had vented his wrath on them for the feds usurping his authority and pulling their shenanigans with the railway companies. We found out later that he challenged them to explain why the rails would cooperate fully and generously with the Trekkers in Vancouver, throughout B.C. and Alberta, but then suddenly ask for RCMP help in Regina. And suddenly ask for help, not from the Attorney General of Saskatchewan, to whom the RCMP answered in Saskatchewan, but bypass their line of authority, going to the Commissioner in Ottawa, who had no jurisdiction in Saskatchewan for these matters. He obviously knew that this was Bennett's baby and that Bennett didn't expect to win many votes in Saskatchewan anyway. Much later we found out that Premier Gardener threatened to order the RCMP to arrest CPR security bulls as well as any others that 'initiated violence' if a riot began that night at the rail yards. I suppose if we had known his stance we might have even tried to leave that night, thinking that his orders might make a difference. But how does one commandeer a train without being charged with grand larceny, and I mean grand?

"Evans arranged for the ministers to meet with a delegation from the Trek; this happened later in the afternoon on Monday. Red Walsh, Doc Savage, Mike McCaulay, Paddy O'Neil, Jack Cosgrove, Pete Nielson and Tony Martin were chosen to accompany Art Evans. The Mayor and provincial representatives were there, but it was clear that this was between the Trekkers and the federal government ministers now. Evans reviewed the history of the strike, the demands, the failure of the MacDonald Commission. Manion replied by defending Ottawa's so-called reasoned approach and blamed the worldwide recession for the problems. Apparently Evans cut him off at that point and objected to playing politics by passing the buck to world conditions, when the issue was whether we would be prevented from going to Ottawa to discuss our six demands. Manion objected that he was not playing politics, and that he had the right to set out the federal government's position. He made the point that the government couldn't afford work and wages for so many, but then he rushed into his proposal. The cabinet would like the Trekkers to send a delegation to meet with the Prime Minister in Ottawa at government expense, while the Trek stayed put in the Exhibition Grounds fed by federal funds. Our delegation wasn't exactly surprised by the proposal, but they insisted on taking it back to the full body of Trekkers.

"We all met that night and Red Walsh chaired the debate. Many brought up the fact that this was a ruse to bring in more police and possibly military troops. The Strike Committee pointed out that this would play out badly in the conservative press if they refused an offer to negotiate with the Prime Minister. They would accuse us of not wanting to negotiate, but wanting to threaten the security of the capital. Of course it was a ruse to stall and bring in troops, but the alternative seemed like a public relations coup for Bennett. It was an emotional and long debate. Division One seemed most set against the delay, but it looked like the hard liners might just barely be outvoted. Evans, although initially against it, finally abstained from debate and promised to be bound by the majority vote.

"Finally it was a charismatic voice from Division One that broke the tension in an ironic way. Comrade 'Hold the Fort' Marsh waved and shouted for the floor from the middle of Division One, and naturally Red Walsh recognized him. When his audience was listening, he dramatically shook his fist to a deep resonating bass chant emphasizing each separate word with an accentuating fist.

"'Scorn... to take... the crumbs... which fall... from... the rich... man's... table!' Then pausing to scan the whole crowd, and daring them to follow, with one raised clenched fist, he screamed, 'ON TO OTTAWA!!'"

Sammy and Cam were giggling and looking at Daniella and me for permission, which made us giggle too.

"A loud rousing cheer mixed with hilarious laughter released the tension and made it clear that the men all loved this guy, their accordion-wielding piper, whose concertina bellows, not to mention the bellows of his own lungs, had led them into battle numerous times. Ironically, they realized that there was more emotion than substance in his appeal; the men were ready to vote, when someone called the question. The proposal to send the delegation passed more easily than expected, so the chair asked if we wished to cast a unanimous ballot and the men agreed — this from Red Walsh, captain of Division One. It seemed Comrade 'Hold the Fort' could galvanize us and unite us even when he was opposed to the majority. That was the democracy and unity that we were so proud of. Well, there was a motion to send the same delegation that negotiated with Manion and Weir, and that passed.

"Evans was given permission to negotiate for stronger conditions before we would agree to send the delegation, which he negotiated quite successfully. He ensured that the men would continue to take vouchers to the restaurants instead of being fed at the Exhibition Grounds. That was a popular move. Sleeping quarters, latrines and laundry were all expanded. The feds had to agree not to disrupt the Trekkers in any way while the delegation was gone, even by media attacks. In exchange we agreed to not encourage more recruits while in Regina other than the 300 plus that were coming in from the Dundern camp, just south of Saskatoon, the next day. We also agreed to obey the law and not attempt to board trains while Evans and company were in Ottawa. The deal was accepted.

"Well, the next day was to go down in Canadian labour history in a way that we could hardly realize till a few scattered radio reports late in the day began the rumours — rumours that turned into headlines in the June 19th papers. While we welcomed our reinforcements in gala style, and preparations were made for Evans and company to leave for Ottawa on the cushions in the evening, something sinister, which many of us had feared, was happening back in Vancouver. The date was June 18th — easy for many of us in the labour movement to remember, because it was the day of the Battle of Ballantyne Pier. Some call it Bloody Ballantyne, or the Ballantyne Massacre. My story comes largely from Fred Wilson's account in a book titled *Fighting Heritage*."

The waitress tiptoed in reverently. Cam's hand circled, ordering a round for everyone, and Charles didn't object.

"You see, the longshoremen had gone on strike up and down the coast to protest a lock-out and scab replacements at Powell River. The strike started just as we left Vancouver, and it turns out that the government and industry bosses had actually been planning to provoke such a strike and had planned a major union bust. Why? Because a more militant membership had inspired the once-docile Vancouver and District Waterfront Workers Association to act like a real union. I say 'real union' because this was really what we call a 'company union' or a quasi-union set-up when they had violently busted the original Longshoreman's Union on the West Coast in 1924. They'd been nothing but a phoney shell for years, but with the election of Ivan Emery as president and Oscar Salonen as agent, all of a sudden the phoenix of the Longshoremen's Union was rising from the ashes, and the powers that controlled the lucrative docks and ports weren't going to accept it, democratic votes or not.

"So on June 18, World War I veteran and Victoria Cross winner Mickey O'Rourke led a march of longshoremen down to the docks to ask the scabs to come out and join the union and the picket lines. Mayor Jeremiah Jesus McGeer had brought in extra police and banned picketing on the waterfront, a situation under which no strike could be won. So rather than defy that ban directly, the union was going to present their case en masse to the replacement labourers, to join the union and be guaranteed longer-term security when the longshoremen took back the waterfront. Well, the trap had been carefully planned with the help of the city police, Mayor McGeer, the RCMP and the Shipping Federation. Chief of Police, Colonel Foster, led a delegation to meet O'Rourke but didn't tell them that they were surrounded by troops hidden in strategically placed boxcars and by mounted troops behind some other freight cars. When the longshoremen insisted that they had the right to lay their case before the replacement workers, Foster withdrew just in time for the first gas canisters to come sailing in. The papers estimated that there were 5000 men trapped by the charge of the Mounted Police, the city police and the hired guns of the Shipping Federation.

"The Mounted Police charged, swinging their clubs viciously. Waiting police cars screamed into action cutting off the retreats, and two shotgun blasts from police-cruiser windows felled some of the fleeing men. The road to the Ballantyne Pier was cleared quite quickly, but the sadistic beatings and blood-lust continued for more than four hours. The horsemen continued pursuing small groups of men down side streets, into yards, up onto verandas, trampling people who accidentally got in their way, even on their own property. Homes were raided. Tear gas bombs were thrown into tenement buildings. It is remembered as the bloodiest and darkest hours of waterfront history. Two youths suffered gunshot wounds, scores of men were treated for the most serious injuries in hospitals, and some were treated by first aid administered by the Women's Auxiliary in a nearby union hall. Emery was arrested, Salonen was arrested, even one of the Canadian Labour Defence League Lawyers was arrested for working too hard in the legal defence of some of the union leaders."

"Jesus," Sammy said under his breath, and all six of us were shaking our heads.

"Jeremiah Jesus McGeer boasted to the nation's presses that 'Communism had not been able to take control of Canada,' at least not in Vancouver. He felt he had shown the nation his ability to deal with 'agitators.' The strike was to struggle on for six months, but the Longshoremen's Union had effectively been crippled for the second time. The phoenix wouldn't rise again from the ashes until after World War II. By then they had learned the necessary steps and precautionary measures to make it last. I doubt it will ever be broken again. But that's another story.

"Back in Regina, June 19th, when the morning news broke in all its bloody horror, Premier Gardiner wrote a letter to William Lyon Mackenzie King, who would be overwhelmingly elected Prime Minister a very few months later. Of course we wouldn't find out about that letter until years later when the historians did their work on this moment in Canadian history. The core of the text reads like this: *I'm convinced, the more I look into this Trek and the decision in B.C. to allow them to move east, the more I'm convinced that the whole thing*

*was planned by the CPR, the Shipping Federation, and the governments involved. They
knew the longshoremen's strike had to come on the coast and they knew the relief camp
strikers would support them, so they made sure these guys got well east into the prairies to
divide the two forces. Both the federal government and the CPR spokesmen kept repeating
the same hackneyed story as if they'd memorized the same script about a communistic plot
that was all planned to explode into revolution this summer and it was their unpleasant
duty to stop it in its tracks.*

"Well, Gardiner had seen more of their side of the plans than we had,
so he was in an excellent position to call it that way. Many of us commented
that we wished we had all been there to march with the longshoremen, and
that our numbers and discipline might have made a difference. It took years
of investigative journalism and historical research to put the full stories of
the 1935 waterfront and the relief camp strike into perspective. Now that
we have that fuller perspective, and more of the evidence is in, I've heard
Doc Savage call the Trek and their strategy in Vancouver and Ottawa, the
'Greatest Rooking in Canadian History.' I didn't even know that a 'rooking'
meant a swindle when I first heard him use the term. Those first years as a
boy in northern England gave him a slightly different idiom than the one
we prairie boys inherited.

"Nevertheless, his point is well taken, that the working folks in Canada
were robbed of something significant, that summer of '35. We were 'rooked'
into two separate blind alleys. And the Cossacks, as Evans called them, were
prepared to smash those separate forces of working-class energy, at the right
time, at the appropriate dark moments. Oh, it's not that Doc isn't aware of
the great things accomplished both by the longshoremen and the Trekkers
that summer. He just also sees, in retrospect, the ruthless strategies and alliance of corporate greed and conservative governments. After all Bennett
and McGeer, like Mulroney so many years later, worshipped and supported
that corporate right to power and greed. And they're not the only guilty ones
of course.

"But to get back on track, there we were, stuck in Regina, entertaining
the good folks of the city with our snake-parades and public rallies, while
they entertained us with another picnic, some recreation and a welcoming
town. We sent a delegation to Gardiner apologizing for our unexpected strain
on his hospitality and promised to ensure a disciplined and respectable presence. We enjoyed the hospitality of the downtown cafés: Ryan's Café, The
Greenaway, The Sandwich Shelfe, The Opal, The Austrian Kitchen, The
Silver Gray. Most of them — I suppose all of them — are gone now or have
changed names, or been renovated several times over. But there in those cafés
we met the working folk, the business folk and the unemployed over soup
and sandwiches, over endless coffees. The proprietors loved us and nobody
saw us as communists or revolutionaries bound for some Bolshevik coup in

Ottawa. You had to live far away from main street and the coffee-shops to believe horseshit like that."

A click cut off his voice.

"Okay," I said. "I edited out the rest. He took a break, and the rest was more scattered Q&A."

"Wow. How many of these tapes do you have Paul?" asked Tom.

"Quite a stack of them. Most of them aren't quite that organized."

"Matt was certainly organized," Daniella reflected. "Maybe because of his eyesight."

"He was organized and polished, which made me think he was always aware that he was on record, that future generations were listening," I offered.

Daniella, Charles and I still had beer to spare, but the other three ordered again, talking about Regina 1935 and Grande Prairie 1997, about how to keep our club alive through the winter.

"I'm a little worried about Daniella," Charles said, "trying to drive the Pine Pass four times through the Rockies at Christmas, just to get Doc, bring him here, and take him back again."

"You are such a sweetheart," Daniella said to Charles, touching his arm. "I want to adopt you as my father. Mine is too far away."

"Yes, Doc's getting a bit frail to take the bus that distance," I said, joining our general theme of concern. "And Daniella says that he isn't that comfortable flying."

We were all worried that our BJ's portal to this particular story was closing.

14

THE SLIM EVANS STORY

PAUL ON THE LIFE AND TIMES OF ARTHUR (SLIM) EVANS

ROBERT "DOC" SAVAGE COULD NOT visit Daniella here in Grande Prairie that Christmas, but she flew to Prince George and rented a car to drive down to see him. Doc had suffered from malaria that he contracted years before serving in the Merchant Marines during World War II, near India and Burma. The health of his immune system seemed compromised for the rest of his life, and I recall that he loathed mosquitoes almost as much as capitalist exploiters. But that winter he fought for his health in that draughty World War II house of his in Quesnel, fighting off respiratory infections, and we feared we might not see him in Grande Prairie again.

The Tuesday Club continued meeting informally, sporadically for some. However, in June of '98 Daniella informed us that Doc was much improved and that he was coming by bus to visit in a couple of weeks. We passed on the word to everyone. The Tuesday evening before he came there was a bit of the old magic as we all entered that BJ's portal stage-right with a planned agenda and a renewed focus for the Tuesday Club. Charles and Daniella were smiling and chatting, while Cam and Tom told Sammy to sit down when they saw me at the lectern.

"All right folks," Cam's bass voice rumbled, "the prof has got the floor."

"So Tuesday History Sessions are back," I said as I pumped the air with one fist to some cheers, "and next Tuesday night, as you all know, Doc Savage is going to be here again, if all goes well. And we're getting him to tell the story of the delegation's meeting with Prime Minister Bennett. That's all about Arthur (Slim) Evans and his little confrontation with the PM. Doc's the only surviving member of that delegation, and we'll probably be the last ones to hear that slice of history from an eyewitness and a participant. So if you've got friends that you think might respect a scene like that, they're welcome."

"So," Cam said, "Daniella says you're going to entertain us tonight with a different story?"

"Well, the first order of entertainment is my cold beer, and one for everyone on me." I was cheered by Sammy. "Once that's taken care of, Charles will introduce our BS session for the evening."

"Well, you know," Charles began, "Paul and I were speculating last

Tuesday that someone could make up a little session on the early days of
Slim Evans. These old-timers keep referring to these intriguing vignettes out
of his past. Bullets in the leg. Three-year prison sentence only to get sprung
after a few months due to public pressure. Ginger Goodwin. Joe Hill. I mean
I'd like to hear those stories if somebody like Doc or Paul could pull them
all together."

"And you talked Paul into doing it," Cam prompted.

"I told Charles that I could tell you all I know on the subject before I
finished my second beer."

"Hell, we should be out of here by midnight," Tom said, "if he's going
for two whole beers."

"Tom, you'll have to hand me back that copy of *Work and Wages* for a few
minutes. I'll need it for reference. Evans' daughter, Jean, collaborated with
Ben Swankey in Vancouver to write this book. Best thing I've come across
on Evans' early life. Then too, I've got some notes from Evans' testimony at
the Riot Inquiry, which includes a sketch of his early life. Lord only knows
why they needed that. I suppose they were trying to find out the makings of
a communist or some damned thing."

"I'll roll the tape," Charles said.

"We don't really need the tape. This is no first-hand account. This is just
me reporting on what I've read. No archives will be interested in my voice
when they can go to the sources."

"We're taping it, Paul," said Daniella with her eyelashes narrowing her
eyes to a glint that bored right into mine. "The archives don't set the rules
for the BJ's History Sessions."

Everyone chuckled as she paid for all of our beers before I could get my
wallet out.

"She's the boss now, Paul," said Cam. "She's talking Tom and I into
producing a CD of all this stuff when we're done. We can sell it under-the-
counter from the bar there."

"Should be a huge black-market demand," Tom laughed.

"Now don't worry, Paul," Cam assured me, "we're not planning on
profiting off your work or exploiting the generosity of Doc and Matt. But
we are kind of serious about the CD. We'll burn all the tapes onto a single CD
and duplicate a few. Especially if you want to give them to several different
archives."

"We're calling it The BJ's Canadian Club Lectures." Trust Tom to think
of whiskey.

"Or maybe The BJ's I-Am-Canadian Sessions." Trust Cam to think of
beer.

"Sounds like a good idea to get it all on a single CD," I agreed.

"Yeah, and Cam and I think that we should add some of Utah Phillips'

Wobbly songs," Tom said. "Maybe a few Joe Hill tunes and Woody Guthrie. Pete Seeger maybe. Set the mood for each session. Billy Bragg does some Woody Guthrie. Maybe Maria Dunn, if she'll lend us a track."

Cam added, "And Daniella decided she'd compile a bunch of leftist Bible passages to give it extra flavour."

"I draw the line at Bible verses," I said in jest. "This thing will be preachy enough without Bible verses,"

"Hey, it's probably easier to get copyright permission for the Bible verses than it is for Billy Bragg," said Cam. "We're just brain-storming, anyway. Mind you, I never knew there was such a thing as leftist Bible verses."

"You might be surprised how many!" Charles said.

"And so would most right-wing Christians," I added.

"Anyway, CDs are cheap and we have the technology," said Cam, "so we figured we should roll the tape on anything that goes down here, in the way of history, and you and Daniella (and Charles maybe) can worry about editing and putting it all in some order later."

"All right, already. Roll the tape. It's only tape, but I warn you I'm not prepared like Doc Savage. And the archives aren't likely to be impressed with extra sound tracks and Bible verses."

"Like Daniella says, it's our history, not theirs," Cam said, smiling at me over his beer.

I could feel an energy building that had nothing to do with me and everything to do with the knowledge that Doc Savage was going to be with us at least one more time. I hoped my dry history lecture style wouldn't dampen it.

"Okay, point taken. Where to begin. Here we go. Arthur Evans. Most of this stuff comes from *Work and Wages*, written by his daughter and Ben Swankey. Arthur was born in Toronto, April 24, 1890. His mother was Mary Ann Bryan, originally from Ireland, and his father, Sam Evans, immigrated from England. His dad was a house painter and his mom a chambermaid. He had an older brother Bill, a younger sister Annie and a younger brother Percy. They were the only brothers and sisters that survived infancy.

"Arthur left school when he was thirteen because his father was often ill, and the burden of support was on his mom. When she became ill, Arthur's formal schooling was over. He sold newspapers, drove a team of horses and learned the carpenter's trade. He left Toronto in 1911 with a union ticket as a journeyman carpenter. He worked at odd jobs in small communities between Winnipeg and Saskatoon before heading south to Minneapolis in December of 1911. They don't tell us why, here. I guess the standard reason was the possibility of decent wages somewhere else.

"Anyway, in the American Midwest, Evans was introduced to the IWW, the Wobblies. Most of you were here when Matt Shaw mentioned the Wobblies and explained their origins. Industrial Workers of the World. They didn't believe that the AFL (American Federation of Labour) was really interested in ordinary working folks beyond the few crafts they represented. But the AFL was the only game in town back then. So the Wobblies decided that the industrial labourers and unskilled labourers needed the representation, collective bargaining and leverage of good democratic unions, and no one was prepared to help them with that. The IWW was closer to anarcho-syndicalist beliefs than to Marxist communism. That meant they didn't have much use for the trappings of the state and the so-called democratic options of joining a political party, or voting, or lobbying politicians for change. They believed in the goals of a cooperative commonwealth of workers who would militantly but non-violently acquire the ownership of means of production through negotiations, strikes and direct action.

"The Wobblies were the first to advocate the need for solidarity and respect between all workers: black, white or brown, regardless of language, religion or citizenship status. That was radical in 1905 in America. Like the communists, they believed in the eventual natural decline of capitalism and its replacement with workers' cooperatives and community ownership of industry first, then of services and utilities eventually. Small business was never in the sights of their revolution as far as I can tell. The first target was, of course, resource-based industry where the bulk of unskilled and semi-skilled labourers desperately needed collective bargaining and organized cooperation. I mean the bosses were absolutely ruthless in exploiting the individual worker, or anyone depending exclusively on their own working ability to earn a decent wage.

"So, that early relationship with the Wobblies provided the real education of Arthur Slim Evans. He must have joined the IWW within a week or two of entering the States, because within a week he got a job in a meat-packing plant in Kansas City where he ended up in the middle of a free-speech fight. Kansas had banned free speech, especially for union workers in the middle of labour struggles, so on Christmas Eve, 1911, Slim Evans was arrested for standing on a makeshift stage on the corner of 12th and Oak Street in Kansas City and reading the Declaration of Independence. He claims that reading it is all he did, and all it took to get arrested and to receive a three-year sentence.

"The Leeds Farm Prison near Kansas City set him free in less than four months for bad behaviour. Yes, bad behaviour. Apparently he helped organize the 1500 inmates to get a hearing for their grievances. When certain conditions were intolerable, they would get two hundred of the inmates to pound on the cells with their shoes until someone came to address the complaints properly. He and most of the free-speech prisoners were paroled to preserve the good order and discipline of the institution. As soon as they got out, they were invited to help with the free-speech action in Des Moines, Iowa; so one can understand that his first prison term hadn't exactly rehabilitated him.

"Apparently, the Wobblies had organized a Cooks and Waiters Union, and Art got a union card which managed to get him casual jobs as he worked his way across North Dakota and Montana and eventually out to Seattle, then back to Great Falls and Minot and other northern Montana centres. Some early labour pamphlets suggest that Evans was organizing for the Wobblies, but he would never speak of that since the Wobblies had been declared an illegal organization in both Canada and the U.S. and much of what is known about Slim's American activities come from his own limited testimony at the Regina Riot Inquiry, where lawyers for the Crown were trying to paint him as a communist revolutionary.

"Perhaps it was Wobbly business that took him south to Ludlow, Colorado, in the fall of 1913. The coal miners of Colorado had a strong union that had won major concessions, such as the eight-hour day, regular paydays twice a month, abolition of monopoly company stores and the right to elect their own check-weight man. These things had even been enshrined in state law; however, the owners decided to ignore the law, since these laws weren't made for the companies or the bosses, and certainly not for J.D. Rockefeller, who was the biggest shareholder in the company. So the miners had to strike in order to bring public attention to the company's illegal actions. Well, the company hired an agency to break the strike. These agencies were experienced in hiring professional thugs and gunmen, who were eventually joined by the national guard from the state government.

"Well, the miners were evicted from company housing, so they set up a tent camp. The hired guns were given militia uniforms and allowed to terrorize the tent camp by firing live rounds into the camp at night time. When that didn't break the strike, the militia and the hired thugs attacked the camp. They got to the strike leader early in the attack. Witnesses say that he was clubbed into unconsciousness with a rifle butt. Then the militia men fired several rounds into his body. With that accomplished, the militia raked the camp with machine-gun fire, cutting down men, women and children as they fled. They also found time to soak tents with kerosene and burn the camp to the ground. Two women and eleven children were murdered that day, besides a number of strikers, and some of the children's bodies were found burned in the ashes."

"To America the Beautiful," said Sammy, raising his beer.

"What so proudly we hail," Tom raised his glass and they clinked together with Cam's.

"Somewhere in this attack Evans took two bullets in the leg. Evans never gave any details about his involvement other than that he was not resisting the militia, but was crossing a bridge when he got hit, probably trying to escape the crossfire on the camp. It took him eight or nine months in the hospital to recover, and he walked with a permanent limp as a result. Though it seems he wouldn't speak of that atrocity easily, it coloured the way he would approach labour conflict from then on. Nevertheless, he steadfastly refused to condone violent confrontation as a tactic, though I'm sure he was not against defending oneself from violent attack.

"Many labour publications from later times report Evans as having worked with the famous Joe Hill, Big Bill Hayword, Frank Little and other Wobbly leaders. His daughter, Jean, who passed away in Vancouver recently, recalled his anecdotes about these men, as did many of the Trekkers. She said that he also used to sing Joe Hill's songs and some of the old Wobbly standards like 'Where the Fraser River Flows,' 'The Preacher and the Slave' and 'Rebel Girl.'

"Tom, I know you've heard Utah Philips sing some of those Wobbly songs at the folk festivals. Utah's a regular at the Vancouver Folk Festival, and he's just about old enough to remember the guys he sings about."

"Absolutely. He's going to be part of this CD," replied Tom, stroking his long beard.

"Anyway, by the time Evans returned to Canada, about the middle of the Great War, he was an experienced trade unionist and a committed leftist who felt an obligation to activism on the job site as opposed to activism in electoral politics. One of the Canadian labour leaders that he worked with in B.C. was Ginger Goodwin. This was probably at Kimberley, where Slim got his first experience in Canadian mines.

"Goodwin's last assignment was as secretary of the union in Trail, where he was called up for army service but exempted due to his tuberculosis. Even in his failing condition, he led a strike in Trail to achieve the eight-hour-day standard. Well, someone in the echelons of the military made sure he was called up before the draft board again and declared fit for service. The union decided that this reversal to draft Goodwin was an order that should not be abided, so they decided to support Goodwin in hiding on Vancouver Island in the bush near Cumberland. The miners of that area honoured him for the labour victories he had achieved in their areas, so they hid him and fed him, until in July of 1918, a special agent hired by the police, and condoned by the government, shot Goodwin in the back and killed him. The special agent was exonerated in the investigation and never even charged with the murder if I recall right."

"Jesus, Paul, do these things make the history texts?" Cam asked.

"Not the texts they used in my high school, that's for sure. A lot of university texts ignore his murder as well. What topic would it come under, you see? Anyway, the entire community and nearby miners showed up for his funeral and the anger in labour circles in Vancouver triggered a one-day general strike. I think it was Canada's first general strike. For Slim Evans, this event taught him that Canadian police forces, Canadian companies and Canadian governments were just as capable of violence and murder when it came to labour leaders as the worst of the right-wing Americans.

"Later, Evans often spoke of Goodwin's murder to his own children and to the men involved in strike action, to advise them of the reality of reactionary extremism when one stood up for the right to bargain collectively. More often, though, Slim Evans was telling lighter stories and anecdotes about the union heroes or Wobbly tactics. Apparently he was a great storyteller and could pour morale into a picket line or a sagging strike through his colourful tales and Wobbly songs. His leadership role in such strikes began with his involvement in the OBU's founding convention in Calgary in March of 1919.

"OBU stands for One Big Union and was unique to Canada. It started because of a ruckus at a Trades and Labour Congress convention in Quebec City. I think that was the Canadian affiliate of the AFL. The AFL is the American Federation of Labour. Too many acronyms here. They were the umbrella congress for most trade unions in America and Canada at the time. The western delegates to this labour congress in Quebec decided that they wanted to unionize all of the industrial workers, including those who weren't in the formal trades. They wanted to head towards more militant policies and aggressive organization. When it became clear that the union leadership was ignoring their wishes, they called this Calgary Convention for March, 1919, with the intention to vote on breaking away from the TLC and the AFL. So they voted to form the OBU to create broad-based industrial unions as opposed to small local craft unions. They dreamed of signing up all unorganized workers into a more action-oriented union, one totally free of the established American control.

"That founding convention of the OBU decided against any partisan political action, though the vote was split on that issue. They limited themselves to collective bargaining and direct job action. I don't know if you remember a movie called *Reds* with Warren Beatty and Jack Nicholson, but it reflected the surge of excitement and more radical labour ideas in the years following the Russian Revolution. The infamous American propaganda machine had not yet had time to make villains of the Ruskies and all things Russian. So the rank-and-file workers had some hope that democracy and workers' rights would take a huge step forward due to the Russian Revolution, and the other imminent workers' revolutions that seemed poised to happen in places like Germany, Italy, France, Sweden and the like. Well that was the atmosphere into which the OBU was born.

"For example, the OBU founding convention called for immediate withdrawal of all Allied troops from Russia. Remember, these were the days of the western nations forming the White Army alliance to fight against the Red

Army of Russia and her allies in the old Russian Empire. This was really a continuation of World War I in which western imperialist nations decided to quit their squabbling and centuries of war just long enough to gang up on the Johnny-come-lately imperialist nations like Germany and its Austro-Hungarian allies. When the Russian Revolution took one of the old-guard empires off-side and out of the war, the remaining western empires never forgave Russia. When they were done with Germany and the Ottoman Empire allies, they turned with a vengeance on the new Soviet state, which they felt had betrayed them. Lenin and Trotsky were to be toppled, and world dominance was to be shared by England, France and the Americans. But the OBU was against all empires, including western ones, because they saw them as the protectors of the new world power brokers, the big multinational corporations that could buy and sell millions of workers in a single deal.

"World War I had brought unprecedented restrictions on freedom of speech, freedom of assembly and freedom of association in the so-called free world. The OBU immediately called for a general strike for June 1, 1919, to back up its call for the restoration of these freedoms and the release of political prisoners jailed for union activity or restricted party affiliation. The Canadian Government was beginning to ban certain political parties that they didn't like — for example, Section 98, which made it illegal to belong to certain political parties. The birth of the OBU and its ideals had a huge influence that year on the Winnipeg General Strike. Many of the referenda in union locals that officially endorsed the OBU were conducted while the Winnipeg General Strike was in progress. Several of the Strike leaders became the leaders of the upstart OBU. It was to have a meteoric rise and fall, but an influence far beyond its short-lived history.

"Anyway, that was the OBU, and Slim Evans became its district coalfields organizer out of Calgary and his first assignment was to organize the Drumheller coal mines. There were more than thirty mines around Drumheller at the time. He started by organizing the Monarch Mine near Nacmine, west of Drumheller on the south side of the river. They had no union so he not only organized it; he also was elected secretary and checkweighman. He cooperated with other union leaders who were discussing a sympathy strike to back the Winnipeg General Strike. They agreed to hold referenda, and the entire valley voted to switch from the United Mine Workers of America to the OBU. Then they voted to walk out in sympathy with the metal trades and building trades in Winnipeg. Perhaps a quick review of the Winnipeg General Strike might be in order. What do you think, Charles?"

"Your call, Paul. The mic's all yours tonight," said Charles.

"Go for it, Paul," Tom said. "We've got a full jug of draft here yet." Everyone nodded.

"Okay," I chuckled. "In Winnipeg, the employers had refused to negotiate a contract with some of the locals, and that had been the trigger for a general walkout by the Trades and Labour Council workers. The demands were simple: the eight-hour day, a living wage and the right to collective bargaining. Of course, other contributing factors were rampant unemployment, terrible inflation and disillusioned returning vets who did not appreciate the string of broken promises to them.

"So the Winnipeg General Strike began in mid-May of 1919 and it triggered some of the most repressive legislation in Canadian history, including the notorious Section 98, which took only forty-five minutes to pass the Canadian Parliament. With 35,000 workers on strike, including the city police, the employers needed the help of Ottawa to back up their so called 'Citizen's Committee' with its volunteer strike-breaking militia. Many of the returning vets lent their support to the strike, so, when a gathering of strikers and vets was attacked by the RCMP and the 'special police,' I suppose it isn't all that surprising that the strikers fought back with the help of these vets and held the streets against the attack. That caused even more paranoia with company owners, who spread the paranoia to Ottawa. A week later they arrested the strike leaders in the middle of the night, and demolished the union offices in the Trades and Labour Temple, destroying their files. Four days later there was a huge march in protest of these actions, since the strike had considerable public support. Anyway the police and the 'specials' attacked in full force. Two citizens were killed, more than thirty were injured and one hundred were arrested.

"During that attack called 'Bloody Saturday,' a young fourteen-year-old boy named Tommy Douglas got part of his working-class education from the roof of a downtown Winnipeg building. He spoke about it many times in later years to the citizens of Saskatchewan, myself included.

"So, about five days later, the strike was called off, near the end of June, I believe, but the unholy alliance between Ottawa, the employers and the American Union head offices continued to pursue thousands of workers, including anyone whom they suspected to be in leadership roles, right down to insignificant shop stewards who were just trying to do the jobs they were elected to do. Thousands were blacklisted, and police continued to raid homes and union halls.

"Back in Drumheller, Slim Evans was instrumental in leading the sympathy strike beginning near the end of May and destined to last a lot longer than the Winnipeg General Strike. That's because the other main issue was recognition of their new union, the OBU. But that same unholy alliance that broke the Winnipeg General Strike had the taste of union-busting success in their mouths so they weren't about to let the OBU into the Alberta coal fields without a full and vicious fight. Again the Minister of Labour, Gideon Robertson, worked with the local companies and the American Union head

One Big Union mine workers on strike, organized by Slim Evans, Drumheller, 1919.
Glenbow Museum Archives, Calgary. NA-2513-1.

offices in Indianapolis to break the strike by violence and intimidation. By late July and early August, the coal companies had permission to hire large groups of 'special constables,' and Slim's first strike, where he was in the leadership, turned into a nightmare of street violence, mostly in night-time raids.

"Now this is where some of my Drumheller contacts come in, because the stories of this strike were passed down through the generations and told to me by locals like Wilf Cunningham and old-time miners who had heard the stories from their fathers. The company and the government played their race card, always accusing the strikers of being aliens, bohunks, wops and all that despicable language of the KKK. And yes, the KKK took an active part in anti-labour activities in that valley. I worked for more than two years in Drumheller in the mid-seventies and heard certain fellow workers still speaking in support of the KKK as late as 1977 in regard to new immigrants in our community. Although many of the strike leaders in 1919 were of British heritage, labour politics always brought out the right-wing racists back then. Sometimes, I get the impression that a minority of their grandchildren haven't come all that far from that sort of thinking.

"Anyway they used surprise attacks in the early hours of the morning, often after being plied with liquor for several hours previously. One night they attacked the miners' shacks along the river near Rosedale, Wayne and East Coulee. They didn't dare do these things too often in the day since the miners were taking to travelling in groups with pick handles for protection, due to the terrorist tactics of the specials. Wilf Cunningham, a First Nations counsellor at the Drumheller Penitentiary, was the one who told me the story for the first time.

"The specials captured Thompson, one of the strike leaders. By this time they were shooting at fleeing miners indiscriminately. They strung up Thompson by the feet in a barn and poured horse urine down his throat."

"God, Paul. You don't intend to spare us the gory details, do you," Tom said. He looked comfortable, beer in hand, leaning his chair back against the divider that separated us from the deserted dance floor room.

"Hey, they didn't stop there. Two other strikers were hung up against the barn, upside down, crucifixion style. Mrs. Babyn, the wife of one of the union leaders had to defend her home with a .22 calibre rifle since she was alone with the family. She was arrested by the police for that and sentenced to three months in a Lethbridge prison. It was obviously okay for the specials and the company goons to use guns, but not for terrorized miners' families. After that infamous attack on August 11, 1919, the striking miners were given an ultimatum to sign up to the old United Mine Workers Union of America or be driven from the town. The companies even issued a public statement that hiring preference would be given to returning vets (especially those they'd hired as specials of course), then to white Anglo-Saxons and, lastly, to *aliens*. Wilf Cunnigham figured that Metis miners, of whom there was quite a community, came somewhere down the line after aliens.

"Shortly after that, the OBU leaders met secretly to discuss how to respond. The specials raided the meeting, arresting the union leaders, Christopher, Kent, Sullivan and Roberts, who were tied to telephone poles and tarred and feathered. Only the Monarch Mine in Nacmine, led by Evans, managed to hold out against the campaign for a while — God only knows how, but it seems that Evans was very open about their defiance. It also seems he had broad public backing. A secret referendum in October of that year showed 95 percent of the Drumheller miners still supported joining the OBU. Evans was becoming somewhat of an 'underground' local hero if you'll excuse the pun.

"By mid December 1919, the UMW American administration had cut an agreement with the local mine owners that if they all instituted a closed-shop policy, meaning no work without a UMW card, then the union would send in organizers to help get rid of the OBU. But apparently the Monarch Mine owner never cooperated, perhaps not wanting to face a picket line led by Art Evans. He probably knew the coal would be mined and sold on time as long as he recognized the OBU. During the following year the OBU local opened an athletic club and held a ceremony and picnic on Victoria Day to re-christen Drumheller Valley as OBU Valley. A World War I flying ace gave the participants rides in an aeroplane and Slim Evans was the first to ride, christening the valley with bottles of Coca Cola since liquor was frowned upon by some OBU leadership. Art himself was known to have a few drinks once in a while, usually when no strike action or organizing action was happening, so the Coke was probably a statement of conciliation to other OBU leaders. The public celebration was no doubt aimed at showing other miners in the valley that the OBU was there to stay and was not intimidated by the new closed-shop policy.

"That same summer Evans married Ethel Jane Hawkins, from a mining family of ten children. I've tried to track down some of the Hawkins family descendants in the Drumheller area, but it seems most of them have moved away. Shortly after his marriage, the OBU tried again to expand starting with the Wayne Mine. Wayne has been a ghost town for all the years that I remember except for a quaint little bar, the Last Chance Saloon, that is still there upholding the working-class traditions of the old days. That bar has witnessed it all, including a famous alcoholic mule named Tinker that used to come into the bar and order a drink by stamping one foot twice. The owner of the bar and the mule would set up a beer for the beast and the mule would take it in his teeth and drain it. Soon everyone would be trying to buy drinks for the mule, till the owner had to kick him out with a broom and lots of loud braying complaints. A relative of that owner still runs the establishment today. But that's another story.

"So where was I before that mule got in here? Yes, Evans and the OBU called a meeting of the Wayne miners and they all signed up. The mine owner promptly locked them out, and the OBU called on all its locals in southern Alberta to down tools in support of the miners. Some of them did, but some of them were holding two union tickets, UMW and OBU tickets, so it's still unclear as to how many were striking as OBU unions, since each local had other issues besides the Wayne lockout on their agendas.

"This same summer Evans was promoted to the Calgary offices as district secretary for the OBU in southern Alberta. While places like Fernie and Nordegg joined the OBU strike, the Alberta Crow's Nest Pass mines did not walk out, and that was a blow to the OBU. Apparently that strike was the beginning of the end for the OBU. Some influential people in the industrial union movement, like Tim Buck and the Trade Union Educational League, began to strongly advocate reform from within the established unions, like the UMW, rather than starting new unions. The strategy was to run slates of officers who were more democratic and in favour of industrial union philosophy. That's probably a major reason for the Crow's Nest Pass response to the OBU.

"While the OBU reached its zenith with about 40,000 members just as Slim began his position in Calgary, it declined to less than 5000 active members in the next two years, largely due to the charisma of people like Tim Buck and Annie Buller who worked tirelessly from union hall to union hall convincing the members to run progressive slates and to work towards Canadian autonomy and industrial union philosophy within their locals and districts."

I paused as I noticed Sammy screw up his face, so I nodded to him.

"So wait just a minute here now, Paul," Sammy said. "I heard of this Tim Buck. Leader of the Communist Party when it was still around, right?"

"Right. I think it's still around in some Canadian cities."

Sammy planted his elbows on the table and reached his hands out to me, pleading for clarity. "So you're trying to tell us that this commie was some great supporter of democracy and not the great defender of Marx and Lenin and Stalin and gulags. I mean I don't even know exactly what a gulag is, but I sure as hell don't wanna get to know one that badly, you know what I'm saying?" He leaned back in his chair, to let us know he was finished his point.

"Yeah, I know what you're saying. I'm not trying to sell anybody on the glories of Soviet Russia or even the merits of the Communist Party of Canada. But from what I've read and heard of Tim Buck and Annie Buller, they were strong defenders of democracy, especially at the local level and in the unions. Now I've heard lots of stories about undemocratic unions; I've never witnessed that myself, but many others claim to have. I'm just suggesting that according to my best understanding of Canadian history, the majority of people who knew anything about Buck and Buller and guys like Tom McEwan generally saw them as defenders of street-level democracy. Now their ideas about Communism, as practised by the Russians, Maoists and North Koreans, certainly seemed to evolve over time, from naive to more realistic. But in their work with Canadian unions they seemed like strong democratic advocates, at least to most careful observers that I've read. And that's as far as I'll go on that, because I sure as hell am not an expert on the history of the Communist Party of Canada.

"Anyway, I've been going on a long time about Evans' role in the OBU and labour history that's bound to be boring to some of you. That's what you get for asking a history professor to speak on anything. But it gives one a notion of the kind of issues that dominated the life of Arthur Evans. Just to mention, many of the OBU local leaders were blacklisted, effectively shut out of all mines." I paused for a swallow of a fresh cold beer just set up for me by Sammy.

"Hell, if I could have got my Social 30 credits over beer at BJ's on Tuesday nights with Paul as my teacher, I would have aced those high school finals," Sammy said.

"BJ's Tuesday History should be part of the provincial curriculum," Charles chuckled.

"Damn right," Sammy agreed raising a glass.

"Thanks, friends, but don't go encouraging me too much or you'll be here all night. Anyway, then in 1922, a few months after the birth of his first son, Stewart, Evans supported and encouraged a sympathy strike with the miners in Sydney, Nova Scotia. The district UMW president ordered them all back to work. Evans was increasingly targeted by the UMW, but remained popular with its Drumheller membership. Eventually Evans started to recognize the necessity to work from the inside of the UMW, so when the Atlas Mine local asked him to be the business agent for their union local he agreed. He was in that position when the Drumheller Valley faced a huge knock-'em-down, drag-'em-out strike that lasted for about six months. The union locals were learning to walk out together instead of separately, industrial union style. However, the UMW refused them strike pay, so the union executive met and agreed that Evans should keep 60 percent of the dues in Drumheller and use them to feed the miners who paid those dues. That, of course, was against the Union charter, but it helped them win that six-month strike. However, this was what the Indianapolis Union bosses, the RCMP and the local companies were waiting for. They charged Evans with theft of $2500 dollars.

"Well, the Canadian Labour Defence League took up his case and gathered about twenty witnesses to the distribution of the money, so the union and the Crown decided to change the charge to fraudulent conversion. This prevented the witnesses from giving evidence since they were involved in the conversion and it is not admissible evidence if it might incriminate the witness, so they got their conviction. Evans got three years in the maximum-security Prince Albert Penitentiary for feeding miners from their own union dues. I don't know if you know about the PA slammer but it's one of the dark hellholes of the earth.

"The Canadian Labour Defence League and Slim's local union drew up a petition, which they got their MP to present to Parliament with 8700 signatures, mostly from Drumheller miners and residents. It convinced the Solicitor General's Department to release Evans on a ticket of leave after serving only nine months of his sentence. Apparently Slim warned them, when he left the pen, that he would not refrain from the union activity that got him there in the first place.

"When he got back to Drumheller, he found that the stress of the trial and sentence and separation had been hard on his wife and young son, so the three of them decided to move to Vancouver to avoid being harassed by police and company blacklisting. The men had made so much progress in union cooperation by 1925 that his union card was recognized by the Carpenters Union in Vancouver, so he got a job quickly. He was almost immediately appointed shop steward and was elected as delegate to the Trades and Labour Council as well as the negotiations committee.

"But soon after the move to Vancouver their young son Stewart contracted diphtheria. The doctor gave him an injection which seemed to make it worse — he died within a few hours of the injection."

"Oh, my God, Paul," said Daniella. I had never heard her use that expression.

"Yes. One can't really imagine the impact that must have had. Jean Evans Shiels, their daughter who was born to Art and Ethel the year after Stewart's death, said that her mom and dad would never allow the doctors or schools to give her any injections or inoculations due to their trauma with Stewart's death." As I glanced at Daniella again, I could see she was fighting back some tears. This threw me a bit and I paused for a drink of beer that was no longer cold. When I had collected myself I continued.

"I suppose it was during this time that Arthur Evans experienced a kind of evolutionary conversion. Under the influence of his new union responsibilities and the radical efforts of the Trade Union Educational League, he was won over to the arguments of the Communist Party that the militant industrial unionists should avoid breakaway movements like the OBU, and concentrate instead on making their own mainline unions more democratic and active. Tim Buck and Annie Buller likely had a lot to do with that conversion. He finally joined the Canadian Communist Party in 1926 in Vancouver. Many years later, when the Regina Riot Commission lawyers for the federal government attempted to show evidence that he was a menace to Canadian democracy, they asked him how long he'd been a commnist. Since the Communist Party was outlawed after 1931, if he answered truthfully, he would be admitting a violation of Section 98 of the Criminal Code. He told them that he'd been a communist much longer than he'd been a member of the Communist Party. He said he thought he had been a communist ever since he started working all across North America, seeing the conditions of the mining camps and the rotten working conditions in general. Then he told them without hesitation when he had joined the Canadian Communist Party.

"To put that in its historical perspective, many of the miners in communities like Drumheller, Nordegg, Crow's Nest Pass and the Hinton-Robb district (not to mention many Ukrainians in communities like Spirit River and Vegreville) used to vote communist in great numbers in the twenties before the party was outlawed and removed from all ballots in 1931. In those days, long before the heavy and enduring propaganda of McCarthyism on both sides of the border, it was not uncommon for intellectuals and working people to support both communism and full participatory democracy as complementary goals for economic and political progress.

"Most of you know that Pincher Creek had an avenue named after Tim Buck until recently, when right-wing elements felt embarrassed by it. May Day parades in the mining towns were large popular affairs where communism was celebrated as an ideal for working folks' progress. Most of those towns are now right-wing bastions that vote overwhelmingly for Ralph Klein and have sometimes flirted with other extreme-right options, like Western Canada Concept, Confederation of Regions and the enduring Social Crediters.

"Anyway, I suppose many of the communists of those days had their blind spots too, but it seems to me their blindness was often mild compared to the gaps in the knowledge of many of our Alberta friends and families today, who know little of their history, or the fights for the many privileges and the lifestyle which they take for granted."

"That damn preacher heritage is creeping up on you again there, Paul."

"Ah, thank you, Sammy," I smiled broadly. "You keep me on the straight and narrow. I'll try to stick to history and not politics, if such a thing is possible."

"Sammy, do you need to have your comments on every tape he makes? He's gonna dump all of these tapes in some provincial or national archives some day and serious researchers of history will hear your input for decades to come." That was Tom, part of a regular defence league forming for me.

"I don't know about archives for this one, Tom," I said. I sensed that Sammy had a point, that parts of my spiel were dry academic labour history in comparison with Doc or Matt.

"Well maybe those archives are just dying to hear from your average rough-neck too. Is there a history of the Patch? Could be fascinating reading," Sammy said.

"Jeez, I hope you're not average, 'cause then this province is in a helluva lot worse shape than we feared." Tom wasn't going to give him the last word. I had to intervene.

"Okay, guys, cut Sam some slack. He just gets a mite skittish when that 'C' word comes up too often. It's one of the hazards of history and our inability to wipe out the stuff we don't like. Sammy's really on our side here. He's been a faithful disciple of western Canadian history for some time now."

"Jesus Christ, I've never been accused of being a disciple before. This party is getting too rough for me." He grabbed his cap and wiped the sweat from his hairline with his forearm.

"Pay no mind. Just trying to match insults with you, Sam. It's a strange custom, but I think that's the way we try to let you know how much we appreciate your input and interest."

"Right! Exactly how much these bums appreciate me is fairly clear."

"We certainly do appreciate you, Sammy," Charles joined in. "You're going to be awarded a Ph.D. in history from BJ's Academy for piling it higher and deeper just like the rest of us."

That's Charles for you. Blessed are the peacemakers and the believers in tolerance, especially in BJ's Bar and Cue Club.

"Anyway guys, I'm just about done for the evening. I get carried away with the moralizing sometimes. I've been trying for five years to get a handle on who exactly this guy Evans was and where he was coming from. The interesting thing to note about his era is that, whenever a government was faced with war or economic crisis, they turned to fascist tactics and fear-fed scapegoating. Hitler blamed the Jews, the unions and leftists; prime-ministers of Canada and presidents of America blamed unions and communists for their troubles. Instead of trying to address the real problems in 1931, they were busy outlawing political parties like the Canadian Communist Party and the Workers Party. Sort of like outlawing the Green Party because you've heard that some of their supporters endanger loggers by spiking trees. It only makes sense to someone with a fortress mentality and a *Mein Kampf* mind.

"So in 1931 the RCMP raid offices of the CCP right across Canada and arrest Tim Buck, Tom McEwan, secretary of the Workers Unity League, Sam Carr, Tom Hill, Malcolm Bruce, Tom Cacic — all the best speakers and leaders in the CCP — and charge them under Section 98, and most were sentenced to five years in Kingston Pen, another of Canada's dark outposts of hell. In 1932, a guard fired several shots into Tim Buck's cell without any provocation, and narrowly missed killing him. It was considered okay to shoot at communists in those days. It was a patriotic thing for some.

"In 1931, three miners in Estevan, Saskatchewan, who were participating in a parade with their families to protest mine conditions, were gunned down and killed by the RCMP in cold blood. Forty others were wounded and the doctors in Estevan were ordered not to treat the wounded and dying. The miners took the wounded to Weyburn — over an hour away on gravel roads. Nobody complained too much publicly in the atmosphere that prevailed, because our famous Mounties were ready in those days to frame you and jail you if you spoke too loudly. Annie Buller and Sam Scarlett went to prison over the Estevan issue, for 'rioting,' even though they were nowhere near that Estevan parade, but had defended it as legitimate and democratic protest. Now, in defence of some great folks who serve in the RCMP both today and back then who have, and had, a healthy conscience, I should state that some RCMP refused to take part in that action against the Estevan miners; there was also a rumour that some RCMP refused to take part in the attack on the crowd in Regina at Market Square. Unfortunately those aren't the ones that have set the tone for RCMP behaviour over those years.

"The crime of these Estevan folk that the police harassed was that they supported the unions organized by the Workers Unity League. So it isn't any wonder that they went after Slim Evans when he was sent to organize the Princeton miners and to help them with their strike. The RCMP no doubt had a file on Slim that convicted him in absentia for being dangerous to the nation's best interests. When he was appointed as District Organizer for the

B.C. chapter of the Workers Unity League, he led what was then called a Hunger Strike, in Vancouver. It was basically a peaceful protest march against low wages, high unemployment and miserable working conditions. His 3000 marchers attracted a crowd of 30,000 for the protest meeting on the Powell Street Grounds. This happened without incident, but the paranoid right wing of the RCMP decided that the next hunger strike would be challenged. So the Edmonton Hunger March just a few months later was met with force and brutality from mounted RCMP and city police as they gassed and clubbed any of the 14,000 farmers and workers who couldn't get out of their way fast enough. Since, miraculously, nobody died in that bloody attack, it doesn't even make the history books, but that was December 3, 1931.

"So you can understand that the authorities thought nothing of arresting Slim Evans for helping to organize a strike in progress at Princeton. For one thing, Section 98 was a foolproof weapon. One no longer needed to catch Slim feeding starving mining families from their own union dues. Now all you needed was a few stool pigeons to testify that they'd heard Slim say something in a speech which was meant to inflame the audience or advocate the doctrines of an illegal party, to which he belonged. In the atmosphere of the early thirties with scared investors looking for scapegoats and the wealthy willing to build walls around their fortune, it wasn't hard to put union activists behind bars. Uneducated people who were vulnerable to propaganda often cheered it as a coup for democracy, cheering just as loud as the bankers and the company brass.

"Canadians, when they criticize the silence of the German citizens during the rise of the Nazis, are really ignorant of how silent Canadian citizens were between the wars. They're ignorant of how many German unionists and leftists did protest the Nazi activity, and how their fates were so similar to the union activists and leftists in Canada during the previous decades. Even the rhetoric and rationale were similar; it is amazing how often the Jews were blamed for the leftist activity here in Canada, too.

"Somehow, we believed that if we could defeat Hitler, Mussolini and the Japanese, this ugly racism, bigotry and imperialism that enslaved so many people would be dead and democracy would be saved. We didn't want to admit that we were merely defeating the most blatant of the empire moguls, so that the slightly sanitized and more sophisticated versions of empires and emperors could continue on their merry way, 'living off the avails,' so to speak.

"Okay, that's it. Sammy's right. I've gone from history to preaching again. Anyway, that brings the life and times of Slim Evans up to the time that Doc and Matt spoke about. It gives you a bit of an idea about the man that went face-to-face with our Prime Minister Bennett. Doc Savage is going to tell us about that on Tuesday night. And I think I need another beer because this throat's getting awfully dry."

"Holy shit, a three-beer evening for Paul. This one's on me to celebrate a first in beer-drinking history." Cam got up to find Stacy.

"Thanks, Cam, I appreciate your encouragement of my drinking career."

Daniella stood up and came towards me at the lectern with eyes almost as full as when she struggled with the death of Slim Evans' child. Then she reached for me and, as is the fashion at upscale parties these days, gave me a hug. But it surprised me, and I wanted to hold on because of those eyes, but she was just coming up to thank me, formally, sort of. That's what she said. And everybody smiled. But it was the first hug from her, formal or not, after a whole year of Tuesday nights. Then we sat down for that last beer, to talk of CDs and Doc Savage and Slim Evans and us.

15

HIGH NOON IN OTTAWA

DOC SAVAGE ON PM BENNETT VERSUS ARTHUR EVANS

IN LATE JUNE OF 1998, EXACTLY sixty-three years after meeting with Prime Minister Bennett, Doc Savage stood before us again as the last surviving member of the Trekkers' delegation of eight to Ottawa. We were in our usual chairs with Cam, Tom and Sammy at one table already pulled in next to where Charles, Daniella and I were sitting with Doc. Over the winter though, the Grande Prairie rumour mill had been at work, and four brave and curious musician friends of Cam and Tom joined us, pulling a square table over to join our two round ones. Daniella had the honour of introducing Doc, so she also welcomed the new folks from the pulpit. Doc rose slowly with determined effort, placing his folder on the lectern and opening his journal, while the waitress set down his pot of tea next to a mug and a glass of water, the beer having already arrived. Doc welcomed the newcomers again and explained that it would be impossible to review the story so far. However, he briefly reviewed the impasse that Trekkers had reached in Regina and the decision to send a delegation of eight to Ottawa. Tom and Cam's friends nodded their appreciation every other sentence, as if someone had warned them that they were entering holy ground.

"So the seven delegates," Doc explained, "that accompanied Arthur Evans in the negotiations with Manion and Wier were the same guys the boys chose to continue negotiations in Ottawa. Let me see, besides Evans, there was Jack Cosgrove. I guess they decided they could spare the marshal since we weren't likely marching anywhere, and everyone trusted Black to take care of the temporary reorganization. Besides we wanted older experienced men and Cosgrove was thirty-five. Paddy O'Neal was in his mid-thirties. Pete Neilson was late thirties. Tony Martin and Mike McCaulay were about thirty. Just Red Walsh and I were a bit younger; he was twenty-five, and I was a month shy of twenty-four. Evans had a decade on the oldest of us so I guess it's no wonder I'm the only one left of the eight. Pete Neilson and Paddy O'Neal were killed in Spain, while Tony Martin and Red Walsh survived the fascists in Spain to die of old age. Martin died in England, and Walsh back in Vancouver not so many years ago.

"So anyway, the eight of us rode the cushions to Ottawa, first class, served on linen placemats with linen serviettes and more forks than we knew

The Trekker delegation to Ottawa: from the left, Tony Martin, Art (Slim) Evans, Bob (Doc) Savage,
Red Walsh, Mike McCaulay, Paddy O'Neil, Jack Cosgrove, Peter Neilson.
Saskatchewan Federation of Labour document.

what to do with. I'm sure Manion and Wier were amused by our lack of so-phistication, since we were all on the same train and had to share the dining car. On the way we had several stops where local organizations requested that we address them. Slim did most of the speeches. At a couple of stops we noticed RCMP troops travelling back west. This was what we had feared in agreeing to send a delegation, that the government was merely stalling for time to amass sufficient police forces in Regina. Then they would force a confrontation that the dutiful press would inevitably interpret in favour of 'Canada's finest.' But it wasn't anything we hadn't expected. The boys in Regina were expecting police action of some kind and had strict orders to give no provocation; we had patrols to enforce those orders.

"When we got to Ottawa, they put us up in a hotel with private baths and the works, and we had a day to feel our nerves before we met with the Prime Minister and his inner cabinet. Well, we didn't exactly get to relax because the likes of J.S. Woodsworth and Tom McEwan came to visit us. Not together of course; the leader of the CCF did not consort with known communists in those days. It confirmed to us, if we had any doubt, that we were indeed the centre of national attention. There was some victory in that already. For a youth of twenty-three, just to be there was something.

"So June 22nd we were escorted to the Prime Minister's office in lim-

Arthur (Slim) Evans, union organizer, On-to-Ottawa Trek leader.
Glenbow Museum Archives, Calgary. NA-3634-7.

ousines with RCMP escort. There were about ten Ministers there besides old 'Iron Heels' himself, and we at least recognized Manion and Weir, though they hardly gave any indication that they'd met us before, let alone travelled across the country with us. The Minister of Defence, Grote Sterling, had this dour look as if he were at a war council and some enemy vermin had been dragged in for interrogation. They had secretaries and sentries and, all in all, we fairly filled the office. So if you don't mind, I've gathered a fair bit of photocopied material over the years about the Trek. Lot of the boys share this stuff with each other, if they get their hands on some part of the record. So I got a transcript, here, that Ronnie photocopied for me, of our little meeting with Prime Minister Bennett, as recorded by someone called

Prime Minister R.B. (Iron Heels) Bennett.
Library and Archives of Canada, Ottawa. C-007731.

H. Oliver, Official Recorder. It might jog my sixty-three-year memory gap here. Let me tell you, memories do wondrous things to history. We've had some great debates about what this Oliver character recorded and what she left out. She certainly tended to clean up the vocabulary, let me tell you.

"Of course the only guy that spoke on their side was 'Iron Heels' Bennett. I think Manion spoke up once, but it was clear that only the commander had authority to speak at this war council. Bennett seemed to know who Evans was. He started by asking our names, beginning with Evans, in a very gruff authoritarian manner as if we were high school rogues called to the office.

"'Your name!' he says to Evans.

"'Arthur H. Evans.'

"'You use to live in Alberta, as I recall,' says Bennett, the prosecuting lawyer.

"'Various places, yes.'

"'Drumheller in my time!' Cross-examination you know.

"'Yes.'

"'Where is your home now?' Bennett asks it as though he's unlikely to have a home in the accepted sense of the word. Then he's finished with Evans and goes to Cosgrove. 'Name!'... 'Your home!' Then it's my turn. 'Robert Savage.' 'Vancouver.' He went through the eight of us and seemed definitely disappointed that he didn't find more Ukrainian, Galician or Jewish names perhaps. And if you think I'm impugning his motives, well, let me tell you that later on he got to asking where we were all born: when he found that most of us were born in the British Isles, they made sure the papers said 'all but one were *foreign born*' and left it to Canadians' imagination what that might mean.

"When Bennett established that Evans was to be our primary spokesperson, it became a two-person prosecutor-witness dialogue for the first half-hour. Evans was well prepared to lay out the grievances and demands; I don't know when he prepared, but he certainly had it organized.

"I remember this example he gave of blackballing and Department of Defence harassment.

"Evans says, 'The man was distributing working-class literature in the camps on the Princeton road.'

"Bennett interrupts, 'commnist literature you mean.'

"'Not necessarily commnist literature, it was...'

"'But it was commnist literature!' Bennett bears down on him again.

"Evans, still fairly cool despite the provocation, says, 'As I was saying, it was the *Relief Camp Workers' Journal*, which is not a commnist journal. He was savagely attacked at night by Department of National Defence personnel and the provincial police. At 2 a.m. they let him go and he had the gall to show his condition to his fellow workers. So for that they arrested him and charged him with resisting a police officer.'

"Crown attorney Bennett interrupts, 'In other words, he got into a fight with a police officer.'

"'In other words he was dragged out of bed at 2 a.m.!' Evans retorts.

"'Before he went to bed he hit an officer!' says Bennett.

"'That is simply not correct.'

"'What was it then, he got into a fight with the provincial police?'

"'No he didn't. He was lying in his bed...'

"'He got his wounds before he went to bed then.' Bennett the bulldog, you know.

"Evans had had enough, 'I tell you that you haven't a clue what you are talking about.'

"Bennett seemed to relish the response, 'Well, let's just finish this then, shall we.'

"Evans says, 'I'm trying to. The man was distributing working class literature, and the foreman told him he'd have to leave camp. He refused. The police came at 2 a.m. and attacked him. When people in Princeton saw what happened, people were angry, so the police came back and arrested him two hours later for resisting an officer.'

"Slim went on to attack Defence Minister Sterling's record of news releases, accusing the union of harbouring a red element that had plans to burn the camps down. Slim showed how he was continually raising the red bogey; that is, the 'red menace,' which was the term used in the later McCarthy era. Apparently Sterling had no authorization to reply because he sat silent as Evans went on the attack, outlining the grievances and the horrendous response of the Defence Department and the police. Evans ridiculed the McDonald Commission, pointing out the farcical nature of the questions, the political agenda and the obvious biases in the commissionaires.

"Slim then reviewed our six demands and the rationale for each. He was concise, articulate and confident in the face of all that pomp and prestige surrounding us — lawyers and millionaires, the peak of the conservative establishment in that cabinet. Maybe I should remind you of just how simple and rational those demands were. First it was for work with wages. (Terribly radical, that one.) Second, workman's compensation and adequate first aid in the camps. (Oh, that's communist.) Third, recognition of our elected camp committees. (Downright Bolshevik, that one.) Fourth, removal from the jurisdiction of National Defence. (What? We're against military slave camps?) Five, unemployment insurance. (Ugh! The root of all evil and sloth, to a Tory.) Six, the right to vote. (Lord have mercy; what will they ask for next?)"

Daniella, Charles, Cam and Tom were chuckling again — a good sign, and I noticed the newcomers looking at them and grinning, glad for permission to relax. But nobody seemed inclined to ask questions. Even waitresses entered discreetly; a different world existed this side of the portal.

"Well, Slim said we had no authority to alter or dilute the demands," Doc continued, "but we would like an official reply, preferably in writing that we can take back to the men. In closing, he objected to a breach of the spirit of our agreement in coming to Ottawa — that there would be no attempt to harass or threaten the men in Regina. He pointed out that even the press was reporting on what we ourselves had witnessed: that is, RCMP in large numbers converging on Regina. He then objected to the short half-hour allotted and firmly asked that other members of the delegation be allowed to speak and to represent the strikers, as was expected of them.

"Well, old Bennett interrupted that proposal as if the peasants had asked for cake instead of bread: 'How old are you, Mr. Evans?' he demands.

"'Forty-six.'

"'How old are you, Mr. Cosgrove?'

"'Thirty-five.'

"'How old are you, Mr. Savage?'

"'Twenty-three.' I was positive that was going to be the full extent of my contribution to these negotiations, but the old boy surprised me. I was still on the witness stand.

"'Where were you born?' He narrowed his eyes.

"'Birkenhead, England.' His face registered a small victory. I'm sure he would have preferred Leningrad, Odessa, Berlin or a shtetl in Poland, somewhere a bit more suspicious than England.

"'Where were you born, Mr. Cosgrove?' He went all the way through the delegation, finding only England, Ireland, Scotland; Paddy O'Neal was from Newfoundland (which was foreign-born in those days), and Pete Nielson was born in Denmark. Bennett was downright disappointed and suspicious when Slim told him that he was born in Toronto and that his people had been in Canada for more than a century. Now he could only report that all but one were 'foreign-born.' He didn't bother to ask how long we'd been Canadian or even if we were Canadian citizens. Not only was he bigoted; he didn't mind playing to the bigotry and racism of the majority of the people at that time. But when Bennett paused, Cosgrove jumped in, taking the opportunity to speak about workman's compensation. Hell, Jack wasn't going to come all the way to Ottawa to see the cabinet and then be shut down just because the Prime Minister was playing intimidation games. Martin then pointed out that Slim had covered things in general and that our time might be better spent getting down to business about the six demands. Well, old 'Iron Heels' took that as a signal that we were done, but he certainly wasn't.

"So he starts his speech or lecture, which was going to go on for the better part of an hour, all about putting us in our place: 'We've listened with interest to what you men have to say. With the exception of one of you, who has a criminal record which we will not discuss, you were all born outside of Canada, and in your native country, I was informed, there are a million or more men who have no work and probably never will have.'

"I guess he couldn't have been speaking of Newfoundland, or Denmark, or Ireland. Then he proceeded to tell us of how good we had it here, and how we couldn't expect something for nothing in the middle of a worldwide depression. He told us we were the dupes of communist agitation in the camps and that there was no way his government or this dominion would ever allow our demand for 'soviet committees' and 'commnistic boards' within these camps.

"'Let there be no misunderstanding,' he wags his fingers at us. 'Our form of government will be maintained by this government and our successors at any cost.' A regular Winston Churchill, this windbag.

"'Unfortunately for you,' he says, 'Your brethren in these camps have

206

become the victims of this propaganda. How much some of you men may be responsible for this delusion and may have misled these young men is not for me to say at this moment. You, illegally, in clear violation of the law, trespassed upon railway property, endangering human life, inducing others to do what they would not have done on their own.'

"He went on to inform us that the railways would swear in as many special constables as needed, and that the RCMP and the militia would be there, if necessary, to enforce the law and to stop the 'trespassing and endangering of life.'

"Then he went on to claim that we had induced others to join in 'rising against law, and against the institutions of our country!'

"Then he had the gall to claim that we didn't really want work and wages but just wanted relief handouts, that we weren't interested in work, but in this 'adventure,' as he called it, in the hope of organizing something that would 'overawe the government and break down the forces of law and order.'

"'I never thought that I would live to see the day,' he said, 'when people who openly admitted that they were breaking the law, would try to censure the elected government for sending police forces east or west to do their job of maintaining law and order. The police will move west, they will move east, they will move in increasing numbers wherever it is necessary to maintain law! Take that down, Mr. Cosgrove.' He jabs his finger. 'Tell Mr. Cosgrove to take that down, Mr. Evans!'

"I guess it must have bothered old Iron Heels that Cosgrove was making notes on what was being said. Now he wanted to make sure that Jack's longhand scrawl could keep up to his rising threats. He then took to forcefully refuting our demands and the need for action on any of them. Then he started harping on our willingness to violate laws, to endanger lives and to 'march on Ottawa.' At this point Jim, that is, Walsh, couldn't take it anymore, so, when the windbag asked the rhetorical question, 'march to Ottawa for what purpose? What purpose, I say,' Walsh broke in.

"'Could I answer that? You've accused 2000 workers of being lawbreakers and endangering human life. But, as I said to the boys in Vancouver, we have done our damnedest to get the government to negotiate the issues. Now, because you'd rather use force than negotiate, then it is this government's fault if someone gets hurt.'

"'Thank you!' Thundered the old blunderbuss. 'You have made it perfectly clear, though we do not require much more proof of it. Your agitating propaganda has made it perfectly clear that you intend to illegally take possession of trains and to march on Ottawa. But to what *purpose*, I say?' It wasn't a question; it was a shouted accusation.

"Evans broke in to get them back on track, 'The purpose is to demand from you this program of work and wages.'

"Bennett was full steam, 'And we have made it perfectly clear that these camps were not established for that purpose!'

"Evans cut him off, '*That* is just passing the buck. We want work and wages, and…'

"And Bennett interrupts, 'Now just a moment…'

"But Evans had had enough of his lectures, 'You just referred to us *not* wanting work. You just give any of us work and see if we will work! This is an insidious attempt to propagandize the press on your part. And anybody who professes to be premier and uses such despicable tactics is not fit to be premier of a Hottentot village!' Well, Bennett went red, then purple. Now I know what you're thinking. That comment wouldn't exactly pass standards for racial sensitivity today, but I've seen Slim in action with every race and he was surely no racist, unlike old Iron Heels across the table."

Doc paused and reached for the tea. His energy was high; his listeners sat in rapt silence.

"Anyway, Bennett was boiling," Doc resumed.

"'I come from Alberta,' he thunders. 'I remember when you embezzled the funds of your union and were sent to the penitentiary!'

"Oh! So much for not discussing his record.

"Evans points his finger at him and narrows his eyes, 'You are a liar!'

"God, the electricity just crackled around that table.

"'I was arrested for fraudulent conversion. Those funds were used to feed the starving, instead of sending them to the agents at Indianapolis. And I again say that you are a liar if you say I embezzled. And I will have the pleasure of telling the workers throughout Canada that I was forced to tell the Prime Minister of Canada that he was a liar. Don't you think you can pull off anything like this. You are not intimidating us a damned bit!'

"Bennett was shaken a bit, but bitterly angry, 'I know your record in the penitentiary at New Westminster and your record in the penitentiary elsewhere…'

"Evans cut him off, 'I was *never in* the penitentiary at New Westminster. You don't know what you're talking about!'

"Bennett was backing up from the stiff jabs and swinging a bit wildly now, 'You are at present on a ticket of leave?'

"'I am.'

"'It has lapsed now, hasn't it?' Bennett was trying to regain his Crown Attorney dominance.

"'There are a lot of things you don't know,' Slim said, speaking to the larger issues again.

"Bennett changed tactics, but he was still seething, 'You are deluding a number of young men.' He had the gall to sort of gesture at Walsh and me.

"But Evans was a street fighter. 'I have stated that I used the funds for hungry people instead of sending them to Indianapolis to a bunch of pot-bellied business agents. For you to bring this question up like this shows the absolute bankruptcy of your position. You have raised the suggestion that we really didn't start this action for work and wages. I tell you, we *want* work and wages.'

"Bennett was still with the personal stuff, below the belt. 'I was referring to your second time in the penitentiary.'

"Evans counter-punched, because Bennett was wide open. 'Where was this second time, and where was this ticket of leave? I was never sent a second time to a penitentiary!'

"'Jail, then,' Bennett counters.

"'Yes, under Section 98, for leading miners in a strike.' Slim said it proudly, with deliberate and delicious contempt in those words, Section 98. The rest of us were galvanized by Slim, and, damn it, we wanted some of this action. Paddy O'Neal couldn't stop himself.

"He pointed at Bennett. 'You have accused us of all sorts of things — wanting to set up Soviet committees…'

"Bennett breaks in, 'Nobody has told you the facts and I am trying…'

"Paddy wasn't finished. 'I have ridden boxcars in France, too. You call us foreigners…'

"Cosgrove cut him off. He wanted a lick in here and his chair grated backwards as he stood to his full six feet some: 'I take exception to any personal attacks on this delegation and will not tolerate…'

"'Sit down Mr. Cosgrove!' Bennett bellowed.

"'I will not!' Jack says. Slim's courage was contagious, obviously.

"'Then you will be removed!' Bennett thunders like some imperious potentate.

"'Then the entire delegation will be removed,' Evans said evenly. He knew Bennett had lost this round. Only Bennett seemed unaware of that.

"'Sit down, Mr. Cosgrove,' he didn't quite have the same credibility now.

"Cosgrove answered determinedly now. 'I will. But when I have said this. I fought in the Great War as a boy, fifteen years old. I have the interest of this country as much at heart as you have.' And he sat down no longer a young man being lectured to."

Daniella chuckled and Doc looked up and smiled at me over another sip of tea.

"Bennett spoke a bit more carefully from then on. He hadn't done his homework, and in Canada at that time, war vets were to be treated with respect by politicians, everyone knowing by then the dirty job the boys had done on behalf of the politicians and the bloody British Empire and all. Bennett tried to sum it up and close it down.

"He said something like, 'All right then, that is good enough. So far as we're concerned these camps were prepared and offered for the purposes mentioned, and are still there for you if you need them. Your program of work and wages will not be forthcoming from these camps, because that is not their purpose.'

"He went on to reiterate the status quo position that everyone was familiar with. But he couldn't finish it without trying another low blow.

"He said that if something went wrong in the camps we had no right to 'go and take the government by the throat and demand that anything which pleases your sweet whims be done.'

"Paddy wouldn't take that: 'It isn't about our *whims*. It is about the will of more than 2000 unemployed men waiting in Regina.'

"Bennett whips back, 'Well who put them into this state of mind?'

"'You are responsible for that!' O'Neal fires back.

"But Evans could see that we had no more to gain from this sort of sparring, so he decided there was nothing left to win here except for some kind of official response, so he said, 'Look, I propose we do not interject any more. We have heard enough of these idle statements from our Prime Minister. So we will take the rest of what he has to say back to the workers and citizens of Canada.'

"Bennett snapped back, 'That is your privilege. So long as you keep within the law. And the minute you step beyond it, Mr. Evans, you will land back behind bars where you were.'

"Well, it was his office, his cabinet, his staff. At his whim all this high-priced talent would remain quiet, apparently to admire his so-called leadership. So he decided he'd take another stab at refuting each of our six points. The men were bolder now and jumped in to correct him when he didn't know what he was talking about. For example, halfway through his lecture Bennett tried another cheap shot.

"He says, 'I would certainly assume that whoever is in charge of the camps might well ask them to take the oath of allegiance for the purpose of trying to prevent communistic agitation being carried on for the destruction of the camps.'

"Cosgrove struck back, 'That is a weak insinuation.'

"Bennett said, 'That is a fact!'

"Cosgrove says, 'Well, I'm an old soldier familiar with many kinds of government...'

"Bennett cuts in, 'Well, thank you, from every member of the government.' We were fairly sure that he wasn't thanking him for his service in the Great War but sarcastically thanking him for wanting to share his insights into government.

"Bennett's refutation of our demands was a case of classic evasion. On our democratic right to vote he merely said, 'Every worker has the right to vote if he comes within the provisions of the *Franchise Act*, and if he does not, he has not.'

"So I guess if the *Franchise Act* violated our right to vote, that must be okay, because that, after all, was the law. A classic case of the problem with law-and-order stances."

Doc's hands paused from their energetic punctuation to turn a page or two in his notes, which he seldom followed. Daniella and I smiled at each other with half a head shake, acknowledging the old man's tenacity.

"Bennett finally concluded in his patronizing way, saying something like, 'Well, that is all there is to say. I warn you once more, if you persist in violating the laws of Canada, you must accept full responsibility for your conduct.'

"'And you also!' Evans countered.

"'I am prepared for that,' Bennett says.

"'So are we,' Slim says.

"Bennett needed the last word, of course, so he takes to lecturing. 'I suggest to those who are continuing to mislead their fellow citizens that they have a great responsibility, for we will govern and enforce the law. Let there be no misunderstanding. And you can tell that to those that are with you in Regina. They may go back to the camps, and if public works become available, they may have the opportunity to work, but if they continue trespassing and endangering life and property we will not tolerate it. Good day, gentlemen.'

"Slim would not let him off that easy.

"'In conclusion then,' Arthur continued, 'you brought up the question of our responsibility. We realize the responsibility we are confronted with. We are confronted today with a greater responsibility than when we first came here, due to the Prime Minister's statement that the government will not deal with the questions raised here. Instead he attempts to raise the red bogey. So our responsibility is to take this back to the workers, to see that the hunger program of Bennett is stopped.'

"Bennett was red and purple again, 'I have nothing more to say. Good day, gentlemen! We have been happy to listen to you.'

"And that was finally the end according to H. Oliver, Official Debates Reporter for the PM's office."

Doc was straightening his notes, tapping the folder on the podium and shutting his journal, but he continued with a finger in the air for his final point.

"We were ushered out, but, as we were leaving, Red Walsh looked back at these luxurious full-length drapes that covered this window alcove. He was probably wondering why we couldn't have had them open to shed some daylight on the affair. And there at the bottom hem of the curtain, he noticed a shadow and the toes of boots, jackboots, like the RCMP wear. He hardly had time take a second look because everyone was hustling us out of there. Well those boots have become an Ottawa Trek legend, and I've heard some fairly spiced-up versions of that discovery. But, if he saw correctly, it would be entirely in keeping with old Iron Heels' paranoia. So that was a fitting end to our high-noon confrontation in Ottawa."

"Doc," I said, wanting to pursue the story, "one of the Trekkers I interviewed told me that Slim Evans saw those boots under the curtain, pushed his chair back a bit, grabbed the drapes and casually pulled them open with a bit of a flourish at the end, revealing several armed Mounties, and exclaimed, 'Well if it ain't our friends the yellow-legged hummingbirds!' I take it that's a slight exaggeration?"

"Didn't happen, Paul!" said Doc. "But I've heard the story enough that I can almost remember it that way. I suppose the truth of that story lies in the storyteller's recognition of the incredible courage that Evans revealed in the face of real intimidation. That courage was contagious, and the seven of us that accompanied him were never the same after that day. We learned from a master of integrity how to speak truth to power, as the young folks say."

So Doc sat down with us next to Daniella to a round of applause, Sammy clapping the loudest. He had been amazingly well-behaved. We all ordered another round of beer as usual, and Charles invited the four from the table beyond Cam's to stick around. A couple of them agreed gratefully, but two of them came over to thank Doc, bending over to shake his hand, telling him what a privilege it had been, and that they hoped to do it again sometime, but they had work in the morning and spouses who were waiting up for them. Daniella and I leaned back in our chairs, relaxing and occasionally smiling at each other, happy that we'd managed to put history on the stage one more time. The other fellows asked Doc some questions, and he was delighted to answer over a glass of water.

"What do you think of our chances," I said in a low voice to Daniella, while the rest were listening to Doc, "of getting him back here during the summer?"

"It's a busy July," Daniella's pitch revealed some apprehension, "and all of us have plans to be away at different times."

Since I was thinking of the six-month gap from his last lecture, I voiced my worries directly to her grandfather: "Doc, you've got to promise to come back to do a session or two about the riot itself. I think you were the highest ranking Trekker on Market Square after the police arrested Evans. You're our best eyewitness."

"Well," Doc said, "rank didn't count for much when the police decided to riot. I'll do what I can to come back, Paul. It's a grim story, though, and no one had much to be proud of that night. A night full of fear and fury and stupidity. Not to mention clubs and bullets and blood."

"We'll get you back here, Grandpa," Daniella said in a low determined voice. We heard the grit in her voice and we all knew that this chapter of the Tuesday Club could not be complete without the story of that Dominion Day Riot. And Doc wasn't getting any younger.

16

BY MIGHT AND BY POWER

CHARLES ON MULRONEY, CHRÉTIEN AND CO.

W E DIDN'T MANAGE TO AGREE ON dates for a decent quorum of Tuesday Club members that summer. Near the beginning of my new semester at the college, Daniella called with the news that Doc had slipped on a bank by the Fraser River, where he always panned for gold; he had injured his hip. A foreboding fog descended from my brain to my throat as she filled in details of how he reached the hospital. My breathing passages constricted. I feared for Doc, no doubt, but now that I think back, I realize that the fear was for all of us back at BJ's, too — perhaps for all Canadians — that we might not hear those final sessions promised by Doc, our last eyewitness. Doc was a historian's delight because he would cut through the romance and the exaggerations. He had often corrected for me the written accounts in national magazines, in memoirs, in published works, where the authors no longer knew the objective truth, or where paid writers relied on the national media of the day, mistaking it for objective history. Doc couldn't be replaced, so now I was increasingly aware of his mortality. At our BJ's rendezvous, Daniella shared with me her increasing apprehension, yet somehow even that drew the two of us closer —it seemed we needed the Tuesday Club on a number of levels. We tried for more than two years to get him back to Grande Prairie, but his hip was giving him too much pain for travelling. We even discussed the possibility of the six of us driving to Quesnel, but it never happened.

We still met most Tuesday nights because I enjoyed the company of Daniella and Charles. For Charles, it was a very short walk, and provided regular affordable social therapy. Cam, Tom and Sammy were more regular than just Tuesdays — liquid therapy perhaps. Cam and Tom had mastered a fairly sophisticated CD with the best of the Tuesday Sessions, but everyone knew that it was incomplete without the account of the riot that Doc had promised. In the spring and summer of 1999 Sammy had to work out of Fort Saint John in the B.C. Peace Country for a while; when he came back Cam told the Tuesday Club that Sammy had taken to drinking in the Lions Den across from the college. He inferred that Sammy was drinking more than usual.

"He did invite us to join him there," Cam said, "but if we do, we might want to join him while he's still on his first five."

Daniella just shook her head and said something like, "Daniella in the Lions Den just isn't happening." We laughed because that establishment had a bit of a reputation, and we suspected that there would be no magic portal to history at that bar. We were worried that our door to history might be closing for us all at BJ's too, but there were other reasons for a beer at BJ's. Besides Cam virtually owned this bar — he certainly would have owned it if he had been purchasing shares with each drink. We appreciated his ability to defend us to the younger patrons at BJ's, not all of whom understood the Tuesday tradition. For example, we often ended up in political discussions around election times, whether federal, provincial or municipal, and we all enjoyed the slightly raucous discourse. Political debate is not a regular feature of northern Alberta bars, and could be considered deviant by some at BJ's.

In the spring of 2000, as we got closer to the June anniversary of the Trek events and closer to July First, the anniversary of the riot, we frequently brought up the need to finish the CD as a tribute to Doc and Matt and the Trek. In June, Cam pushed us on the matter; he was proud of the production quality of the CD, but he knew it was incomplete. Charles agreed; he suggested a 65th anniversary of the Trek and Riot at BJ's, with Doc as the guest of honour. We tried, but Doc was sick again and unable to travel. He promised Daniella one more time that he would make it back to Grande Prairie some day soon. We decided to have a 65th anniversary celebration at BJ's anyway, so I went to look for Sammy at the Lions Den a few days earlier to invite him to join us. He hadn't shaved for a while, but he greeted me warmly, even standing to shake my hand.

"Hey professor," he hailed me loud enough to grab the attention of everyone in the bar. "Great to see ya. They let you out of them hallowed halls across the way?"

We had a beer, but when I mentioned the Tuesday Club I noticed that he was a bit reticent, not really ready to explain his absence. I thought perhaps his isolation in the oil patch had driven him deeper into his addiction and that he was embarrassed about it. He promised to consider my invitation to the July First informal celebration at BJ's.

It turned out to be more of a party than a history celebration, with lots of talk of the good old days of the Tuesday Club in '97 and '98. Sammy showed up clean-shaven and smiling, as if he'd never missed a beat, and we all took our cues not to make it a big deal, but we toasted the reunion and the Trek. The only thing we recorded was about fifteen minutes of good wishes from all of us to Doc, which Daniella delivered to him in person on July 30th, Doc's birthday.

The rest of the summer was another lost cause for the Tuesday Club, though Daniella brought back greetings, thanks and another promise from her grandfather. While she was in Quesnel, she had insisted on setting up extended physiotherapy for Doc's hip and some sophisticated steroid treatment for his bronchial passages, to help him deliver on his promise. It took months, but, by Christmas, Daniella told me that she now believed that it was going to happen. In March 2001, after two more postponements in the winter months due to weather, we heard that he had set a date to see us in early April.

When Daniella announced this officially at BJ's, she also informed us that the week before Doc's appearance we would tape a warm-up session, where Charles and I would tell the stories about our minor confrontations with premiers and prime ministers over the years. We had casually shared some of these anecdotes with her since Doc's last presentation. Neither Charles nor I thought that this was a topic worthy of the recorded sessions; it certainly couldn't rival Doc's sensational story of Evans confronting Bennett. However, as usual, Daniella got her way. I think she just wanted to test the magic, to remind the old BJ's portal that it had to open at our command. So, at the end of March, I phoned Sammy; he had joined us more frequently at the Tuesday Club throughout the winter. I let him know that we planned a taped Tuesday Session, sort of as a warm-up for the coming sessions with Doc. He said he'd be there, because "the pros never missed a warm up" or something like that.

Tuesday night we were all in our places, two pitchers of draft on the table for Cam, Tom and Sammy. Daniella was trying to introduce us from the lectern, but neither of us would think of using her portable pulpit, so we insisted on remaining around the two tables, "seminar style," Charles called it, winking at me. Charles and I were a bit self-conscious about the whole affair.

"I'll never forget Doc speaking that last time," Charles said, "about how Arthur Evans faced down an old bear like Bennett in his own den. That ain't easy when you're on their turf, and they're out to intimidate you."

"The Rev knows whereof he speaks," I said. "If I recall, he, himself, faced down a couple of prime ministers and at least one famous premier, am I right?"

"No, no, no… it wasn't the same kind of thing at all," he said. "This thing we heard from Doc was a direct and personal attack by a prime minister on his own home turf."

"Sounds like there's definitely a story or two here. And the Rev is trying to stonewall us on it, in the name of modesty," said Tom.

"Hey, we can't have that sort of nonsense. Modesty is a dangerous thing, in excess," said Cam. "Help us out here, Paul. If he won't tell us, you have the burden of obligation, having brought it up."

"Well, I was there on one occasion, but the other two I just heard about secondhand, so Rev, you'll have to correct me where I've got it wrong. Okay?"

"Ah Paul, this stuff doesn't even make decent anecdotes. They pale in comparison to the issues Evans was dealing with."

"Yeah, well we can't all lead a march on Ottawa, and call the PM a liar to his face," Daniella said. "But history's about more than just those moments. I'm with Cam and Tom on this. I promised them these stories."

"Well, if I recall," I began, "the Rev started his record of confronting first ministers with the legendary Peter Lougheed. 'Course who knows how many he'd put in their place before I caught up with him. Anyway, the Premier was up here in Grande Prairie for reasons forgotten and the Rev had the nerve to confront him about the Lubicon land claims east of Peace River. Lougheed had been stalling and using some underhanded legal manoeuvres to continue allowing his pet oil companies to drill on land that was supposed to have been declared a Lubicon Reservation years ago. I was with Charles that time — I don't think Lougheed even deigned to offer an answer, right, Rev?"

"No, he just looked at me as if I'd threatened him, and kept walking. That was the signal for his burly bodyguards to block my way," said Charles. "It's their way of telling you that you're a pain in the ass and not to be taken seriously. Lougheed wasn't always like that, but towards the end of his tenure, he was less approachable than Chrétien guarded by his missus." That was a reference to Mrs. Chrétien scaring off an intruder at Sussex Drive. I looked around at the listeners and everyone of them was nodding as if they knew the story. Sammy was hard to read though; I doubted that he listened to the news regularly in those days.

"No, if you want to talk about approachable premiers, it's Tommy Douglas who wins hands down. The stories are many and legendary. He once stopped on the highway when he saw a stalled car on the way from Weyburn to Regina. The folks he stopped to help were the Vanstones, some friends of Paul's family. His offices were so notoriously open that farmers would come sixty miles without an appointment to blow off steam in Douglas's office about this thing or that thing. People trusted him and he'd make them feel at home. He was head-and-shoulders above Lougheed as a leader, in my experience."

"Now you're just trying to get us off track on the Rev-versus-the-Prime Minister stories," said Daniella, pretending to punch Charles's shoulder.

"Well before you leave Mr. Lougheed, you should ask Paul to tell you the story of how he cross-questioned the young lawyer Lougheed during the '71 campaign when he first got elected," said Charles, smiling at Daniella's teasing.

"I don't remember telling you about that," I said, surprised by my friend's knowledge of my youth.

"Your father told me about it years ago, not too long after it happened," said Charles.

"I can't even remember telling him. But I suppose I would have. He still supported the Social Credit government in those days. I voted for the New Democrats that year. The Grant Notley early years. And he voted for whoever succeeded his hero, Ernest Manning. Harry Strom wasn't it? Anyway, the Rev's trying to get us off the scent of a good story, again."

"So get us back on track, Paul, and we'll get your Lougheed story when we're finished with the Rev," said Daniella. Tom and Cam sat back, beers in hand, smiling at our modest evasions.

Sammy leaned forward, arms on the table, "Daniella you're just going to have to point your whip at the one you want talking or these guys will play tennis with this ball all night."

Tom chuckled, "Yeah, Sammy's right. We've got a session to record here. We'll call this one 'Taking It to the Top.'"

"Taking it to the top and talking to a wall," Charles said. "I mean, it didn't go anywhere."

"Yeah, but we want to hear it," Daniella said. "Come on Paul, you've got to deliver the goods if Charles won't."

"Well the most recent prime minister to come face-to-face with the Rev's scrutiny was none other than the Honourable Jean Chrétien," I said.

"The Yawnable Jean Chrétien, the little guy from Shawinigan," Tom imitated his accent and raised a glass in salute. "You asked a question; then he strangled you, right?"

"Damn near… if I heard it right," I said. "Come on, Rev. You caught him on one of his famous walkabouts, right? As he glad-handed it with the crowd in Muskoseepi Park, the way I heard it. You asked him about cutting the transfer payments to the provinces, right?"

"Yeah, I guess I did. It was back before they cut the federal transfer payments. But the rumour was out that they were going to do some deficit fighting on the backs of the provinces, cutting money that we use for health care and education, so I just told him that we couldn't afford to deal with that kind of cut, and that he would be hurting people like me if he did it. He stopped smiling and his grip on my hand got a little rigid. He stared at me for a minute… and, I swear, I remembered that look from the TV news. You know the story. That face just before he strangled the protester? I recognized that look. It was the one I stared into, in his moment of silence there. But then he composed himself and said carefully, 'Okay, I have heard you,' which meant 'you've had your say, and it was rude to ruin my good time here in this walkabout.' Anyway, that's all there was to that great encounter. It didn't even attract the media. Like I said, Paul's building you up for expectations that these little encounters just can't deliver on." He waved a hand dismissing it all.

"Well, I don't know about that. There's a pattern here, of standing up and holding these guys accountable, as best one can, anyway. And the incident with Mulroney is a classic. The press got that one cold. I witnessed this one so I can tell you the story and spare you the Rev's modesty."

"With friends like this, who needs enemies," Charles smiled, as he crossed his arms, ready to listen to my version of his story.

"So Brian Windbag Mulroney," I began, "is touring our Muskoseepi Park, charming his way along the walk with his huge security gorillas and the national media cameramen all in tow. Charles and I kind of take up a position right in their path and stick out our paws to shake hands. Introduce ourselves, and, sure enough, Charles starts asking him about the Lubicon land claims and why his government is dragging their feet, while Bernard Omniyak is struggling to do something positive for his people. And why he would delay the reserve agreement when there'd been fifty years of stalling already. Well it's no sooner clear that Mulroney is going to have to field a political football, when the national television and radio microphones descend on us. These crooked booms with mics come down from above us, the cameramen jostle for position, and the security gorillas start moving in on us like we're holding Molotov cocktails or likely to pull a switchblade. All of sudden it's just packed in there with Mulroney stacked against us so close we know each other's deodorant brand, or lack thereof. Well, Mulroney was never at a loss to fill in a Kodak moment, so he starts off this lofty homily about how close his government came to striking a deal on Aboriginal rights and self-government in the Charlottetown Accord.

"'We came that close,' he says, thumb and finger measuring off an inch or so. 'We came that close to signing an agreement recognizing Aboriginal rights across this nation, and…'

"Well, Charles here cuts him off, because Brian is obviously off topic, as usual, and the Rev isn't going to stand for the kind of bullshit they all take from this guy in the Commons, right? So the Rev says, 'Now hold on a minute here. Aboriginal rights and self-government is one thing, but it's got very little to do with a promised reservation and honouring Treaty Eight with this band that's been…'

"Well, Mulroney's been embarrassed that someone finally called him on his typical evasive answers, so he cuts off the Rev with an injured tone of voice.

"'Do you want to hear my answer or not?' asks the windbag.

"Well, the secret service boys squeeze us a little tighter because they feel it's their duty to punish us or threaten us for embarrassing their charge. The network mics descend from above a little closer, and nobody can breathe, we're that vacuum packed in there. The Rev says he definitely wants to hear the answer, but not a speech about the Charlottetown Accord; he wants him to answer the question. So Brian 'the charmer' Mulroney ignores that brazen reply and continues his Charlottetown Accord speech with thumb and forefinger measuring out that small gap between him and history book glory. As if the Charlottetown Accord would have brought running water to Lubicon Lake and the Little Buffalo Cree.

"So when Brian was finished talking to the camera and letting us all know the tragedy we'd caused by not supporting his constitutional coups, the secret service gorillas moved between us and his majesty — our moment in the spotlight is over and we can breathe again. The *National News* covered it that night, suggesting that the PM's peaceful tour of the Peace was interrupted by a lone voice from a distinguished-looking Afro-Canadian questioning his sincerity on the Lubicon negotiations. God bless CBC. They still call them like they see them, even when they're being cut to the bone. Not that they don't see them through their own coloured glasses usually, but at least they got the story straight and didn't kiss ass. Excuse my French." I paused for a drink.

"And I," Charles said, "even voted for the damned Charlottetown Accord, warts and all. But it certainly had nothing to do with the question I asked him."

Tom grabbed the pitcher and poured another beer, "Now that's a helluva story, Rev, and to think you were gonna hold out on us. I can't help thinking that if Paul had been there to witness the other two confrontations, we might have two more *High Noon* gunfights to relish."

"Come on, guys," said Charles as his hand came up shoulder height. "You're lacking a sense of perspective here. *High Noon* in Canadian politics doesn't come that often, but if you want *High Noon* confrontations, I'd say you better look at the October Crisis and the guys that stood up to Pierre Elliot Trudeau and his notorious ego. Let's take a more critical look at who the greatest leaders of that era were. Let's take a more critical look, not just at his charisma, but also at his character flaws that partially prevented us all from realizing his 'just society' in his time or in our time."

"That's true," I said. "People often forget that Trudeau had just as dangerous an ego as Brian Mulroney, and, whether you're right-wing or moderate or left of centre, that's a dangerous thing in a crisis. That was R.B. Bennett's problem."

"But I think that is connected to my original assertion," Charles said, "that we have a tendency towards nostalgic revision when it comes to our history — maybe not as bad as the Americans, but an awful lot of Canadians know better. A lot of Canadians have long ago come to the conclusion that Trudeau deceived us during the October Crisis, practising the shoddiest of partisan politics and opportunistic grandstanding. Yet we absolved him long before he died."

"Seriously," Daniella said as she found some Splenda, from a stash in her purse, to stir into her tea. "I agree with you, Charles. He went too far with the *War Measures Act*. It was a fairly cavalier grab at civil liberties from what I gather from the CBC specials, though I wasn't old enough to pay much attention back then. I guess we're just too Canadian in our willingness to forgive and forget. But, Charles, you started talking about someone who stood up to him back then, didn't you?"

Charles looked like he was still contemplating, but Cam leaned forward to engage him. "I bet you Charles means the reporter who asked him why he needed all the tanks, and how far he'd go… the time when Trudeau said, 'Just watch me!'

"No!" I chimed in. "Dimes to dollars he's referring to Tommy Douglas."

Charles laughed and cocked his head, "Well, Paul wins. I mean I thought that reporter had guts and asked the proper questions. But he didn't have the opportunity as a reporter to address the bigger issues. But Paul knows me too well. It was Douglas in Parliament who went to the core of the issues by challenging Trudeau and his motivation for such a blatant attack on civil liberties. If it had been a lesser statesman than Trudeau, or a less notorious action on his part, it wouldn't be such a classic Canadian *High Noon* confrontation. But you've got to remember that he had 90 percent plus support for his actions in English Canada and 85 percent support among Francophone Québécois. The *War Measures Act* was his most popular moment, when he got more popular support than at the height of Trudeau-mania. Yet Douglas smelled a rat and had the guts to call him on the deceptions."

"And Douglas got terrible harassment in question period when he spoke up on this," I added, my hand on a mug of ale that had long since lost its chill.

"God, these Saskatchewan boys are a regular fan club for Tommy Douglas," said Cam, pouring another draft for Sammy and gesturing at my mug as if he were giving up hope for my drinking career.

"Hey, I'm northern Ontario, born and bred," Tom said, "and I'm part of the fan club, too. But I've never heard this part of the Douglas story. What do you mean, he smelled a rat?"

"Well, if I recall correctly," Charles said, " they had municipal elections coming down on them, and francophone Montreal was threatening to support FRAP, a coalition of nationalists, unionists and progressives. I can't even remember what the acronym stood for. Some kind of Front Populaire. Many of the people arrested in the crackdown belonged to FRAP or the Parti Québécois. Hey, the PQ were hard on the heels of the Liberals in Quebec then. Many of these folks who were arrested were sincere democrats — nonviolent, highly educated people, many of them. Most of them were arrested, then released much later without charges. But they were all tarred with the same heavy brush as that small minority of FLQ members who actually broke the law. The Liberal establishment in Quebec was in trouble in the polls. A very right-wing establishment, by the way. And Trudeau knew that he could rescue it with his high drama and his strong-man tactics. Because not very many people had the guts to speak out publicly against him, when he was sticking it to the French separatists."

"Even some of the most ardent Québécois nationalists," I added, "had to shut up during that time, because no one wanted to be associated with defending terrorists. Years later we found out that Trudeau told the Premier and the Mayor of Montreal that, if they sent him a letter requesting troops due to an 'apprehended insurrection,' he would not question their definition of 'apprehended insurrection.' He would declare the *War Measures Act* with the implication that the election would be saved for both of them due to the public reaction to troops in the street. Tommy Douglas suspected that kind of partisan shenanigans long before that dirty agreement ever became public. You know, Rev, I think I've got parts of those speeches Douglas made during the October Crisis at home in a book. I should bring it one of these nights for an informal session, some night when Doc's finished."

"Yeah, why not?" Charles said. "Read it into the record. Part of the BJ's Canadian History Sessions. No sense having those great moments sit there in Hansard in the archives where no one ever reads or hears them. We'll add it to Cam's CD."

"Hey, the Rev's catching the entrepreneurial spirit of this venture," Cam said. "We'll all take a cut of the profits from the sales."

"A Tommy Douglas speech would certainly out-sell a speech by Paul. No offence, Paul," Tom chuckled and raised his glass toward me in appeasement.

"None taken."

"I hope I get a copyright cut for coming up with this idea," Daniella said. "I haven't told you guys, but I need to study up on my Quebec history and culture in the next few weeks anyway because I've decided to take some holidays the last half of April and go down to Quebec City for the Summit of the Americas meetings."

"Holy shit!" Tom buried a hand in his long hair. "Another Battle of Seattle shaping up for that one."

"Watch your tongue, boy!" Daniella wagged a finger at him. "We're going to have to give you several Hail Marys as penance for inappropriate language, and for scaring middle-aged women."

"Now if you were my priest, Reverend Arthur, I'd probably take up going to confession again after my thirty-year absence," Tom smiled, clearly unrepentant.

"Flirting with the clergy, and you a married man," Daniella said. "Yeah, I've been thinking seriously of Quebec City ever since I developed those social justice units that these two recommended for my summer camps."

"Well, congratulations," said Charles. "I've always admired those that plan holidays more stressful than their normal lives. Are you taking a gas mask?"

"Hey, I'm not going to participate in a riot." Daniella rolled her eyes. "You of all people shouldn't be stereotyping protesters of economic globalization."

"No stereotype intended," Charles said. "I just noticed that a lot of people that got gassed in the Battle of Seattle hadn't intended on being in any battle zone, either."

"Speaking of *High Noon* Canadian match-ups," Cam said, "can't you just see old Jean Chrétien getting his hands around the Right Reverend Arthur's throat. And the headlines: 'PM Strangles Protesting Protestant Clergywoman.'"

"'Orange Lodges Across Canada Protest Catholic Attack on Protestant Clergy.'" Tom's one free hand highlighted a half-meter-long headline before our eyes.

"Guys really! I'm not going there to confront police or the Prime Minister. I'm there to show solidarity with thousands who don't want to sit quietly at home while our rights to a safe planet are traded away for the convenience of big business."

"Does your boss let you preach like this on Sunday, too?" Tom asked.

"I like it when she preaches," Sammy's beer moved with his hand. I was thinking that he'd knocked back more than usual.

"Don't pay them any attention, Daniella," I said. "They're just as proud of you as we are. I just worry about the Sécurité de Québec. They're conditioned to think of every young person out there as a Black Hood in disguise."

"*Young person?* I like that. But what's a Black Hood?" Daniella queried, eyes locked into mine.

"They're the ones that the media and the police call anarchists," I said, looking away from those direct eyes. "In fact they call themselves anarchists, but they're not classic anarchists in the tradition of the Wobblies and the European anarcho-syndicalists. As best as I can discern, the Black Hoods are just a few members of the Black Bloc who cover their faces with black tuques. The Black Bloc believes that sometimes symbolic or calculated acts of violence can help oppressed people more effectively than the ballot box or non-violent political activism. In other words, they don't mind getting the police to attack a crowd if they think they can get good numbers of the crowd to fight back. They tend to think that a little blood covered by cameramen in close-up shots is worth the effort. And they just hope to hell it's someone else's blood. Some of them remind me of the worst elements of the FLQ in 1970. More full of themselves and their revolutionary image than full of concern for the people they purport to fight for. The Black Hoods are the ones Chrétien will refer to again and again when anyone defends the majority of peaceful protesters like Daniella, who just want to exercise their right to dissent, not to mention improve the world. Unfortunately these Black Hoods help create a general stereotype for protesters, which the media loves."

"You're trying to scare me, right?" Daniella put her hand on my arm.

"Nope. I know you don't scare that easily. I can't even remember why I brought it up. Oh, yeah, because I said I was worried about the attitude of the Quebec police toward protesters in general. Be careful, Daniella. That damn fence is going to be the centre of attention for police and the Black Hoods. If you see them put on the hoods and head to the fence, that's a good time to head the other direction. Don't even stay with the crowd at that point, because they'll panic and stampede if they're gassed."

"Hey, I kind of like that gallant concern for the lady. Can I take you with me to keep me out of trouble?" Daniella smiled.

"You could, but your congregation might not agree that I was there to keep you *out* of trouble," I said.

"I just love it when she flirts like that," Tom winked at me. "It gives me hope for mankind. I mean the male kind, in general. And the clergy in particular."

"Seeing more clergy in trouble with their congregations," Daniella countered, "over their private lives would make you feel better about the world, more positive about religion? Is that what I just heard?"

"Well, I do feel better about the world in general when I'm smiling," Tom replied. "I don't think I inferred anything about more positive feelings about religion. But I do have the same kind of feelings as the Rev and Paul there, when it comes to your adventures in Quebec. Take a gas mask along. Take your own secret can of pepper spray. Take lots of cash to bail yourself out of the slammer, and take the phone numbers of two good lawyers in case one's not home."

"I like this. I would have done this a lot sooner if I had known I could generate all this concern for my personal well-being," said Daniella sipping her tea and smiling smugly.

"Phone us every night at 10 p.m. to tell us where you are," I said.

"And again at 1 p.m.," said Tom, "especially if you're being led into temptation by one of those young Québécois protesters."

"And don't talk to any police officers," Cam leaned back in his chair, "or trust what they say. They're out to get you, in my experience."

"So these Frenchie cops are as bad-assed as the LAPD, are they?" Sammy inquired. He definitely had had a few more beer than he should have.

"It won't just be Quebec provincial police. There'll be CSIS, Canadian army, certainly RCMP," I said, as if I knew for sure.

Sammy smiled. "Canada's finest, eh?"

"Now Paul," Charles said, "from the details you were giving her on police action, it sounds to me like you've had some experience with this sort of thing. You want to come clean on this one and supply a few details?"

"Nothing to brag about on that account," I said. "I'm a lot more comfortable doing the one-on-one protests or asking questions at a microphone, or writing a letter, or organizing a campaign. The one occasion that I faced a police line was enough to convince me that not much is won in those encounters, and I don't get off on the fear that runs riot through a person's blood on both sides of those police lines. I unfortunately got training in riot control when I worked in the penitentiary system. They even made us case-workers go through it all. Fear is the object in riot control and the motivator of the men in uniforms. I've had to swing those swivel batons in practice, in unison. It all makes me sick."

"I vote we hear about the one occasion he faced a police line," said Cam.

All hands shot up in a mock vote: they laughed when I sighed and closed my eyes.

"Come on, brother Paul. It's your duty," Charles said.

"Well, let me see. It was in Ottawa," I said. With this crew it was easier to tell the story than to try to get out of it.

"See, that's farther than the Trekkers got," laughed Cam.

"I was down for some convention or council meeting," I said.

"Probably plotting some socialist action," said Tom.

"Probably. But we had a lunch break in which some of us went down to lend support to a protest rally about Premier Harris's cuts to women's shelters. The women were running the protest so it was very organized and civil. This wasn't in any danger of escalating to anything. We were at a T intersection on Laurier Avenue down on the edge of Strathcona Park, about a block away from the Russian Embassy at the end of Laurier. There's a restaurant there at the top of the T intersection, right on Laurier, and Premier Harris was coming there for a swanky five-hundred-dollar-a-plate fundraiser. The women who were acting as marshals for the protest wore yellow armbands and were damned efficient at keeping us across the street from the restaurant and off the street entirely. We could stand on one corner of the T intersection or the other, but the minute one of us put a toe across the curb to stand on the crosswalk or to stand in the gutter for more room, the yellow armbands would approach and ask us politely, but firmly, to move off the road. There was plenty of room on the Strathcona Park side of the road, but somehow I was across the road on the other corner of the T — the side with the houses, a hedge and some parked cars. It was crowded. The women had instructed the crowd about what was and wasn't going to take place and, like I said, they weren't going to tolerate any nonsense from some young punks who would risk the safety of their kids. Many of them had their children there."

"I've got a bad feeling about this," said Daniella, reaching for the pretzels.

"Well, I didn't at the time, at first. There was one traffic cop directing traffic and making sure that drivers kept moving their cars instead of gawking at the signs and the crowd. He talked on his radio every now and then, and, after one of these chats, he called the women in charge of the yellow armbands over to him. I saw him motion to the crowds on the corners and to the crosswalk. I heard him say something about blocking off the bottom end of the road at the base of the T, so that it didn't matter if they let the crowd stray onto the crosswalk, as long as they didn't come further toward Laurier Avenue than that crosswalk.

"Then I saw the confused look on this woman's face and her half-hearted instructions to the women in the yellow armbands. He obviously only half convinced her that it was a better idea for crowd control. Anyway, in less than two or three minutes, we were blossoming out onto the crosswalk, and now that it was not off limits suddenly everyone wanted a front line position along the crosswalk facing the café. Well the women in yellow armbands stood facing them, making sure they didn't get within six inches of the edge of that crosswalk, so that Laurier Avenue remained uncompromised. My first indication that something was wrong was when I noticed cars still coming up the stem of the T, the street running into Laurier. They hadn't blocked off the bottom end, and now these cars were trapped and busy trying to turn around. Then I saw the Gestapo round the corner a block away in front of the Russian Embassy. The crowd kind of jeered, but damn it, they had riot helmets with visors and plastic riot shields, and those riot batons that look like a peace pipe but are absolutely the scariest and deadliest riot baton in use. I won't bore you with the technique of using them, except to say they swing in a swivel motion from under the forearm and they reach speeds double and triple the speed of an ordinary straight baton. Anyway, they goose-stepped right up to that crosswalk, covering it end-to-end and then some. They turned left on command to face the front row of protesters face-to-face along that crosswalk. And, just like that, the TV cameras were there, shooting that dramatic sight of police in full riot gear facing the protesters, less than a metre between them."

"Holy Christ, they set you up," said Tom, hand buried in that hair again.

"Exactly! There was no good reason for letting us on that crosswalk except if someone wanted dramatic television coverage and a confrontational setting. I was racking my brain as to why the police would do that, when someone next to me said that some protesters had thrown eggs at the Harris limousine the day before in Kingston and this was Harris's way of letting everyone know that he could play rough. Well the women in charge of the yellow armbands was obviously annoyed and felt betrayed. She used her megaphone to warn us to back away and not say or do anything that would provoke the police. 'We have our children here,' she said, 'and we don't need any of this nonsense. Back away and shut up.'

"Already some of the young male teenagers were taunting the Gestapo, because what do you do when someone tries to intimidate you when you're seventeen? The protesters couldn't back up very easily; they were six or seven bodies deep before there was any space to manoeuvre."

Tom leaned in and rested his forearms on the table, "Where were you, Paul. In the front line, I suppose."

"Not on your life, Tom. I could see no earthly good coming out of that front line. I left that for the seventeen-year-olds. Tom, I was scared to death. I'd occasionally imagined myself in a crowd in some kind of protest, but I never could have imagined that gut-wrenching fear that something here was going to snap. I tried to figure out what to do, to do something positive, but, damn it, one person is so small and helpless in that kind of crowd. I was behind this solid wall of protesters, and I noticed how snarled we were getting with the cars behind us trying to turn around. The cars back of the front ones were not giving them much room to manoeuvre. I could see us all being forced back right into this mess of stalled cars, so I decided something could be done about that, and started barking orders to the cars, trying to help them turn around to get out of there. For every one I got turned around another two seemed to show up at the bottom of the street to lock the others in. I was cursing the police for lying to us about blocking off the bottom of that street. And finally I saw that it didn't really matter which of these cars got caught in the panic of our retreat. I wasn't going to get rid of them all.

"As I paused for a helpless minute, I noticed this guy in a very sharp brown suit and dress shoes right beside me, behind the lines like me, staring hard at the line of confrontation. I couldn't help wondering if he were a plainclothes police officer or a secret service agent. So, with all subtlety, I asked him who he was and what he was doing here. 'I'm Russian,' he said, and told me his name. 'I work at the embassy over there, and I just came over to watch,' he says in an unmistakable accent with this odd nervous voice. Then he said something I'll never forget as long as I live. 'I've seen this in Russia,' he said, 'but I never thought I'd see it here.' He shook his head. 'They're going to come at us!' he said.

"Just then, the black limos pulled around the corner in front of the Russian Embassy and onto Laurier. Everyone knew it was Premier Harris, but, in case we had any doubts, the front line of the riot police got a snappy order, at which point they flicked their batons out in front of them in unison and shoved them within inches of the protesters' chests in the front line. At least half of the people up front spoke up angrily, and some of the young guys started taunting them. The woman with the megaphone was talking to us desperately now, but, in my twisting guts, I suddenly knew that the Russian was right. He'd been there.

"A young guy in the front row grabbed a baton that probably was poked into his chest… I can't say for sure… but he pushed the baton back hard at the police officer. All their visors went down like that, not quite in unison, while the officer gave a violent push back to the kid, freeing his baton. Someone screamed. They obviously thought the batons were coming. And that scream was a bit too threatening for all concerned. They started pushing and shoving to get the hell out of there, and in the chaos some were shoved forward. On command the police took one step back and brought their shields around. Then they moved forward, and screams and shouts escalated. Most of the protesters were trying to turn and run, but some poor suckers who were pinned by those shields, started swearing at the police, and I just recall the sounds of sudden fear, escalating voices and straining bodies. I remember knowing in my bones that some of these officers, like the prison guards where I was trained, were high on the adrenalin rush at the moment, knowing they had been given licence for assault."

"Jesus Christ!" Tom said. Then he looked at Daniella and touched his forehead, "Oh, I'm sorry, Daniella, I just…"

"Never mind," she said softly, but firmly. "Those were the exact words I was breathing."

"Well, then I noticed the Russian quite some metres away, walking briskly between the cars into the more ample space of the park. But I had backed off the other direction toward the hedge so I was cut off by the retreating stampede. I had a choice of fleeing over or between parked cars, or jumping a formidable hedge, or turning around to face the riot shields and batons."

"You didn't!" Daniella said.

"I didn't. I dove over the hedge into the yard," I laughed.

"Good man," Charles's fist touched the table lightly.

"Scratched up my arms and body some, but protected my face somehow. I couldn't imagine them coming over that hedge in riot gear. I was surprised that I seemed to be the only one taking this escape route, but, sure enough, someone tried to follow my lead, and this middle aged woman, maybe not quite middle-aged, got halfway across the hedge and got stuck. It was fairly high — about shoulder height, you see — and quite dense. She looked at me with this sickening look in her eyes. I realized my eyes probably looked the same. I told her to give me her hand and I tried to pull her over, but too much of her weight was still not on top of the hedge, and she was scream-ing, either in fear or in pain. I told her to roll onto her back and pull her legs up if she could. She finally managed it, and I helped pull her over. She was shaking badly and had blood on her face from a bad scratch. But she just wanted to find her way out the back of that yard. We found a gate that we could get through in the back and both of us were shaking and talking, incoherently probably. Just sharing the anger, you know. Not to mention the fear and the indignity of the whole mess. Just raging at the senselessness of the police.

"She wouldn't let me tend to her bleeding scratch. I guess she was in shock. We were finally silent when we got a block away, stopping now and then to see what we could hear or see. We were assuring each other that there was nothing more anyone could do back there in that mess. She wondered what happened to the kids, and I told her that the parents with kids had backed out of the line before the police advanced. I had to believe that all of them did that. But I had some doubts. Finally I asked her if she had some place to go — the hospital perhaps, and if I could walk her there. She seemed offended that I would suggest the hospital. I told her that the scratch needed some serious attention. 'I'll fix it when I get home,' she said. I asked if I could walk her home, because she was still shaking. So was I, for that matter. She just shook her head as if she were angry at me and said that she needed to be alone and that she'd be okay. She thanked me again for helping her. Then she assured me that she wasn't afraid of me walking her home. She just needed some space to come down a bit, alone. I must have told her that I was at the convention centre, because she told me that I could go back to the convention because she'd be okay.

"I've even forgotten her name now. Though it always seems like it's right on the edge of my memory. I finally realized as we separated that she was acting a lot like a woman who had just been raped or sexually assaulted. Then I realized that I felt somewhat the same way. Humiliated to the very core. They had used terror and force on us and both of us were old enough to know better than to resist, yet both of us were probably humiliated that we didn't have the satisfaction of striking back. Humiliated that we didn't stick around for more blood and concussions. It didn't make sense, but I'm sure we both fantasized about hurting the police in some way, but how do you hurt a damned robot in riot gear, and how would that help the world anyway? You know what I mean?" I paused for a breath.

There was a moment of silence till Sammy reached for his beer and Daniella kind of sighed, "Jeez, Paul, I don't think we can possibly know what you were feeling. But I sure as heck appreciate you sharing the story." She gave me a tentative smile, which I returned.

"That's for sure, brother," Charles said.

Cam held up a warning finger, "I've a feeling, Daniella, that Saint Paul's sermon here is aimed directly at someone sitting close to him. So when storm troopers appear — three themes — head for the hills, duck and cover, and no sticking flowers in their gun barrels."

"I'm staying clear of the riot police, believe me. Green Zones. No Red Zones."

"Your grandfather will be proud of you," Charles smiled. "Have you told him yet?"

"Oh yes, and that was his advice. Stick to the Green Zones. Red Zones are for trouble. He reminded me that, in spite of all the militancy of the Trekkers, they were taught to be non-violent."

"Just watch for the Russians," Cam said, "and when they leave the scene, follow them. They'll know when to leave."

17

THE RIGHT REVEREND SAMUEL EAST

DOC ON THE ATTEMPT TO FINISH THE TREK

I PHONED DANIELLA TUESDAY MORNING to ask her if she minded picking me up on her way to the Greyhound depot to welcome Doc. He had
insisted on taking a bus through Prince George, refusing to let Daniella
come for him due to the seven hours each way. Flight connections between
Prince George and Grande Prairie were next to impossible, involving stops
in both Vancouver and Edmonton, and he hated airports. When we finally
saw him carefully stepping off the bus, I saw that he no longer stood quite as
straight and that he had lost a lot of weight. There were careful hugs, slow
movements and lots of catching up over supper.

Later, as the three of us entered BJ's through the front lounge area, the
only two waitresses on shift who were still with BJ's from the last time Doc
visited stopped what they were doing and came up to greet him nodding
their heads and shaking his hand. I noticed concern in some of their eyes.
The Tuesday Club members were all there to welcome us, pride on their
faces. There was a bit of a lull as some customers tried to figure out who
this ancient mariner could be. We walked slowly toward the bar and took
our usual right turn; some ten people disappeared through that portal into
the relatively empty south-west corner. A couple of guys shooting pool shut
down their game quickly when they noticed a lectern being set up for this
elderly patriarch with files full of notes. They discreetly exited to the lounge
for a beer.

Daniella introduced her grandfather with what I suspected were tears
glistening in her fierce and pride-filled eyes. She finished with the simple
words, "He promised to come back to finish what he started. And he did."

We clapped and Sammy whistled as Doc eased his way to the pulpit.
The waitresses took orders quickly, bringing Doc a glass of ice water and a
pot of tea. Finally Doc straightened up a bit with his hands on both sides of
the lectern. He had decided to stand as long as he could. He surveyed us all
for a few seconds.

"I can see some of you doubted my return," he began, holding back a
smile in response to our nervous laughter. He continued with the formalities,
the sincere thanks and a sentence or two of introduction.

Then he got down to business. "I believe I left us all hanging in the nation's Parliament in Ottawa last time, as our delegation got the boot from Bennett's cabinet room, after our leader, Slim Evans, called the Prime Minister a liar. We had another day, compliments of the PM, before boarding the train back to Regina. So Evans and the rest of us attended a mass meeting at the Rialto Theatre in Ottawa on Sunday, before heading back west that same night. I remember Evans powerfully condemning the Prime Minister for refusing to negotiate any of the demands and for making no counter offer of assistance at all. We had arranged for meetings at stops in Sudbury, Port Arthur (Thunder Bay, I guess it's called now), Winnipeg, naturally, and Brandon. Evans spoke at all the meetings; he was galvanized, to say the least, by his confrontation with Bennett. At Sudbury he told a crowd that the arrogance and veiled threats from the Prime Minister had convinced him that inviting a delegation to Ottawa was indeed a ruse to buy time to send more police and militia to Regina in preparation to 'smash the Trek in a welter of blood.' The *Winnipeg Tribune* and the national media distorted that statement, suggesting that Evans had threatened 'blood in the streets' of Regina should they try to stop us. So in Winnipeg Evans gave another powerful speech, overshadowing even Tim Buck, who was also there on stage to express his support for broadening the strike to a national movement. But Evans was careful to state forcefully this time that we must go to Ottawa in an organized and disciplined manner.

"'If you don't want to go that way,' he told the crowd, 'you had better stay at home.' The press, however, chose to ignore this and to emphasize that he appeared with Tim Buck and that he proudly admitted that he was a member of the Communist Party.

"When we reached Brandon, we got a telegram from George Black, informing us of the federal government's plan for us. It was clever and hardnosed. It involved forcing us into a concentration camp between Craven and Lumsden, under the authority of the Dominion Department of Labour. They didn't call it a concentration camp, of course, and they were careful not to leave it with the Department of Defence for the sake of public relations and media coverage. What they didn't tell the press was that this had been a suggestion by RCMP Assistant Commissioner Wood, who had actually used the term 'concentration camp' in describing his solution to his superior, Commissioner MacBrien in Ottawa. Remember, this was two years after Hitler had taken power in Germany and had begun to use concentration camps for Jews, union leaders and any leftists who opposed him. So concentration camps were beginning to be a human rights issue throughout the world, yet Wood was willing to use them as his solution to the Trek. Commissioner MacBrien was just as bad in his communications, suggesting that Wood could use Section 98 to arrest the Trekkers if they tried to move east from Regina, resisting Wood's orders. That doesn't say much for his grasp of the law.

"But Wood acted very quickly. He found a site for the proposed camp the same day that the Department of Labour got authority to set it up. That was on Monday while we were on the train across northern Ontario. On Tuesday the Regina representative of the Department of Labour, C.P. Burgess, issued the ultimatum to the strikers that they would register for transportation to the Lumsden camp or else they would not get further food vouchers, starting Wednesday after breakfast. It turns out that this was also recommended by Wood. He had argued that we were getting our orders from the 'Communist Bureau of Canada,' though there was no such bureau and clearly our decisions were made by democratic vote. The next day he claimed that Tim Buck was in town secretly, not appearing in public. Buck certainly didn't contact us if he was.

"Anyway, the feds' ultimatum also promised that the camp was temporary and that we would be processed and sent home sometime in the future. This Burgess character was in charge of building the concentration camp and registering the future victims. He set up a registration booth right in the Grain Show building on the Exhibition Grounds where we were bunking. In the three or four days that it operated, that registration booth was mighty lonely. Even when they cut off our food supply, no more than twenty-five of the 2500 Trekkers registered to go to Lumsden. Do you know that relief camp workers from Dundern who failed to join us in Regina were forced to build that camp, to dig the latrines? So here they were, like slave labour, building a prison for their buddies who chose the Trek rather than twenty-cents-a-day slave wages? Kind of ironic when you think about it. Reminds one a bit of Auschwitz.

"So when our delegation got back to Regina, early Wednesday morning, that's what we were faced with. Most of the boys marched the mile or so to the train station to greet us and to hear a preliminary report from Slim on the Prime Minister's response, though they'd already read about it in the papers. It was great to see over 1500 Trekkers out to greet us that early in the morning. George Black had taken to leaving one division behind at camp at all times for security reasons, since more and more police and troops seemed to be converging on Regina while we were gone. After Slim's brief address from the bumper of a taxi at the train station, we marched back to get our breakfast vouchers, the last meal ticket to be issued, and we held a Strike Committee meeting to discuss our predicament."

Doc hesitated, reaching for a glass of water, while I glanced across to Cam's table, where even Sammy was leaning forward with a concerned look.

"Evans spent most of that day," Doc continued, "trying to get Premier Gardiner to guarantee relief, protection from police and aid in leaving the province. Gardiner made excuses on the last two requests, saying that they were beyond his authority, but suggested that, if we registered as transients with the City of Regina, the province would pay the bill for our food on the City's behalf. He sent us to the Mayor and the Mayor sent us back saying he needed an order. They sent our delegation back and forth till Evans asked the Mayor to speak directly to the Premier. Not even that could cure this buckpassing. After the Premier had a visit from Colonel Wood of the RCMP, it seemed he had to contact Ottawa before issuing money or relief to feed the men. Slim laughed at him.

"'You're telling me,' Slim said, 'that we don't already know that Bennett is going to say "send them to Lumsden where they will be fed and cared for?"'"

"Still Gardiner wouldn't do anything without receiving a wire from Bennett.

"'Why did you keep us running between the city and the Legislature all day,' Slim asked Premier Gardiner, 'if this was your answer?' He left in disgust and went to plan the evening rally.

"Interestingly enough, the Reverend Sam East had been at the side of Evans all through this. Apparently, he had become chief spokesperson and activist for the Citizens' Emergency Committee. Now Matt Shaw probably mentioned Sam East in his presentations. He got to know him better than the rest of us since he travelled to Toronto with him. East was a Methodist minister who was without a church at the time. So I guess he had more time for that greater congregation: the unemployed and the Depression victims in Regina. And, by God, he took that congregation as his own and went about representing and ministering to them as if he were being paid full salary to do it.

"So there he was those next crucial days, at Slim's side, representing the Citizens' Emergency Committee, the core of citizens' support in Regina. And he was ready at all times to berate the Premier, the Mayor, the councillors, and any officials that came in his path for not recognizing the moral high ground, urging them to do their duty in representing Canadians, in dealing with the devastation of the Depression. He was simply amazing; one couldn't help but feel that he had been waiting his whole life for a moment such as this.

"Within no time Evans started bouncing ideas off Sam for solutions to our quandary. That was unusual because normally Slim needed to have seen a man prove himself before he'd confide in him. Slim asked the Reverend whether he thought they could charter some CPR passenger cars at excursion rates to take the boys into Manitoba. Immediately Sam East got on the phone to find out the rates, suggesting to the CPR officials that he was interested in a church outing or something like that. Perhaps he really believed we were his congregation. Of course later when the CPR found out that it was for the Trekkers they told us clearly that an order had gone out to all transportation companies not to move the Trekkers. That didn't surprise us.

"Anyway, East was ready and able to act. He spoke that night at the public rally where we had about 6000 people. He was an inspiring orator, who had a history of conflict with his more conservative colleagues in the Methodist Church. I remember reading some of his testimony from the Regina Riot Commission in the Saskatchewan Archives. Apparently he had been investigated, wiretapped and spied on by the RCMP because of his willingness to bring in J.S. Woodsworth to talk about the Winnipeg General Strike. East was a bit older than the rest of us, probably early fifties, so he remembered the RCMP repression following the Winnipeg Strike in 1919. He talked about some Methodist ministers being blackballed unofficially in some Methodist conferences because of their support for Woodsworth and for the 1919 Strike. I don't doubt he was one of them. That would explain his absolute fearlessness in the face of police harassment."

Doc shifted his weight from one hip to the other, his hands on both sides of the lectern. His balance didn't seem as steady. Daniella started rising out of her chair, but Doc kept on talking, so she sat back and relaxed again.

"Reverend East seemed to believe that a thorough application of New Testament teaching would lead to a utopian state similar to communism: 'From each according to his ability to each according to his need,' he'd say, and then he'd cite the early church's practice of holding property in common. Well, I don't know much about theology, but that sounds like enough to get anyone in trouble with his employer.

"So while the Reverend Sam East's speech soared and inspired us all to a better world, Slim Evans focused his speech on the problem at hand. He repeated his statement in Sudbury that the Prime Minister seemed prepared to smash the strike by force in a welter of blood, so that we'd be foolish to try to force the issue by taking a train. He therefore called for folks to volunteer trucks and vehicles for a massive convoy to take the Trekkers into Manitoba. He gave out the phone number of our office at the Unity Centre and suggested that folks contact us there if they could help us out. He also enjoyed working the audience, getting them to respond to Bennett's judgement that relief camp conditions were adequate, getting them to respond to Bennett's decision to starve us into submission.

"Well, by late morning the press was carrying stories that an order-in-council had been passed by the cabinet forbidding citizens to give any aid to the Trekkers. Actually the alleged order wasn't really an order-in-council but an order from the RCMP Commissioner interpreted by Colonel Wood. The original only mentioned a ban on aiding the Trekkers to move east, but the press reported it as though it were a ban on any aid at all, and that scared a lot of Regina citizens into withdrawing from any public shows of support. But not the Reverend Sam East. He announced in a public speech that the order-in-council was invalid and that people should ignore it. Apparently an order-in-council could not be passed while Parliament was sitting.

"So all of Thursday was spent on the phones trying to get the necessary trucks together to transport the men, but it became quite apparent that the public believed Colonel Wood and the papers that aiding the Trekkers was illegal. Apparently the Mayor in his one moment of courage and sanity in the whole affair refused to publicly broadcast or post Colonel Wood's decree that it was illegal to aid Trekkers leaving Regina. I guess, he didn't believe that such a draconian law could possibly be legal. Nevertheless, all of Regina and Canada heard it from inaccurate and misleading media reports and were led to believe that any aid whatsoever was illegal.

"So only one truck and three automobiles could be mustered; obviously there was not going to be a miraculous exodus from Regina. Slim had the sense to go to the Highways Department and obtain permits for transporting people in trucks, so we decided that we should at least test the legality of all these permits against the draconian measures announced in the press, to see if the police were actually going to restrict freedom of movement without any reasonable grounds. So Jack Cosgrove and the Reverend Sam East volunteered to drive two of the vehicles to lead a small body of strikers east, just those we could crowd into the one truck and into the two cars that were finally chosen to go.

"Well, hell, they got to the Imperial Oil Station on the outskirts of Regina before they were ordered to stop by an army of fifty mounted RCMP brandishing weapons. There were more Mounties on foot in full riot gear as well. There was a crowd of citizens that had come along to the outskirts on bikes and on foot; they got to see the show that followed. At first, no one was arrested, because they all obeyed the order to stop. The Reverend Sam East presented his permit to transport passengers and the RCMP looked at it and gave it back. So people just milled around. The police didn't seem to know what to do. It turns out from evidence later that Wood wasn't sure that he had any real law under which he could lay charges or seize the vehicles, so he had wired the commissioner — get this — 'requesting necessary government action immediately to declare camp strikers in Saskatchewan an unlawful association within the meaning of Section 98 in order that we may legally seize trucks, cars, property, and control actions and destinations of strikers. Could such strikers be held in Craven Camp under escort?' he asks, and continues with 'Advise if prosecutions should be instituted.'

"Can you believe this? Relief camp Trekkers fall under Section 98? Part of the blame for Wood's clearly illegal action was that his boss, the RCMP Commissioner in Ottawa, had given him some really sloppy orders, without proper legal foundation. So Wood was quite willing to arrest and seize property; he just wanted to know what he was going to put on the paper work.

So he was giving his boss some suggestions, you see.

"The wife of the owner of the truck sat with her husband, crying, while the Reverend Sam East consoled her with his assurance that the police had nothing to charge them with, that they had done nothing wrong. He probably even told her that she had acted as a good Christian should. We only know part of what happened from his testimony at the Regina Riot Commission and much later reports from some of those that were there.

"Apparently one of the drivers asked if they should turn around and go back to the stadium. The RCMP said that if they moved they'd be arrested. East phoned Evans and explained their crazy situation. Evans told him to do exactly what the police told them to do. In the meantime, in the dark, and with the crowd growing rather than dwindling, one of the cars turned out to be empty. Apparently the driver and the Trekkers slipped out the doors into the crowd before the Mounties realized that they had no one to arrest in that vehicle. Finally, the RCMP told Mr. Hallabard, the owner and driver of the truck, that he could turn around slowly and follow the escort vehicle. As soon as he started it and put it in gear to move forward, another officer stepped forward and told him he was under arrest. Then another officer told him again to follow the escorting vehicle back towards town.

"Well, later evidence showed that the head of the RCMP, Commissioner MacBrien, had sent a vague and misleading answer to Wood stating that the 'government is taking action under *Relief Measures Act* declaring national emergency so as to maintain peace, order and good government. This will protect you against such actions and seizures which you consider it necessary to take…' The fact is that no such action was taken by Ottawa, though they were contemplating it. The Commissioner was in fact encouraging Wood to follow through on illegal seizures and arrests, since the drivers had complied with all orders from the police. Wood, of course, realized this, being the brighter of the two, but he arrested East, Cosgrove, Edwards and Bell. The other Trekkers vanished into the crowd. Hallabard and Lennox, the two owners of the vehicles, were arrested also. They were taken first to the downtown station, and then to the RCMP Training Academy, where they were held prisoner in the horse stable. East described it as a huge riding compound with heavily armed Mounties all around them as if they were expecting a herd of unruly colts. The Reverend East protested the conditions, the floor being wet, etcetera, and he did it with such authority and confidence that they moved the prisoners into the Academy's library. East grabbed one of the chairs that the guards had brought for their own convenience, and of course the guard didn't challenge him. And that is exactly what I'm going to have to do: grab a chair, because…"

Daniella was up and beside him quick as a cat, holding the chair for him, repositioning the lectern to the stool beside him, moving the water closer.

I was surprised at her agility and grace. On cue, the waitresses descended, collecting empties and replacing them with another round for Cam, Tom and Sammy. And peanuts and pretzels for all. We waved off the drinks at our table, but the other waitress brought more ice water and replenished the teapot with hot water. Doc smiled, thanking Daniella and the waitresses; he was ready to continue.

"Sam East's wife — now wouldn't you like to meet the woman married to this guy? — his wife apparently was phoning the police checking into the status of her husband's arrest; she was finally told that he was free to go because they weren't charging him. So she phoned Sam to tell him, but Sam seemed to be having so much fun that he decided to stay."

Now that Doc was seated, we felt more comfortable, laughing and chuckling at his humour.

"To be fair, he probably felt responsible for Mr. Hallabard, and even more for his distraught wife, who felt obligated to stay with her husband. Ironically, eventually someone came around to inform East that he was charged after all, with 'acting contrary to law, order, and good government.' Wonder where they dug that one up? Probably thought they better find something for the books or they'd get in trouble for holding East overnight. Finally the order came that the Reverend East was released. Charges dropped. And there was a car waiting to take him home. Apparently his wife was preventing several officers from getting their work done and Wood wasn't getting any sleep worrying about lawsuits from the Reverend East, who he knew was adept at reading the law books and couldn't be intimidated or BSed, if you know what I mean.

"Well, to make a long story shorter, the Reverend East just wouldn't quit. The more ironclad the clampdown, the louder the man spoke up. When the *Regina Leader-Post* finally published the actual text of the rumoured order-in-council, the nefarious threat to the citizens of Regina, Sam East declares in a prophet-like voice to a public meeting on Saturday, that the order-in-council from Ottawa is null and void because Parliament is sitting and they're not allowed to pass orders-in-council while Parliament is in session. He points to chapter and verse. Turns out that the so called order-in-council was a hoax perpetrated by Colonel Wood.

"But in the meantime Sam East implores the God-fearing citizens of Regina to step forward in good conscience to feed the Trekkers, quoting from scripture, *I was hungry and ye gave me food. I was naked and ye clothed me. In prison and ye visited me.* He told them to come out to Wascana Park and provide the boys with food, family nurture and moral support. The man was a singular menace to fascism. Even the most hardened agnostics among us, who were sceptical of his motivation, were eventually won over. I know, because I was one of them.

"And you know what? The people of Regina responded, came out to Wascana Park on Sunday and threw the boys a picnic. Wasn't as big as their first one for us, but it was a big victory of common decency over fascist intimidation, and we won't forget the people of Regina for the way they stood by us. They stood by us before July First, on July First and after July First.

"The boys were impressed enough with the Reverend Sam East that they voted for him, and for Matt Shaw, to represent us at Maple Leaf Gardens in Toronto, where the Workers Unity League and other progressive groups were sponsoring a mass rally in support of the Trekkers. Now there were lots of popular Trekkers and fine leaders among them who were nominated to fill those two slots, and no one was surprised that Matt Shaw would be elected, since we knew he was one of our best speakers and communicators with the press, but for the boys to elect an outsider like Sam East to ride the cushions to Toronto, well, that was something. I doubt they could have given him a better thank you. So while we were battling the Cossacks on Market Square in Regina, Sam East and Matt Shaw were riding the cushions to Toronto, missing all the fun. But I tell you what. We knew damned well that our fight wasn't limited to Regina.

"I've always thought that if there were more men of the cloth like Samuel East, the churches might just fill up again. But I think the Reverend Sam East is what they call an anomaly, not your average preacher, Daniella here being the other exception of course. And that's about all I got to say for tonight folks."

He reached for his tea cup and took a sip. The applause was sudden and sustained, and the outside lounge was quiet even after we sat down again.

Daniella stepped up behind the pulpit and cleared her throat. "Well Doc," she said, "Samuel East is an inspiration to this clergywoman, and so are you. Folks, for those of you there who are new to this group, he's going to be back here next Tuesday night to tell us the story of the July 1st, 1935, Regina Riot. This is sort of the climax of a four-year story that's been happening at BJ's. You've probably heard the rumours. You all feel free to invite friends, but, if you want to hear the earlier chapters of this story, you need to get a CD from Cam here, so that the final chapter will make more sense when you hear it live next Tuesday. Now my friends here are warning me to keep an eye on the police when I go to Quebec City in a couple of weeks to the Summit of Americas. But Doc's story of Sam East has inspired me to look right past the police. He almost makes me want to join the Methodists."

"Hey," Charles said, "any denomination that could spawn J.S. Woodsworth, Tommy Douglas and Samuel East has got to be doing something right... or maybe something left."

I smiled, "Well, I suspect that particular genetic code of the radical Methodists has mutated into the genes that created this particular United

239

Church Minister." I put my hand on Daniella's shoulder for a second.

She chuckled, "Not the Presbyterian or Congregational genes, eh?"

"What the hell are you two going on about?" Sammy was shaking his head.

"History, Sammy. Church history in this case. It's mostly irrelevant to what's happening these days," Daniella said.

"History of churches, eh? Remind me to skip that session." Sammy grinned at us and was one of the first to shake Doc's hand. "Can I buy you a beer, Doc?"

"I just might take you up on that, Sam," Doc smiled up at him.

18

DOMINION DAY FIREWORKS, REGINA, 1935

DOC ON REGINA'S POLICE RIOT

A S WE PULLED UP TO BJ's Bar and Cue Club, knowing it was probably Doc's last session here, I couldn't help noticing the new stylish brick façade, where there had been unfinished plywood for so many years. Only if you parked around back would you see the aluminium siding adjoining the main stucco siding, where our BJ's History Club corner had been patched on to the south side of the stage in years gone by. I couldn't help thinking that the Tuesday Club had added some class to this old tavern. But certainly not from the profits from our tables.

When we walked Doc slowly up the entrance aisle of the main lounge area, unlike the previous week, everyone seemed to know what was happening and who the ancient mariner was. People we never talked to before greeted Doc and welcomed him to BJ's. Everyone had heard that this was the last of the eyewitnesses to something or other. We waved to the bar staff and they nodded as if we were the owners. Then we walked Doc through the portal one last time. There were seven guests — the most in Club history — and all were acquaintances of Cam and Tom. The guests all sat at two larger tables between our group and the bathroom toward the exit to the main bar. Cam told me that two of them had bought the CDs that he had burned for them.

Daniella's introduction was slow because she paused to control her voice and the emotions welling up again. Charles closed his eyes as if he were praying, and I guess I was kind of choked up myself, not from anything she said but just from the reaction of two close friends. Finally, Doc was behind the pulpit and holding on to straighten up that frail and fading frame one more time, as the applause filled the room. Daniella sat down close beside me with Charles across the table, closer to Cam, Tom and Sammy's table.

Doc straightened a pile of notes and clippings. "Well folks, I'm not sure where to begin, except that I promised Paul I'd cover the events of Dominion Day 1935 and Regina's Market Square that evening. I have a great need to thank Paul and Daniella, but maybe I'll save that for the end… if there can ever be such a thing as an end to this.

"So I'll try to summarize what I know first-hand, and what I've learned since from other sources. This much is certain — that from the time our delegation returned from Ottawa, the Strike Committee for the Trek knew we were in a tough situation. It appeared to us that martial law had been declared, from what we had read in the papers and what we had experienced with the arbitrary arrests of our people trying to travel east in private vehicles. In reality, we found out months later through the Regina Riot Commission that in fact no order-in-council existed and that Assistant Commissioner Wood, head of the RCMP in western Canada, merely had orders to prevent any Trekkers from moving east, through arrest and seizures of property if necessary, and that aiding and abetting the strikers could perhaps be prosecuted under Section 98, which contained some vague references to aiding or renting facilities to unlawful organizations.

"Commissioner MacBrien's orders were vague and sweeping, including the arrest of the leaders of the Trek and anyone else Wood thought necessary under Section 98. Colonel Wood must have realized that he had been given a blank cheque to do whatever the hell he wished and that MacBrien and Bennett were prepared to back him up. So he fabricated this thing about an order-in-council, and the western Canadian media bought it without checking it out, as everybody out west thought that Regina was under martial law. Under cross-examination at the Riot Commission hearings, he causally referred to his fabrication by saying 'what I called the order-in-council was the orders I received from Commissioner MacBrien.' And what do you know, the polite lawyers let him get away with that.

"Interestingly enough, Saskatchewan's Attorney General, T.C. Davis, was supposed to have authority over the RCMP in Saskatchewan, but the RCMP Commissioner MacBrien usurped that authority, ignoring the federal-provincial agreement. That was already clear two weeks earlier. Months later, of course, we learned that during this time Attorney General Davis still felt some responsibility for police actions in his province. So he wired Hugh Guthrie, Minister of Justice in Ottawa, requesting clarification on the orders. Let me read the wires to you.

Regina, June 28, 1935. I am given to understand instructions have been issued from Ottawa to police officers here requiring them to prevent movement of any marchers by any means from this city and furthermore preventing any person from rendering assistance whatsoever by way of food or otherwise while in the city. I would be very grateful if you would send me by wire at once information with respect to any order so given, and furthermore advise me under what authority, act, or Order in Council you are proceeding in issuing such orders, in the event of the same having been issued, as I am unable to find any legal authority under which such orders could be issued.

"Then he inquired about arrests or charges already laid against the 'Eastward-with-Reverend-East Cavalcade' on a previous night. This was signed, T.C. Davis, Attorney General of Saskatchewan. So you see, not everyone was fooled. The Justice Minister finally tried to clarify it on June 29 after repeated wires by Davis focusing on the existence of an order-in-council. Here are parts of two replies: *No Order in Council of any kind has been passed.* And the second on the same day: *No instructions have been issued to prevent persons rendering assistance by way of food or otherwise,* signed Hugh Guthrie, Federal Justice Minister. One can see Truth on the sacrificial altar of expedience when it comes to dealing with people they don't like, don't understand or don't wish to see in Ottawa.

"But despite Colonel Wood's blank cheque to arrest anyone he saw fit to detain, it also became apparent during the Commission hearings that Wood knew there wasn't sufficient evidence in Regina to charge the men with much of anything, so he was busily collecting evidence in Vancouver, Edmonton and elsewhere. He had the offices of the Workers Unity League and the Relief Camp Workers Union raided in Vancouver, and the infamous Sergeant Leopold — who was the undercover officer instrumental in fabricating enough evidence to incarcerate Tim Buck, Tom MacEwan and company in 1931 — this same Leopold was in charge of bringing in enough evidence to Wood for the arrests of Evans, Black, Cosgrove, Shaw, Tony Martin, Paddy O'Neal, Jerry Winters and others. Wood had twelve on his list and I think when the evidence arrived on July First his lawyers felt he only had sufficient evidence for warrants for seven of them, all under Section 98.

"We knew none of this of course, so the Strike Committee was faced with the impossible task of keeping the Trek together when our treasury had run dry on Saturday, because food vouchers were no longer provided by the provincial government or by the city of Regina, so our funds were feeding the boys until they ran out. 'Surrender to Lumsden Camp internment or starve' was the ultimatum from Commissioner Wood. He was turning out to be quite a law unto himself, since he had been freed from his duty to obey the Saskatchewan Premier and the Saskatchewan Attorney General. Thankfully, the Regina citizens had responded with a picnic lunch for us on Sunday, but we couldn't organize that every day during the working week. Many of the citizens were afraid to contribute money or aid, despite the Reverend Sam East's crusade to challenge the truth or legality of any order-in-council. Most everyone other than East, including the Trek leadership, believed that the order was real, because we saw Colonel Wood as having all the force and will to act on the reported order-in-council. The Trekkers had maintained solidarity by refusing the Lumsden Camp, where they would have arrested the leadership anyway, interrogated whomever they pleased and generally humiliated us on the assumption that it was their right to do so. Only about twenty-five Trekkers registered to go to Lumsden and, to our knowledge, only about a dozen actually went. This happened despite the RCMP and the Department of Labour publicizing the fact that it was no longer necessary to register, that anyone could show up at Lumsden or ask for assistance from the police or other officials privately and they would be taken care of.

"Evans had been working on establishing our own camp outside the city limits, but we finally gave up on that and decided to negotiate a return to Vancouver on our own terms, as a united body of Trekkers. Some of us thought we would be more useful now helping the longshoremen, who were still trying to hang on to a viciously battered strike on the docks of Vancouver. So that's what we were doing Dominion Day while Colonel Wood got his arrest warrants in order; we were negotiating with Premier Jimmy Gardiner to send us back home on the cushions, and we finally agreed to allow anyone who wanted to go to homes somewhere other than Vancouver to accept one-way tickets to those destinations. The final deal included the right of each Trekker to go at least as far as the centre from where he had originally joined the strike. The deal was struck and Evans was prepared to announce the details of the deal to end the Trek at the public meeting at Market Square at 8 p.m. that evening.

"Actually Evans and a Strike Committee delegation had met with Burgess, representing the federal Department of Labour, and a stenographer for the RCMP at a 10 a.m. meeting, and again at 2:30 p.m. with Colonel Wood and Inspector Mortimer of the RCMP. The identical proposals that were accepted later that afternoon by the Saskatchewan Premier were rejected rudely by Colonel Wood, who said that we would 'take Lumsden or take the consequences,' and that the strikers just wanted to go back to cause trouble in the longshoremen's strike in Vancouver.

"Evans forcefully told Wood that he was determined to prevent any physical confrontation between police or armed forces and the relief camp workers. He even offered himself as the exception to immunity from arrest, in effect telling Wood to arrest him and let the others go home on the cushions. The federal plan was to send us home on the cushions anyway, once they had arrested the leaders. Here's Colonel Wood sitting with warrants ready to be executed, for Arthur and some of the others there at the table, just awaiting final signature, yet pretending to negotiate in good faith.

"Anyway, Evans and the delegation told Premier Gardiner and several of his cabinet at their 5 p.m. meeting what Colonel Wood had said. Gardiner and company were obviously annoyed with Wood and Burgess, and resolved to end this thing at provincial expense. So the tentative deal was struck and we were on our way home, except for the plans the RCMP had for us that evening. Wood claimed under oath that the warrants were signed by the magistrate at 6 p.m. just two hours before the public meeting, but the arrest warrants were ready and certified by his legal counsel already that morning. Colonel Wood admitted under oath to making the decision to arrest the leaders of the Trek at the public meeting at Market Square. He obviously had the police operation planned by this time. So the Dominion Day fireworks were destined to be a bit different this year, with audience participation, shall we say."

The audience laughed, anticipating the fireworks to come, as everyone hung on Doc's every word. My students were rarely this attentive. Daniella got up and quietly asked him if he would like to sit down while he spoke, but Doc waved her off saying he was fine.

"Of course no one knew of the plans for that evening," Doc continued, "except the RCMP commanders perhaps. The public meeting began about 8 p.m. in Market Square in downtown Regina. We'd had other public meetings in the Square before. Our Wednesday night meeting, the day our delegation returned, was held there, for example."

"Doc?" I said, "Would you mind describing Market Square for those who have never been there — what it was like back then, I guess, is the question."

Doc nodded at me. "Sure. Market Square is a full city block between 10th Avenue on the north and 11th Avenue on the south. Eleventh Avenue could be considered the downtown main street today. And back then, too, I suppose. Tenth Avenue is now merged with Saskatchewan Drive, I believe, these days, just south of the rail yards. But some of the original buildings still surround this block, especially on Halifax Street — the eastern boundary of the Square. The old fire hall is still there right on the south end of the Square facing 11th Avenue. Beautiful building. On the south-east corner of the Square facing Halifax Street is the city police garages and what used to be the city police station and their holding cells. We didn't know it, but the entire city police force was assembled in there, about forty-five or fifty, I believe. That place is still there, slightly expanded now, but I've seen their old jail cells still there. To the north of these two buildings, the Square was mostly just an empty dirt and cinder lot, I'd say something over a hundred yards north and south behind the fire hall, and maybe not quite a hundred yards east and west. It was used for a farmers' market on weekends and some of the stalls were hardly shut down by the time our meeting started. There was a city weigh scale on the west side of the Square just off Osler Street, the western boundary of the Square. It was toward the south-west end of this relatively vacant area, across the street from the Regina Hotel, so we had a couple of flatbed trucks together near the scales to act as a stage, just a few yards north-east of the scales, into the Square, so that we could run power from the scales, and the crowd would surround the stage on three sides, north, south, and east, but mainly north and east I would say. The stage was only about thirty yards north of the back wall of the fire hall. Most of that whole area where the crowd stood is now covered by a newer Regina city police building today. They built it right over the bloodstained scene of the police assault. They've even got a little historical sign at the front entrance, facing

Osler, mentioning the Trek and the 'Regina Riot,' as they call it. For anyone that was actually there on the Square that evening, the words 'Regina Riot' are a mite provocative, but I'll get to that.

"So anyway, estimates range between two and three thousand people in attendance that evening, not quite as large as the Wednesday night meeting, because no one knew that we were announcing the disbanding of the Trek. It had been advertised as a public show of support for the strikers. Only between 200 and 300 Trekkers were reported to be in that crowd. I frankly think it was less than 200. Some of the Trekkers at the meeting estimated that there were not a whole lot more than fifty who were actually there to start with when the police charged us. There were probably another hundred or so at the downtown cafés and coffee-shops who came on the scene later. The other 2000 or so Trekkers were either at the baseball game that we'd been invited to or at their quarters at the Exhibition Grounds. Already, word was out in the ranks about the probability of an agreement to disband, and the meeting was seen as a last chance to ask for funds, food and supplies, and to inform the citizens of our agreement and the reasons for it — also, to thank them for their wonderful support over the past two weeks or so.

"Since the Reverend Sam East and Matt Shaw had just left on the train to Toronto, the Citizens' Emergency Committee was represented by a guy called Toothill from the CCF. As the lead speaker, he spoke for maybe fifteen minutes. During his speech several of the Trekkers and citizens noted three large moving vans pull up, one just north and west of the stage on Osler Street, one on the north end of the Square on 10th Avenue, more to the north-east end, as I remember, and another moving van on Halifax Street directly east of the main crowd. One of the Trekkers came to the stage and informed Slim Evans that the vans were filled with Mounties. A Regina citizen passed a note up to George Black informing him of the same thing. Evans says Black asked him if they should inform the crowd, but Evans said, 'No, it'd just cause a stampede. Besides, we have nothing to worry about. It's a peaceful meeting.' Evans was to be the main speaker, and it must have been hard to imagine that anything could happen now that they'd agreed to go home peacefully."

Doc stopped for a drink and scanned the audience for a couple of seconds, "Are you ready for this now?" We all giggled nervously, glancing at each other.

Doc appeared to be ready for the riot one more time. "Well Gerry Winters — Tellier was his real name — got up to give a pitch so that we could pass the hats and collect a little travel money. He'd barely got started when a shrill whistle blew and out of the back doors of the police garages the city police charged, four abreast, yelling like banshees, clubs raised in front of them. They headed west — north-west from their building — straight into the heart of the crowd. They weren't even aimed at the stage directly, so it was obvious they weren't coming just to arrest someone. People started screaming, 'police! police!'

"Evans said that he noticed the RCMP unloading from the vans as well, so he looked over his shoulder at Inspector Mortimer who had negotiated with him just a few hours earlier. He had noticed him standing there with a number of plain-clothes officers earlier. Sure enough Mortimer and company were coming straight for them. I was near the north-east corner of the stage, and I remember Evans saying to me, 'Watch it Kid, they're here.' In seconds these goons were on the stage. I was making my way north out of their path and got separated from those on stage. Now much of the rest of this story comes from a variety of witnesses, most of whom testified at the Riot Inquiry Commission. But, I'll try to make it clear what I witnessed personally.

"Evans and Black jumped down behind the stage and only took a couple of steps before they were jumped by Mortimer and his plain-clothes Mounties. One put a stranglehold on Evans from the rear, while several others took care of his arms and legs. They propelled him to a smaller van, whereupon eight of them piled into the rear, the single prisoner being Evans.

"Evans said, and I quote, 'Some damn fool bull threw a tear gas bomb close to the truck, completely filled the truck with fumes. We were coughing and spitting. The bulls yelled to the driver to go. He pops the clutch with a jerk and throws one of the Mounties out the back end on his ass.'

"Clarence Mason, one of the boys from Division Five, grabbed Inspector Mortimer in an attempt to liberate George Black, but he was overwhelmed by officers and arrested, too. Gerry Tellier says he kicked at one of the of-

Regina Police Riot. RCMP and city police burst out of parked moving vans, using tear gas and clubs to disperse meeting, Regina, July 1, 1935. Glenbow Museum Archives, Calgary. NA-3622-19.

ficers who was storming the platform and they both fell off the stage. Tellier apparently got away.

"Well, in the meantime, the city police were the first ones to reach the crowd, so the thousands of citizens surged in panic mostly toward Osler Street on the west side of the Square. The city police had brandished what looked like sawed-off baseball bats from the opening charge and they began using them when people couldn't get out of their way because of the press. These city cops had billies and side arms too, but at this moment they were swinging these baseball bats. Some started turning to defend themselves when the police were swinging at them, but most just headed for the streets trying to get off the Square. It didn't help things that the Mounties from Osler Street advanced, forcing the crowd to choose south or north on Osler, and that caused chaos clearing the Square. A woman got shoved hard and her baby carriage tipped. The crowd was desperate to get away from these screaming maniac city cops, so she was torn away from the carriage and screamed to get back to help her baby. I think someone else must have picked up the baby who was sprawled in the dirt. One witness testified to two baby carriages overturned in those first few minutes, but the babies were picked up immediately. Everybody who was there seems to remember this.

"You can't imagine the fear and anger an attack like that can generate. Inspector McDougal, who led the charge of the city police, had the gall to lie under oath to the Commission that they touched no one on their charge to the centre of the Square. That was an outrageous insult to anyone who was there. Fortunately, the legal counsel representing the Trekkers and citizens of Regina put a few witnesses on the stand that had been clubbed in that first

Police attack a public meeting at Market Square, where most people were Regina citizens not Trekkers, Regina, July 1, 1935. Glenbow Museum Archives, Calgary. NA-3622-18.

charge, but there were many others that never got that satisfaction. Agatha Sentes was in a chair just north of the stage; she was struck on the back by a baton and fell to the dirt. From there she witnessed an older lady knocked to the ground and trampled; she heard her scream, 'Holy Mother of God,' as her leg was broken. She was finally picked up and carried over to Osler Street. Steve Fustus was there in front of the stage with his wife and daughter when the charge arrived. He was carrying their baby and tried desperately to get his family off the Square together, but they were separated in the panic. He sees a man down bleeding from the head and he calls for help, but it's just chaos. Sometime in the next seconds he raises his arm to protect himself and the child from a baton and takes a blow on the wrist. He finally finds his wife and daughter safe on Osler Street, and Stanley MacKinnon witnesses his swollen wrist.

"Since I was to the east and north of the stage when the city cops charged, moving west with that stampeding crowd didn't seem like a good idea, so I and some of the boys from Division Three retreated north-east towards Halifax Street and Tenth Avenue. You see, the Mounties from the van on Halifax had marched west across the Square to join the city police, while the Mounties from the van on 10th Avenue, to the north of the Square, had marched south toward the centre of the Square. Our part of the crowd was

Police beat Trekkers and citizens during the Regina Riot, Regina, July 1, 1935.
Glenbow Museum Archives, Calgary. NA-1609-4.

not close enough to the stage or far enough west to get to Osler Street and we sure as hell didn't want to be in the middle of the Square when the cops converged.

"Now, some of the boys were so angry and indignant — I mean, you've got to understand the fear and humiliation that happens when police start treating you like some kind of criminal or animal — so some of the citizens, some of our boys included, started picking up rocks and chunks of concrete or brick from around the intersection of Halifax and 10th, and they ran back onto the Square in small groups in a south-westerly direction, hurling these rocks and chunks of broken bricks at the Regina city police. Well, McDougal and his men charged toward us, driving the rock throwers back, and then the city cops tried to reassemble, but now that some had started fighting back, many of the citizens of Regina and some of our boys started a regular guerrilla campaign of rock throwing. McDougal's men charged again, but not in neat ranks this time, and pretty soon the Mounties who marched south from 10th whirled about and charged north again to clear the space behind them that was filling up with rock throwers, and others of the crowd that weren't sure what they wanted to do, but had obviously decided that they didn't like getting pushed around for no good reason. Or maybe they were just fascinated by fascism in action, I don't know.

"Anyway the Mounties were starting to lob tear gas canisters. Since it was hot and not much of a breeze one never knew where that gas was going to blow. Some of the guys would pick up these canisters and throw them back at the police. That would guarantee a police charge, because they seemed to believe these canisters were their property to be used against us only. McDougal's city cops in their blue uniforms and bobby helmets had broken formation entirely and were engaging in individual forays, or small group forays, against the crowd that was throwing rocks and occupying the north-east corner of the Square, where I was.

"A couple of brave constables named Splitt and Hogan grabbed one of the rock throwers and started dragging him toward the police station, which is connected to the police garages, but some of the boys ran in front of them and challenged the officers to release the fellow. One of the rescuers is reported to have said, 'Hey guys, let him go. He hasn't done anything more than everyone else here. You'd better let him go.' Obviously this was one of the first attempted arrests, other than the arrests of the stage participants, because nobody would have stopped to discuss the matter later. Apparently Constable Hogan tried to argue with him; somebody hit him with a rock and he went down, bleeding. Constable Splitt started wrestling with someone, while Hogan tried to get up and take the prisoner, but they both fell to the ground, Hogan being struck again with some flying missile, so the prisoner fled back to the safety of the crowd.

"The police became particularly brutal at this point, and apparently equally brutal in all areas of the Square, not just our north-east corner. Jacob Brunner owned a garage on the north-east corner of Halifax and 10th, so he came out to witness some of this action in our area. He gave evidence about an incident that many of the boys witnessed, where three of the city cops had descended on a man that one of them had knocked down.

"Here's what he saw: *Just wherever they could hit him, they were hitting him on the head, and anywhere they could — arms and everything, and, well, he was kind of smothered there with blood, you couldn't tell who he was... you could see it was a man... And I walked towards them... and I saw one of them that I knew, a sergeant, Tommy Logan, and I said to him, "What are you doing here, are you trying to kill him? If you are trying to kill him why don't you shoot him and be done with it? If you are trying to arrest him why don't you take him in? He is on the ground there; you could take him in. Why do you keep pounding him?"*"

Of course Logan claimed under oath that he struck no one, but Brunner knew most of those city cops since their office was only half a block away and it wasn't a big town or a big force in those days."

Doc shuffled some notes; he knew the material so well that he always got way ahead of his notes and occasionally had to catch them up to his presentation. Daniella poured him an extra glass of water as he drank the rest of the first one. As she sat back down she put her hand on my forearm and squeezed it lightly for a second or two, her eyes glued to her grandfather.

"Thanks Daniella," Doc said and continued like a professor getting paid to deliver the goods.

"On the north-west corner of the Square, at Osler and 10th, the Mounties from the Osler Street truck had wheeled and marched north against a group of citizens, mostly, who had taken to throwing rocks and fighting back. Now the Mounties were in their brown serge jackets with those jackboots and steel riot helmets, riot batons and .45 calibre colt pistols in their holsters. Official police witnesses say they had no ammunition with them when they first attacked us. I'm not so sure. Again witnesses saw citizens beaten on the ground, here, when caught in their flight from the Mounties. A couple of Mounties also went down here. Well you see the people started to realize that the Mounties, too, were clubbing anybody within reach with these two-foot weighted batons they carried, and some of the citizens were picking up cordwood to defend themselves or, in a few cases, to fight back. They got this from one of several farmers' market stalls. Farmers had brought it in over the long weekend to sell for firewood. It was about an inch and a half to two inches thick cut into three- or four-foot lengths.

"I've often thought that these cudgels were just too handy to believe they were there by accident, and that maybe Colonel Wood made sure they were there to tempt the citizens and strikers and lure them into striking back so he'd have an excuse for a full scale dustup. I admit I had one in my hand most of the night, because I'll tell you, fear can make a young man fight for his dignity, and for all our discipline, we weren't like Gandhi's protesters who could lie down and take a licking without fighting back. Anyway, these two-inch clubs didn't look like firewood to me, but some of the Regina witnesses at the Inquiry said that this was typical of the firewood sold in the Market every weekend, because that was the size of the willows and poplars that the farmers would cut in ravines or bluffs on the farms around Regina. I guess they don't get huge native trees growing in that area of the prairies.

"So, according to testimony at the Inquiry, an RCMP Constable Parsons went down in that north-east corner and testifies to receiving several blows and kicks, but he admits that they quickly left him alone when he stopped resisting. A Constable Francis led a charge into a group gathered at that intersection of Osler and 10th, but he was so excited to get his licks in that he arrived ahead of his troop and was confronted, disarmed and knocked to the ground with his own baton and possibly cordwood. He testifies to receiving a few kicks and punches before being rescued by other Mounties from the Osler Street contingent. So as you can see, people on both sides are going crazy with fear and anger. But remember, none of these citizens came to Market Square with the knowledge that they would be clubbed and chased like animals.

"About that time the final contingent of Mounties joined the battle on horseback. This troop of Mounties had been hiding out at Osler and 12th Avenue apparently, and they charged right through the crowded intersection at 11th and Osler at a trot, through the bulk of citizens who were attempt-ing to escape the Square. Now Osler and 12th Avenue, where they had been hiding, isn't far from the centre of downtown Regina, but it is seven or eight blocks from their barracks, and nobody keeps fifty horses in town, so one gets the idea of how completely this attack was planned. And just think about how sinister it was to cut off one of the only safe and natural ways to retreat, and how calculated this chaos was. I'll come back to these mounted chaps later, but it's important to remember that this all happened in the first fifteen minutes, by 8:30 p.m.

"It was about that time that an older city cop, Detective Charles Millar, was standing in the city police garage at the south-west corner of the action. This is where the city police charged out from, and now, for some reason, both Colonel Wood, who planned this whole mess, and Chief Bruton, head of the city police, were in the doorway watching the carnage. They watch, as Detective Millar, a reservist who is not supposed to be out on the Square, decides that he is going to head out to some carts and machinery for road work that are sitting behind the fire hall on the south side of the Square. He must have been worried that some of the hostile crowd seemed to be interested in grabbing some of the contents of those carts, possibly to be used as weapons or projectiles. I can't imagine what would be in them of use. But this, of course, means that various parts of the Square were now being challenged and could no longer be described as cleared.

"Anyway, Millar was an older officer, a World War I veteran with a steel plate in his head from a war wound. His commanding officer, Bruton, and Colonel Wood didn't stop him from going out there, for some unknown reason. Sometime after Detective Millar gets to the nearest cart, he is attacked by someone — one, two or three men, depending on which eyewitness we believe. Most say a single assailant. He is hit over the head with something. One witness, Ernest Doran, had just retrieved his eight-year-old son who got in the path of Millar in his hurry to rescue the contents of these carts. Doran testified to the following: 'A gentleman coming over from the Market Square, from the north, he ran down and *en route* he picked up a piece of cordwood... three feet long... and he arrived just at that moment... and lifted the piece of wood over his head and struck Millar on the head.' Other people claim they saw a Mountie's baton hit him, since Millar was not in uniform and could have been mistaken for a striker. One Trekker, Robert Lundie, witnessed Millar bending over someone on the ground whom he thought Millar had hit in trying to protect the contents of that road machinery cart. He then saw a Mountie coming from the west who hit Millar over the head, mistaking him for a Trekker. He then testifies to seeing the Mountie continue across the Square.

"Many Trekkers later asked the question why any citizen or Trekker would think that Millar was a policeman in his civilian clothes. Anyway, the witnesses could never agree on a description of the man who hit him. Some might have been witnessing other clubbings. There were plenty of them going on. So somebody hit Charles Millar, and I guess they lived with that on their conscience to their grave, because if you don't know already, Detective Millar never recovered from that single hit. It's thought that the steel plate injured his brain as a result of the blow."

Doc paused, a bit agitated, searching for the words, and then he looked straight at Sammy, who was leaning forward hanging on everything Doc said, including the pause.

Doc spoke with emotion now, "I don't excuse whoever it was who hit him. And folks, neither do I excuse Chief Bruton standing in the doorway a few feet away, for ordering that crazy police charge, and I don't excuse the man standing with him, Colonel Wood, who carefully planned this mayhem, and I don't excuse Iron Heels Bennett who gave him the licence and incentive and opportunity to do it. Who really killed Millar? You know what I'm saying?

"Constable Alex Hill saw Millar in a kneeling position seconds, probably, after he got hit. He testified to the following: 'I ran towards Millar, and some people were around him. They backed away. I thought he had been knocked out.' Hill reached down to lift him up and apparently was struck with something on the head, possibly a rock because all kinds of things were being thrown this direction by this time. Horseshoes from the livery stable, junk from the city forge on Halifax, it could have been anything, perhaps not even intended for him — there were no official witnesses. Anyway, another constable by the name of Anderson carried Millar back to the city police garage and then went back to get Constable Hill, who seemed to be okay because he testified that he went back into the combat zone for more action. Anyway, a few minutes later, a Constable Don Magee got orders from the police station to the city police garage to take Detective Millar to the hospital. He testifies that Millar's eyes were glazed over already when he laid him in the vehicle and that he died a few minutes after arriving at the hospital.

"Some of this Constable Magee's testimony, many years after the fact, is illuminating, if he's at all representative of the city police. He testified to being in an altercation with Stanley McKinnon. This was the fellow who witnessed the swollen wrists on the father that was trying to escape the Square with the baby in his arms. Well, Magee knew McKinnon, but that night they seemed to be on opposite sides. Magee claims he was assaulted by Stanley, whose father worked for Imperial Oil, but then part of his testimony is very revealing.

"Magee says, and I quote: *Lost my billie. Bust it over his fuckin' head!* He was charged with rioting. He told the judge that it was a kangaroo court. Said, *You old goat gonna die of apoplexy one of these days. You're drinking too much whiskey.* Stanley was then ordered into the judge's chambers. Got six months.'

"There, that gives you some idea about the attitude of some of the policemen in Regina, and at least one citizen's idea of the reputation of law and order in that fair town.

"Several citizens and Trekkers witnessed severe beatings of men already down on the ground by Mounties who kept pounding them long after they had stopped responding. One of these tragedies was Nick Schaak, a fifty-two-year-old Trekker who was brutally beaten by city police and, after cursory treatment in the hospital, was left without medical attention in city cells for six weeks. He died in the hospital three months after the beating, unable to recover from complications that resulted from his weakened condition.

"A Regina blacksmith by the name of Fergus Blane was in the vicinity of the Osler and 10th intersection. He testifies to seeing two Mounties beating on one striker. A fellow striker comes to the rescue, grabs one Mountie and drops him with a single punch. The pugilist, as Blane calls him, then grapples with the other Mountie till some city cops charge over and drop the pugilist with a baseball bat blow to the shoulder. In that same area Blane sees a striker with a red armband. These red armbands signalled our designated first-aid medics. We had at least a couple in each division. Blane sees this Trekker go to the rescue of a Mountie who is downed in a mob of citizens. He picks up the Mountie and carries him to safety, but other Mounties come and pick up their trooper, and arrest the medic.

"In the same area, Fergus Blane witnesses three Mounties beat up a fellow that tripped. Blane says 'What the hell ya doin', boys? You're gonna kill him.' Two of the Mounties came over to him and threatened him. Blane says they were in a very ugly mood. Blane also testified to people throwing rocks at the police, and police throwing them back at the civilians."

Doc paused, looked at his notes, glanced down at the chair provided for him in case of need. Daniella tensed, but didn't rise this time. I even noticed Cam and Tom preparing to stand and help. But Doc raised his chin high and his eyes told me that he was back on Market Square, imagining himself a lot younger than he felt at the moment. He looked determined to finish this.

"Back on the south end of Osler, the mounted troop of thirty-eight Mounties broke into two troops and patrolled the west side of Market Square aggressively. One of the cavalry chased a man into the lane between the Regina Hotel and the automotive garage and coldcocked him from his saddle with his baton. A Regina woman runs out and stands over the fallen fellow shaking her fist at the rider. Then she single-handedly drags the fellow into the safety of the hotel. Another citizen, John Lynch, is nearly trampled and grabs the bridle and reins to avoid going down. He's dragged along the sidewalk until he lets go and hits the cement. Another local man who lives on that street is clubbed by a mounted officer; he retreats to the steps of his rooming house, where a friend tends to his wound until the mounted officer charges them again. They retreat inside the building but the officer rides right up into the doorway. Another man tries to get out of the way of the cavalry against the service station on the corner of 11th Avenue and Osler. But the rider harasses him and the horse bites him on the scalp. The other troop begins to clear the northern intersection at Osler and 10th, even chasing the curious patrons from the Metropole Hotel back inside the safety of the bar.

"By 9 p.m. the cavalry has tipped the balance of power and the crowds at the two northern intersections along 10th Avenue have diminished to small bands of raiders who are easily chased. By this time about twenty constables from the RCMP and the city police have been injured such that they need aid at the hospital. McDougal, who led the initial charge of the city cops, has taken a horseshoe on the head. Market Square is littered with rocks, bricks, bottles, chunks of concrete and pavement, horseshoes from the livery, cordwood and other junk that folks found along the railroad to the north and behind some of the local business along 10th and Halifax. Apparently five truckloads of this kind of ammunition, mostly rocks, was cleaned off Market Square the next day — an outpouring of anger and indignation you might say.

"About 9 p.m., while the Mounties and their cavalry were not quite so busy mopping up little pockets of resistance around the Square, the police raided the Unity Centre, which was just east of Brunners Garage by about a half a block. That was our temporary office. I can't imagine that they came up with anything very interesting there, but I suppose they were desperate for any evidence which might help them charge some of us under Section 98. I mean, how do you prove that a bunch of unemployed relief camp workers have a union that should be declared an unlawful organization and a danger to the national government? The only danger was that we were exposing their bankrupt policies on the economy and workers' rights. So the raid was a non-event. Nobody resisted the raid as far as I know, though they faced some rock throwing as they moved east along 10th from the corner of Market Square. The manager of the Unity Centre had the temerity to ask the Mounties for their search warrant. He was shoved aside and they promptly cut off his phone line."

Doc paused, holding onto the lectern and scanning his audience before looking directly at his granddaughter. "Daniella I think I need to sit down," Doc said, and she moved like Catwoman. She had this routine down; in seconds he was comfortable with the lectern lower beside his chair.

"We've only covered the first hour of a long summer evening folks, so you best have another beer or two," Doc said as we witnessed those waitresses' perfect choreography and timing. How did they do that? I took a mental note to thank the manager and waitresses. A pitcher of draft this time for Cam, Tom and Sammy, and a round for our table.

Doc's notes were ready. "Most of the Trekkers that were at Market Square, some of whom took part in the rock throwing, had begun to make their way west through town in smaller bands, either along 10th Avenue or 11th Avenue, which took one right down the main drag of downtown businesses.

"I didn't personally witness this part of the evening because I had headed west a few minutes earlier to the fair grounds and ball diamonds, where about half of the main body of Trekkers were, with the idea of getting some help. Some of the Trekkers I met along the route came back with me, but our Trek security detail at the game soon got orders not to allow any more of the boys to go downtown. Other Trekkers had made it back to the Exhibition Grounds and there, too, our security pickets were ordered not to allow strikers to go downtown. At the time I thought that for the safety of the boys downtown, reinforcements were desperately needed, but I understand in retrospect the cooler heads of those who had not been assaulted by a full-scale police attack and didn't want to expose the main body of strikers to the senseless violence.

I mean, that brutal attack at Market Square had changed many disciplined strikers into fearful but enraged street fighters, as might be expected.

"Anyway, some of us who returned to the downtown area eventually met up with the Trekkers and citizens from Market Square in the middle of downtown in front of the Post Office and City Hall, about four or five blocks west of the south-west corner of Market Square. The story of how we all got there and why is a bit of a complex maze. You almost need a map of downtown Regina to follow the different stories.

"For example, Willis Shaparla, one of the boys from my division, tried to head west along 10th avenue with twenty or thirty or so of strikers in an attempt to get back to the Exhibition Grounds. Whenever the cavalry or other Mounties came in sight, they would holler 'Look, we just want to get back to the Grounds.' This seemed to work until they got near Cornwall Street about five blocks west of the Square. There some Mounties came charging at them, drew their guns and fired shots. Nobody seemed to be hit, but there were all kinds of citizens besides the strikers there at the time. They were confused naturally, and backed off to Scarth Street the next block east. What they hadn't realized is that they were perilously close to the RCMP city headquarters where Evans and Black and other prisoners had been taken, and the RCMP claimed under oath that they thought this handful of Trekkers might be trying to storm the RCMP headquarters. Well, they either had aw-fully fertile imaginations or they were just annoyed that they were away from the action on Market Square. Apparently they weren't the first officers that night to fire live ammunition, and they sure as hell weren't the last.

"According to police testimony, after a telephone call from the Cornwall Street police station that, quote, 'rioters are in the vicinity,' Inspector Brunet is ordered to provide escort for a constable who issues twelve rounds of .45 calibre ammunition to each RCMP officer. This would probably be a few minutes before 9 p.m. when the troops at Market Square get their orders to head west to the centre of town following the mass of citizens and the strikers. Sergeant Griffin and twenty troopers on horseback are sent straight down 11th Avenue to reinforce the town station on Cornwall. Then Wood sends Inspector Brunet and the remaining constables in his division by the same route. One wonders why they were sent down 11th Avenue, which was bound to be the most crowded.

"McDougal and the bulk of the city force were actually the first to march west from Market Square along 11th Avenue, because Chief Bruton had received a call from a hardware store two blocks further west even than the Cornwall Street police station. It turns out that the Trekkers, whom the store owner was worried about, had no intention of bothering his store, and MacDougal's troops found nobody there but the embarrassed owner when they arrived. But this goes to show that some of the Trekkers were already halfway back to the Exhibition Grounds when the police decided to chase the Trekkers who were headed downtown. These Trekkers might have been some of the first to arrive back at the Exhibition Grounds. In fact, most of them stayed at the Grounds when they got back there, due to the decisions of the leadership there.

"Also at least three Regina citizens besides our own strikers testified that they'd heard one or more of the strikers call the Trekkers to form ranks near Market Square and on 11th Avenue to maintain discipline and to march back to the Exhibition Grounds. All of the Trekkers along 11th Avenue tell about their attempts to march on home. However, the police managed to make that a bit difficult. The Trekkers marching west met other Trekkers like Shaparla and crew who were already there at Scarth and 11th.

"This could probably be called the centre of town. There are at least four huge highrise towers on or near that intersection owned by four major banks today. At least two of those were there in earlier and older decor back then. I, and a few strikers from the baseball game, joined the group there. All of the Trekkers in this area, that we know of, that is those gathered by the Post Office and the old City Hall, joined into our usual four-abreast columns, and we headed west toward the Exhibition Grounds, because by then we can clearly see the RCMP horses to the east on 11th Avenue and they're headed our way. Again there were never more than about forty of us together at one time there, or at any other time during the whole evening. Mostly it was groups of a dozen, twenty, or thirty at the most, with citizens old and young hanging around, some trying to be helpful. Many of the Trekkers had fled the Square and headed south, north, some even out of town, thinking we'd all be arrested. And remember, there were about 500 cops, all told, chasing us around the downtown area.

"Anyway, at this point we tried to move west in a disciplined fashion, but as we passed Cornwall Street we could see a police barricade of automobiles across that street and a fair number of Mounties getting loud orders, and some tear gas canisters were lobbed. I don't think any of us realized that Arthur Evans was held prisoner north of that barricade, and that was possibly one reason why so many police were descending on this one area. But anyone who thought that these boys were inclined to storm an RCMP station that night had no idea how effective their terrorizing attacks on us had been. We continued as far as the Grand Theatre on the next block when we ran into Trekkers who told us there was a police force about to cut us off — they suggested we don't proceed. Much later we found out that a squad of Mounties had rushed west from the police station, behind the Grand Theatre and into a used car parking lot to cut us off and hit us from close range. We felt like we'd walked into a trap, because now Sergeant Griffin and his mounted Cossacks were close behind us; one could hear the clatter of the hooves over the general noise and crowds along the street. So we decided to dig in where we were. We told the boys to build our own barricade of cars across 11th and Cornwall from the north-west corner to the south-east. That would protect us from the police to the north and the cavalry from the west. I guess we didn't really realize that the cavalry was coming not just to harass us ('a show of force' was the order), but also they were to relieve the officers who supposedly thought they were under siege at the Cornwall Police Station.

"So we commandeered cars from around the theatre and near that intersection. One man is reported to have volunteered his car. And we took them out of gear, pushed and steered them, lined them up door to door across the intersection. I suppose we realized then that we were all likely to be arrested if our barricade didn't hold. So then we picked up rocks and chunks of pavement to hurl at the approaching riders. Somebody had thrown more tear gas canisters and there was a good deal of gas east of that barricade. Perhaps some of the boys had lobbed them that way when the Mounties north on Cornwall threw them at us. Anyway most of the horses turn aside, and I think some of them must have gone north on Scarth and over on 10th to relieve the Cornwall Station. A few of them ran the gauntlet, one or two at a time, turning north at Cornwall right in front of our barricade. They came under quite a barrage of rocks from the boys and from the crowd as well.

"Incredibly enough, kids on bicycles were riding up and bringing us rocks and broken bricks and ammunition to throw. One or two had done this at Market Square as well. We seemed to be successful for a while, turning back the cavalry and Brunet's constables on foot. At one point, during a lull in the action, some of the boys began a heartfelt verse of 'Hold the Fort,' which seemed a lot less metaphorical and a lot more literal at that moment.

"Then someone tells us that there's a radio reporter broadcasting live from a building above us and that he's telling all Regina how brave the cops are and what a terrible situation they are facing and that they have acted absolutely heroically. I don't know who had time to listen to a radio during all this, but in retrospect it might explain why the crowd of Regina citizens seemed to be getting larger despite the fact that there had been shots fired, tear gas in the streets and barricades erected. Finally one of the boys hears his ridiculous commentary from street level and threatens to climb up there and wrap the microphone wires around his mouth. His technician then guarded the way up with a club, as if we would have really bothered with him when we had cops coming at us from all directions.

"But he apparently got shut down by his station later on when a number of shots could be heard live over the radio waves. Also the reporter, with a bit too much relish, described a man going down from a cop's club. That was possibly too much enthusiasm for the managing editor's taste back in the radio station. I'm not sure if he covered the Mounties shooting of the Trekker in the alley behind us south of the Grand Theatre. The two fellows in the alley must have thrown a rock at the police line, so a couple of officers rushed out and fired at them. Later we found out that they hit one of those boys through both thighs and he was lucky someone at the back of a café there dragged him inside and stopped the bleeding.

"Anyway, I guess between the gunfire and the clubs dropping civilians, it was a bit too sensational for the radio station manager, so he pulled the plug on that budding police-drama romance writer up there at the top of the building. The damage had been done though, as hundreds of Regina citizens decided that they should witness history in action, with the result that they all came down to join the chaos. With that gunfire the police were a little bolder and started advancing on us from the north and the east. They fired over the heads of the crowd, and that effectively scattered most of them temporarily. The riders then laid into us with their riding crops, backed up with scores of Mounties on foot and we retreated south on Cornwall. The Mounties pushed a few key cars out of the way to give the cavalry better access. It was absolute mayhem. There were dozens of citizens along every block now, some just watching and some joining in — throwing rocks or helping us with barricades.

"Now apparently, while we retreated to 12th Avenue, Inspector Cooper arrived with the second troop of cavalry, aggressively attempting to clear all citizens from 11th Avenue. He probably couldn't tell who was a citizen and who was a Trekker, but testimony suggests that he forced his column all the way past the Grand Theatre right out to Albert Street four blocks west of Cornwall. Apparently, citizens and Trekkers stoned them all along the route: he and his men chased them into yards, up alleys, over low fences and the like. When he runs out of action at Albert Street, he wheels his troop and comes back east for more action. When he gets to Cornwall again and our breached barricade he turns south, possibly due to the heavy tear gas still settling over that intersection.

"The main body of Trekkers who attempted to stick together rather than flee the downtown core, had to retreat east on 12th Avenue due to the presence of city police to the west and RCMP cavalry nearby. So, with the help of some of the crowd along the streets, we erected another barricade of cars across the intersection at 12th and Scarth Street. One of the boys directed the traffic away from the intersection as much as possible. One fellow came out of a theatre and noticed his car lined up in the barricade and came over and asked if he could have his car back. He was told to go ahead and take it. So he manages to squeeze into the door, starts it up and drives it away straight toward the advancing city police and some Mounties who were behind them.

"Then the police were on us again. MacDougal and the city police arrived from the west and marched right at us along Victoria Park, which is just south of 12th Avenue and runs two blocks between Lorne and Scarth. We threw a barrage of rocks and chunks of debris up in the air to rain down on them, thinking they might take the hint and back off.

"In fact, describing this intersection years later in an interview, our notorious Constable Magee invented this flight of fancy. Let me read it: *Then there was Leo Disken's little yellow truck. Leo, the old bugger, was a communist. Still is probably if he's still living. His truck appears in front of the Capitol Theatre with a load of stones. Dumped them there for the boys to use against us.* Turns out that was a mutated version of a story repeated so many times in police circles that it turns up in various testimony at various places with various coloured trucks. The original truck that spawned the story appeared at the north-west corner of Market Square, far from 12th Avenue; it had been borrowed without proper authorization from the owner by someone who wanted to see the action. The truck actually had cream cans, not rocks in the back, and some of the boys had grabbed these cans to pound on the pavement to break it into something they could throw. Amazing what a brainwashed mind will remember.

"But that intersection of 12th and Scarth was brutal. MacDougal claimed at the Inquiry that it was the worst assault on his troops that night and that none of them escaped injury. That exaggeration was his excuse for giving the command to fire their revolvers. Most of them fired over top of us, but some of them fired at us and three men fell, wounded. With that crowd of citizens around, McDougal must have been crazy if he thought no one would get hit by stray bullets as he claimed. Ricochets alone were bound to claim some victims. One of the wounded was an orderly on his way to work. The wounded were carried to the safety of buildings nearby that had not yet locked their doors. The Trekkers had been advising people to close up and to get off the streets.

"At the gunfire, the crowd scattered and we tried to take cover north of the intersection on Scarth. Inspector Cooper and his cavalry arrived behind the city police and attempted to breach the barricade. I just want to make it clear, here, that at the time we had no idea of the names or identities of these officers. I got these names and the movements of the police from later evidence, mostly submitted at the Riot Inquiry. Anyway, one of the boys hit one of the horses in the head with a rock: I remember it stumbling as it tried to breach the barricade. The gunfire had pretty well had its desired effect and citizens and Trekkers alike had scattered in all directions, wherever looked safe.

"So Cooper had no real trouble charging his cavalry north on Scarth to 11th; I don't know where he went from there, somewhere east. Apparently McDougal entered a store and used their phone to demand that more ammunition be couriered to him at that intersection. That call was placed about 9:45 p.m. The sun was probably getting low but it was still light out. However it wasn't too early for Dominion Day 'fireworks' that year."

Doc paused and stretched a bit. "You know this water is not doing anything for my energy level. I could use a beer, or something that this old blood can run on." Cam and Tom craned their necks looking for a waitress through the door to the bar, while one of the guests went to find her. In the meantime Sammy grabbed Doc's empty water glass and poured him the last remaining draft from his pitcher. Doc smiled and thanked him. The waitress later brought a bottle of Canadian for Doc and a pitcher for Sammy. Doc was never going to run short of beer this night. He drank part of the draft and set it down as he resumed the story.

"Shortly after this, several Trekkers and many citizens report witnessing a black sedan, probably a Buick, speeding east on 11th Avenue past City Hall, just east of the Post Office. Both of these buildings had been refuges for Trekkers and citizens throughout the last hour. From the windows of this car gunfire was sprayed carelessly. It ricocheted off the stone walls as the car accelerated east. Bystanders all expressed amazement that no one on that main thoroughfare was hit by the car or by the gunfire, to our knowledge. It was as if someone was shooting a gangster movie in downtown Regina, but on this night everyone was acutely aware that we weren't dealing with fiction or romance. Yet incredibly, the same car comes racing back a few minutes later, and the officer inside fires shots again as they cross Rose Street before approaching Hamilton. Witnesses say the car swerves to barely miss another car and crashes into a garbage receptacle, backs up and speeds away again. We now know that the car had been sent to pick up and deliver more ammunition to McDougal and the city police.

"There were a few of us — some from the original group that barricaded at Cornwall and again at 12th and Scarth — a few who were still together on 11th Avenue again, twenty Trekkers possibly, including those who joined us from the shelters of the Post Office and City Hall. Some were hiding behind some stalled trolley cars on Scarth and 11th Avenue. Most were just trying to avoid Cooper's cavalry, who were flailing away on anyone who was in reach on the streets, so it seemed like a good idea for the Trekkers to stick together to avoid getting beat up separately.

"Yes, there still seemed to be hundreds of citizens who wanted to watch this thing to the bitter end. Some of them have been watching in shock and silence. Some have been cursing the police. For example, a citizen named Victor Olson overhears a group of ladies near Cornwall Street, not the safest of locations this particular night, discussing the situation in decidedly British accents. In the words of Olson, they were 'talking about their rights as British subjects, and British justice being trampled on by these yellow-legged bastards.' Maybe the folks in Regina felt so much at home in this part of town — the usual centre of night life, movies and late-night restaurants — that they just couldn't believe that their downtown could be taken away from them like this. All I know is that there were a lot more spectators and civilians in the vicinity of Scarth and 11th than there were Trekkers resisting the police at this time.

"Some of the boys behind the streetcar and some of the spectators spot McDougal and his blue-coated bobbies — at least that's what they looked like with those helmets and bats — they spot them coming out of the shadows along the sidewalk on Scarth. The sun is low and light begins to fade after 10 p.m. No one could know that they had just received more ammunition and were itching to use it after their success in breaching the barricade and scaring the civilians and Trekkers into flight a few minutes earlier. Some of the boys start throwing rocks from behind the stalled streetcars. A few men were right in the intersection of 11th and Scarth. Rocks start raining down again on McDougal's men, but McDougal no doubt is still feeling the anger and humiliation of that horseshoe in the head at Market Square. They say he suffered blood-poisoning from it due to not getting it treated immediately. Whatever his reasons, even after his men had unlawfully shot down three citizens at the intersection behind him, Inspector Duncan McDougal orders his men to draw their loaded .38 calibre revolvers. This time he orders them to fire right at the rock throwers to bring them down. More than a dozen men are cut down by the withering barrage that many mistook for machine-gun fire. They fired at least two rounds each, more in some cases, and it had the desired effect — screams, people fleeing, bodies and blood on the ground.

"Tony Tomachuck is hit in the leg; he crawls beneath the trolley car, hoping to escape further fire. McDougal orders him to come out from under. Trekker George Foley is down with a bullet in the foot. Two men who are hit stagger into Ryan's Café at 1761 Scarth Street just north of the Bank of Nova Scotia, north of the 11th Avenue intersection. One boy is hit in the shoulder and one in the leg, according to Francis Ryan, owner of the Café. She literally has to drive away a mounted RCMP who tries to follow the boys into the Café, still mounted on his horse. Trekkers Alf Waalerud, Tom McMurray and Jack Johnson are all down in the street with bullets in the legs. Griffith Jones has been hit in the knee. Robertson has a bullet in his back. Dave Lyon has been hit in the stomach. MacDonald has been creased by a bullet across his face. Clarkson has a bullet in the shoulder. All of these were Trekkers.

"Regina citizens and non-participating spectators, Ephraim Delmage and James Cross, have been cut down, Cross with a bullet in the hip. Bill Rogers, a citizen on his way to a church a block and a half north on Scarth Street, is hit in the chest. Joe Rothecker, having a beer with his father-in-law at the King's Hotel three blocks east, is hit in the shoulder by a ricochet and falls to the ground. Joe Slabick, a CPR section-hand foreman, is hit in the hand near Railway Avenue to the north on Scarth.

"Red Walsh and I didn't really do a body count at that moment, but as close as we can reconstruct it, there were ten or so men hit, who were down on the ground in the immediate vicinity of the Scarth and 11th intersection, who needed quick attention. The people who were not terrorized into fleeing the scene went to work trying to get the wounded into cars or ambulances and to the hospital. A couple of our red-armband Trekkers, Red Cross medics we called them, who were trying to help with the fallen were arrested, just because they were Trekkers.

"There is no rock throwing or fighting between police and civilians now. Everyone is a hell of a lot more sober, and our grim anger is directed toward doing what we can to save these guys from bleeding to death. The hospital records show only a dozen relief camp workers treated for gun-shot-wounds that night, and most of those fell in that deliberate carnage at 11th and Scarth, except for Philips who was shot in the alley by the RCMP from Cornwall Street. The five Regina citizens that I have named were also treated for gunshots. It is still unclear who two of the men were that fell ear-lier at 12th and Scarth the first time the city police fired, and whether either of them were taken to the hospital. Most assuredly there were others who were treated by doctors outside of the hospital; I saw Anderson treated for a bullet crease, and the elderly doctor who treated him would not answer our questions about other covered bodies he had in his clinic. Both citizens and Trekkers fled the vicinity without being professionally treated rather than risk arrest at the hospital, which was the fate of the twelve Trekkers treated for gunshot wounds there. Walsh, Brodie and I, and any other Trekkers that were on the scene, were all convinced that some others were killed that night and the evidence suppressed. I'll try to defend that belief a bit later."

Doc took another drink and said, "I think this beer is doing the trick, boys, recharging this old blood a bit so I'm going try standing again for this final push."

He looked at Daniella and smiled, but the way she tensed and gripped the table, I could tell that she wasn't sure this was a good idea. But Doc was standing up, so she did his bidding restoring the pulpit to its higher calling. Sammy set a beer beside the pulpit and Doc thanked them both with a nod and a grin. Notes on the lectern, hands holding on to either side of it, he was ready to push on. I wasn't entirely sure if he was on 97th Avenue, Grande Prairie, or 11th Avenue, Regina, at the moment.

Doc began again with determination. "Well folks, Sergeant Griffin and Inspector Cooper continued their cavalry patrols, splitting up to do mop-up work because there wasn't any real organized resistance any more. But individuals and small groups were spread over a huge area as dusk slowly deepened. They were patrolling more than fifteen blocks east and west, and four or five blocks north and south, so I suppose I'd be misleading you to suggest that I've covered all the action that night. I know that at Scarth and 11th Avenue there in front of the Post Office, down the block from the City Hall, Red Walsh and I called for the few remaining Trekkers to assemble. McDougal finally came toward us and asked if we were ready to vacate the streets and return to the Grounds. Walsh said, 'Mister, we've tried to do that several times tonight, in case you hadn't noticed. Yes, we're marching back to the Grounds if you're prepared to let us.'

"McDougal retorted, 'Well, that's good because if you don't we've got orders to clear the streets any way we have to and I'll use bullets if I have to.'

"We just marched off, thinking that he probably didn't have to convince us of that, considering the blood and bodies we'd just been dealing with in the street. A body of Trekkers on 12th Avenue was also witnessed about that time, assembling in rank and marching west again toward the Exhibition Grounds. Almost all serious collective action by Trekkers and citizens was over at that point. Eleventh Avenue behind us was littered with car barricades, rocks and chunks of debris, and broken glass. I had no idea how many broken windows there were along 11th Avenue. Apparently someone, probably only a handful of young men or kids, had fled down 11th Avenue fairly early on, before 9 p.m., breaking windows as they went. I suppose that's why, when they heard those reports, the police assumed that the Trekkers were rioting. However, we had many witnesses testify to the number of times different groups of Trekkers attempted to return in orderly, peaceful fashion to the Grounds. One witness saw the police shoot out a window when they fired over the heads of a crowd. I'm sure disgruntled youths, caught up in the fever, did their fair share as well.

"So I couldn't even really tell you now if it was twenty, or if it was thirty, of the boys who finally marched unimpeded west along 11th toward the Exhibition Grounds. I think it was well after 10:30 when they got there. I'm not sure because I had left them by the time they arrived. Most of the boys had already straggled in, in small groups coming by various routes. Apparently, between 10 p.m. and about 2:30 a.m., when the RCMP threw a heavily armed cordon of officers around the Exhibition Grounds, some seven or eight hundred, perhaps a thousand, slipped out of the Grounds. Or, like myself, perhaps many decided not to return to the Grounds and risk arrest. Being a captain of a division and a member of the Ottawa delegation, I certainly expected to be arrested. Slim Evans sent word from prison later that they were looking for me, though I haven't found a record of a warrant for me at that time. I chose to stay in seclusion a few days at the home of a CCF member of Parliament. Then I chose to make my own way back west, heading north-west through Wainwright first, and eventually back to Vancouver.

"I'll tell you what happened to the main body back at the Exhibition Grounds as well as I can from second-hand accounts and the few history books on the subject. Of course I had close friends like Steve Brodie, Red Walsh and Mike McCaulay who filled me in back in Vancouver. Mike McCaulay realized that Evans, Black and Cosgrove were all in prison, and that left a pretty big hole in the leadership of the Trek. He also remembered that we had struck a deal with the Premier, and that Gardiner had probably already discussed the deal with the cabinet members, so Mike borrows a phone somewhere in a downtown café at about midnight after the streets are fairly well deserted, and he calls Premier Gardiner at home. Gardiner tells him that he had met with the cabinet late into the evening after supper and had got permission to close the deal on sending us back on the cushions. He hadn't heard about the riot until he got home late from the Legislature. He promised to meet with McCaulay and a delegation of strikers at 10 a.m.; he said he would wire Ottawa of his intentions before that. So Mike got back to the stadium just barely before the RCMP tightened their noose around it. I had expected that to happen even before Red Walsh and his boys got back there at about 11 p.m. In fact many of the boys downtown had got the impression that the Grounds were already guarded by RCMP.

"Apparently the boys didn't get much sleep that night. Even at 4 a.m. when it must have been the darkest, some of them noticed RCMP take up positions high in the stadium stands with rifles. Come morning light the strikers all saw the grim reality of a machine gun mounted, sandbagged and pointed at them from the top of a boxcar on the rails that went through the southern part of the Exhibition Grounds. The RCMP had rifle positions all around them and nobody was fed or allowed to leave. So they finally had their concentration camp, with or without permission. The Strike Committee decided to go along with McCaulay's hope that Premier Gardiner could get the boys out of this mess. They didn't have a whole lot of options.

"McCaulay and delegates were stopped by RCMP as they attempted to leave for their meeting. Mike was hit in the stomach with the butt of a rifle. He asked to see the officer in charge because the Premier was waiting to see them. It took a long time, but they finally got the Attorney General to speak with Colonel Wood. Apparently the balance of authority had shifted back to Premier Gardiner by that time. Then they were escorted to see the Premier and his cabinet.

"By the time they met with the Premier, Gardiner had already wired Prime Minister Bennett informing him that Bennett's federal representative had rejected an offer by the strikers to disband and go home, just a few hours before an unprovoked police attack. He told Bennett that the Saskatchewan Cabinet was closing a deal to send the Trekkers home at provincial expense when the police attacked a public meeting without notifying the province or the Attorney General of their intention. Considering the fact that a policeman was dead and scores of strikers and citizens injured, he requested, with an edge of politeness, that he be allowed to proceed in cleaning up the mess and negotiating the return of the men, bypassing the Lumsden plan.

"He also mentioned that the RCMP apparently planned on starving the men into submission, since they had not been given food in more than twenty-four hours, and that they had the Exhibition Grounds under siege. He warned of further trouble if he were not allowed to act quickly. The Prime Minister blustered a bit in his reply as usual, but he gave in with the words: *We have no intention of interfering with any action you may decide to take that does not involve these men in violation of the laws of the country.*

"Well, it took several wires back and forth that day, but with that bit of leeway, Gardiner and Attorney General Davis announced to Colonel Wood that they were now taking control of matters and that the RCMP would answer to them again from then on, as per the federal-provincial agreement, or else. They concluded the deal with McCaulay and our delegates, the same deal we presented to the feds the day before, which Burgess and Wood rejected. The Trekkers were to be fed and registered for train tickets, and only those that the police had warrants for could be touched by either police force.

"By 4 p.m. they finally had food in to the Trekkers. The RCMP had counted the Trekkers at the stadium in the morning and found only 1100. That's out of about 2500 at our peak in Regina. I guess many found shelter with people they had met in Regina, like I did, and the rest had left town at night during the riot."

Doc shuffled some papers looking for something. He found his page and set them all down with that one on top, then raised his head again. "Only 1358 registered for train tickets to their homes or to the nearest station to where they joined the Trek. Perhaps you'll allow me to do a breakdown of that number for you, so you can see where they were all from: 857 went back to B.C., 172 to Alberta, 151 to Saskatchewan. That would be Saskatoon mostly; there were more from southern Saskatchewan who might not have used the train. Fifty-four to Manitoba, 71 to Ontario, 38 to Quebec and 15 to the Maritimes. So you see we had representation from across the nation.

"Anyway, let me back up here a minute to the police attack. More than 100 injured people were admitted to the Grey Nuns Hospital or other medical facilities. Of course the injuries ranged from mere bruises and lacerations to gunshot wounds and skull fractures. Many others that were hurt called doctors to their place of residence, because doctors would still do house calls in those days. Others with serious injuries were treated by friends and family to avoid the possibility of arrest. In the next few days, Steve Brodie joined a committee of women from the Mothers' Council searching for boys who were missing and perhaps dead. They attempted to get information from morgues, clinics and hospitals, but were denied access and treated rudely at times. I suppose confidentiality was the excuse. They even searched the fields around Regina for signs of illicit graves. The only hard evidence, of course, was circumstantial, but persuasive; several Trekkers were never seen again by family or friends, and the last they were seen was at Market Square or downtown Regina during the police attack.

"I'll give you one example and leave it at that. Testimony from Red Walsh: *I know personally of one family here in Victoria... one of them I worked alongside in the ship-yards... the younger brother in this family by the name of McElroy disappeared from the face of the earth in Regina on July 1, 1935. This boy never failed to write his family, at least twice a month to his mother. His last known existence was on Market Square that night. Of course there were people killed that night.* Well that issue is a whole story in itself, and the jury is forever hung on that one.

"Anyway there were about a 120 people arrested that night, about 63 were listed by the courts as strikers. Most of those people arrested were charged with vagrancy, yet denied bail. The vagrancy charge was just a temporary general charge to keep them behind bars, because most of those charges were dropped and the majority of the arrested were turned loose within a couple of days. About thirty-seven strikers were charged with rioting and these were not given bail or released, some of them, for several months. Seventeen of these were still denied bail as of September 25, and five of them were not released on bail till about November 11. Ultimately, only twenty-four were charged with rioting, two of whom were citizens. These were token charges, really, so they wouldn't look like they were only going after Trekkers. The trials were delayed again and again; they didn't commence till April 1936 and by the end of April only nine of the twenty-four were found guilty of rioting or assault and received sentences ranging from three months to eighteen months. Nine, folks. Just nine. A few others were committed to mental asylums without trial. Does that bother anybody out there?

"Arthur Evans, George Black and Jack Cosgrove (Jack was still in jail as a result of the aborted attempt to drive east in trucks) — these three were all charged under Section 98, 'belonging to an unlawful organization.' Ivan Bell and Ernie Edwards were also charged under Section 98 for belonging to the Relief Camp Workers Union. One can only wonder what special reasons they had for charging those two and not the rest of us with that same heinous crime. It goes to show they really didn't understand much about the leadership of the Trek. Anyway they dropped the charges against those two though they kept Ernie in jail for seventy-two days before dropping charges against him.

"Matt Shaw was the fourth Trekker who actually stood trial on Section 98 charges. The RCMP arrested Matt Shaw in Toronto after he spoke at Maple Leaf Gardens on the same stage as Reverend Sam East and Sam Carr. A crowd of 6000 or so apparently gave Shaw some great ovations and carried him on their shoulders while an orchestra played 'Hold the Fort.' Of course the Trekkers were the centre of national attention that week, and for weeks to come. Well, silver-tongued Matt got the plum assignment there; although he missed the police assault in Regina, he was still favoured by the RCMP as one of the top four candidates for Section 98. We used to tease him about that when we saw him, but we all knew that he did a good job of representing us on many stages across Canada.

"You see, there was a huge legal and populist effort to get those four out on bail, and people like Reverend Sam East and the Citizen's Legal Defence Committee led by T.H. Newlove, finally forced a stubborn conservative bench to grant them bail early in August after only a month or so in the slammer. They let them out just in time to help the rest of the thinking Canadians to defeat Iron Heels Bennett and his Conservatives in the federal election. I've got more to say about Bennett in a minute, but you know they continued to harass Evans after he got bail. They threatened him with contempt charges, but they couldn't intimidate him; he insisted on his freedom of speech rights. At public meetings and on a speaking tour right across the nation, he became a ruddy folk hero as he continued to denounce the cover-ups, the bought-and-paid-for legal system and the lies of R.B. Bennett and company. He kept this up right through the election and right through his much-delayed trial, when all four were eventually found not guilty, at the end of February. Not guilty, folks! Not guilty of contravening Section 98. The winds were changing by then. Bennett relegated to the Opposition benches."

Some people clapped at that last statement, and Doc took that opportunity to pour Sammy's beer into a glass for a couple of swallows. I could feel Daniella's anxiety as to whether his energy would last.

"Speaking of those lies that Evans challenged, let me take you back to July 2nd for a minute. Bennett stood in the House of Commons the morning after the carnage and said: *There were no cartridges in the hands of any members of the Mounted Police last night. Yet this afternoon there are mounted policeman lying in the hospital shot with bullets.* Folks, there were no policeman shot, nor was there any witness in the courts or in the Riot Inquiry that saw anybody but policemen with guns, let alone shooting guns. In fact, an affidavit placed into evidence by an eyewitness says that Western Cycle and Rifles just off of 11th Avenue suffered no damage or pilfering, and, furthermore, that a Trekker was heard advising others to keep clear of touching any guns.

"Referring to the police, Bennett said in the same speech: *One of them died in the discharge of his duty, killed by those who defy law and challenge authority.*

This is a lawyer in the highest position of influence willing to prejudice a case before any evidence or charges or investigation has advanced. Witnesses couldn't agree on the colour of shirt, the kind of clothes, the weapon used nor the number of men nearby when Millar went down; yet Bennett knew in Ottawa what had happened?"

Doc's voice was gaining strength and his passion was rising. The portal was fully open and there was no explaining his energy. No one was leaving. No one even dared to whisper.

"Again, same speech, same liar: *Last night's assembly was an unlawful assembly.* The truth is there were no charges of unlawful assembly, no *Riot Act* read, and no evidence to support that claim because everyone in Regina knew that, until the police attacked the crowd it was a peaceful, lawful assembly, altogether like many others of its kind in Market Square.

"In the same speech, the same propagandist says that the Trek was *not a mere uprising against law and order but a definite revolutionary effort on the part of a group of men to usurp authority and destroy government... an organized attempt against the national life of Canada... [towards] the rule of commune and the guidance of the soviets.* Charges under Section 98 of course would have had to prove those assertions, yet Bennett is willing to try them in the press — a press over which he has a lot of influence, a press that dutifully reports his words as gospel.

"And the press bought the lies of the police and the lies of the federal cabinet, helping spread them for several days — especially Conservative-owned-and-operated presses like the *Regina Star*. Some reporters for the *Regina Leader-Post* and some of the eastern papers actually started digging for the facts, after a few days, and soon the truth could not be hidden, except for those who preferred to believe that their beloved police and their federal leaders could not have done the things that they did. By federal election time, we'd seen thousands of people meet in many major cities across Canada to protest the police attack, the loss of civil liberties and the abuse of the legal system. Slim Evans, Matt Shaw and the Reverend Sam East crisscrossed the country telling our story.

"The game was over. On October 23, 1935, Bennett's Conservative Party went down to humiliating defeat; R.B. Bennett managed to retain his own Calgary seat only because Premier Bible Bill Aberhart chose not to run a Social Credit candidate in that riding. As Ronnie Liversedge used to say, 'I don't know how Calgary has ever lived down the stigma.' A couple of years later Bennett resigned and left Canada for England. The king gave him a title, Viscount Bennett of Calgary, for his defence of empire values, I suppose. He is the only Canadian prime minister to be buried abroad. May Mother England keep his bones, because every Trekker I know was proud of the fact that we helped bury him."

Doc looked up and scanned the crowd. His eyes had a hard glint that sixty-five years could not diminish —I imagined that he was seeing R.B Bennett one more time.

"And I think that's probably enough for one night," Doc said. "It's been a long one, but then so was that evening of July the First, 1935."

Folks started clapping and standing, but he held up his hands. He had something else that needed to be said, although he didn't look too steady when he wasn't holding the lectern. He was clearly exhausted. We all ceased applauding and listened.

"I need to say one thing before I finish here. In case you never figured it out from the way these folks are fussing over me, this is likely my last session here at BJ's. It's been a good run. And there are some people we need to talk about. You know First Nations people have certain elders called keepers: keepers of the drum, keepers of the medicine, keepers of the ghosts, keepers of the lore, or the stories. In your community you are fortunate to have some keepers. Daniella and Paul have been keepers, at least of one old ghost here." He smiled and people laughed softly.

"And there are other keepers here among you." He raised his hand like a strange benediction toward Charles, and then towards Cam and Tom, "Keepers of music. Keepers of the stories. This session tonight feels like one of those final stories, like a climax, we call it. But folks, there is no *final* final chapter. Just exit chapters for certain characters. So honour your keepers."

His hand did that benediction again toward Daniella and me. "It is the First Commandment. Good night."

The applause poured from us. We were standing, and Daniella was beside him to ease him into the chair. And for the rest of the evening we honoured a keeper.

19

I AM CANADIAN HISTORY

DANIELLA ON QUEBEC SUMMIT POLICE VIOLENCE

O NLY A FEW DAYS AFTER DOC returned to Quesnel, we heard the startling national news that Quebec City had been transformed into a virtual war zone, as the third Summit of the Americas erupted into a chaos of riot police, tear gas, plastic bullets, black hoods and failed security fences. Our Daniella was there somewhere. A day or so later she finally called from Quebec City: the news was grim. She had been arrested and incarcerated, a story that all of us would need to hear. Other than that she was okay and on her way home, but we knew then that there would be another chapter to the *BJ's I Am Canadian History* CD.

Unfortunately, Daniella was busy with work and her youth camping program in June and July, so we finally all got together for the next taped BJ's History Session in late July 2001. I was to have the privilege of introducing Daniella as the guest speaker on "Police Repression of Dissent in Canada Today." We had about fifteen guests, besides the Club members. Eight of the new guests were Daniella's friends; she was busy finding them chairs and making them feel welcome. Two of the guests with Tom and Cam were known to me: their presence came as a bit of a shock. Dana and Deb, the wives of Tom and Cam, seldom accompanied them to the bar anymore to my knowledge, but both wanted to hear Daniella's story. Daniella was delighted when Tom and Cam introduced them to her. Sammy was sitting next to Charles for the first time, and I thought to myself that, what with the needs of the one and the experience of the other, this unlikely combination had some potential.

"Break a leg, Daniella!" Tom called to her. He was a man of the stage.

"You're our closer, Daniella," Cam shook her hand before sitting down. "The BJ's Sessions CD couldn't exist without you." Charles and Sammy waved and smiled.

Finally all twenty or more were seated, crowded into our club's corner at BJ's. From behind the portable pulpit, I tried to explain how we got there. I was excited that the spark plug behind the sessions would now finally be one of the voices of history.

"Welcome to BJ's Tuesday Club. For all our visitors, we thought we'd meet tonight one more time, to add another session to the now notorious *BJ's*

I Am Canadian History Sessions. We are burning some CDs with the full record of these sessions going back over four years now, six years if we include the Matt Shaw tapes from Regina. We hope to have the CDs on sale at cost before September, from the bar there through that doorway.

"The decision to add at least one more chapter was partially due to the way this album of historical vignettes evolved. Several of you here tonight did not have the opportunity to be at any of those sessions, and some of you were only there for Doc Savage's last session on the 1935 Dominion Day Police Riot in Regina. Tonight we have a distinguished guest who is going to talk to us about her experience with police repression of human rights at the Quebec City Summit of the Americas in April of this year. I'm not certain, but she might also be touching on the Battle in Seattle and the APEC Summit in Vancouver of the pepper spray fame.

"But before I introduce her, I'll try to give you folks who are new to this a brief summary of the past BJ's History Sessions, partially as a pitch for our CD."

As everyone laughed, I thought about how much I liked the atmosphere of the larger but compact audience. I tried to gage how much they needed to know.

"We began with the some stories of the Depression and how the massive unemployment among single men led to the relief work camps across Canada. We were privileged to have Doc Savage and Matt Shaw describe the conditions in the camps and the organization of the Relief Camp Workers Union. We heard about the appalling conditions and the virtual slave labour for road work, with the men paid at twenty cents a day. They told us about the strikes, the two months of protests in Vancouver in the spring of 1935 and the emerging leadership of Arthur (Slim) Evans.

"The space between these sessions was anywhere from a week to several months, due to that terrible two-year gap when Doc wasn't well. We filled in the gaps some Tuesday nights taping some of us *younger* folk recalling chapters of our own histories of Alberta and Saskatchewan, from stories of Bible Bill Aberhart to Tommy Douglas. From Christian fundamentalism to Pierre Trudeau and the *War Measures Act* — somehow it all seemed to fit in to our weird collage of Canadian history. Daniella always insisted that we all have important roles in our province's history, so it seems fitting that we are ending with Daniella's story."

People clapped and few raised timid cheers of "Yeah, Daniella."

"One of our topics has been the repression of dissent through police violence, which some of us have experienced personally. So tonight, I'm sure you've all heard the news reports about the infamous fence at the Summit of the Americas in Quebec City, about indiscriminate use of gas and plastic bullets on peaceful protesters in April. Tonight we have with us one of those

273

very civil dissenters who was not engaged in physically challenging the fence nor even in civil disobedience, but nevertheless suffered the same police attacks and arrests as might be expected for the worst criminals on our streets. May I introduce Grande Prairie's own Reverend Daniella Arthur, Associate Minister at Saint Paul's United Church. We've asked her to tell her story and we are all anxious to hear it.

"But just before we hear from Daniella, I'd like to include a comment from one of the stars of our BJ's History Sessions, Daniella's grandfather Robert Doc Savage, who sends his regards. I mentioned to Doc that a colleague of mine from the University of Alberta had cautioned me about including current events in the BJ's History Sessions album. Apparently he mistook my description of our endeavour for a more academic enterprise. He's obviously never had the privilege of a beer at BJ's."

Folks were laughing again, which I appreciated, considering how long my introduction was running.

"He suggested that our tapes' value for the historical archives might be destroyed by including contemporary voices and contemporary issues like the globalization of trade and the Summit of the Americas. I asked Doc Savage what he thought of that. He said, and I quote, 'The problem with your academic friend there is as widespread in the hallowed halls of learning as it is in the rest of Canada today. Folks don't understand that they are part of history and that their actions, their attitudes, even their apathy, all influence history, even as they have been influenced by history. If your friend can't see the connection between the police riot in Regina 1935 and the police riot in Quebec City in April, he is no true historian. Just ignore him. In fact Matt Shaw's testimony and my testimony are made more valuable by Daniella's testimony and those others that dare to declare our struggle a living breathing story rather than a dead relic of a bygone era. Just ignore the academics and keep that tape rolling.'"

Applause filled the room, and I waited. "That was Robert Doc Savage, folks. So now we'll do what the man said and keep the tape rolling for his very special granddaughter, Reverend Daniella Arthur." Before I finished, the applause erupted. Many had heard the rumours of her story. Daniella rose and strode to her place behind her portable pulpit, scanning the crowd, then looking into my eyes.

"Thank you," Daniella said. "Thank you, Dr. Wessner, Known to the regulars of the Tuesday History Club as our own Saint Paul. And thank you, Grandpa, Doc Savage, for teaching me how to be Canadian. Those two men surely know how to make one feel important and significant, don't they? First, I'd like to thank you all for your presence tonight, which indicated to me your interest and concern for the story that I'm reporting on. Second, I'd like to compliment the owners and managers of this establishment for not being so focused on their niche market and the almighty dollar that they didn't have time for the offbeat and novel ideas of Dr. Paul Wessner and company, who first stimulated a grass-roots interest here in the stories of these veterans of the On-to-Ottawa Trek. I understand that BJ's Tuesday nights started out (and I quote), 'as nothing more than anecdotes and bull sessions.' I want to make it clear to any Saint Paul's United Church board members here tonight that I wasn't a party to those inauspicious beginnings."

We all laughed and she continued, "But BJ's management moved with the flow and when Dr. Paul Wessner requested some space for recording an early Doc Savage talk, BJ's came through. When it grew to a semi-regular tradition, BJ's supported it. I don't know of any other bar or pool hall that has held a series of history seminars, unless perhaps the Legion, and then I'm sure it wasn't about labour history." Our laughter set a light and engaging mood.

"Finally, I'd like to thank Doc Savage, Matt Shaw and Paul, as well as Charles, Cam, Tom and Sammy, our Tuesday Club regulars, for teaching me so much about my country and about my historical identity. After all, the BJ's Sessions played a role in motivating me towards this Quebec City trip. So let me explain." Daniella took a deep breath and continued.

"I went to Quebec City in April to protest against the Summit of the Americas, and America's assumption that our planet Earth, its resources and its people were created for the profit and privilege of a few large corporations to do with as they see fit. I went to participate in the program of the NGOs that were running a parallel conference. Most of these NGOs were there to prove that some of the ideologies and interests of the people behind this movement toward broader unregulated trade were not in the best interests of the average working folks in this country, let alone the average working folks of the Latin American countries.

"Now I know what you're thinking: 'Saint Paul's United obviously doesn't have enough work for her to do or she wouldn't be kibitzing around the country getting into trouble.' Actually, it was my work assignments for the church that led me to take my holidays in Quebec City. Several years back I was developing a youth summer camp program for our Naramata Youth Camps, and that led me to a chat with Charles Quamina and Paul Wessner about their experiences in running youth camps. That was over a lemonade here at BJ's. That memorable evening — parts of which have become one of the *BJ's I Am Canadian History Sessions* by the way — that memorable evening inspired me to included a Peace, Justice, and Social Awareness Unit for our youth camp that would encourage young people to be more engaged with the larger issues of their society, and more active in the social and moral issues of their community and nation and planet. In creating this program, I became increasingly conscious that one of the greatest moral issues of the last two decades is this ever-shifting battlefront between the forces for freer trade and the forces for freer people."

Daniella smiled and took a sip of water. "Now again, I know what some of you are thinking — 'More Luddites wailing and crying wolf about the evils of free trade.' But I submit that very few of us Luddites are suggesting that freer trade and freer people are always mutually exclusive or incompatible. However, we are claiming that the two are certainly not partners, nor always headed in the same general direction. For example, not everything that makes Bill Gates richer is bound to make us poorer. But from that true premise some people would fallaciously leap to the conclusion that whatever makes folks like Bill Gates happy will eventually make the rest of us happy. At least with the world of Microsoft, most thinking people can see that this is a fallacy. Strangely, many have a hard time extending that logic to other economic empires.

"The twenty-first-century attempt to remove all restrictions from global trade is in fact an extension of nineteenth-century empire building and twentieth-century economic empire building. Gandhi, Nelson Mandella and Martin Luther King had one thing in common. They all were fighting the fall-out from this progression of empire building. In India they were fighting against classic empire ideology. In South Africa, it was the chaos and racism left behind by British and Dutch colonialism that they opposed. In America, when I was a young girl, Martin Luther King was fighting against the remnants of slavery, which was and still is a major weapon of nineteenth-century empire building, and of twentieth-century economic empire building, and of twenty-first-century corporate globalization.

"The APEC Summit in Vancouver, the MAI talks in Paris, the Battle in Seattle, the Quebec Summit, the Genoa Summit and the G8 Summit in Kananaskis next summer all have a main agenda described benignly as liberalizing international trade. Many folks across the globe know by now that this is a euphemism for corporate globalization, which attempts to give privileged status to larger corporations so that they don't have to be limited by silly little national or provincial governments that might have concerns about environmental issues, labour standards or human rights. Corporate empires don't want these issues impacting on their corporate right to do business as they've always done business. At least as they've always done business in Indonesia, Mexico, the sweatshops of Asia, the labour camps of Nazi Germany (I'm not speaking of the death camps) and the relief camps of Canada in the thirties.

"Oh, I'm sorry for including those last two; I know it is not nice to implicate present world leaders and corporate leaders with such nefarious slave labour conditions. But actually when one starts looking objectively at this, Suharto's Indonesia and many other third-world and first-world regimes often condone labour situations just as horrific as the labour camps in Germany and the relief camps of Canada, with all their ugly racism and right-wing stench. But many of these corporate empires have raced to build factories and do business in such countries, because they don't like to be bound by national or provincial laws that enforce human-rights standards, environmental standards and quality-of-life standards.

"So people like me protest these summits to protect the quality of life, the quality of work and the quality of the environment in our backyards, and also in our neighbours' backyards, in the third-world countries of our planet. Most of these dissenters are educated people with foresight and conscience. The vast majority are not people looking for an adventure with police riot squads.

"Oh, yes, there are always a handful of people like a small minority of the Black Bloc in Quebec, or the Weathermen Underground in the early seventies, or a few of the FLQ in the sixties who, through some twisted logic and personal angst, believe that their violence will miraculously lead to a better world. But my friends, the vast majority of those who protest against corporate globalization are dedicated to democracy and peaceful solutions to conflicting ideas.

"So, folks, when the Quebec Provincial Police threw tear gas grenades at me for sitting on public grounds with other folks with signs protesting the security fence and protesting the agenda behind that fence, in the Green Zones and not the warning areas, when they arrested me for that small expression of my feelings and when they fired plastic bullets at people fleeing the tear gas, I have to ask myself why more people don't stand up and ask, 'Hey, isn't this Canada?' I have to ask myself as a person of conscience and as a person of faith, 'Which is worse? To be behind bars for protesting, or to be a free Canadian — silent and hoping that the problem will go away?'

"And as the heads of first-world nations begin to condone and encourage police violence to defend the sanctity of empire building agendas, that atmosphere of open season on dissenters has led to the death of one dissenter in Genoa, the maiming of an innocent dissenter in Quebec and the brutal attacks and arrests of peaceful protesters in Vancouver, Seattle, Quebec and Genoa.

"However, when the Canadian government raised its voice against the MAI in Paris and sanctioned the participation of NGOs in these talks, the world stepped back from this sort of fascist violence and reaction for a couple of months. Unfortunately, it seems that certain interests were only regrouping. Still, we have a lesson to learn in the grass-roots victory against that Multilateral Agreement on Investments. Because we educated our government leaders, they were forced to take our message to other heads of state. This was accomplished through organized peaceful dissent, and communication, education and international cooperation between NGOs. This didn't just happen with picket signs on the streets of Paris; it happened because progressive grass-roots movements in Canada used their email, their telephones and their old-fashioned postal service to lay the groundwork for victory in Paris.

"In our fight to expose the WTO and the free trade agendas that seem to dominate Group of Eight summits and OECD meetings, we need to remember that victory is not possible if we only depend on last-minute protests at the meeting site. The people of the world, and the governments of the world, need to be prepared ahead of time to look at the issues. That is not to say that legitimate and effective peaceful protest at the sites of these meetings should be downplayed, nor is there any excuse for police violence and repression of peaceful dissent. Nor is there any excuse for our Prime Minister's tacit condoning of that violence and repression of civil liberties. But I am suggesting that we need to prepare the ground for those expressions of peaceful dissent so that they have more chance of succeeding in their purpose." Daniella paused for a drink.

"Excuse me, Daniella, sorry for interrupting. Could you explain for me what kind of CD is an OECD and what the hell's an Enjy OZE?" The guests laughed. Cam rolled his eyes. Tom took a drink. Charles put his hand on Sammy's back to show that we weren't disowning him. Guests were smiling and glancing from Sammy to Daniella to see their respective reactions.

"Hey!" Sammy shrugged, feigning innocence, as if to ask us "What is the big deal?"

"Hey, no kidding," Daniella chuckled. "They've got so many of these organizations, I've forgotten what all the acronyms stand for myself. Who remembers what NAFTA stands for? MAI, GATT, APEC, OPEC, WTO, OECD, NGO? All I can remember most days is that all of them are plotting to get more of my money, except the last one. And that's only because the NGOs just openly send me donation requests." We laughed again.

"Sam," she said, "I'm glad you asked that question because most people in Canada are not familiar with the term NGO or with the OECD. And we often need to apologize for adopting jargon instead of communicating the issues clearly. NGO stands for non-governmental organization, usually a grass-roots organization that is trying to educate the public about corporate globalization or environmental problems. Usually several will meet outside of the official agendas and the official summit meetings, often running parallel conferences or information sessions, attempting to educate and influence both the public and the decision makers. They are an important and growing part of democracy in action."

"So they're good guys?" Sammy wanted it to be clear. He wasn't fazed at all by the laughter.

"They're good guys usually, but sometimes the big corporate interests form their own NGOs to distribute propaganda to confuse the public. The OECD stands for Organization for Economic Co-operation and Development, if I remember right. They are from about twenty-one nations, a first-world big-business front that would like to organize world trade to their advantage and convenience. Sammy, most of us went to Quebec to support the NGOs, to educate ourselves on corporate globalization and to share information with people on-site and with people watching through various media venues. I attended as many of the educational events as I could and was invited to speak at one. I also attended the mass rallies to protest the closed agenda of the Summit and the infringement on charter rights represented by that huge dehumanizing security fence that suggested that we were some kind of livestock that needed herding or corralling.

"Now, depending on the time of day, there were from twenty to fifty thousand protesters, dissenters who like me came to Quebec City specifically to peacefully express their feelings about the summit's agenda and that hated fence. These included the Council of Canadians with Maude Barlow, CUPE members from Ontario, Alberta and elsewhere, nurses' unions, Greenpeace, the NDP and PQ caucuses, Green Party members, many other non-radical labour unions — the usual suspects, according to right-wing media. Probably at least that many ordinary citizens joined us from Quebec City, to swell the march to what many estimated to be about one hundred thousand peaceful marchers.

"There were from fifty to two hundred people on Saturday who self-identified as the Black Bloc. Some describe these as anarchists who believe in the right to 'defend their streets,' as they say, with direct action. Some sources say there were as many as five hundred in the Black Bloc, but, if so, I didn't witness those numbers. These few were prepared with gas masks and some with grappling hooks, wire cutters and other equipment. They clearly intended to breach the security fence that divided neighbourhoods, and this fence created a general backlash, especially in downtown Quebec. Now I was warned by my Tuesday Club friends here of some sinister troublemakers called the Black Hoods who sought to provoke violence at peaceful protests. I did see perhaps fifteen of these young people with hoods among the Black Bloc, but they just seemed to be the least prepared and equipped of the very organized Bloc — those who couldn't afford a gas mask I suppose. Surprisingly to me, the Black Bloc members that we encountered were very helpful in warning the rest of us where the Green Zone was (supposedly free from danger of confrontation) and where the Red Zone was, where police reaction might be expected. This was not the behaviour the media had taught us to expect. They did not seem to need or want our help; they did not want us to put ourselves in harms way."

Daniella looked directly into my eyes, and then at each Club member who had warned her about these dangerous people; we all knew the questions behind that look, and none of us had the answers.

"On a signal, these gas-masked Black Bloc members, with those few Black Hoods among them, rushed the fence: within five or ten minutes, they had breached a three-metre heavy-gage fence in a significant way. The police initially backed off a ways until the well-armed riot troops arrived, so some of the people in the Yellow Zone, between the pacifists and the Black Bloc, joined them on the lawn inside the forbidden zone. Before that happened, these 'dangerous provocateurs' rolled in a catapult that launched teddy bears." Daniella stared directly at Tom and me again for a few seconds while the crowd responded with surprised laughter.

"I must say that this was not the kind of incitement to violence that Paul, Charles and Tom had warned me of. However, the riot police when they arrived never bothered to try to arrest all those within the forbidden zone. They marched into the crowd with riot shields, helmets, batons. Tear gas canisters were fired not just in front of the crowd but into all areas — Red Zone, Yellow Zone and our Green Zone — zones that the police themselves had designated. Their first actions were to throw tear gas canisters all throughout the crowd near the fence, to put on their gas masks and to begin firing plastic bullets at anyone in the front of that crowd before they had time to react.

"It reminded me very much of the accounts I have read of the police attack on the Regina citizens and Trekkers of the On-to-Ottawa Trek, which you've been hearing about in these BJ's History Sessions. Except these police started with gas and plastic bullets rather than gas and clubs. The bullets came later in Regina, and the clubs came later in Quebec. But, in both cases, the police decided to attack the peaceful crowd with the same weapons as they used on those more aggressive protesters, in this case the Black Bloc fence-wreckers with their teddy-bear catapult. It didn't take long before our Green Zone was attacked with gas and plastic stun bullets.

"Why would the police do that? There can be only one reason. They were trying to tar thousands of peaceful, intelligent, educated dissenters with the same brush as the, quote, 'anarchists' and the Black Bloc. Now before you start to believe that I condone the teddy-bear revolutionaries, let me be clear that, after fighting with and escaping from baton-swinging riot police and mounted police, a handful of the Back Bloc went on to smash several windows of the CIBC Bank and tried to torch it. Some of the peaceful protesters tried to prevent them from this unforgivable and senseless property damage. This did not seem like a pre-planned attack since most of the Black Bloc actions were well executed and well-thought-out.

"I have to admit that many of the Green Zone protesters, who didn't witness that vandalism, were increasingly sympathetic to the Black Bloc as long as they stuck to symbolic fence-felling and teddy-bear launching. In fact there was considerable cheering when someone announced that the many kilometres of security fence had five major breaches. However, those handful involved in serious property damage got the attention of the media; that was the whole story initially, just as it was in Regina in 1935, and at the Battle In Seattle in 1999."

Daniella stopped for some water, and surveyed us intensely as if her congregation needed to concentrate for the crucial point of a sermon.

"Many of the police and most of the press showed a cheap, dishonest and callous willingness to close their eyes to violations of human rights for the sake of smearing the reputation of the democratic folks who wish to express a dissenting opinion. For example, I was one of those peaceful observers who had come there to learn, to share information, to let the governments of these leading nations know that there were other citizens in their countries that needed to be heard on the subject. Yet they threw tear gas my way, though I was nowhere near the fence and not headed toward it or threatening any aggressive action. Neither were the people in my immediate vicinity, yet they fired this known carcinogen at us and fired plastic bullets at us, hitting a woman near me in the leg. I don't know if you are familiar with these bullets, but they pack a wallop that is meant to injure, and they just about killed a young man there by hitting him in the throat. He has not yet fully recovered the proper use of his voice and breathing as a result.

"Arrests became more random as the day continued. The leader of the Green Party and Jaggi Singh, a well-known activist, were arrested by undercover agents early on despite being far into the Green Zones and not engaged in any illegal actions. Finally, not just known people, but seemingly random peaceful protesters like myself were arrested. I was sitting near a teach-in site for one of the NGOs when police started arresting the present-ers. When I told them that we understood this to be a Green Zone, I was pushed against a wall, handcuffed and told that I was obstructing justice. New Democrat MP Svend Robinson was also shot in the ankle by a plastic bullet and has filed a formal complaint against the RCMP."

Now her voice rose with passionate appeal, and her left hand rose with one finger pointed skyward. "Yet somehow the right-wing of the Canadian press decided that this was the kind of fun we had all come for, that we wouldn't be there if we didn't expect violent conflict with the police. Folks. that is exactly the kind of thinking that Hitler depended on when he prom-ised his law-and-order agenda, which was just an excuse, as we now know, to violently attack his democratic opposition. When everyday middle-class people refuse to speak up in Germany, in Indonesia, in Columbia, in Mexico, even in Canada, then police repression of human rights increases. I am not hear to preach at you folk, because, by the very fact of your attendance here tonight, you are demonstrating your concern and your determination to know the truth about these matters."

The audience members that I could see focused on her without so much as a twitch; I was impressed with her stage presence.

"But I made my own personal decision," she said, "to hold these men accountable for their illegal actions. We cannot achieve peace and security through violent repression of peaceful dissent and violation of human rights. Thus, I am in the process of launching legal action against the RCMP who fired those shells and tea gas canisters in our Green Zone area, who made indiscriminate arrests. I want to hold them responsible for the physical assaults and the assaults on my dignity and my reputation. I'm sure that everyone throughout history who was assaulted, like I was, wanted to pursue legal action against their assailants, but many were not in a position to do so. I like to think that I am taking this action in part for them, as well as for my own injury. I believe that an assault against a morally concerned and civilly engaged citizen is an assault against each one of us and against our collective human rights."

Some guests responded with light applause, and some looked like they wanted to respond but weren't sure what was appropriate.

"In Genoa, Italy, the police killed a protester last week, and savagely beat up on protesters and journalists alike. They didn't discriminate. Anyone there was in danger. The police became terrorists like the brown-shirted thugs of Mussolini. There is no difference, my friends. The folks who buried their heads in the sand during Mussolini's reign of terror thought the same thoughts that folks who bury their heads in the sand in America and Canada think. Many good Christian folks defended the Ohio National Guard when they shot and killed four students for protesting against Vietnam because they thought at the time that the local policing of civil unrest or dissent could not be all that bad. Yet plastic bullets have killed people, and crippled people, too. But they continue to use plastic bullets against peaceful dissent in Canada. Tear gas is a proven and virulent carcinogen, yet they use it in Canada against peaceful dissent. They got away with it at Quebec City, and our Prime Minister bragged about the job they did, and suggested they could be tougher at Kananaskis. He might as well have quoted his mentor and said, 'Why, just watch me!' That is certainly what he meant.

"It worries me that my right to disagree with the agenda of a meeting, and my right to express that peacefully, but publicly, is being denied. The police humiliated us by strip-searching us as if we were drug addicts suspected of smuggling drugs into the prison. Why must Canadian police continue that tradition of humiliating people whose ideas they don't understand, humiliating them with physical and psychological brutality?

"Friends, I'm hoping that by now some of you are thinking, 'Yes but what can *I* do?' Perhaps you're thinking, 'I'm not the type that gets active for any cause. I don't like it, but what could I possibly do to change it?' If you're thinking like that, I've got something that you can do that will only take fifteen minutes or less from the comfort of your home or office. We've found that emails and phone calls and letters to the proper place are extremely effective, perhaps a hundred to a thousand times more effective than a vote at the ballot box, which can be misinterpreted as support or lack of support for almost anything. So if you believe in your duty to vote, why not do something that takes less time, but has far more impact.

"I am passing around this short list of email addresses of the Prime Minister's office, the Attorney General, the RCMP Commissioner, key cabinet ministers. I also have phone numbers where you might not get to talk to these same people, but you will talk to people who will take down a message that will be read by these people. Make sure you write down briefly what you want to say to make it concise and cogent. We have included some sample messages, brief and to-the-point, about police repression of civil liberties, and about corporate globalization of trade. They might help you make up your own personal message. Direct and personal is the key, and sign your name. If you believe in voting, then 'cast your whole ballot,' as Thoreau says, not just an X beside a name."

Again the audience applauded, more freely this time. I thought I could see a fierce love in the faces of some of Daniella's female friends.

"If you would like more information, I have listed some web-sites and email lists that you might want to sign on to for awhile. And as parents, I suggest that you let your children see what you are doing in this regard. Believe me, it will be one of their longest and fondest memories of you in the decades to come, even after we parents are gone from this world.

"Thank you for listening and thank you for caring."

As applause erupted, everyone rose to their feet. Pride shone in the faces of the Club members, not to mention her friends at the other tables. I felt what I imagined was a collective urge to celebrate this woman's spirit. I wanted to give her and the audience time to savour this, so I came forward to thank her, to keep her up there.

We smiled at each other. "Thank you, Reverend Daniella Arthur. I am reminded of Paul and Silas and Peter and John and a host of those other early Christians who went to prison for their beliefs. I think, two thousand years ago Daniella might have caused an earthquake in those prisons too. Questions for Reverend Arthur?" I waited. The waitresses were collecting bottles and glasses, but no one was getting up to leave.

Tom took the lead, "How long did they keep you in jail and what did they charge you with?"

"They initially charged me with interfering with an officer in the discharge of his duty, but they dropped the charge in the morning and let me go, since I hadn't interfered or resisted at all. They tried to suggest that just by sitting there in an area that they wanted to clear was interfering with an officer. In fact it was similar to what Doc Savage said about arrests in Regina in '35. They weren't serious charges, just something vague so that they couldn't be accused of frivolous arrests, which many of them were, I think."

"Did they give you a reason for the strip-search? And who conducted it?" It was a woman, who asked this one. I took this opportunity to sit down.

"There was a police matron there at the station; the five women who were arrested with me were ushered into this fairly empty waiting room next to the showers and told to do whatever the matron ordered, or else. She explained that this was all routine and that we had to empty all our pockets into some trays with our names and leave our bags or purses with the trays. We were told we'd get the items back eventually. Then we were told to strip and to leave our clothes in a neat pile next to our tray and bags. One girl was having her period and asked if she could be excused from the exercise. She was told no one was excused from this. I'm sorry if this gets too graphic or if my voice chokes up a bit on this subject."

Daniella paused for a deep breath and forced her head to one side as if stretching out tense neck muscles. "The girl asked if she could at least keep her panties on and keep some pads with her. She was told, no, she had to take everything off and that they would bring her institutional-issue pads, along with the institutional clothing that we were issued. So she had to go through this extra humiliation. Then the matron apologized, but said that she had her orders and that we all had to bend over hands touching the ground, legs spread. Routine security check to see if we were hiding any contraband in certain places of our anatomy, she explained. The girl with her period was trying to hide the fact that she was crying, which caused me to choke up."

Daniella paused again. "I'd never before experienced tears of anger and hatred like this, hatred for a system that allowed this kind of degradation, just because they wanted to teach us a lesson about authority and what they thought of female protesters. The matron just walked behind us inspecting us; she didn't touch us. I don't think she was enjoying it, but I suppose it was her job. Anyway, then they made us all shower and use a vile-smelling soap and shampoo that was suppose to kill lice or something. It felt like it was capable of killing hair roots, too. I think it turns the skin raw wherever it touches. Some of the women prisoners testified that male guards herded them naked into the disinfection shower rooms.

"Anyway, I'm starting to shake just thinking about it. Friends, forgive me, I'm not great at responding to off-the-cuff to questions. Perhaps, I can answer other questions later, one-on-one."

I got up quickly and spoke as I approached her, "That would be fine, Daniella. I mean Reverend Arthur," I corrected myself. I wanted to put an arm around her but wasn't sure about doing this in public.

"Daniella's fine, Paul." She grinned at my embarrassment, as the people applauded again.

"Thank you," Daniella said, looking from face to face in the audience, her friends smiling back at her. "You've been terrific and understanding. If I could leave you with one thought, it is this: if more people today refuse to be silent about police violence and repression of human rights, even as those good people of Regina refused to be silent sixty-some years ago, then our children's world will be better for it. And I realize that some people have different levels of comfort with expressing their beliefs in public ways. So this sheet we've handed out will help you find a medium or a forum in which you can be comfortable, yet still express your feelings and beliefs. Or perhaps you might just want to find out more information. Information and education are the bedrock of healthy democracy. Thank you again."

We all clapped and cheered. Even though there were only twenty people in the chairs set up in our corner room, the patrons near the bar in the next room were silenced by the repeated applause. Everyone wanted to talk to Daniella, and her friends came up to give her hugs. She smiled and engaged them all even though I knew she was tired. Even Tom, Cam and Sammy hugged her. I was sorry I hadn't embraced her immediately before the rush, but I was exhilarated, as I had been thirty years earlier at those sawdust trail meetings, perhaps.

When Daniella's guests and the friends of Tom and Cam finally took their leave, BJ's regulars, along with the wives of Tom and Cam, lingered a bit to say goodbye, since we all suspected that we'd just seen the end of the BJ's History Sessions, even if remnants of the Tuesday Club continued informally.

Charles was the first to make a move to take his leave and head for home, since he tended tire out before the "younger bucks," as he ironically called us. So Charles shook my hand, but held on to it while he reached for Daniella's hand with his left.

"Listen you two," he said with his fatherly voice, "we've got to get together next week to put some order into these history sessions, do some editing and go over Paul's journal to see what we can use to fill out this project of ours. So you two might want to put your heads together and give that some thought. Give me a call when you're ready. You're welcome to come on over for a coffee at my place." He finally released our hands from his joint benediction.

We all said good bye to Charles, with hugs all around.

"That's more hugs than I've had in the last decade," Charles said. "Do I get one from you or not, Sammy?"

"Handshakes are as much as I can handle with the brothers," Sammy smiled, shook his hand and clapped his shoulder. He teased Charles about having to get home early, and then Charles was off.

It appeared to me that Dana and Deb were ready to take their husbands, Tom and Cam, home early for a change, so Daniella and I shared a quick meeting of the eyes that said that we were not willing to shut the place down with Sammy. Since she had walked that evening, I offered to drive her home, and she accepted. That certainly got the attention of the guys.

"Now, it's not my place to meddle," Sammy said, "but accepting a ride home from a bar with a professor on the prowl could be a mite risky."

"Especially one with an inherent lack of respect for the clergy," Tom added with a wink. I shook my head and rolled my eyes. What could I expect?

Cam just laughed and gave Daniella a bearhug. Tom and Sammy followed suit, giving Daniella hugs and clapping me on the shoulder as if they knew a chapter had closed. Dana and Deb gave Daniella and me polite hugs, since that seemed the order of the day, and then we walked out of BJ's together.

When we arrived at her place, she invited me up for a nightcap, and I accepted with mixed emotions, wondering if this was something the Saint Paul's United Church Board would approve of.

As I write this I even worry that my potential readers of this journal might not approve. Not the moral question but the genre question of the author including an evening nightcap with an attractive female in what was supposed to be the history of western Canada. But even the inhibitions of a middle-aged insecure author have some potential for humour and history. So forget about questions of genre and protocols of formal discourse; just wait there on the couch with me in her apartment for that cold beer Daniella is bringing. Even this casual beer fits into the history of western Canada, if you allow it.

All right folks, perhaps you don't need the blow-by-blow account of our conversation on the couch over those mugs of beer. But you do need to know how we ended up planning a final chapter for the *BJ's I Am Canadian History* CD.

As I remember it, I complimented her presentation and she apologized for being too graphic. I thought she should take the story to the people, run for Parliament. She thought I was flattering her, and I argued that I honestly admired her. Then she admitted that she just wasn't used to sincere compliments from successful senior men of status.

I remember her saying at one point, "Truth or dare, as they used to say when we were young." I think in context she meant that one could rarely dare to be truthful, but that is not the way I remember that game. I could never tell throughout the evening if she was flirting with me or if it was just my fertile imagination.

Thus, in my insecurity, I tried all evening to stick to a proper academic conversation like the church's stubborn refusal to address women as fully human and equal. I suggested that this was the issue that finally turned me, severed me from the church and from religions generally. I even said something corny like "As Luther said, 'Here I stand; I can do no other.'" She laughed at me and asked if that was really my final Damascus Road conversion to secular Christian status. Apparently she considered me a secular Christian just because I still acted altruistically.

When I asked if that meant there was hope for an alliance between the left and the peace-and-justice movements in the church, she suggested that the two of us were a great example of such an alliance. She managed to personalize every ideological direction I followed.

"Maybe not exactly in the same bed," she grinned, looking me in the eyes, "but at least sharing in the same movement."

Well I think it was after that comment that I decided that she was flirting. I think my face might have heated up a bit from the directness of her eyes. She was much more comfortable on that couch than I was. On the other hand, Daniella was too good a friend now for me to make a mistake in reading her signals.

After what seemed like a couple of tantalizing hours, I finally found the plan for the ending of the evening and the ending of BJ's CD. I looked her straight in the eyes and told her what a lovely evening it had been and that I could not remember the last time a woman that I liked had invited me up for a drink and fine conversation after a long evening. I was obviously suggesting that I was headed home. But I was still getting to my plan.

I mentioned that her granddad, Doc Savage, was turning ninety on July 30, just a few days away, and that if she were contemplating a trip there to celebrate it, then I would like to offer her a ride there and back. She had Monday off, and that was his birthday. Then I explained my excuse for the offer. We could take him out for a meal and maybe get him to do just one more tape to wrap up the BJ's CD. I suggested that Doc had a few loose ends about Slim Evans and the Inquiry Commission that could make a fitting close to the CD, and that he wouldn't mind talking with a tape running if Daniella would ask him to do this as part of his birthday celebration.

Well, folks, I seem to recall Daniella smiling through that long pitch, and I could tell she was looking right through my scheme. She mentioned that it was a long way and that we couldn't possibly return in one day. Her eyes were staring into mine because we were already standing, and I could tell she wanted me to be up-front on this delicate question of getting a hotel room. I admitted that we would have to stay in Prince George Monday night and that there were some reasonably priced hotels, if she could take Tuesday morning off. Usually I don't smile enough; at that moment, I couldn't stop smiling, and my eyes weren't even tempted to drop.

"You know," she said as she slowly started to smile back at me, "I don't have anything on till Tuesday evening. I don't think anybody would miss me as long as we got back by 8 p.m. I think I'd like to spend that time with you."

She went on to say that she was looking forward to it, that the Pine Pass should be wonderful this time of year. Fourteen hours or more on the road with "her favourite conversationalist" was the way she described it, as she followed me to the door.

I stopped with my hand on the door knob. She kept following and smiling. But then she came right up to me with obvious intentions, and I let go of the door knob just in time to almost respond appropriately, but still off balance, to her good-bye hug and a quick kiss on my cheek.

"That's thank you, Paul, for a wonderful evening."

She stepped back and we looked at each other, grinning. I was forty-eight and divorced; she was forty-two, single and a United Church minister. I remember at that point thinking about Sammy. Sammy would be bound to ask her outright about this evening. And then what could she say?

"Hey Daniella," I could hear him. "We warned ya, didn't we, about this Romeo. You can't trust these lefties. They have sinister intentions. They support women's lib for a reason, you know. It is all about friggin' seduction to these academics."

Nevertheless the main point here was not about the six days of eager anticipation, the trip to Quesnel ahead of us or the road home. The main point was that we would be working out the details of the conclusion to this story, this history of which we had been a significant part. There would be time for second thoughts for each of us, let the denouement come, come what may.

The door was open, and I was stepping through, the two of us waving and smiling. I noted that she, too, had decided not to clarify the number of hotel rooms needed in Prince George. And I was happy that Sammy was not around to challenge the validity or relevance of this chapter's conclusion.

20

ALLEGIANCES

DOC SAVAGE ON THE RIOT INQUIRY, THE SPANISH CIVIL WAR AND EVANS

I PICKED DANIELLA UP AT 8 A.M. on July 30. She was packed and set to go. Smiling, she remarked about my readiness; I just grinned foolishly. We were determined to arrive early enough in the afternoon to have some quality time with Doc who would be waiting for us. We had wonderful conversations, a stimulating breakfast and lunch, and the only topic we didn't get to was the hotel in Prince George at the end of the day. In Quesnel, Doc was a gracious host, taking us on a tour of his world including the gravel bar in the Fraser that had been his place of employment, so to speak, for the better part of two decades. He introduced us proudly to some of his remaining friends, who joined us for birthday cake. We helped him organize his files, editing them to a manageable amount for this last kick at the Trek lectures. Some of his friends stayed sitting around the kitchen table with us to be a part of this last session.

"So Robert, one last recording," I said. "Happy birthday from all of us here!"

"Thank you."

"Happy ninetieth, Grandpa," Daniella said. "We're honoured to be a part of this little celebration."

"Well, the nice thing is you can't expect me to remember anything now that I'm ninety. So it could be a short tape," he said.

"Yours is the best and most detailed memory of any of the Trekkers that I've interviewed, Robert," I said.

"Well, there aren't a lot left to argue with you on that account," he said.

"That's a fact. Maybe you can start by telling us what things of interest happened after the relief camp workers went home on the cushions. What happened with the Riot Inquiry Commission in Regina, and what happened to Art Evans after he and the other three were finally acquitted? Whatever you find interesting."

Of course, Doc had friends watching so he was well prepared with notes and script. Like Matt Shaw, he now was very aware that history was finally taking notes, that the archives were finally hearkening. He began in full speech mode as if Art Evans had asked him instead of Matt Shaw to represent the grand cause to Maple Leaf Gardens. Maybe to all of Canada, down through the generations.

"The thing you have to keep in mind about the Regina Riot Inquiry Commission is that it was set up by Premier Gardiner, who was still furious at Prime Minister Bennett for usurping his authority over the RCMP and precipitating the chaos in Regina. Bennett then pulled all the tricks in his powerful bag to delay the inquiry till the federal election was over in October. Of course, then Mackenzie King and the Liberals were in power and it was no longer expedient to get the general public riled up about unemployed workers and violent and vicious police. So there was a marked change in the rationale and goals of the Inquiry. The whitewash for establishment interests soon became evident. Nevertheless, our single lawyer for the Trekkers, man by the name of Cunningham, did a fairly thorough job of bringing forward scores of credible eyewitnesses to the events of July First. So the transcripts of the Inquiry contain some fairly illuminating testimony as to what happened that night.

"Of course, the other side had four lawyers to our one. The feds had these two shysters who had scrounged up the evidence to charge Evans and Shaw and company. So of course they did their damnedest to prove we were violent communist revolutionaries, since their reputations were at stake. The city police had their lawyer there to make sure the Commission wouldn't be allowed to admit evidence too embarrassing to the bobbies, though they couldn't avoid testimony of them drawing pistols and firing directly at a crowded intersection. And the Commission had their own lawyer who seemed to protect the interests of the federal government, as well as to rant and rave if Evans or anyone criticized the biases of the Commission itself. On the bench, the Commission had three judges: Chief Justice Brown, who was chairing it, Justice Martin and Judge Doak — all conservative establishment folk naturally.

"This Inquiry started on November 12, after the federal election, and continued virtually every working day until it concluded in April of 1936. So, as you can imagine, the transcripts include scores of files and photos and thousands of pages of testimony. I've collected a few photocopied samples from the Saskatchewan archives there, well, more than a few, I suppose. Reporters, Trekkers, citizens. Very interesting to hear the events from different perspectives, different locations.

"Let me give you a few examples. Harold Kritzweiser, reporter for the *Regina Leader-Post*. He was on site and witnessed the carnage at many of the hot spots, especially downtown at 11th Avenue and vicinity. He worked for a paper that is not quite as biased as that conservative mouthpiece called the *Regina Daily Star*. He wrote out his account and they read from it at the Inquiry, and questioned him, asked him for clarification, etcetera.

"Listen to this for example: *These two men came to the head of the alley and came out into the lamplight, and some missiles were [thrown] — I don't know what they were — at the policeman, and two Mounted Policemen shouted something — "get those... sons of guns" — or something like that; and two Mounted policemen detached themselves from the group of police and ran to the entrance of the alley and fired.* Now this is his written testimony. *Mounties yanked out their revolvers and blazed into the darkness. They got their quarry, one striker being hit by bullets in both legs.* That was Phillips who I told you about at BJ's who was pulled into the back door of a restaurant from the alley west of Cornwall.

"Listen to his description after the city police gunned down the folks later at Scarth and 11th: *Two striker's Red Cross men came across the street to render aid to the fallen man on the sidewalk. Two policemen first stopped them, then sighting the red armbands let them go... Another Mounted [police] man stopped them. The strikers pleaded they were not fighting and explained their armbands. At this point up ran Ed Stern [Regina coal dealer] who, armed with a police club, was with the city police. He interrupted the explanations, shouting that the men were strikers anyway and that the armbands made no difference... They were hustled away.* Meaning arrested.

"How do you like them apples? Listen to this later in his testimony. One of these shysters for the feds, in charge of making the Section 98 charges stick, asks him this:

Question: In fact, as we follow the events that transpired that evening, is it not fair to say, and a fact, that the police were trying to get them away from the centre of the city?

Answer: No, I would not say that, that they were trying to get them away.

Question: But you told us that the police were warning the people to get out of the way, and wanting them to go home?... Did that not apply to strikers as well as citizens?

Answer: I do not remember any instance where a policeman was talking to a striker to get him to go home.

"Interesting, in light of other witnesses — another radio reporter for example — who saw the RCMP from the station scurry to cut us off when we were past Cornwall and their police station and on towards Lorne heading to the Exhibition Grounds. The reporter saw them outflank us in that car lot on the other side of the Grande Theatre. Pretty clear they weren't done smashing us up and they weren't interested in us getting back to the Grounds until after there were bodies shot down in pools of blood in the street, and that sobered them up a bit.

"Another thing the transcripts reveal is the disdain which most of the Crown lawyers had for the status and credibility of working-class Regina citizens and the unemployed. Many of the witnesses sensed this, and reacted to it in various ways.

"Corson, a Regina printer, testified to the Mounties clubbing indis-criminately and to one of them firing a gun near the crowd around the Post Office. So the shysters for the feds cross-examined him, pointing out that he did printing for the Unity Centre where our temporary office was.

Would you say you are strong in your sympathy for them? And, You think they are absolutely right? And, Would you say that you are a big booster for them? These are the insidious questions.

"Corson finally answered, *No. I am not a booster for anybody. I am a human being, though. I was brought up poor. And yes, I respect the poor.*

Question: You never attacked the police? Why would he single you out? Are you sure he said those words?

Answer: I will swear before Almighty God, that's what he told me. I wouldn't have repeated it in court unless the Judge had instructed me to. He said, "You son of a bitch, get out of here." I had my arm up to protect my head and replied, "Give me some time, and I will get out.

"Another case where the mucky-muck lawyers couldn't conceal their disdain for the witness was when Mrs. Frances Ryan testified. She was owner and operator of Ryan's Restaurant at 1761 Scarth Street, just north of the intersection with the worst shootings. She refused to hide her disdain for the police and their actions on that particular night, and this annoyed the shysters. Describing the action, she suggested that after the Trekkers and rock throwers had held the intersection for a while, *the police stood around feeling sorry for themselves.* The lawyers warned her that she wasn't at liberty to speak impressionistically, that she was to stick to what she'd seen and heard. She ignored them and told her story her way, impressionistically.

"When she helped the men who had been shot and were taken into her establishment, she describes the intruding Mountie: *I find this Mountie on horseback in the front entrance. I told him to get the hell out. It wasn't a stable.*

"She was one of the witnesses who described us getting into our ranks, four abreast earlier, before the shootings, to head to the Exhibition Grounds. She said, *The mounted police closed in on them from both sides. Police got hitting them right and left and the boys retaliated, and I don't blame them.* The lawyers repeatedly warned her, indignantly, not to make assumptions like where we were headed, and *not* to comment about her feelings. She just refused to be intimidated and told it her way. Could any here use some more tea? Daniella? Jake?"

Over Daniella's objection, Doc was getting up from the kitchen table, headed for the stove to get the kettle and to make some tea. As I paused the tape, I noticed how well Doc was doing.

"You get to fuss over me in Grande Prairie, but here I get the privilege of waiting on my friends." He looked like he was enjoying turning ninety and entertaining the friends who were honouring him. Finally, after serving us all, he settled back in the chair and signalled me that he was ready to go again.

"So one of these witnesses, John Cheers, who was trying to keep his wife from harm downtown, testifies to hearing strikers pleading with citizens to go home because they didn't want any more hurt. He also witnessed the strikers on 12th Avenue line up in ranks and try to head for the Exhibition Grounds. The shyster lawyers couldn't stand this kind of testimony, because it undercut their contention that the boys were there to riot, attack officers and cause trouble.

"The only one they didn't dare try to humiliate was Evans. They were very careful with him because I think they sensed his fearlessness. There is one point in Evans' testimony where the federal lawyer felt an obligation to defend his master, the Prime Minister. I have to read you this:

Evans: [about Bennett] By this time he was quite angry. He said, "Work and wages! This is impossible. Where will we go to get the money for this?" He barked this at us.

Lawyer: I don't think this witness can be said to be fair to Mr. Bennett when he said he barked at him.

Chairman: I think we understand what he means.

Lawyer: It is quite obvious it is intended to prejudice Mr. Bennett.

Judge Doak: We can understand that the witness is perhaps a little biased in these matters.

Evans: I am going to take objection to that. I am not biased. There will be eight delegates who will give evidence before this commission that my statement in connection with the treatment of the delegation by Mr. Bennett is quite correct. If this Commission is going to take the attitude that I am biased...

Judge Doak: Don't start criticizing the Commission.

Evans: I say I was not biased!

Judge Doak: The language you use in respect to Mr. Bennett shows you are biased.

Evans: I think when the other delegates report to you it will assure you that I am not biased. The words used by Mr. Bennett were arrogant, domineering, and cynical and quite uncalled for!

Justice Martin: We just want to know what took place. I don't care about any criticism of Mr. Bennett. I want to know the facts.

Evans: Those are the facts! I merely raised the objection to the statement that my statements of fact are biased.

"And with that they forgot about the lawyer's objection and let Evans continue. They never made further insinuations about his judgement that I could find. The Chairman eventually complimented him on his credibility as a witness.

"Anyway, I suppose we can't go into almost ten thousand of pages of testimony. Despite the overwhelming evidence presented, the Commissioners summarized the riot as being the result of a well-intentioned attempt to arrest the leaders of the Trek. Nobody paid too much attention to their summary, because the trial of Evans, Black, Shaw and Cosgrove had established their innocence, and the vast majority of Canadian people had judged the Trekkers and former Prime Minister Bennett at the polls. Regina itself elected a city council that fall where the United Front leftist coalition took virtually every position, and that says something about the mood of the voting citizens of Regina following this affair. By the time the Commission ended with fifty-two volumes of testimony, the relief camps were about to be abolished and Section 98 was in the process of being repealed by the King government. I think Evans, Shaw, Black and Cosgrove were the last four to be charged under that statute."

"Doc," Daniella asked, "can you tell us in brief what became of Evans, perhaps some of the highlights of the rest of his life?"

"Well, let me see. His speaking tours during and after the Inquiry and the trials, of course, not only helped to pressure the government into shutting down the camps and Section 98, they also made him a very popular, in-demand speaker among leftist circles from one end of the country to the other. So that same year another struggle took centre stage for the Canadian left. That was the Spanish Civil War. As I mentioned before, several of my closest friends on the Trek enlisted. Well, Arthur took up that cause and eventually was sponsored on a speaking tour on the subject of the fascist threat to Europe and the world."

"Doc," Daniella said, "I know we've mentioned this in the BJ's Sessions before, but give us a brief idea why you see this as so connected to our story here in Canada."

Doc looked at her and nodded with a chuckle. "Brief eh? Okay. In 1936 the Spanish had an exciting election, too. They elected a Popular Front coalition of several progressive parties: the Left Republicans, the Socialists, the Anarcho-Syndicalists, the Basque Nationalists and the Communists. Immediately the banking and the industrial establishment joined forces with the biggest landowners and with the Catholic Church hierarchy to plot their overthrow by financing General Franco and a minority of extreme right-wing elements in the army. So Franco was able to purchase the support of an entire mercenary army from Morocco and elsewhere, and he launched a powerful invasion backed by Italy and Germany, who were more than willing to supply major armaments, and to export technicians to accompany the hardware. For Hitler and Mussolini and their generals, this was like a scrimmage, preparing for the greater games. They were the new kids on the block when it came to empire ambitions in Africa (not to mention Europe), so Spain was the perfect launching pad.

"Governments in America and England were kind of infatuated with Hitler and Mussolini. Remember the Olympic Games in Germany? Did you see the movie *Tea With Mussolini*? Those women's reaction to fascism was typical of our upper classes, too. Britain, Canada and America pretend now that it wasn't so, but we collaborated, and now there's a deathly silence and cover-up of that collaboration. But these three countries joined Hitler and Mussolini in blockading Spain's ports much like America has done with Cuba for years. As Ben Swankey said in *Work and Wages*, the policy of appeasement didn't start with Chamberlain and Munich in 1938, as our history books state. It started with Canada, America and Britain, directly aiding Hitler, Mussolini and Franco in the overthrow of the democratically elected progressive government of Spain, from 1936–1938. The rationale was that, if we sell Spain down the river, maybe Hitler in appreciation would go beat up on Stalin for us and then the British, American and French empires wouldn't have to worry so much about these lesser Eastern European empires wanting a foothold elsewhere, like in Africa or the Middle East or the Far East where the big money was.

"But through all this, democrats around the world found it offensive and rallied to send medical aid and funds to the people of Spain to help defend their fragile democracy. Norman Bethune was a big part of that in Spain, inventing and initiating mobile blood transfusions there on the battlefields for the first time in history. Arthur Evans was a big part of that in Canada, raising money for Bethune for ambulances and supplies. So, as we said previously, the young idealistic men and women from England, France, Mexico, Russia, Canada and elsewhere responded to the Spanish government's call for help. Thousands travelled to Spain to enlist in the International Brigades

Arthur (Slim) Evans toured to rally support for the Canadian Medical Mission (of Norman Bethune fame) for the forces fighting fascism in Spain 1936–37. Glenbow Museum Archives, Calgary. NA-3634-17.

to fight Franco. Twelve hundred Canadian volunteers formed the Mackenzie-Papineau Battalion. Some estimate that over 400 of those were boys that had been with us on the Ottawa Trek. Only half came back.

"Funny how these 'unemployed bums' and 'dangerous communists,' as the right-wing press and governments called us, were some of the few 'educated' enough to see the danger to Europe and the world in 1936 and '37. Canadians, as usual, had a hard time seeing how our democracy was threatened by a war over there. But Canada actively aided the demise of democracy in Spain, participating in the blockade — sort of like Americans who couldn't see that by aiding General Pinochet's murder of President Allende, and by aiding his squelching of democracy in Chile, that they were threatening their own democracy at home. Even the Pentagon Papers and Watergate couldn't fully awaken a brainwashed, apathetic public. That's the way it was in Canada back in '36. We turned away a boatload of Jewish refugees fleeing concentration camps because the wealthy opinion makers were too comfortable in fortress Canada. I really believe that the wealthy in Canada are often more comfortable with the Liberals in power than when some right-wing conservative government like Mulroney's begins to wake up the slumbering consciences of the educated.

"So that was Slim Evans' next big fight. And of course I connect it to this story you're working on because my friends are buried there in Spain — Pete Nielson, Paddy O'Neal. Some of them returned, like Red Walsh, Tony Martin, Perry Hilton and Ronnie Liversedge. But what they witnessed in Market Square and downtown Regina drove them to be a little more sensitive about fascism than the average Canadian. And I think we owe an apology

Arthur (Slim) Evans organizing in Trail, B.C., circa 1938–1939.
Glenbow Museum Archives, Calgary. NA-3634-19.

to the ones buried in Spain, and to the ones that came back, for turning our eyes away from it all, and thereby fostering a much larger war in Europe.

"Okay I'm preaching. But as for Evans, he fought a few more big union battles before the war broke out, like organizing Cominco in Trail. The goons demolished his car in that one at Trail. When he left that assignment, Arthur was tired and disillusioned, and I think that one is just too long a story. He decided his young family needed to see more of him, and they spent the summer of 1939 sluicing for gold around Lillooet. His daughter, Jean, always remembered that summer fondly. When the war broke out, he moved the family to Vancouver, bought an old house eventually, probably a carpenter's special, since renovating houses was how he fed the family. Then he got a job in the West Coast shipyards and ended up helping them reinvent their unions. I think he was happy those years, being just another working union man and finally a family man.

"But on a Saturday night, January 22, 1944, it says here, he was at-tending a provincial convention of his union as a delegate from his local. Evans was urged to run for the executive and was nominated from the floor for president. The meeting ran till near midnight, so he caught a streetcar after midnight to his home at 5355 Taunton. He got off the streetcar near Kingsway and Joyce, exiting from the rear, and, as he went to cross the street, he was struck by a car, operated by a young driver. He was thrown a hundred and fifty feet, and it smashed his body up terribly. For twenty-one days he was in a coma, regaining consciousness once to greet his wife. Then he died at the young age of fifty-three, not all that much older than you, Paul. He's buried in Ocean View Cemetery in Vancouver."

"I'm going to take a bathroom break," Doc said. "Daniella I'll let you pour tea this time." Doc was standing, so I paused the tape, and some of us stretched, remarking on his organization and his memory. Finally we were ready to roll again.

"So I guess I'm not much on funerals, and ceremony, and eulogies, but whenever I tell someone about Arthur Evans' death, I feel that something more needs to be said. I can't help it. So, if you two don't mind, I'm just going to read the last part of something my good friend Steve Brodie wrote to remember Evans. Steve and I faced a lot together, like Bloody Sunday in '38, when they clubbed us senseless for leading the unemployed in a sit-down protest at the old Vancouver Post Office. Steve was always the one who had a way with the written word. He should have written a book on the fights we faced back then. There were a lot of them, there in Vancouver, in our struggle for dignity through those hungry thirties. Well, his is my favourite eulogy for Slim. Here goes, from near the end of it:

He had that feeling of urgency that we must struggle to avoid another world war or fascism. To him there was no time to waste and he kept this picture in front of people wherever he spoke to them.

He spent every day of his life actively combating what he knew was going to be the fate of the world — war and fascism.

The only time that I can recall Arthur Evans in a relaxed mood was when he was in one of his favourite places, in the Finnish settlements around Shushwap Lake, in Sorento and Glen Eden. Evans was welcome here as in no other part of the world.

It always impressed me the way the older people in the Finnish community treated him, the way their eyes would brighten up when he came into their homes, the way they gathered at whatever farm home he was holding his meeting. As they came in, they immediately sought Arthur out, shook hands with him and held on to him.

I always got the impression that they saw in Arthur, this man burning himself up with zeal for the cause, a reflection of their own folk heroes in the old country.

The older Finnish women mothered him. They could hardly speak to him, they didn't have enough English, but they were forever running to see that he had the best chair in the little farm house, that he was protected from the drafts. They knew exactly how he liked his coffee. They kept pressing him to have some soup, have some coffee. They took it as a personal insult when he came to their homes as a long skinny string bean of a man, just burning himself up, and it was always a disappointment to them if he didn't eat a real good meal before he left their houses. They seemed to want to devote their lives to making him look like a man who was well-fed.

This was their way of showing him, although many couldn't speak to him, that they loved him and respected him. It was a unique thing to see.

The old men would be sitting listening to him and he'd be telling the story of the need for unity among the farmers, of a cooperative method of working, and so on. He'd dig up some reading material that he had brought with him and he'd read them something. Then he would divert to a story of some of his experiences somewhere.

It was a treat to see the old Finnish farmers sitting back and listening. There was always a second or third generation member to give a running translation of what Evans was saying. You'd see the old white-haired gentlemen with their white moustaches and sometimes with their white beards sitting there all wrapped up in what Evans was telling them. And you'd hear the murmur from the corners all over the room, "Arthur, I foresee that. Yes, we know that is the truth. Yes, that is so," and so on.

And then after the formal discussion was over would come the questions, asked for the old men by the grandson interpreting. Arthur had a unique way when he was listening. He never took his eyes off the old men who were speaking or asking the questions through their interpreters, even though they spoke in Finnish of which he didn't understand a word.

He was a unique leader in their lives. They saw him as few others did. To keep peace in these communities he had to move from one home to another to share himself among them. They knew Evans was the genuine article.

Arthur Evans didn't belong to the commnist movement alone. He didn't belong to the Workers Unity League alone, although he was one of its mainsprings. He let it be known at all times that he belonged to the working class of Canada and he devoted his whole life and his whole energy to it.'

"Well, that was Steve Brodie all right, able to see something of the opposite side to the obvious in every event. When most of us think of Art Evans, we don't think of a man living in the idyllic community that he dreamed possible, but of a man in the middle of a storm and a struggle to achieve that community. Well that's what eulogies are for, I guess."

Doc looked around the table at us all and took a sip of tea. Daniella smiled, "That was absolutely inspiring, Doc. I'm glad you took the time to read it to us."

Doc nodded, "Well you know, I've got all these papers and books and photocopies so mixed up I forgot to read you something from the Regina Riot Inquiry that I wanted to share with you. And then I'm done. This is the shyster lawyer wanting to establish a case for his Section 98 charges against Evans.

Question: Mr. Evans, how long have you been a commnist?

Evans: Much longer than I've been a member of the Communist Party, which I joined in 1926. Ever since I began to travel across this country and saw the conditions of the workers, the mines and the mills, I think I was a communist since then.

Question: You have allegiance to a party that advocates the overthrow of our present system and government.

Evans: No, the Communist Party disagrees with the use of force, but will try every legal means to address the rights of the workers. And to change those laws which make justice and the legal system ineffective for everyday working people.

Question: Isn't it a fact that you as a commnist, you do not consider that you owe allegiance to any particular country?

Evans: I owe allegiance to this country, but not to the parasites who own this country at the present time.

Question: Whom do you mean by parasites?

Evans: Mr. Holt and Mr. Bennett, and those that own the mills, mines and factories and all the good things of life that are in this country. I owe allegiance to the country. I am very patriotic towards this country. I want to see it become a beautiful place for people to live in, but not for those men that take these utilities and close them up, who close mills and factories, and have elevators filled with food stuff to overflowing with every good thing, yet denying the possibilities of sharing in these good things to the people who are not given work.

Question: You do not include His Majesty the King in the terms you have just used?
Evans: No I do not include His Majesty the King.
Question: Mr. Evans, the oath of allegiance is not an oath to Holt or Bennett.
Evans: There is quite some room for argument as to whom allegiance is sworn.
Question: Is your first allegiance to King or the Communist Party?
Evans: I owe allegiance to the common people to see that they have a better life.'

"There. It is finished!" Robert "Doc" Savage declared.

Well, we talked some more, got to know his friends, ate some more left-over birthday cake, thanked him again, wished him happy birthday again. He offered Daniella the tiny spare room, which was really just storage space, and he offered me a mattress on the floor in the living room, but we declined, as I think he knew we would, and we said our good-byes. We headed north in my car towards Prince George.

"I hope we see him again," she said.

"I hope so too. I'm not sure I liked the way he said, 'It is finished.'"

"Yeah, I know," she said. I was silent for a bit, thinking about Prince George and how I had postponed the decision on booking a room. But Daniella fixed that within two minutes of getting into the car.

"So. Did you reserve a room with a big king-size bed and a bottle of champagne for the two of us?" she asked with this sudden big smile.

I caught my breath and smiled back. I looked at her courageous smiling face and I just wanted to keep looking at her, so I pulled over to the curb, still in Quesnel, and leaned her way, reaching out two hands that beckoned her to come a little closer. She moved right over and I gave her the kiss that I wanted to give back in her apartment.

The End

Yes, the end, I think. Except that I can hear my chief critic, Sammy.

"Now wait just a goddamn minute. What the hell you doing, Saint Paul? Isn't this supposed to be a popular history book? Recording voices of actual historical people? What you doing headed toward a hotel bed with a United Church minister at the end of a friggin' history book? Is this history, or is this a fuckin' Harlequin romance, for God sake?"

Ah, Sammy. Count on Sammy to be there for you.

But now you need to back off, Sammy. So what if we broke a few rules? If you know so much about the rules of fiction and non-fiction, then you write the story. Anyway, interrupting Daniella and me at such a touching moment is just plain rude. Go back to Alberta, please, and leave us alone. We're happy here in Lotus-Land, for the moment. We'll be back to Alberta's version of realism in the morning. In the meantime, *find your own story*.

And honour thy keepers.

FOR THE RECORD

ACKNOWLEDGEMENT OF SOURCES
AND DISCUSSION OF GENRE

A S THE AUTHOR, I WISH TO acknowledge how disconcerting the border
between historical fiction and creative non-fiction can be to the historian,
the genre critic, the academic and the critical thinker who wants to know what
creative licence the author is taking with the facts of history. Thus I believe I
owe the reader some explanation beyond a bibliography of sources. My primary
sources were a series of personal interviews with the two primary narrators
Robert Savage and Matt Shaw, plus other Trekkers, including Andy Miller,
Rudy Fedorowich, Bobby Jackson and George Taylor. Other sources included
reporter William Davies (later Minister of Health in the CCF government during introduction of medicare) and Doreen Rust (my wife's grandmother). Other
eyewitnesses, whose voices are not actually used, sometimes contributed memories that influenced the narrative. Most of these interviews took place between
July of 1995 and July of 1999, though I've spoken to Robert Doc Savage on the
subject as recently as September 2005. The Savage and Shaw narrations are
not just their voices, but a compilation to help narrative flow. The only known
travesty of historical objectivity in their narrative is that Doc's account of his
expulsion from the work camp near Merritt is actually the true story of Matt
Shaw's blackballing. Doc came out of a camp near Squamish. I apologize for
this. The narrative flow tempted me to shuffle those stories.

The second most important and extensive sources were the *On-To-Ottawa
Trek Files* and the *Regina Riot Inquiry Commission, 1935–36 Files*, both found in the
Saskatchewan Archives in Regina. Information from these sources was sometimes
put into the mouths of the narrators. The secondary sources are listed here in
order of their influence and the amount of material that influenced the narrative:
1. *Work and Wages*, by Ben Swankey and Jean Evans Shiels, daughter of Art Evans
(Vancouver: Trade Union Research Bureau, 1977). This is normally quoted in
italics and credited within the text. Steve Brodie's eulogy in the final chapter is
quoted from this work also. 2. *Recollections of the On-To-Ottawa-Trek*, by Ronald
Liversedge (Toronto: M&S, 1973). Liversedge was not only a Trekker but an
activist in the Relief Camp Workers Union and on the Trek. 3. *We Were the Salt of
the Earth! The On-To-Ottawa Trek and the Regina Riot*, by Victor Howard (Canadian
Plains Research Centre, University of Regina, 1985). 4. *Fighting Heritage*, edited
and partially written by Sean Griffin (Vancouver: Tribune Publishing, 1985).

Secondary sources two to four were mainly used to help order the narratives chronologically. Some of the anecdotes have been described over the years from multiple perspectives; I acknowledge my debt to all of these sources for several borrowed anecdotes. Sometimes it was obvious that my eyewitnesses had also read some of these works.

All Hell Can't Stop Us, by Bill Waiser (Fifth House), was published in 2003, after my initial drafts were finished. I did not discover it till 2006, whereupon I read it immediately. He used many of the same sources for the Trek and Riot except for the primary source interviews that are crucial to my narrative. I do not believe that there is anything substantial in this book that comes via Waiser. I have not had his book in my possession since reading it and I did not make notes. I think all the factual material was already established in the drafts. I enjoyed reading Waiser, but, of course, his is a proper academic study and very different in genre and mode.

The even-numbered intercalary chapters (2 through 16) and the openings of each chapter are characterized by the fictional frame of the BJ's History Sessions. The bar is based on a drinking establishment in Grande Prairie with a similar name. The interaction between the characters at the bar is fiction and merely a creative frame for the personal narratives told there, which are all historically accurate, witnessed by me in most cases. The Douglas speech, however, is a composite of several T.C. Douglas speeches witnessed by me. Daniella is fictional, and no such granddaughter lives in Grande Prairie, but her story about police abuse in Quebec is based on an eyewitness report given at a political meeting by a young female NGO member reporting on the police actions at the Quebec City Summit of the Americas meetings in late April of 2001. I interviewed her after her presentation and have also heard some description of those events from Svend Robinson, another eyewitness to that scene.

The other "audience" characters, like Sammy, Cam and Tom are fiction-alized or composite Grande Prairie characters with fictional dialogue. Political experiences described by Charles and Paul are almost always from my own history. The fictional parts of the creative frame (BJ's Bar) and the ending all attempt to examine historical objectivity and the oral event itself as history.

The character Daniella argues that the audience at BJ's (and the readers) actually participate in history, usually without knowing it, and that it is important to recognize one's place in history and to assert that narrative. Our First Nations argue that the oral narrative is also a historical artefact. Our interaction with history orally is an integral, genuine and researchable part of history. The book's form and content argue a postmodern approach to narrative and history. Should it be read as a historical novel? Some would say yes. Many academics would classify it as creative non-fiction due to the pervasiveness of primary sources. One way or the other, it is a very Canadian narrative.

Elroy Deimert

ABOUT THE AUTHOR

Dr. Elroy Deimert is a City Alderman, a college instructor of English Literature, and a political activist in Grande Prairie Alberta. He is on the national executive of the NDP as well as the author of the novel *Engedi* and several dramatic monologues produced by CBC.

praise for *Pubs, Pulpits & Praire Fires*

Labour history is always subversive. It demonstrates that our daily life is not the product of those men and women who can, with a straight face, permit themselves to be addressed as "Right Honorable." Elroy Deimert offers a documentary-film style narrative of 1935 On-to-Ottawa Trek participants speaking of solidarity, vision, success, setbacks, and oppression. Their voices are gripping. Deimert never loses sight who really makes history, who decides what is worth remembering, and who history addresses. Deimert's book challenges us to decide whose Canada we will take for our own.

    — Tom Wayman, Associate Professor of English, University of Calgary,
    poet, and author of many books of poetry and fiction, including,
    A Country not Considered: Canada, Culture. Work.

This lively historical novel recreates the drama of the Great Depression, the On-to-Ottawa trek, the excitement surrounding Bible Bill Aberhart's questionable social credit ideas, and much else from the lives of working people in the Dirty Thirties. The Tuesday History Club provides the locale for a concoction of individuals of different generations to compare notes. The RCMP billy clubs that stopped the On-to-Ottawa trek in Regina mingle with more recent suppression of dissent, from the War Measures Act in 1970 to the Quebec City marches against the Summit of the Americas in 2001.

    — Alvin Finkel, Professor of History, Athabasca University, author of
    The Social Credit Phenomenon in Alberta *and co-author*
    (with Margaret Conrad) of History of the Canadian Peoples.

Anyone who says Canadian history isn't exciting should read this thrilling tale while eating their words. Elroy Deimert writes a terrific yarn and it has the added attraction of being true. Why this tale has waited so long to be told can only be because the right author needed to be found.

    — John Wing, Canadian poet and international comic

An engaging read that connects us with the passionate, courageous and ever-relevant voices of the young unemployed men whose thirst for dignity and rights led them to plan and participate in the 1935 On-to-Ottawa Trek.

    — Maria Dunn, Canadian Folk Singer